I0831932

Vigilia's Tempest

Also by Stephen Poleskie:

The Balloonist: The Story of T. S. C. Lowe, Inventor, Scientist, Magician, and Father of the U. S. Air Force . . . *a novel 2007*

The Third Candidate . . . *a novel 2008*

Grater Life . . . *a novel in stories 2009*

Vigilia's Tempest

Stephen Poleskie

Author's Note

This book is solely a work of my imagination. Names, characters, descriptions of places and events are used fictitiously. To this end I have altered and embellished reality, extended real people into imagined space and time, and invented incidents and dialogues. I make no attempt to furnish factual answers to any of the theories or questions raised in the text.

Order this book online at www.trafford.com
or email orders@trafford.com

Most Trafford titles are also available at major online book retailers.

Printed in Victoria, BC, Canada.

ISBN: 978-1-4269-2946-5 (sc)
ISBN: 978-1-4269-2947-2 (dj)

Library of Congress Control Number: 2010903611

Trafford rev. 3/18/2010

www.trafford.com

North America & international
toll-free: 1 888 232 4444 (USA & Canada)
phone: 250 383 6864 • fax: 812 355 4082

To my wife, Jeanne Mackin

Acknowledgments:

I would like to thank the following people, writers and friends, who have read and encouraged my work over the years: Diane Ackerman, David Borden, Marvin and Pat Carlson, Patrice and Steven Demory, Antonio Di Renzo, Rebecca Godin, Jack Goldman, Lamar and Amparo Herrin, Edward Hower, Nino Lama, Alison Lurie, James and Gladys McConkey, David Pollock, James Michael Robbins, Thaddeus Rutkowski, Nick Sagan, Gary Weissbrot, Paul West, and Danielle Winterton.

With special thanks to:

Lise Lemeland; artist, aerobatic pilot, educator, and mother of three, who read through the manuscript and made valuable comments.

One

I come
To answer thy best pleasure: be 't to fly,
To swim, to dive into the fire, to ride
On the curl'd clouds. . . .

Shakespeare *The Tempest I. ii.*

The boy's hands held a death grip on the hot, rusty iron ladder. The world below him seemed to be rolling off its normal course, spinning, things were beginning to blur. Frozen with fear, he found himself unable to go on. The blood pounding in his head had turned the green pine-covered hills around him to pink, and yellow, and red. Seen through the afternoon haze they should appear blue or gray. Aerial Perspective was what Leonardo da Vinci called this visual phenomenon in his notebooks. The boy had once thought that he wanted to be an artist, a painter; but there was no art in his town, so he had painfully worked his way through Leonardo's text, hoping to teach himself all that he needed to know. It was in these notebooks that he had found his design for a flying machine.

A cold blast of wind rattled the water tower. Sweat coated the boy's palms. On the ground it was a fine summer day, with only the occasional strong breeze. A sudden gust tore at the knapsack he had strapped to his back containing the fabric for the flying device, threatening to lift it free. The pack's straps dug into the boy's shoulders, the bundle of thin bamboo poles tied onto the bottom swaying to and fro. He hesitated. If he would be an aviator he must learn not to fear the wind.

Others have done it long before I was even born; so why not me?

Time seemed excessive, still, raw and sterile, of no use. Risking a furtive glance, the boy saw that he was higher than the hill where he lived, and where he had first tested his device from the roof of his father's garage. Grinning into the cool sky, he began breathing normally again. He had six rungs remaining before he reached the top. There was another puff, but not as strong as before; could the wind be dying down? Glancing up he wondered what came after the ladder reached the rim. Were there handholds continuing onto the roof of the tank? He had never been up here before. Fighting his fear, the boy forced himself to climb another rung. His movement, or was it the gusting wind, caused this ancient iron structure to vibrate, its motion giving off a hum, demoniac yet singsong.

Over I'll go and see what happens.

What curiosity had drawn the boy to the water tower? What kind of degenerate, unstable elevator had whisked him to the top floor of the building, opening opposite the dim stairway to the roof, leaving him receptive to this abnormal temptation, the highest point on the highest structure for miles around? You could never get lost in this small mill town; wherever you were, just look up and there was the water tower.

The colorless, and mildewed, door to the roof had opened on a beautiful and fantastic vista, unvisited for many months, perhaps even years. This neglected roof exposed a seam in the boy's ambition, the sense of space, of being above it all, in touch with his hero, Leonard, in his tower, writing in reverse in his notebooks, penning ink drawings for parachutes and flying machines. The rough, mottled doorway to the stairwell was gone, melded into the wall; there could be nowhere to go except up.

Over I'll go and see what happens.

Looking around the boy's breathing slowed; the nearby hills had gone back to being medium blue, the ones farther beyond to a paler gray, just as Leonardo wrote they would. With apostolic zeal the boy's purpose returned, if not his courage. Slowly, he climbed another rung, and another, and then, making a rapid spurt, the final three. Pulling himself up against the weight of his burden, the boy gazed at the pitched top of the water tower, uninhabited except for six startled gray pigeons that took flight at his emergence. With jealousy he watched them leave; what a glorious gift they enjoyed he told himself.

If only flying were so simple for me.

Bathed in luminous midday sunlight, the slanted landscape below beckoned, but the boy still clung fast, immobile. He was unwilling to trade his grip on the last rung of the ladder to reach for the first of the handholds. Traffic went on in the streets below, a few people passing by. The small town looked unchanged, much like the old engravings that he remembered seeing in a yellowed book in the library. Were these pictures early aerial views? Perhaps the artist had gone up in a balloon, or had he climbed this very water tower?

The sky around the boy had become crowded with various species of birds, circling on an endless track, sounding his intrusion into their private space. Down below him people were walking around, grounded in their own realities. Few had an immediate need to contemplate death. If they chanced to look up their assumption would be that the figure on the tower belonged there; he was working, it was the time of the day for work; they were working, or on their way to work, or going to look for work. People did not necessarily think much about death until confronted with it, ignoring the irrational need to turn it into something of value. The boy knew that he was born to die, but first he wished to fly, and if this choice might hasten his death, then so it would be.

Over I'll go and see what happens.

His flying machine was a simply made affair of nylon fabric and bamboo sticks, lashed together with cord. The boy had assembled his device many times, but the pitch of the roof, and the wind, were making it difficult today. An audience had gathered in the streets, and a few people were waiting at the base of the water tower, with lifted heads and clucking among themselves. No one was brave enough, or foolish enough to climb the rusting ladder to try to get him down, but someone had called the police and the fire department. The boy could hear the wailing of the sirens as these public servants raced each other through the labyrinth below.

His fragile glider assembled, the boy slowly drew himself upright. Holding his wings open wide, he imagined himself a living crucifix taking possession of the sky. People in the crowd were shouting now; he could hear their voices wafted up from below. A fireman was speaking something through a bullhorn, perhaps addressing him. All the sounds were unclear, only background to the many thoughts that were beating in his head, and the wind rushing in his ears.

A sudden, strong gust knocked the boy down; for an instant the would-be aviator disappeared from the view of the crowd below. No one could see him grasping fearfully at the handholds. And then, in a flash, he popped up again, his courage returned. Had he lost all reason? Walking mincingly along the very edge of the water tower, he waved to his watchers, but that was not enough.

If only flying were so simple for me.

The boy could hear them clearly now; even if his audience did not dare express its pleasure it would never forgive him for stopping here. Their shouts compelled him, demanding everything. He gave it to them.

Over I'll go and see what happens.

Stepping from the edge of the tower, the boy felt the cold rush of wind on his face and the downward pull of gravity; a gentle jolt lifted his body as the homemade wings caught the air.

I am free; I am flying.

But below him all the sadness of the world still waited.

Two

We are such stuff
As dreams are made on, and our little life
Is rounded with a sleep.

Shakespeare *The Tempest IV. i.*

Nine minutes later than he had anticipated the rocky, ragged shore of Lake Erie slowly unraveled itself from the blinding glare of the summer's day. The head winds were stronger than had been forecast. The pilot glanced down, checked his aircraft's fuel gauge, and then set his gaze back outside, over the cowl. Seen through the beating arc of the propeller, the water and sky appeared to meld into one band of faded blue. Since this ancient open-cockpit biplane was not equipped with an artificial horizon, a modern day instrument useful for keeping the wings level on low visibility days like today, the haze was making flying difficult. Peering out through the network of struts and wires, the pilot concentrated on keeping his Bücker Jungmann level and on course. This lack of forward visibility presented yet another significant problem. Air mass thunderstorms were fond of forming on hot June days like today, and it was possible to fly right into one without knowing it—until it was too late to turn back.

He hadn't intended to come by this way at all, but was behind schedule, having gotten a late start from his home airport due to passing thundershowers there. His biplane was not equipped to fly at night, so the pilot needed to be in Wisconsin by this evening. The aerobatic competition he was scheduled to fly in began on the day after tomorrow, and he wanted to be there early, in time for the practice day.

A quick mental calculation led the pilot to believe that he had enough fuel to fly diagonally across the lake, which had not been his original plan, and then to fly over a thin strip of Canada. To go around this vast body of water, which for safety reasons he would have preferred to do, would entail the delay of an additional fuel stop. Checking his watch and fuel gauge one more time, the pilot made his decision. Banking slightly to change direction, he pointed the nose of the Bücker toward the middle of the lake.

The weather was hot, and dizzy with bright sunlight. Despite the altitude, and a stiff, steady breeze from the northwest, the direction the biplane was heading, the pilot could smell the freshness of the water. The great lake in front of him reflected the sun, its color a slant blending of blue and green. Directly below him the Erie was like glass. In other spots the surface had taken on a polished quality that at present made it appear almost solid.

Lettered on the side of the fuselage of the multicolored biplane, just below the curve of the rear cockpit, the one used when flying solo, was the pilot's name, John Vigilia, the words "The Stunt Flying Professor" and the name of his hometown, Elmira, New York U.S.A. John had the sign painter add on the U.S.A, as he secretly dreamed of competing in the Olympics of flying, the World Aerobatic Competition on the United States Team. Considering that his aircraft was not one of the latest competition models but only a rebuilt 1938 Bücker Jungmann, an airplane previously used by the Germans to train *Luftwaffe* pilots for World War Two, and that John Vigilia only competed in the Sportsman category, three categories below the Unlimited level of international competition, fulfilling his world team ambition was doubtful. John was, however, by trade a creative person to whom fantasies came easily.

The title The Stunt Flying Professor was kind of a joke, a sobriquet bestowed on him once by an air show announcer that had stuck. John was indeed a stunt flyer and a college professor. At the age of thirty-three he had obtained a position at a small college teaching writing, becoming a run-of-the-mill pedagogue, expounding in turgid, ponderous language ideas that were by then somewhat less than original. To achieve the status of a third-rate professor, and the steady salary that came with it, John Vigilia had given up some nine years of promise spent in Manhattan, where he had worked construction during the day and written at night. During that time he had completed an unpublished novel, and thirty-three short stories, six of which had been published in obscure journals that had since disappeared. John had also suffered sever depression and a broken marriage, and done any number of stupid, and sometimes illegal, things just to get by.

Without any warning the aircraft's engine began to vibrate. John reached forward, adjusted the engine's mixture control and the Lycoming O-320 smoothed out again, producing the regular sound of 2400 beats per minute. Engines always seemed to run rough over water, and he was definitely over water, having lost sight of the shore some time ago. Sliding his hand down between him and the side of the fuselage, John Vigilia patted the boat cushion his behind rested on, the only thing he had if the engine should fail and the airplane went down in Lake Erie. The Jungmann would sink in a few minutes, hardly enough time for John to unbuckle from all his safety harnesses and get out. And no one would know where to look for him, as John had not filed a flight plan. At that moment John wished he were back in Elmira in the old gazebo.

The college John Vigilia taught at had a gazebo in the middle of its campus that supposedly had been used by Mark Twain when he had lived in the town. John regularly visited this weathered structure, and sat there for hours, perhaps hoping for some inspirational message from Twain's ghost. Afterwards John would retire to his office and stare at a blank computer screen, unable to make letters turn into words, words into stories. Posing no direct threat to his lackluster colleagues, after six years Professor Vigilia was granted tenure. He told himself that every man should be content with what he was—but John could not deny that he was not.

Despite having a loving wife, a fine Victorian carriage house located in the *good* neighborhood professors were supposed to live in, two cars, a motorcycle, and his airplane, John felt that he was, neither cynically nor hopefully, still wanting for something else. It wasn't friendship. His acquaintances were many, but they were unintegrated. The people who were John's friends were not friends of his partner, nor were they friends of one another. The college was a place filled with people escaping the prison sentence of their own personal history, a history that had lost its promise and destiny.

The realization that his own promise had been false was slowly dawning on John with the passage of his years. He was living out his own prison sentence; that of bearing witness to the steady attenuation of his sense of limitless possibility. He was not the same John Vigilia who, as a youth of thirteen, had wildly leapt from the top of the town water tower wearing homemade wings.

John Vigilia's soul had developed a kind of amnesia, a loneliness. John had lost hold of what he knew, and if he could not hold on to what he knew he could not take in any new experiences, and without new experiences there was no change. He realized that in the past his strength had lain in refusal, in his ability not to give up. But now his life had become an endless remembering of what had been.

Abandoned by his muses, John had returned to the few heroes of his youth: Leonardo da Vinci, the Wright Brothers, Charles Lindbergh, and did what he had always wanted to do. He learned to fly. And furthermore, having earned his license, and not content with the straight and level, John Vigilia had become a stunt pilot.

The visibility had diminished to about a mile, barely legal for flying by visual flight rules. Nevertheless, as John judged himself to be more than half the distance across the lake, he considered his best alternative would be to continue in the direction that he was heading. His main effort now was keeping the biplane steady in the growing turbulence. John locked his concentration on the altimeter, and the turn and bank indicator. The Bücker was skimming the cloud bases, rocking up and down in the billowing, ragged fingers of mist clutching at him as he flew along.

John Vigilia had started across Lake Erie at 8500 feet above sea level, an altitude that would have put the Jungmann about 8000 feet above the surface of the water, as high as he could go with the cloud ceiling, but not high enough to glide safely to the other side should his engine fail halfway across. The sky and water around him had turned from hazy blue to a bowl of murky gray Jell-O. With his single radio set to the Aylmer VOR beacon for navigation, John clung hopefully to its narrow beam, his eyes searching for a thin spit of land identified on his chart only as "Long Point." As clouds were gathering below him, and he needed to keep in visual contact with the ground, which in this case was the water, John descended to 6500 feet, and then to 4500. At this lower altitude the radio signal was becoming extremely weak.

John checked his watch. The Stunt Flying Professor should have been to the other side by now. Was he fighting a head wind considerably stronger than he had earlier? Above the beat of the engine John thought he heard the distant sound of thunder. He didn't know why, but John Vigilia was getting an increasing sense that this flight had the possibility of becoming something worst than any of the wildest adventures of his past.

Raising his head, John peered over the side of the fuselage and down through the grayness, straining for a sight of land. Long Point would not be wide, and very probably rocky, but at least it would be land. His fingers fumbled with the boat cushion he was sitting on, just to reassure himself that it was still there.

Now the cold, damp whiteness of the clouds was all around him. Pulling back the throttle, John descended once again, hoping to get back into clear air. The altimeter unwound, as he passed through 2500, and then 1000 feet. He leveled off, stopping the descent. At this point he was running along just below the ragged cloud bases, but barely 100 feet above the surface of the lake. John could clearly see the white caps churning on the water as the wind kicked up the waves. The radio's course needle swung back and forth a few times, and then came to rest on the left stop. The biplane was too low to receive the station's signal. All that John could navigate by now, as the aircraft bobbed up and down in the choppy wind coming off the lake, was his compass. Frantically John Vigilia folded and refolded his sectional chart, searching to find the number for the magnetic disturbance in the area that he thought he was passing over.

The fog was closing in on all sides, but John dare not descend any lower. A prudent pilot would have turned back miles ago, but John Vigilia had not listened to his own reason and pressed on. It was probably too late now; however, John decided that he should at least take a look to see what the conditions were behind him. Putting the

Jungmann into a steep bank, he executed a tight 360 degree clearing turn, his wingtips a scant fifty feet above the water. To his horror, John saw that the opaque white vapors completely surrounded him; there was no turning back. The gusty wind was making holding a compass heading all but impossible. John realized now that his only hope was to find Long Point. He pressed on, flying so low that the wind-whipped spray lashed at the Bücker's landing gear.

John Vigilia could feel his brain pulsating beneath his flying helmet, his mind telling him that he was hopelessly lost. Suddenly, John caught a glimpse of a shape in front of him. Or was he just hallucinating? He wiped the condensation off the inside of his windscreen and peered through the small clear spot. Something was apparently out there in the mist just ahead of him, a large and dark mass. Was it the rocks at Long Point? John had flown over them several times before, but never this low, so had no idea how high above the water they might extend, or how they looked close up.

Pulling back the power, John and his Bücker slowly approached this zone of darkness. It seemed to be going away from him, yet hovering, like some kind of phantom presence. John Vigilia had read a book once about the Great Lakes Triangle in which the author claimed this area, which John was now in, though not as well known as the Bermuda Triangle, was just as mysterious—and actually more deadly. It had swallowed up many boats, and more than a few airplanes, over the years, traces of which had never been found.

Then, as suddenly as it had appeared, the dark mass was gone. John increased power and slid into the mist. Whatever it was that was out there, he did not want to loose it. Anything was better than the rolling nothing of the fog and wind, and now it had begun to rain. Without warning the form was there again. This time John saw lights. He quickly pulled back on the power. He was overtaking something. The shape became clearer. It was a ship, a large ship, perhaps an iron ore or cargo boat. John tucked in abeam of it, almost as if he and the ship were flying in formation. As he flew alongside John was barely clear of the water, the Jungmann being actually below the level of the ship's bridge.

John could read the name lettered on the side, *Morgan Sidney,* and the homeport of Liverpool. There were men on deck, and they were pointing at him. John raised his left hand and waved. The crewmen waved back. For some reason John's mind chose to recall the story of Charles Lindbergh shouting from the *Spirit of Saint Louis* to ask directions of fisherman he came upon off the coast of Ireland.

"Which way is it to Long Point?" John yelled through his cupped hand.

John Vigilia could barely make out the response of the crewman over the wind and waves, but was sure he had heard someone shout "Long Point's back that way," and they were all pointing at his tail, in the direction that he had come from.

Had he somehow gotten off course and passed Long Point in the fog? Or had he been flying down the center of the lake instead of across it? John looked at his fuel gauge, which strangely showed less than a quarter of a tank remaining. Then he checked his watch. According to the time that had elapsed, the tank should still be half full. John was confused. He could not reconcile the vast difference in the fuel consumption. It was true that he had been flying into a strong head wind, but he had also been running at partial throttle for a good portion of the time. One thing John Vigilia did know was that he needed to find land, and hopefully an airport, very soon.

When John raised his eyes from his gauges again the *Morgan Sidney* was gone. It had disappeared back into the fog as mysteriously as it had appeared. A brief ray of sunshine flashing across his cowl caused John to look up. Overhead he could see a slight break in the clouds. He pushed the throttle to the firewall and started climbing in a tight spiral. John hoped that this would be his escape. He knew these sudden openings in storm clouds, which seemed to promise a way out, often closed in on you once you got inside them, which was why they were commonly referred to as "sucker holes." Nevertheless, he had no choice other than to keep spiraling upwards into this ragged clear space in the middle of the fog's whiteness. He continued circling, climbing ever so slowly: as if he and his airplane were clawing their way up the inside a giant smokestack.

Time seemed to have no end as the Bücker continued to struggle upwards. Eyeballing the distance John guessed he still lacked about 900 feet to his goal, the top of the clouds. Fumbling with his radio John twisted the course selector knob randomly in a desperate attempt to pick up the navigational facility nearest the area that he believed himself to be passing through. The course needle waggled from left to right unable to find a signal strong enough to lock on to. This was odd, John thought, as he had now reached 7000 feet and should have even been able to pick up the signal all the way from Buffalo. John squinted through his goggles at the now mist-soaked map. Had he misread the frequencies? He found the numbers listed for what he believed to be the closest navigational facility, Aylmer at 114.2, dialed them in and tried it again. Although John was quite sure that this was the correct frequency, his radio still did not pick up anything.

Much to John's alarm, the hole in the clouds above him was threatening to close up before he got there. Huge white hands seemed to grab at the Jungmann from all sides. The throttle was already against the stop. John carefully leaned the fuel mixture, coaxing the last bit of power from his gasping engine. The biplane was rocking up and down, struggling with the downdrafts coming off the clouds. The sky around John grew darker. He raised his tinted goggles, and hunched lower under the windscreen. John could feel the temperature dropping. It was becoming very cold in the open cockpit. Lifting his head back up, John encountered total blindness. He was completely wrapped in the cloud vapors.

The buffeting from the freezing wind forced John Vigilia to duck his head back down inside the cockpit. His eyes fell on the vertical speed indicator. John was startled to discover that the Bücker was climbing at 3000 feet-per-minute, more than three times its normal rate. The biplane was in an updraft. It had been sucked up into the air mass, not an ordinary cloud, but a building cumulonimbus, a developing thunderstorm.

Words memorized from his pilot's meteorology text flashed in John's mind: *The cumulonimbus cloud marks an area of most turbulent air, with probable hail and torrential rain. The sensible pilot never attempts to fly through such a cloud, but always goes around it.*

The textbook had become a reality. The Jungmann was being drawn up into an immense, luminous dome, the damp white insides of which revealed streaks of its own heavenly geography. The aircraft raced upward in air that was becoming difficult to breathe. John peered over the side at the cloud, which was growing darker, a green twilight, almost as if he and his airplane were under water. Rain, mixed with hail, began to beat on the taut fabric covering the wings and fuselage. He was locked in the first stages of a thunderstorm. Until that moment John had not been quite sure of what he was encountering, and so had not known what to fear. With the realization of his situation came terror—a panic that dulled John's responses and slowed his reactions.

Although his hands gripped the control stick, John Vigilia was not flying the airplane. In the violent air the Jungmann had taken on a life of its own, climbing and diving, while all the time being forced upward. The severe turbulence inside a storm cloud was lethal. An airplane, even an aerobatic one like the Bücker, could become overstressed and eventually come apart. He had to slow the airspeed down.

With his left hand, numb from the cold and trembling with fright, John pulled back the throttle. There was no response. His eyes flashed to the tachometer, where the needle rested on zero. It took John but an instant to realize that the carburetor's intake must have iced over. The engine was dead. Looking out the side caused John's stomach to tighten further. The pounding rain was turning to ice—it was as if summer had for some reason hibernated at this altitude. The ice was adhering to the wings and struts, not only adding weight to the airplane, but also destroying the airfoil, decreasing the lift just when it was needed most. This condition increased the speed at which the aircraft stalled, which at high altitudes was not that far below its cruise speed in level flight. John checked his altimeter; the gauge showed the incorrect altitude of 666 feet, the pitot tube was frozen. The Jungmann's airspeed indicator, which shared the same tube, would be inaccurate also.

Fighting his fear, he hunkered down underneath the now completely frosted-over windscreen. The covering of ice did not matter, as John had no outside visibility anywhere. He had to regain control of the aircraft, to fly it by what few instruments that still functioned before it went into a spin. It was cold, extremely cold. John's body was shaking. The attitude indicator showed the aircraft to be in a sixty degree left bank. Tilting the control stick cautiously to the right, John tried to level the wings. The gauge showed no response. The venturi too was frozen over. He felt the airplane beginning to shake, the subtle buffet that came just before a stall which, without the pilot being in control, could turn into a spin. A spin in these clouds would tighten up before he could stop it, and take John Vigilia, in his confusion and helplessness, all the way back to surface of the lake—and below.

John could hear the thin air being breathed in and out of his nostrils, fast and hard like a piston. All the winds of the world were being sucked through his brain. John sat there resigned to the fact that he had never been as important in his life as he hoped to be. This final spin would be the ultimate consequence of his all too many failures. He was considering the possibility of bailing out, abandoning the foundering airplane, as he had abandoned so many other things in his life when they appeared not to be going as planned. Then, as if the forces of nature were intent on denying John Vigilia the innate fulfillment of his tragic destiny, the clouds began to part, and the Jungmann bounced free of the mist and out into the brilliant sunshine.

Three

Be patient, for the prize I'll bring thee to
Shall hoodwink this mischance: therefore speak softly;
All's hush'd as midnight yet.

Shakespeare *The Tempest IV. i.*

The fall of 1923 was not a good time for barnstorming in northern Minnesota. Brisk, cold weather had come on early, and the young Charles Lindbergh was having a hard time finding people who wanted to go up in his open cockpit biplane. He decided to head south. In Wisconsin, however, he found that some other pilot had already passed through the area who had been taking up passengers for half the going rate. Lindbergh always abided by the unwritten rule in use among barnstormers at that time of giving a good ride for five dollars, but not taking anyone up for less. So, he left southern Wisconsin and headed his Jenny towards Illinois. Knowing that the International Air Races were being held in Saint Louis, Lindbergh decided to pass up all the little towns on the way, with their possibilities for flying passengers, and go directly there.

Not far behind Lindbergh, another barnstormer, Francis Angelucci, was also heading for Saint Louis in his biplane. In the front cockpit little Ariel Angelucci, the son of his late brother, had his hand lightly on the control stick. At first glance it would seem that the boy was only following his uncle's movements, pretending to fly the airplane; but closer observation revealed that Francis was sitting there with his arms folded across his chest against the cold. The twelve year old boy, who needed three cushions under him just to see over the cowl and blocks taped to the rudder pedals for his feet, was in complete control of the aircraft.

Outside the cockpit the checkerboard of colors that was the Illinois landscape in fall unraveled its beauty. How different from the view out the window of the Chicago tenement Ariel and his twin brother Caliban had grown up in, the apartment that had burned, taking his mother and father to their early graves. In school at the time, he and his brother had avoided being caught in the fire. Their parents gone, the boys had been separated, and sent to live with relatives. Ariel's brother went to their aunt who had a farm in Canada. The boys wrote letters sometimes, but had not seen each other since they were parted. No one had the money for travel. Caliban wrote that although life on the farm was interesting, and there was always plenty to eat, he was bored most of the time. The farm was about a mile from the nearest neighbors, so he didn't have any friends.

Sitting in the front cockpit, flying the biplane, Ariel Angelucci had no doubt that he had gotten the better of the two choices. He had been sent to live with his Uncle Francis, a real barnstormer. In winters Francis worked at rebuilding airplanes, and so Ariel had to go to school, but as soon as the weather broke they were off in the Jenny. He had traveled all over the Midwest, and seen more places in the past three years than most boys see in a lifetime. And best of all, his Uncle Francis had taught him how to fly.

At first Ariel had just spelled his uncle on long flights. Then he was allowed to make the takeoffs. After some practice he was able to land, Francis said, as smooth as any older pilot he knew. Now Ariel was part of his uncle's act. They had been doing it all summer, and made a considerable amount of money, some of which Francis even gave to the boy, telling him to save it, and when he had enough he could go to college.

Passing over a field near Carlinville, Illinois, Francis looked down and saw another biplane on the ground taking on fuel from a gas truck. They had enough fuel to make it to Lambert Field, where the races were being held, and where Francis was already entered in the parachute jumping competition; nevertheless, he signaled his nephew to circle and land next to the other airplane. As long as a gas truck was there, they would take on fuel and stretch their legs. And Francis thought that the biplane on the ground looked like it might belong to someone he knew.

Craning his head from side to side to see out over the Jenny's cowl, little Ariel greased the aircraft onto the soft turf, and taxied up next to the other airplane. Francis hopped out of the cockpit even before the propeller had stopped turning. The pilot of the first plane was standing on the wing walk tightening his fuel cap; he looked up and recognized Francis.

"Hey! Will you look who's come in after me? If it isn't Frank Angelight," the man said calling him by the Americanized version of his name that Francis used as a barnstormer. "How the heck are you, you old son-of-a-gun?"

"Slim! . . . I though it looked like your battered old hulk from up there. We were on our way to Saint Louis, and when I saw you and the gas truck I thought we'd stop down for some fuel."

"We?"

"This here's my nephew, Ariel," he said motioning to the boy. "Ariel come say hello to Mr. Lindbergh. Everyone calls him Slim. His father used to be a congressman . . .

he flew his dad around when he was campaigning . . . that's probably why his old man lost the election. People figured anyone crazy enough to fly with Slim Lindbergh, shouldn't be in congress. He even flew his mother around with him for a while."

"Pleased to meet you Mr. Lindbergh," Ariel said, extending his hand. "Are you a barnstormer too?"

"You're askin' if he's a barnstormer!?" Francis interjected. "To tell the truth Slim here is the craziest barnstormer of them all . . . he's crash landed more times than anybody else I know."

"Maybe so, Frank, but I think my barnstorming days may be coming to an end," Lindbergh announced. "I'm planning to take the examination for the Army Service Training School at Chanute Field in January."

"Well I'll be . . . good luck to you, Slim. We're gonna miss you . . . not too many of the regular guys around anymore."

"Barnstorming is a hard way to make a living. At least in the service I'll get steady pay, and fly new airplanes with powerful engines that don't have to be wished into the air." Then Lindbergh looked Francis in the eye. "Say, you weren't the one who flew around Wisconsin taking people up for half fare were you?"

"Me? No . . . I'd never do that. In fact I have a whole new act now; me and Ariel here work the fairs and carnivals . . . make enough so's that we don't have to hop passengers."

"How's that?"

"Well, this here little kid can really fly. Did ya see the landing he made coming into this field?"

"I thought it was too good of a landing to be you at the controls."

"Hey, and that's not all . . . I mean you should see him. He can do wingovers, loops, barrel rolls. . . . "

"No kidding," Lindbergh said, looking over at Ariel who was standing there bursting with pride.

"Now you know how I was always good with parachutes . . . well we take the airplane up, only Ariel is so small he can hide in the front cockpit and no one can see him, and the announcer says I'm going up to do a stunt show, making the point that I'm solo to keep the plane lighter. So I do a few things, and then at the top of a loop I pretend to fall out, flailing my arms and legs. And on the ground everyone's yelling and screaming . . . then my parachute opens. And the announcer says 'goodbye to that airplane, it'll probably crash in the next county.' Then he says, all excited, 'no wait look it's coming back!'

"Now Ariel is flying . . . only no one can see him because he's so small. And he comes over, and the supposedly empty airplane starts doing stunts again, right over top the crowd. The announcer keeps shouting that this is crazy, and he hopes the plane doesn't run out of gas and crash down on all of us. And just before the crowd is about to run in panic, Ariel comes around and makes a perfect landing, and taxies up, only no one still can't see him. And when the propeller stops, he jumps out. Everyone is so surprised they start clappin' and wavin' and hollerin' and sometimes they get so excited they even throw money at him. He flies like a little angel."

Lindbergh paused for just a moment before speaking; he seemed to be thinking of something. "Wow! That sure sounds like a great act . . . I mean hiding this little kid in your airplane. I'd really like to see it someday. You're not fibbing me are you? This here boy can really fly that airplane of yours?"

"He sure can; much better than most grown-up pilots. Say, we're headed to Saint Louis for the Air Races, which way you say you're going?"

"I'm heading for Saint Louis too."

"Then we'll see you there. . . ."

Four

Now would I give a thousand furlongs of sea for an acre of barren ground; long heath, brown furze, any thing. The wills above be done! but I would fain die a dry death.

Shakespeare *The Tempest I. ii.*

Safely above the clouds now, the warm sun was rapidly melting the coating of ice off the Jungmann's wing surfaces. John leveled the biplane with the horizon, which at present was the top of the cloud deck. Suddenly realizing that at the moment his airplane was still powerless, and about to sink back down into the freezing vapors, he frantically pressed the starter button. After a few tentative revolutions, the modern engine John had installed in the ancient aircraft came back to life. The Lycoming coughed a few times, swallowing some of the melted ice, and then took full throttle. Gently pulling back on the stick, he climbed away from the billowing clouds below.

Swiveling his head from left to right, John's eyes took in the resplendent whiteness of the world surrounding him. He was like a little bird that had failed in his first attempt to fly, but providence had picked up and put back to try again. John felt a childlike sensation of helplessness, a curious sort of dreaminess. It was as if he had looked at things, but his eyes had seen through them to the other side. A basin of thick clouds encircled the Jungmann. If John could remain in this clear area he would be in no immediate danger; however, the steadily growing darkness showed that towering thunderstorms were forming on all sides. And John Vigilia was getting low on gas; he couldn't stay here forever.

Absentmindedly, he recalled a story from one of Charles Lindbergh's early flying experiences. Caught on top of a fog bank, and running out of fuel, Lucky Lindy had bailed out, leaving his airplane to crash in an Illinois cornfield. Lindbergh wrote that he had crossed his legs upon entering the clouds to keep from straddling a branch or electrical wire when he came down, but had landed on a barbed wire fence. It was after his fourth emergency parachute jump, and four wrecked airplanes, that Lindbergh had begun to think about the New York to Paris competition as another way of making some money.

John Vigilia had considered bailing out inside the thunderstorm, but knew that for him it was not an option. The winds would have torn his thin nylon chute to shreds. The idea, however, had been only a last resort, if the airplane had started to come completely apart. He was leaning on a parachute, which he was required to wear during aerobatic competitions. It would have been a simple matter to slip the straps over his shoulders, tighten the buckles, roll the airplane inverted, and just fall out, perhaps flailing his arms and shouting "Geronimo" like they did in the movies.

John's situation had been somewhat different from that of Charles Lindbergh, who had abandoned U.S. Air Mail Service airplanes. The aircraft did not belong to him, and he usually got a replacement the very next day. John Vigilia not only had paid for his Bücker Jungmann out of a modest professor's salary, but had rebuilt the old airplane with his own hands at the grass strip in Texas where he found it. John had invested a great deal of money, sweat, and love, into this machine. He couldn't just abandon it. Then there had been the distinct possibility at the time that he was still over the waters of Lake Erie.

John banked steeply, putting the Jungmann into a 360-degree turn hoping to assess his situation. The whole scene, somber and grave, floated imperceptibly around him, the clouds shifting slightly in wafting, stealthy movements, fluid bands of gray and white in every shade of those non-colors. As he surveyed that heavy and monochrome aura a great valley opened up in front of him, and almost just as suddenly its bottom fell away.

There, on a northwesterly heading, a fantastic landscape was displayed below him. John Vigilia stared covetously at its woods, and fields, and roads. This was where he wanted to go. The only problem with his newly discovered salvation was that it did not match the image of the earth as he had previously known it. Nor did it correspond to any of the symbols on the multicolored chart that he had open on his lap. No matter, it was land, which John was happy for, and would take wherever it might be. Pulling back the power only a bit, he began to spiral down rapidly, fearing the sickly green violence of the surrounding thunderstorms might close in on him yet again before he got through the hole.

The flying wires howled, stretched taut, as John Vigilia descended at close to the Bücker's never-exceed speed. Then, to his dismay, the lovely hole in the clouds below him closed up as unexpectedly as it had appeared. He pulled back on the control stick and leveled out, not wanting to proceed farther down into the vaporous nothingness at near terminal velocity. Circling, John waited for his opening to reappear. Like a child playing hide-and-seek the filmy mist teased him, offering a brief glimpse of the land below and then taking it away, a hole never large enough, or lasting long enough, to proceed down through. John continued to circle until it became apparent that the game was over. The bottom had sealed up completely and now the sides were threatening to close in on him. A light rain began to drum on the wings. He had to make a decision, anymore waiting and things would only become worse.

Having no idea what the ceiling below was, John Vigilia did not want to just go spiraling down in the blind. He might be surprised to find himself breaking out only a few hundred feet above the ground traveling at a great speed. There was one other way; John could spin down. This was a technique often used by the old-time pilots. While it sounded crazy, it did take you down at the slowest possible air speed. The trick was, once you broke out of the clouds, to stop the spin before you hit the ground.

Pulling back on the control stick, John raised the nose of the Bücker, at the same time retarding the power. The airspeed slowly bled off. The wings, having exceeded the critical angle of attack, the point at which they could no longer generate lift, began to buffet, the signal that the airplane was approaching a stall. Holding the back pressure, John Vigilia stomped hard on the left rudder. The right wing came up and over and the biplane fell of into a spin and was immediately whisked down into the void. John held the stick to his stomach and out of habit began to count the turns, which wasn't easy considering he was looking into a leaden nothingness that gave no references at all.

John Vigilia imagined that this was what it must have been like to be born, going head first down; down, to what you did not know. Suddenly John broke out of the clouds. He released the back pressure on the stick and applied opposite rudder to stop the spin. A good little spinner, as well as a snap-roller, the Jungmann stopped on command. John pulled out of the subsequent dive with room to spare, but he still got a more detailed look at the rocky shore than he would have liked to. The beach was shrouded with a dull gray mist. The surf pounded menacingly. Flocks of gulls flashed shrieking towards the water. Rather than relief, John felt a kind of terror overtaking his soul.

Leveling out below the clouds, John Vigilia found it dark, the difference between afternoon and evening, although it was now, by his watch which he no longer trusted, only three o'clock. On a westerly heading the shoreline below him was on his right, so John took it to mean he was paralleling some part of Canada.

John's altimeter indicated that he had broken out of the clouds at about 1000 feet mean sea level. Guessing where he was at present the map showed the surface to be around 400 feet. Keeping 500 feet above the ground to be legal had the Jungmann flying at 900 feet, and in the raveling scud. With the poor visibility, and rain showers all around, John was not too happy, even though his situation was considerably improved from what it had been only minutes ago. Also, the aircraft's fuel gauge was showing lower than he normally allowed it to read before landing.

But where was he actually? Fighting the wind swirling in the open cockpit, using one hand while still flying the bucking airplane with the other, John refolded his chart to a new section. He banked the biplane and looked out over the wing, hoping to find something on the ground that corresponded with the tiny, colorful, symbols on this piece of paper. The rain showers were getting closer, with lightning flashes not that far away. John decided to head inland, due north, as his best hope of finding some place to set down.

Below him the farms and fields slid by, the trees and bushes swaying to and fro in the mayhem of a land invaded by a summer storm. Above John muddled on, participating in his own sense of space, the only sound in his ears the steady beat of the engine, and his own deep breathing. The great, rather disorderly, and somewhat half-ironical conversation that John had been carrying on with himself in his head was causing his tired brain to long for sleep.

Suddenly, out of the rain and fog, as if it had been put there by some great feat of legerdemain, a very large airport with three intersecting runways appeared off to his right. Rather confused by what he saw John wondered where he might be? The only city in this part of Canada that could have an airport of this size would be Toronto. But that should be far to the east. How could he have approached such a huge facility unaware of where he was heading? There had been no indication; no large towns, no maze of highways, none of the things that usually surrounded a major airport.

John had no knowledge of the control tower's radio frequency, and would have a lot of explaining to do when he landed. He would doubtlessly get a violation; however, John no longer cared. Here was an airport. He would land and get gas, and find out where he was, and get things sorted out. Banking the Jungmann, John headed back. His plan would be to circle the tower, and have them shine a light gun at him to clear him to land, if the tower crew remembered how to use the light gun. And, John wasn't too sure that he remembered the light signals either. Was "clear to land" a steady green or a flashing green? Or an alternating green and white? It was a long time since he had answered that very question when it appeared on his private pilot written examination.

Being uninvited, and not wanting to make too bold of an arrival, John made a cautious circuit of the field at pattern altitude. Much to his amazement he found that the rotating beacon was not turned on, which surely it should be considering the low visibility. As he passed over the hangar area he was further surprised to find no airplanes parked anywhere, neither were there any fuel trucks, nor people on the ramp. Nevertheless, John had made his decision. He pulled back the power and circled low around the control tower waggling the aircraft's wings.

In spite of his frantic efforts to be noticed, no light signals shot back at him from the tower. John Vigilia was about to make another circuit, figuring that the tower personal must not have seen him when, peering through the rain, he observed that the tower windows were boarded over with plywood. The entire place showed no sign of life anywhere. For some reason the large boat he had seen on the lake, the *Morgan Sidney,* and the book about the Great Lakes Triangle returned to John's mind. Had he indeed flown into some kind of a time warp? His mouth went dry at the thought. Or was he being completely irrational? Trying to maintain his senses, he shunted the notion to the back of his brain. This was reality, John told himself, not some kind of a science fiction novel—just concentrate on getting this airplane safely on the ground.

Regardless of the rather ominous appearance of the facility John banked the Bücker and set up for the downwind leg of a standard landing pattern. The rain was drumming heavily on the wings now. He could barely see over the side, and had no forward visibility whatsoever. As he turned his base leg, a bolt of lightning flashed off to the north, striking the earth not more than three miles away; wherever he might be at the moment, ghost airport or not, John Vigilia was going to land.

On short final, John could make out large turfs of grass, at least a foot tall, growing out of the cracks in the pavement. Perhaps there was a better runway, but he was not about to go around and look for it. The wind whipped with a turbulence the tower would have called, if anyone were up there, "severe." John was crabbing about 30 degrees into the stiff crosswind, not a favorable situation for an airplane that had its smallest wheel on the back end of its fuselage.

An instant before the main gear touched down, John kicked the Jungmann straight with the rudder. The old biplane bounced three times just to let him know that he had landed a little fast. With the wheels on the ground John immediately got on the brakes. Unhappy with the wet runway, and the tufts of grass it was rolling through, the Bücker swerved, obeying its natural instinct to head into the wind, which was not the way the runway was pointed at the moment. But he had come too far, and flown the Jungmann too many hours to let it have its way and ground loop now. His feet danced on the rudder pedals, his toes stabbing at the breaks. Finally slowing the aircraft to a comfortable walk, John managed to turn off the runway, and maneuver up the battered taxiway to a row of apparently abandoned hangars.

The doors of these massive, hollow buildings had long ago sagged on their hinges, and most of the windows were broken or missing altogether. Where there should be parked aircraft, and fuel trucks, and a line service technician directing his airplane to a tie-down spot, was nothing but an empty ramp, the pavement cracked and crumbling. John could not see a person anywhere. He cut the engine and, removing his headset and helmet, sat in the cockpit listening to the relative quiet of the storm passing overhead. Thankful to be out of the frenzied sky, John climbed out on the slippery, wet wing walk and stepped down onto the firm ground.

"Hello! Hello! Is anybody here?" John Vigilia shouted, hobbling into the nearest of the hangars on legs stiff from their long confinement in the cockpit, and perhaps a little shaky with fear. "Hello! Hello!" he repeated, his voice raw from screaming at no one but himself for the past half-hour. "Is there anyone here?" he asked again even though it was obvious no one was.

The only answer to John's call was the wind and rain rushing through the decaying structure of what he concluded must once have been a World War Two flight training base. "Hello! Hello! Where is everyone?" he shouted again. What was he expecting? a squad of ancient airman to come marching smartly out of the damp shadows.

John guessed that he was somewhere in Canada. If this were true, technically he was illegal, having landed without first clearing customs at an airport of entry. This was, however, the least of his concerns. John moved into the shelter of a corner of the hangar and unfolded his sectional chart. Straining his eyes in the dim light, John carefully checked, and rechecked, the chart but could not find the symbol for an abandoned air force base anywhere near where he figured that he might be.

As the rain was now gone, and no one had appeared since he had landed, John decided to secure the Jungmann as best as he could. He pushed the airplane nearer to the fence and tied the tail to a post, and then chocked the wheels with fallen bricks. Looking over his situation, John concluded that at the moment the wisest plan would be to walk to what appeared as if it might have been the main gate when this place was used for whatever it had once been. Checking the security of his biplane one last time, John started out in that direction.

Upon reaching the gate John was disappointed to find that the road that lay beyond it appeared as if it had been little traveled lately. The black asphalt was cracked and riddled with pot-holes that revealed numerous layers of pavement which, like the rings of a tree, gave a clue to its age. To the right, just over a hill and at a distance he judged to be about five miles, a bright strobe light flashed on the top of a tall smokestack. This was most likely a power plant, a possible clue to where he might be.

John unfolded his chart and laid it out on the ground, holding it against the wind. His moving finger explored the Canadian shoreline. There was only one symbol for a power plant with a strobe light along the coast of Lake Erie, and it was about sixty miles back, east of Long Point. Yes, he had been flying into a head wind, John considered, but the wind could not have been so strong as to have blown him that far off course. He would have had to have been flying backwards. His finger nervously traced westward along the damp map. Following the shoreline as far as the American border, John found no other power plants. What concerned him even more was that he could not find a symbol for an abandoned airport anywhere near where he had concluded that he might be.

On the horizon off to his left John could make out a silo and a barn, which he estimated to be no more than a half mile away. Since it was the only building he saw, other than the hangars, and the rain had begun again, John started in that direction. Not knowing why, as he tramped along the road, John began loudly singing songs from popular Broadway musical comedies. Was John Vigilia afraid of something? He didn't even like musical tunes, but sang, and then whistled the parts that he did not know the words to. By the time John reached the barn he had run out of songs, and the rain had become quite heavy. Taking refuge in the hay, he hunkered down in the one corner of the ancient structure that did not seem to leak.

After his eyes had adjusted to the darkness, John observed that the shadowy walls were hung with all kinds of leather harnesses and tack, and strange farm implements from another era. In that dank space, with the thunder and the lightning flashing outside, the sharp prongs and hooks gave John the ominous impression of being in a torture chamber. An involuntary shudder ran through his body. To ease himself of this notion, and to get some fresh air as the place smelled heavily of manure, John went over to the far wall and put his head out of a gap in the rotting boards. Lightning struck again, somewhere nearby, illuminating his view of the landscape and revealing a clapboard farmhouse a short distance down the road. Not knowing what else to do, he decided to head for this place as soon as the rain let up a bit.

Five

Mark his condition, and th' event; then tell me
If this might be a brother.

Shakespeare *The Tempest I. ii,*

The thunderstorm ended as abruptly as it had begun, leaving the scent of a new succulence on the earth. John Vigilia heard the birds singing, and the faint barking of a dog, and a train whistle in the distance, all the delicate noises of the country. Feeling good again, he got up from the hay where he had been resting and started to head out for the farmhouse. Suddenly, and without warning, he felt three sharp prongs pressed into his back. John froze in place

"What're you doing here, eh?" a voice demanded behind him.

"Who are you? . . ." John inquired cautiously.

"Never you mind who I am . . . I own this here farm, eh. So now you just turn around slow like."

John quickly did as he was ordered, instinctively putting his hands over his head without being told. Facing his captor, John saw an elderly man wearing a dirty yellow slicker thoroughly drenched by the rain, its hood cloaking him like a monk. On his feet were glistening green Wellington boots. The man's hands were shaking as he wielded his pitch fork aggressively at the intruder he had just discovered.

"What'er you doing in this here barn, eh?" the man asked.

"I was just trying to keep dry . . . I was running out of gas, so I landed my airplane at that old air base down the road. I was hoping to find someone who might be able to tell me where I am."

"Did see an airplane go over awhile ago . . . and then it looked like it was maybe going to land. Thought it might have been in trouble, eh. But I was waiting for the rain to stop . . . so I could go see what happened. I was lookin' out the window there when I see you sneaking into mah barn, eh." The old man had said all this very slowly, as if he was carefully weighing his words.

"So, where am I?" John asked

"You're in mah barn, eh."

"I know that . . . but just where is your barn."

"It's right here, on mah farm."

"I mean what town are we in?"

"We ain't in no town, eh . . . we're here in the country."

John realized that he was getting nowhere; perhaps the man was retarded, or just senile. He put down his hands and reached for the aeronautical chart, which he had dropped on the hay-covered floor.

"Hey! Watch it there, fella. . . ." the old man said, taking a step back and at the same time jabbing his pitchfork in John's direction.

"Okay, okay. Take it easy, I'm just getting my map." John said, unfolding it and pointing to the area that he thought they were in. "Maybe we can find out where we are on this here. . . ."

The old man looked at the large and colorful paper. A puzzled expression came over his face. He rubbed his hand across his grizzled jaw. "Can't read no maps like that there, eh."

"Then what's the name of that power plant down the road, the place with the tall smoke stack and the flashing light?"

"That there be the power plant, eh."

"I know that, but what's its name?"

"Dunno . . . everyone just calls it the power plant, eh . . . that's good enough for me."

"And what do they call that old airport up the road a bit?"

"We just call it the old airport, eh. They kept a lot of airplanes there during the war. I used to go down there and watch 'em fly. But when the war was over . . . they took 'em all away. They used to use it for motorcycle races awhile back . . . but now they don't use it for anything. Yours is the first airplane I see go down there in quite some time, eh."

"Look, I need to find out where I am. I don't have much fuel left, so I can't just get in my airplane and go flying around looking for things. I need to head directly to the nearest airport. Is there anyone around here who might know the name of where we are?"

"Mah aunt does. . . ."

"Then let's go get your aunt."

"Can't, she's not home now, eh. She's gone to, ah . . . to the cemetery. But we can go back to the house and wait for her . . . if ya like."

The old man hung the pitchfork up on hook on the wall, which John took as a sign that the man trusted him. Then, without speaking, the two of them left the barn and walked up the road to the old farmhouse. When they reached the house, the man led John through a battered screen door, which slammed shut loudly behind them. Looking around John felt, upon walking into the stillness of the dark, empty, and neglected rooms, like an intruder in a different, and separate, notion of time and space.

The old man removed his rain hood, giving John a better view of his face and head, which were overgrown with wild and recalcitrant shocks of gray hair, bristling in irregular tufts, not only from his scalp, but from his warts, his eyebrows, and the openings of his nostrils and ears, giving him the appearance of an anxious porcupine. Hanging his wet gear on a peg in the corner, the man motioned John to sit at the table. Without saying a word he sat down across from him. The grim old man was sweating heavily, giving off the odor of damp wool, rat holes, chicken droppings, and musty places between the old walls.

The rain started again. The two men sat there, not talking, listening to the storm beating on the roof. John had the choking feeling that he had lost contact with the real world. The aunt had to return soon, and tell him where he was. The rain had to stop before it got dark. He could not imagine spending the night in this stale place. John waited for the old man to say something, but he just crouched at the table cracking his knuckles.

A half-hour must have passed as the two of them sat there eyeing each other without speaking. The host's face seemed to express a more than usual anxiety. John found something extraordinary in the stillness, a profound, but yet obscure significance, which his thoughts could not succeed in penetrating. Finally, the old man broke the silence.

"My name is Caliban, but they call me Cal, eh. Cal Angelucci. What's yer name then?" he said, an inquisitive look coming across his rough weathered face.

"John . . . John Vigilia," the visitor replied, adding, "and when did you say your aunt was coming back?"

"I got a twin brother too," the old man said ignoring John's question about his aunt, "name's Ariel. But he don't live round here, eh."

"Ariel and Caliban," John mused, nonplused by the revelation. "Your parents must have read Shakespeare."

"My father was damn smart, eh. . . ."

"Really, what did he do?"

"In Italy he taught literature in a university, but in Chicago the only work he could get was in the slaughter houses."

"How'd that happen?"

"They said he wasn't qualified to teach here, eh. He spoke good English, but they said his degrees were no good in Chicago. Can you imagine that? There were many great universities in Italy long before schools like Harvard and Yale were even cow pastures, eh."

John tried to turn the conversation back to his situation. "So when's your aunt coming home, Cal? . . ." He caught himself almost ending his question with the word "eh."

"She's been gone a long time now . . . but she should be back soon enough, eh. Then ya can get yer directions offen her."

"Oh, well I guess I'll just have to wait," was all John could manage to say. He could hear the rain pounding heavily on the roof now. To John, however, the steady monotonous noise seemed not to come from the outside but from deep within himself. His heart was pounding, perhaps with fear. He wanted to start singing the show tunes that he had sung on the way here.

Without any prior warning, and with a surprisingly graceful, feline movement Caliban leapt up and tiptoed to the door, peering out through the screen with utmost caution. Then, with a bashful smile, he returned to the table slightly embarrassed, murmuring and whispering indistinctly to himself: "I thought I heard her coming, eh, but she ain't here yet. . . ."

"Where did you say she was coming from again?"

"She's comin' from the cemetery . . . she visits the grave, eh."

"Whose grave does she visit?"

"Dunno. She gets up early in the morning eh, before I'm awake . . . and just goes there by herself."

John kept silent; not wanting to interrupt the elderly man's conversation, remembering those what must have been hundreds of cemetery visits he had made with his mother after his father died. Who ever forgets such things? She would link her arm in his, her poor emaciated arm, so fragile he could barely feel it through the heavy coat she wore in the heat of summer as well as the cold of winter. Holding on to her son with one hand, her cane in the other, they would walk together through the rows of headstones searching for the graves of people they both had known.

"Your aunt's been gone a long time then," John said after Caliban had paused. "Where's she coming from?"

"Where'd you come from in that there airplane of yours, eh?"

"Elmira . . . down in New York State."

"Took you a long time to get here then, eh?"

John glanced down at his watch. "It shouldn't have . . . but it seems to have taken longer than I planned. What time is it now?"

"Dunno, don't have no time piece. My aunt has one though . . . she'll tell us what time it be when she gets here, eh. . . ."

The rain began falling heavily again. A nearby lightning flash illuminated the room, followed shortly by its clap of thunder, a hoarse screaming as if the earth were protesting and clamoring in sudden pain. To provide a bit of distraction from the morbid speculations that were entering his head, John got up and began to pace about the floor. He shuffled in silence, without enthusiasm, absent of any intention or spirit. The whole situation had taken on the aspect of the unendurable reality of bad theater.

"Kin you fly to Paris in that there airplane of yours, eh?" Caliban asked for no apparent reason.

What a strange question to ask, John thought before answering: "No I can't."

"Why not then, eh?"

"Well, for one thing it doesn't hold enough gas. . . ."

"What iffen you could put in a great big tank, eh . . . with enough gas to get you all the way there?"

"Maybe, but I don't have the right instruments. . . ."

"So do ya have as many instruments as Lindbergh had when he flew to Paris?"

"Well back then airplanes didn't have very many instruments. I probably have even more. . . ."

"Then you're afraid to do it, eh?"

"No! I'm not afraid."

". . . afraid you'd fall asleep and go down in the ocean."

"Well, it is a long flight, I mean I flew to Paris on an airliner once and got tired just sitting in the seat," John responded using the restrained voice of passionate practicality.

"Well then how did Lindbergh get to do it without falling asleep, eh?"

"Look . . . I don't know. I guess he was a brave man . . . and all that, and lucky besides," John said adding, "So when do you think your aunt is coming back?"

"They say Lindbergh was alone," Ariel said, reluctant to leave the subject that he had so strangely introduced. "But I know he wasn't. He had someone with him, a secret copilot, eh."

"There was no one with him. Where did you get the notion that there was?"

"A small boy was hiding in the back. Lindbergh had landed in Nova Scotia and picked him up. The boy knew how to fly, eh . . . so he changed places and sat on Lindbergh's lap and flew the airplane while he slept. If I go with you, and help you fly the plane will you take me to Paris, eh?"

John pondered this strange revelation from a man he now was beginning to realize was madder than he had first imagined. He had a hard time restraining himself from laughing out loud. "So who told you that story about Lindbergh having a small boy copilot? It's the weirdest thing I have ever heard. Everyone knows Lindbergh was alone; that's why he's so famous. And why do you want to go to Paris anyhow?"

"I don't want to go all the way to Paris, eh . . . you can just drop me off in Ireland . . . where my brother Ariel is. I want to find my brother, eh."

John's gaze again circled around the shabby, badly lit, dirty kitchen. The rain rattling on the roof made the empty room seem full of somnolent human chatter and random confusion. He parted a pale blue curtain and peered into the cluttered next room. To his surprise, John Vigilia found a fading photograph of a man and a young boy standing in front of an early Curtiss biplane, a Jenny, displayed on the mantle.

"That there's my brother Ariel, eh" Caliban said coming into the room behind John Vigilia and pointing at the boy. He was standing too close to his visitor and was peering over his shoulder. John could smell his breath, the scent of fried eggs and rotten teeth. "And that there man was my Uncle Francis, a pilot, an early barnstormer, eh."

"Is that so?" John commented moving away from the man, but Caliban closed the gap between then and went on talking.

"Ariel and I used to live in Chicago with our parents, eh. Like I told you, our father used to work in a slaughterhouse . . . he cut up things, pigs and cows, eh."

Caliban's closeness and his reference to cutting up things sent a shudder down John's spine. His eyes were drawn back to the kitchen where he could see a wooden rack holding knives hanging over the sink. Unconsciously he counted them; there were five knives in a rack that should have held six. Had the rack been full when they came in? he wondered. Lightning flashed outside. John moved away from Caliban again. He went to the window and looked out trying to assess his situation. What did he know about this old man? Where was the aunt, and when was she coming home? John took a deep breath, and flexed his hands, trying to reconcile himself to his entrapment.

For no apparent reason, John began to think about his wife's private parts, of the great sex they had had before she started getting her abdominal pains. The doctor said it was nothing, perhaps a problem of her age. But they were not that old. John Vigilia wondered what he was doing traveling around the country all summer long to make a display of his flying prowess, while his wife spent most of her days lying in bed in pain. What was it that he found so attractive in the sky that he did not have the courage to stay on the ground?

The old man kept on talking, as much to himself as to his visitor, his voice going from a lofted melodrama to low, mumbled humdrum. "And then after my father sliced up my mother, he set the apartment on fire, eh . . . then slashed up his own wrists and lay down on the bed to die. Ariel and I were at school, and only heard this story later . . . at first they told us that it just had been an accident, eh."

Reduced to silence by the man's tales, John skulked at the window watching the rain trickle down the glass. Nevertheless, he was listening carefully, almost out of habit, accustomed to the storytelling exploits of his students. But Caliban's Lindbergh story was good, much better than what the Stunt Flying Professor was used to. It was not an old tale repeated, although nothing in the world is ever new, rather derived in some way from something else. But somehow Caliban had come up with something John had not heard before, the idea of Lindbergh having a secret copilot. But it couldn't possibly be true. "So tell me the rest of your story," John said, trying not to sound too eager.

"So after our parents died, I was sent to live with an aunt on this here farm, eh. It was good here, but I had to work hard all the time, almost like a slave . . . but my brother Ariel, he got to go and live with my Uncle Francis, who was a barnstormer in the Midwest. And my uncle taught him how to fly and to do stunts in the airplane . . . and Ariel used to hide in the front cockpit, because he was so little, no one could see him, eh . . . then my uncle would pretend to fall out of the airplane, waving his arms and shouting, eh. And his parachute would open . . . and after he was out Ariel would fly the airplane and do some stunts and then land."

"Are you making this all up?" John said his voice rising in incredulity. Outside the rain had stopped. "And what does this all have to do with you wanting me to fly you to Paris like Lindbergh?" he asked somewhat gruffly. John was growing tired of the old man's stories; he wanted the aunt to come home so he could find out where he was and be on his way.

"You see Lindbergh saw my brother fly, eh . . . and a few years later, when he was planning his trip to Paris . . . there was a contest to see who would be the first. . . ."

"Yes, Yes, I've read the story and know all about that."

"But, you don't know this part, eh . . . nobody does, nobody but me; everyone else who knew it is dead, and now I am going to tell you. . . ."

This revelation, real or not, caused the hair to stand up on the back of John Vigilia's neck. "So tell me, I'll risk it," he said with a bravado that surprised him. For the first time he noticed a clock ticking in the next room. John remembered that the old man had said he didn't have a watch, and that his aunt would tell them the time when she got home. So why had he lied about this simple matter?

Caliban smiled, his teeth forming a crisp line immediately below his nose, giving him an eager, predatory look. "Lindbergh met my uncle and asked if he could hire Ariel to go with him on the flight . . . no one was to know, eh. He had raised a lot of money because he was supposed to go all by himself . . . when several other men had already died flying together in bigger airplanes. . . . Well, Lindbergh realized he couldn't do it, that he would fall asleep. But, he didn't want to lose his chance, eh . . . so he decided to take Ariel, because he was so small and could fit in the little space behind his seat, and also because he knew how to fly.

"The plan was Lindbergh would make a big show of taking off from New York alone, and then land in Nova Scotia, eh . . . and pick up Ariel, who would sit on Lindbergh's lap and fly while he slept. When they got to Ireland . . . Lindbergh would land on a beach and drop off my brother before going on to Paris. If Lindbergh made it all the way, eh, Ariel and my Uncle Francis were going to secretly get a share of the prize money."

"So what happened? . . ." John asked, surprised that his interest was growing in this unbelievable story.

"Something went wrong, eh . . . the men who were supposed to pick up Ariel on the beach in Ireland never found him. Then my Uncle Francis heard Ariel had been caught by the police, who thought he was a runaway, and was being kept in an orphanage run by Catholic nuns near a town called Dingle . . . and he went over there to get him back, eh. But before he could find Ariel my uncle died. . . ." Caliban made a puzzled pause, gazed around the room for some little time, then looked at John Vigilia carefully before going on. "They said he fell off a train on the way there, eh. But I don't believe he fell; I think he was pushed . . . murdered."

Startled, by this speculation, John moved away from the window. Even if he was telling the truth, what could Caliban change now? Would his going to Ireland, or to Paris change, anything? He was listening to the repetition of a series of events that had taken place a long time ago. History had already been written. That was the story so far. Isn't each of us just anyone, John thought to himself, to whom anything can happen at anytime? And after it is written down, that is how it occurred, whether or not the events were recorded accurately.

The clouds had parted and the sun was showing itself again if only for a few brief moments, tragic and pale. Sunshine could be at the same time the gladdest and the saddest thing in the entire universe. In all of John's most painful memories, as well as his most joyous, there was always a little sunshine; coruscating through the whirling propeller as he pulled out of the bottom of a loop; reflecting off the brass handles of his father's coffin as he walked behind it at his burial.

John was now growing impatient. The aunt was never coming back. Caliban, if that was his real name, would begin another story, which would most likely be entertaining, but he doubted could surpass his Lindbergh tale. He wondered if the man even had a brother. Ariel was probably just an empty echo of Caliban, two names he no doubt must have taken from Shakespeare's play *The Tempest.* He supposed that the old man must read a great deal, although he could see no books anywhere. The storm raging outside, John thought, and a perfect stranger having been sort of "washed up on his shores" in all probability had stimulated the lonely old man's imagination.

Doubtless Caliban's next story would be equally inventive, but John decided to take this opportunity to leave, even if he wasn't sure of where he was now, or where he was going. John Vigilia would walk back to the airport, hoping that perhaps he might meet someone else on the way.

"Goodbye, Cal, it was nice talking to you," John said, as he hurriedly worked his way out the door of the old farmhouse. He looked up. On the power lines out front an assembly of sparrows had begun to chatter.

"Goodbye to you, John," Caliban said, standing on the porch. He seemed deeply saddened by his recent guest's departure, but resigned, as if leave taking for him was a common occurrence. "You'll stop on your way back and take me to Paris, won't you, eh? You see my aunt can't say no because she stays at the cemetery all the time now."

Suddenly, for the first time, John Vigilia understood what Caliban had been trying to tell him about his aunt, that despite how much he hoped for her return; she was dead, and would never be coming back.

John looked over his shoulder from time to time as he walked off toward the airport. The old man stood watching him from his front door until John could no longer make him out. He thought about Caliban's strange story. Obviously he lived alone and amused himself by making up these tales. He had been more than happy to have someone as a captive audience. John Vigilia speculated what other stories the man might have told him had he been forced to stay the night. He saw this old man, out of touch with his fellow human beings, living a life that was a permanent lie. Inventing stories was for Caliban both his satisfaction and his pitiful fate.

John wondered where his own stories had lately disappeared to. Had he lost his adeptness with words because his original goal had been to become a visual artist, a painter? Had he only worn a convenient mask, disguising himself as a writer, while hiding from a hypocritical society whose fine art was in a chronic state of decline.

Had he lied to himself? John Vigilia considered. Was the almost constant self-deception a masquerade, which concealed his elitism, and the duality of his very being? John was jealous of the old man's story. A tale about a small boy who was smuggled on board and flew the *Spirit of Saint Louis* while Lindbergh slept was indeed an ingenious story. Make the tale bigger than life, John reminded himself, and everyone would believe it for what it is; or would they?

John Vigilia realized that he had always been an ironic dreamer; unable to fulfill his inner promise. He almost enjoyed watching his carefully worked efforts go down in defeat. He was never convinced of what he believed in. Words were his only truth; yet the right words never seemed to come from his hand. What had he made of his life so far that really mattered? John asked himself as he walked along in the misty wind.

Six

O, the heavens!
What foul play had we that we came from thence?
Or blessed was't we did?

Shakespeare *The Tempest I. ii.*

A stiff breeze had come up from in the direction John took to be Lake Erie. It raked the few trees lining the road, rattling their branches like bones, their wet leaves glistening. The odor of damp cow dung assaulted his eager sense of smell, and somewhere nearby a male skunk was apparently looking for a mate. He kept tramping, the winds in his face creating a deafening roar. Head down and shoulders pumping, John followed his legs with impunity until they finally led him back to where he had come from, the entrance to the abandoned air force base.

The brisk walk in the blowing wind had cleared the claustrophobia from John Vigilia's head. Back at the farmhouse John had encountered moments of panic when he felt like he was going to suffocate. Arriving back at the airport, having met no one on the way, John still did not know where he was. A brief tour of the confused spectacle of crumbling buildings also gave no clue, as every room appeared to have been stripped a long time ago of anything of value that it might have held.

He resisted the temptation to stay on the ground and to attempt to walk to someplace else. It was getting on in the afternoon. With the overcast sky there would be no dusk, and he no longer trusted his watch. John could not shake the notion, however bizarre, that he had somehow flown into another time zone, or perhaps a space warp, a place from which, his irrational mind told himself, he could only escape if he remained unaware of its existence.

As captivating as this fantasy was John's real problem at present was fuel. When he had landed the Jungmann's gauge showed less than a quarter of a tank, hardly enough to get him anywhere—especially if he didn't know where he was going. To save what little avgas he did have John decided not to start the engine and taxi the Bücker out. Struggling over the buckled pavement and the tall weeds growing between the cracks, he dragged the biplane, rocking in the wind, to the end of the runway by its tail first. John planned to take off, and then head west, at reduced power, hoping to figure out where he was, and to find an airport before he ran out of fuel. With the stiff winds, which were still blowing from that direction, it would have made more sense to head east to save gas, but John Vigilia was reluctant to give up one mile in the direction of Wisconsin, even though he now had no possibility of reaching there before nightfall. He pushed in the throttle, roared down the runway, and slowly climbed out, reducing the power and leaning the mixture as he ascended.

The sun had disappeared again, and the low clouds would prevent John from climbing much higher than 1000 feet above the ground, not a good altitude for fuel economy, or if you were stumbling around trying to spot landmarks to determine your location.

Flying across a river, John banked and decided to follow it. Rivers usually led to towns, he reasoned, and towns often had airports near to them. Good fortune smiled on his choice. After about ten minutes a streak of sunlight, as if a gleaming yellow pointer, revealed a small grass airstrip off the biplane's right wing. He turned and made for it. A quick circuit assured him that the only hangar on the field did indeed have a gas pump next to it. He called on Unicom for traffic advisories. While there was, as always, immense chatter from every aircraft in radio range, no one responded to John from what he assumed to be the airport below. Realizing that he dared not go anywhere else, he checked the windsock, scanned for other traffic, and entered the downwind leg to set up for a landing.

To John's joy he greased the Bücker on in godlike fashion, the old biplane being happier on grass runways than on the concrete and asphalt he normally subjected it to. Pleased with the landing and his luck at finding an airport so quickly, John Vigilia was happily taxing toward the hangar, s-turning as one needed to do in a tail-wheel aircraft, when what he saw caused that little courage he still had to desert him. Was the fading light playing some coarse trick on John's already overstretched imagination?

As he taxied closer and confirmed their presence, the row of airplanes parked in purplish shadow behind the hanger gave John such a fright that he almost put the power to the Jungmann and took off again. There, tied down next to a stand of trees so that he had not noticed them when he flew over, was a neat line of five World War Two Grumman TBF Avengers, looking as fit and trim as if they were again about to go up against the Japanese fleet at Midway.

Upon viewing this unexplainable row of ancient war birds, John became more convinced than ever that he should be away from this place. A check of his fuel gauge, however, as the biplane bounced along the rough ground, made him painfully aware that, as much as he would have liked to, John did not have enough gas to go anywhere else. He told himself that there must be some rational reason why this small grass strip in Canada, if he was in Canada, would have a row of U. S. Navy torpedo bombers tied down, the very same type, and number of airplanes that had disappeared while on a training mission off the coast of Florida into the Bermuda triangle in 1942.

Besides the time warp theory, two other possibilities swirled in John's severely puzzled brain: first; that this was a dream, and second; that he might be dead. In either case he would not need anymore fuel, John reassured himself as his hand went for the throttle. Then a line boy appeared out of the door of the hangar, waving him toward the avgas tanks. He pulled up to the pumps and cut his engine. As John Vigilia climbed out of the cockpit the lad gave him a look as if he were seeing a ghost. John guessed he must be dead.

"So you're from the states, eh?" the boy said, reading the registration number on the side of John's biplane. "Where'd ya come from then? Like we don't get many Americans stoppin' here, eh."

"Well, I was going to land at that big airport I just passed buy, but no one was home," John joked, fishing for the answer as to where he had recently been, so he might figure out where he was now.

"What big airport? The only airport of any size near here is Saint Catharines, and that's quite a ways away, ya know," the line boy informed him.

John caught the smell of the avgas as the line boy popped the filler cap from the Bücker's fuel tank. He felt reassured, in dreams you can't smell things, he told himself.

"Oh! My eyes must have been playing tricks," John said, defensively. "I thought I saw an airport with three crossed runways back there just a bit."

"Not 'round here. So where'd ya clear customs, eh?" the boy asked, his suspicions apparently aroused.

"Oh, I landed at Saint Catharines," John lied. "I mean I thought I saw another airport between there and here, but I guess not." John Vigilia couldn't image that he was being taken for a drug smuggler; illegal aviators didn't fly around in multicolored biplanes with "The Stunt Flying Professor" lettered on the side of the fuselage in nine inch high letters.

"Top it off with 80 octane," John said climbing from the cockpit. "I'll be inside."

It had started to rain again, not a heavy downpour, just a spatter from a passing cloud. As he sprinted toward the office, it occurred to John that the line boy might wonder why he hadn't gassed his airplane at Saint Catharines when he supposedly had stopped there for customs. He turned and shouted, "Those big airports make enough money . . . I like to give you little guys my business."

The line boy smiled, but said nothing.

Safely inside out of the drizzle, John looked around hopelessly at the empty room. Up until now every airport he ever visited had a wall-size map in the pilot's lounge, complete with a compass rose mounted over the airport's location and a length of tape marked in miles that rotated from that point, which was used, mainly by student pilots, for flight planning. This one did not. Nor was there a name over the door, or anywhere else, that would reveal to him where he was. At least there was a clock, which agreed, more or less, with John's wristwatch. As no one else had appeared, he would have to ask the line boy the name of the airport when he came back in. John hoped that the boy wouldn't consider his question too dim-witted. Was he perhaps unconvinced by John's parting statement, and wondering why this rather confused visitor hadn't saved time by also getting fuel in St. Catharine's, when he supposedly had landed there earlier to clear customs.

"She only took twelve gallons, eh" the line boy announced coming in the door. "How much does she hold then?"

John was surprised. “Are you sure you filled it all the way up?” He asked. “It has a thirty-five gallon tank.”

“All the way to the top. I was filling ‘er and then she started squirting out the bottom. I put my finger in the neck and she was full, eh.”

“Oh yeah, I forgot to tell you about that . . . I have a special tank installed for inverted flying, it vents from the bottom.”

“So you’re the stunt flyer, eh?” the line boy said, looking at the name on John’s credit card, which matched the name lettered on the side of his airplane. “We don’t get very many famous pilots in here, especially from the states. Would you sign our guest book so that I can show it to people to prove that you really landed here? I wish I had my camera so’s I could take your picture, eh.”

“Oh, sure,” John Vigilia said. That’s just great, he thought to himself. Here he was, in Canada illegally, not having cleared customs, and the authorities would not only have his signature on a dated credit card receipt, but also in the airport’s guest book. He considered signing a fictitious name, just scrawling anything, but the line boy followed him over to the book, where he handed John a ballpoint pen. He twirled the pen over in his hand checking it to see if the name of the airport might be printed on it, but it carried no advertising.

“Ve-gel-ea,” the line boy said slowly, watching the visitor write. “That how you pronounce it, eh?”

“Close enough. Few people get it right, John said. “Thank you, I’ll be on my way now,” He handed back the pen. The rain had let up again. John headed out to the Bücker, with the undeterred line boy following close at his heels.

Grabbing the handhold, John hiked himself up onto the bottom wing and clambered into the cockpit. The line boy climbed up after him. Being careful to stay on the wing walk, he helped The Stunt Flying Professor with his shoulder straps. The boy must have seen an air show or two in his day, John thought. He pulled on his fight helmet, buckled the chinstrap, and swung his head around to be sure the radio cord was free. Shaking the line boy's hand, John thanked him for his service. The boy smiled and jumped down off the wing walk. Glancing around John Vigilia saw that the rest of the airport appeared to be still uninhabited. As much as he wanted to, John refrained from asking the line boy the name of the airport and about the five Grumman Avengers parked behind the hanger. In fact, John hoped very much that the torpedo bombers had been only his eyes playing tricks with him, and wouldn't be there when he taxied back out.

The sound of his engine echoed off the hangar sides as the Bücker rattled past. Turning the corner John saw them clearly. To his dismay they were still there, all five Grumman Avengers, with their big radial engines, lurking in the shadow of the trees. John had not, however, walked up and actually touched them, had he? He kept telling himself that they were just a vulgar figment of his over-active imagination. Looking at the Avengers, John Vigilia felt the same eerie sensation that he had experienced the day when he first was led into the funeral parlor to see his father's corpse, all powered and painted up. Lying in his open casket surrounded by wreaths and flowers, John's eyes had seen a man that had appeared to him then more real than when he was alive. No matter what the story of these airplanes was; he should be out of here as fast as he could.

The clouds had cleared a bit. It was getting on toward evening, the cloud bases streaked with sunlight. John lined up with the runway, pulled down his goggles, and took off into a darkening sky. Climbing up to 3500 feet above the ground level, he could just make out the waters of Lake Erie glistening in the setting sun off to the southwest, so decided to head that way. He would pick up the shoreline and trace it west until he got to Detroit, which he hoped to reach before nightfall.

After about some twenty minutes of following the shore, John came upon a long, dark spit of land jutting out into the lake, identical to the shape of Long Point as it was depicted on his map. Confident that this was the Long Point that he had been looking for, but still confused about how he had gotten so far east, John passed over it and continued on his course toward the rapidly sinking sun. The blazing orange sunset was soaking everything in a warm glow, and gave a vague promise of a nice day for tomorrow. If he got an early start John Vigilia could easily be in Wisconsin before noon, with plenty of time to register for the contest and get in a practice flight before it got dark.

Ten minutes past Long Point John spotted what appeared to be a cargo boat riding on the dark green waves, and roughly paralleling his course. This was the only boat he had seen since departing the grass strip, the name of which he still had not yet learned. Something attracted John, almost tormentingly, to the ship, which for some reason looked strangely familiar. His mind hesitated for a moment. John was eager to continue on his way, but could not resist diving down and giving the boat a quick look over. He swooped low and fell in beside the vessel as it chopped along on the dark waters. Then he saw it; clearly lettered on the bow were the words, *Morgan Sidney, Liverpool.*

John's heart accelerated a few beats. A dreadful silence filled the cockpit. All the fantastic fears that had gripped him for most of the afternoon returned like a nightmare. During the time that he had been on the ground John had forgotten about this boat, and yet now here it was, approximately where he had passed it several hours ago, that is if his rather vague calculations were anywhere near correct. He remembered the crewmen pointing behind him, which would put the *Morgan Sidney* in the position where she now lay. How John had gotten so far east that he had to fly almost a half-hour before he came on to the ship again he could not comprehend. And why had the *Morgan Sidney* not moved farther on during the time, almost three hours, which he had spent wandering about the farm and the two airports. Could she be anchored? He decided to circle around and give the ship another look.

The lake was mostly in shadow now; however, where the sun did break through it painted the surface of the water a burning gold. A shaft of sunlight as narrow as the band of a laser beam sharply illuminated the *Morgan Sidney* as brightly as if she were on fire. John banked and turned. For a few seconds the ship was under his wing and he lost sight of it. When John leveled off again the sun was gone and the lake was wrapped in twilight. Continuing on, he searched the water for the ship. John Vigilia always fancied himself to have keen eyes, but at the moment he could not see the vessel that he was seeking. Guided by intuition, John proceeded to where he had last seen the *Morgan Sidney*. He peered over the side at the dim water. For an instant John thought he caught the silhouette of a ship riding on the swollen and purple swell, but when he refocused his eyes there was nothing there but empty space.

Going lower, his prop wash churning up a wake in the rolling water below him, John circled the area yet another time, however, found no trace of any ship. Had his own eyes gone mad in John's head? Or might he soon wake up with a jolt and find himself still in his bed at 33 Seneca Road in Elmira. As if to test this introspection, with a decisive gesture John simultaneously pushed in the throttle, pulled back on the stick and banked the airplane, swinging around and climbing away from the water. In that instant all the fantastic fears he had been subject to this day fell from him like the bonds of a man suddenly freed from his chains.

Heading west, into the fiery innocence of the evening sky, John Vigilia's mind mulled over the events that had transpired since he departed the New York shore of Lake Erie some six hours ago. Off to his left the lake was slowly expanding, a pool of black treacle. Despite having made several wrong decisions earlier, he was thankfully up here in the sky, not below the surface of that leaden, watery mass. John smiled and considered what an irrational fool he had been. The terrible truth rose in John's mind that despite his preconceptions otherwise, all human life was based on uncertainty—a horrible, horrible, uncertainty.

Seven

What
seest thou else
In the dark backward and abysm of time?
If thou remember'st aught ere thou cam'st here,
How thou cam'st here, thou may'st.

Shakespeare *The Tempest I. ii.*

The contest was over. On his way home now John and his Bücker were approaching Lake Erie from the west. The Stunt Flying Professor studied the changing landscape below him with awe. The storm-ridden body of water that had harried John on his way out was for the moment placid and tranquil, the full afternoon sun soaking everything in warmth. There was something about this blue vastness that always caused John to rearrange his position in the world; to realize how very small he was in relation to the whole of creation.

John Vigilia was vaguely surprised by the large number of birds soaring seemingly carefree in the sky, oblivious to his passing. The fresh wind filled his lungs and cleared his head. Contented in his breezy cockpit, John felt a strange and vivid worth in all the earth around him, and in the sky above. He sensed the love of life in all living things. In the beating of his heart John imagined he could hear the surf pounding on the shore below, and the cry of the sea gulls. Then, like the gray clouds he could see forming to the southeast, dark and heavy thoughts began to permeate his mind.

Fond du Lac, Wisconsin, the biggest aerobatic competition of the season had been a disappointment for John Vigilia, not that he hadn't done well. He had come in eighth in the Sportsman Category, out of thirty-three contestants. Sportsman almost always had the most entrants; it was the beginners' category. Most pilots flew in two or three events in Sportsman and then dropped out of competition flying, finding the activity to be too demanding, or just too expensive.

There was no prize money in these events, only trophies to the top three places in each category. John often came in fourth, which meant that he got nothing out of it but the joy of competing, and seeing his name near the top in the "results column" of *Aerobatic News,* the club magazine. Despite the considerable sums of money that the competitors had spent for their airplanes, plus the high cost of fuel, maintenance, insurance, and travel, this was strictly an amateur sport.

At smaller competitions John Vigilia sometimes placed third or even second, depending on who else showed up. It was not his lack of skill. John could be flying in Advanced or Unlimited, but wasn't going to do it in his ancient biplane. He needed a Pitts Special, or one of the new monoplanes from Germany that had recently come onto the scene. Beginning at $150,000, their price was out of the range of someone who taught English at a small private college.

Nevertheless, John Vigilia had dazzled the crowds at the Saturday air show. "Now here he comes! The Stunt Flying Professor in his immaculately restored 1938 Bücker Jungmann!" the announcer could be heard shouting through the loudspeaker. John kept his program to simple maneuvers, all that the Jungmann could do, but he did them with skill, and close to the ground. Air show fans always liked to see a pilot working his flight right down on the deck. While the spectators were there ostensibly to admire the pilot's flying skills, as well as his daring, more than a few harbored the secret desire to see the aerial showoff crash and maybe even blow up, like everything seemed to do in the movies.

And John Vigilia's old biplane put out a long and thick trail of smoke behind it, which for some reason was also what the crowd liked to see. Then there was the novelty of a college professor, with a funny name flying in an air show. John had used his artistic talents to design a motley colored paint scheme for the biplane, a combination of camouflage, bird feathers, and Southwest Indian art. As a concession to his heritage John had the Polish Falcon painted on the Bücker's tail and in the center of the upper wing. This was indeed a strange decoration for an airplane that had begun its life in 1938 as a trainer for future *Luftwaffe* pilots.

Despite the storms John could see forming to the south and east, where he presently was the sky was cloudless and the visibility unlimited. He was cruising at 7500 feet to take advantage of a brisk tail wind. Surveying the immense landscape unfurling around him, John ventured to think of the loneliness that had first attracted him to flight, the joy of being up high, by himself, freed from the tedium of the world below.

But things were different now, there seemed to be too many airplanes, and too many rules. A man couldn't just go up in an open cockpit biplane and wander about the sky looking at whatever it was he wanted to look at, as things had been in Lindbergh's time. Today, one had to worry about violating controlled airspace, which seemed to be everywhere. Nowadays pilots spent more time with their heads down reading maps, and talking on the radio, trying to make sure they weren't breaking some rule or other, then they spent with their heads up, looking out the window for other airplanes. Regardless of the happiness John was presently experiencing, he was also considering if perhaps his flying days might be coming to an end. Things were getting just too expensive for him. In addition, John had witnessed the accidental death of a good friend.

Aerobatic competitions were supposed to be fun, a bunch of guys and gals, pilots, just getting together to see who would be judged the best three fliers in the various categories. The National Aerobatic Club was fond of pointing to its safety record of never having had a fatality, not even a minor accident, in any competition. They did not, however, keep track of the number of pilots who had died practicing at their home fields. Nor did they count the number of pilots who, inspired by what they saw at an air show or competition, had crashed trying to emulate what they had seen, sometimes without proper training, and often without even having been flying in an aerobatically approved airplane.

Adrian Sebastian had been as close as John had ever come to having a best friend. Adrian was a captain for a major airline and lived in Atlanta, so he and John saw each other only five or six times a year at the various competitions, but kept in touch throughout the year by mail. The bond that brought them together was that they both owned Bücker Jungmanns, the only two of the type actively flying on the contest circuit. Thus at any event they waged their own private little competition within the competition to see who could place the highest in a Jungmann.

The results of Saturday's flying had Adrian in eighth place, and John just behind him in ninth. This was higher than they had both expected to be after the first flight at an event on the national level. The pilots scoring ahead of them had all flown Pitts Specials, a small biplane that normally has the same Lycoming 180 HP engine as Adrian and John had retrofitted in their Jungmanns.

Their Jungmanns, however, were considerably heavier, almost twice the weight of a Pitts, and therefore suffered on all the maneuvers that required vertical performance, that is going straight up.

On the final day of the competition, Sunday, it had become considerably hotter than the day before, so the two Jungmanns were at an even greater disadvantage. John had flown before Adrian, and had managed to have a tremendous flight. Many of the other pilots told John Vigilia that it was the best they had ever seen him fly. John had helped Adrian buckle in for his flight, patted him on the shoulder and wished him good luck. Adrian confided he wasn't feeling quite right, a bit of vertigo, but assured John that he would give it his best shot. He knew that he would have to fly extremely well to beat his friend the professor's score.

As John watched from between the rows of parked airplanes with a group of other pilots, Adrian's flight appeared to be not going very well. John Vigilia had been fortunate to fly in the cooler early morning air; however, it had warmed up quickly and the temperature was clearly affecting the performance of Adrian's Jungmann. He was almost at the low altitude limit, which for Sportsman was 1500 feet above ground level, with three maneuvers left too go. To descend below the lower limit was to have your flight disqualified.

Adrian pulled up into his loop, and floated the inverted airplane nicely across the top, but he was leaving the downside widen out. John sensed what he was planning to do. Adrian would drop the end of the loop below the level of the line he started out from. This would cost him points on his loop, if it was caught by the judges, but a loop was a fairly low value maneuver. The longer arc would give him the entry speed he needed for the half-roll on a 45 degree up line, which came next. To the spectator what looked like a contest of flying skill, was in reality a series of aerial compromises, designed to trick the five judges into seeing a flight that appeared better than it had actually been flown.

Suddenly someone shouted: "He's busted it!" At that John had immediately looked out at the judges, who were still seated in their lounge chairs grading the maneuver. Adrian had not been called for going below the lower limit, otherwise the flight would have been over as far as they were concerned. The judges and their assistants would have gotten up from their chairs and been stretching their legs, chatting, and having a sip of soda as they casually waited for the next contestant to take the stage.

Continuing on Adrian pulled back on the control stick and set the plane into a 45 degree climb. John judged the line to be perfect. He should have been starting the half-roll now, but Adrian was extending the line for a little more altitude. The half-roll would get his airplane into the inverted position. He would lay back at the top of the line, setting up for the next part of the maneuver, a 90 degree down line. Adrian wanted to carry his 45 degree up line as high as he could as he needed more room to prevent his descending below the 1500 foot limit at the end of the down line. What the Jungmann lacked in the climb, it made up for in the dive, going down like an elevator with a broken cable.

The half-roll was not very crisp; the airplane was too slow. Forget about the second half of the line, John thought, you don't have the speed, just set the line and pull the airplane through. But Adrian, probably remembering the long line he had set before the half-roll, and wanting more altitude was holding the line. The inverted airplane appeared almost motionless in the haze. The airspeed was bleeding off, the wings had no lift. Adrian would be applying forward pressure to the control stick trying to keep the nose up. But he must have pushed the stick too hard, for suddenly the right wing came up and over and the airplane fell off into an inverted spin. John could see the nose falling through the horizontal.

At first everyone was calm, waiting for Adrian to recover, but the spinning aircraft just started rotating faster and faster, getting lower and lower—until it was too late. No parachute was seen to open; Adrian Sebastian rode his airplane right into the ground. The Bücker went in with a soft thud in a corner of the aerobatic zone. The boundary judges were running toward the airplane when the crumpled fuselage burst into flames.

When the results were posted John had moved up to eighth place. Shaken, and embarrassed, he wondered if it was because of his good flight, or because Adrian's name had been moved to last, with the notation "WD" after it, as if death were nothing more than a mere notice of withdrawal from the competition.

"Something must have gone wrong with the airplane, maybe a control cable broke," another contestant standing next to John commented wryly. "I don't see why they let you two fly those old clunkers in these events anyway, they're not safe." The man, who was in his other life an orthodontist, and had spent the equivalent of three years of John's salary for his sleek German monoplane, had only managed to come in twenty-ninth out of the thirty-three Sportsman pilots.

John Vigilia felt guilty about Adrian's death. He did not tell anyone that his friend had mentioned he wasn't feeling well just before the flight. Perhaps if Adrian were not straining to beat John he might not have gone up. Or had Adrian become disoriented by the haze, and attempted to recover from an upright spin when he was actually in an inverted spin, which he hadn't recognized until he was too low? Or perhaps something mechanical had actually gone wrong with the Bücker?

John set his eyes back out over the lake studying the storm clouds gathering in the distance, but his ears were in the airplane. Normally while flying along on a cross-country flight John was in the habit of listening to every beat of the engine; but now he listened to every single noise. In the sound of the wind in the struts John imagined creaks and groans in the spars, or a flutter in the tail. Further, he no longer trusted his fuel gauge. Although it had indicated near empty at the abandoned air base he had landed at to escape the storm, at the grass strip only a ten minute flight away the Jungmann had taken on a little less than one-third of a tank. As it had registered correctly at his subsequent stops, John had yet to figure out the real reason for this apparent anomaly.

Off of John's left wing flocks of geese soared in the sky, jockeying forward and back for position in their enormous V formations. They seemed to be heading south, but it was too early in the season for this. It was as if their world were out of kilter, as John Vigilia's had been since yesterday. This was not just due to the death of Adrian Sebastian, but because of an article John had found in the local newspaper back in Fond du Lac. The piece, picked up from the wire service, which he had read over breakfast on Saturday, so perplexed John that he had skulked back to his motel room and reread it over and over. As much as he tried to make sense of it, things did not seem rational. The story was about some divers who had discovered the wreckage of a cargo ship that had been lost in Lake Erie since 1942. The name of the ship was *Morgan Sidney*, and it had been found last week lying on the bottom of the lake just off Long Point.

Now in John's mind he distinctly recalled circling in the fog, and coming upon a ship. It had not been a dream. He had seen the ship's name clearly, in circumstances that made it impossible to forget. It was the *Morgan Sidney*, but it had not been under water, and it happened last Thursday, not back in 1942. And John had flown over it again in the late afternoon, after leaving the small grass strip where he landed for fuel. Although the light had been fading, John had seen it, even if he wasn't able to locate it when he circled back around. He had read and reread the newspaper article, and then torn the piece from the page and tucked it in his shirt pocket, where it was now.

Despite of the beauty of the day, John Vigilia flew on without enthusiasm, idly surveying the vast landscape unrolling outside his cockpit. His mind was weary from the events of the last few days. Then a thought came to life in him, or perhaps arrived from somewhere else, born of a sudden instinct to drive the feeling of lassitude from his brain before it became permanent. For some reason John felt the impulsive need to revisit the abandoned air base, to see the old man in the farmhouse, and the small grass airstrip with the torpedo bombers again. He wasn't sure if he could find these places, if they were really there, but he would give it a try. How relieved he would be to find these things actually existing in reality, not just on a map of his own imagination. Banking the biplane steeply, John advanced the throttle and changed course to the northeast, towards Canada.

Arriving over the Canadian shore he pointed the biplane east, down the Ontario shoreline, reversing the route he had taken only days earlier on the way out, trying desperately to find what he was not sure had even been there before. After about an hour of cruising back and forth, John found that he was running low on fuel. He had not seen anything that even faintly resembled the huge, abandoned air base, or the grass airstrip with the torpedo bombers that he was seeking. He would have to land somewhere and get gas. John consulted his chart. He had passed over several airports during his search that had been located where they were supposed to be; he only hoped that they would still be there when he went back. And despite what John had promised his wife, because of this diversion, there was no way he was going to make it home to Elmira before dark. She would be worrying about him, as she always did when he went flying. He had better call her before it got too much past the time she was expecting him to arrive home.

"Hello, Iris! It's me. Look dear, I'm stuck in Canada . . . no, nothing's wrong . . . I know I wasn't supposed to go to there on the way back . . . but remember the story I told you when I called? about what happened to me on the way out . . . well something else strange has come up . . . you're in bed, not feeling well . . . okay I know tomorrow is your birthday . . . look I'm at a pay phone and someone else is waiting to use it . . . I'll tell you all about it when I get back . . . I love you . . . no, I'll really be there tomorrow for your birthday . . . you can count on it . . . look I gotta go . . . you stay in bed, okay, I love you. . . ."

John was calling from the airport at Windsor, Ontario, where he had landed to refuel, and this time to clear customs. Normally, John Vigilia avoided larger airports like this with their approach controls and towers. Some of the smaller airports, like Chatham which he had flown over, were listed as airports-of-entry, but this usually involved waiting an hour or more by your airplane for a customs agent to drive over from the nearest bridge, and a fee of thirty-five Canadian dollars. Besides, he felt a little guilty about having failed to clear customs on his previous visit, and fleeing in a hurry from the little grass strip after the line boy asked him to sign the guest book, so he wanted to make it very official. John wondered if the customs agents might be looking for him, after all a multicolored biplane with a Polish Falcon on the tail was a hard thing not to spot. But apparently no one was. Everything had gone without a hitch, which made John realize how easy drug smuggling by airplane must apparently be.

At the lounge in the General Aviation Terminal none of the local flight instructors or pilots John asked knew of an abandoned air base near a power plant with a tall stack anywhere in the vicinity of Long Point. The only tall stack on the Canadian shore of Lake Erie that anyone was aware of was the one shown on the charts at Port Colborne, sixty miles east of Long Point.

With customs cleared, his gas tank topped-off, and a few hours of daylight yet remaining, John had taken off again and scoured the shoreline looking for the abandoned air base, or the grass strip with the five Grumman Avengers. As he shuttled back and forth over the green Canadian countryside John realized now that what he really wanted to do was to talk to the old man who had told him the story about his twin brother Ariel who he said had flown secretly as a copilot with Charles Lindbergh. And he also wanted desperately to come upon another cargo ship with *Morgan Sidney,* or better yet *Morgan Sidney II,* lettered on its side. As John flew along, not finding what he was seeking, the wind vibrating through the struts began to take on the sound of laughter, the discordant cackle of his wife's mother-in-law, whose dire forecast of his living a life of confusion and bewilderment seemed to be finally coming true.

The late summer day had no dusk. The sun was beginning to set, lengthening the shadows and turning the landscape into a gray abstraction. The results of his search were inconclusive. John had found nothing that even vaguely resembled the landscape he remembered seeing when he had broken out of the storm clouds last week. Reversing his course, John Vigilia headed for a single runway airfield that he had flown over about ten minutes earlier.

Having happily landed at the small airport at Welland, John arranged for his Jungmann to be topped off with fuel, and then put in a hangar. Antique biplanes just were not tied down out on the ramp. Then he inquired about a place to stay for the night. A call from the girl working in the airport office to a local motel brought a courtesy car out to the field to pick him up.

When he arrived at the fifties vintage motor court John Vigilia was taken aback when the woman at the front desk asked him to pay in advance. "It's because you don't have a car, eh," the woman explained.

"But, I have luggage. And I don't have a car because I came in my own airplane," John protested. "It's worth as much as a Cadillac, probably more. And. . . ."

"And I don't care what you came in, eh . . . it's not parked out front is it?" the desk clerk responded, sucking on her cigarette. "The rules are the rules, eh. If I don't get a license number ya gotta pay up front," she said swiping John's credit card. "Here's yer key, room 39, around the corner. It's the last room in the rear."

John stepped out into the cool night air, carrying his two small bags, reading the numbers on the doors. Most of the rooms in between his and the office seemed to be empty. This struck him as odd, he wondered if the woman might have taken him to be some kind of sex pervert who didn't want to be seen so hid him around the back.

The motel room was small, damp, and moldy, with an ancient TV with large knobs, and no remote, that could only find three channels. John Vigilia made a mental note to himself to try and buy a newspaper when he went out. He took a quick shower, worried that he might run out of hot water, and then went to eat at the brightly-lit burger chain across the street. The Stunt Flying Professor stood there, third in a line of three to order, taking the opportunity to read the menu above the counter. It was not the kind of place he usually ate in—not that he was a snob about dining out. It was just that his health conscious wife did not allow him to eat fast food. "They have too much fat and carbs, and who knows what else they put in," she always said.

The burger place was far from full, but, standing there with his tray looking around, John had a hard time determining where to sit. One corner seemed to be filled with the usual crowd of noisy teenagers, chatting and hopping from table to table. Another section was busy with families, the children playing on the brightly-colored contraptions that were provided for their entertainment by the management. Older people, pensioners out for a treat, a meal that they could afford, had claimed the third corner. John took a place in the randomly occupied fourth corner with those persons mostly alone, apparently truck drivers or night-shift workers. Sitting there munching his super-sized cheeseburger and fries, the flickering neon lights providing an inverted dance hall for black flies and other insects, assaulted by greasy food smells and loud music, John had to admit that he felt a bit out of touch with the rest of the world. What surrounded him was reality. A trip to the mall and a stop a fast-food place on the way home was all that most people seemed to need, or want out of life.

What was he trying to prove? John asked himself. Flying around the country in an antique biplane, risking his life taking part in stunt flying competitions would doubtless strike most people as rather odd behavior. And now he was off on a search for some eccentric old man who had probably made up his preposterous tale about a twin brother who was Lindbergh's secret copilot. He should forget about the strange man and his story, John thought. But what about the boat he had seen? Had it really been a ship called the *Morgan Sidney* that supposedly went down many years ago? There must be a rational answer to what had happened to him last week. He had other things to do with his life, like the book he was planning to write, but never seemed to begin. John decided that if the weather was good enough tomorrow he would get an early start, and be at home in Elmira with his wife shortly before noon.

When he got back to his room John took another shower. He didn't know why, he had taken one only an hour ago. Then he stretched out on the bed with the local newspaper, which he had picked up in the motel lobby. Suddenly, his whole world fell away, even the world of speculation. There at the top of the third page was another article about the wreckage of the lost cargo ship that had been found off Long Point. Accompanying the news story was an underwater photograph of the hull of the ship, across the bow he saw clearly lettered *Morgan Sidney, Liverpool.* The ship looked exactly as John had seen it when he had unexpectedly come upon it last Thursday in the fog.

Just how many husbands have made promises to their wives that they could not keep? John had told his wife that he would be home tomorrow for her birthday, but now he knew he needed to spend more time here in Ontario, looking for the old man and the abandoned air base, trying to discover what had actually happened last week, what was really going on. John reached for the telephone to call her. No, he would get up early tomorrow and fly around the area looking for the air base. If he found it by midafternoon, he could see the old man and still have plenty of time to get back to Elmira before it got dark. If he didn't find the man, John would just go home and forget about the whole thing.

Planning to get up at dawn, John retired early, but could not sleep. He lay in bed wondering what could possibly be the connection between Lindbergh's copilot, if he had had one, and the lost ship *Morgan Sidney,* which John would swear in a court of law he had seen steaming down the surface of Lake Erie last week.

Despite there having been a brilliant red sunset last evening—red sails at night sailor's delight—the next day began foggy and with light rain. With the low ceiling and visibility contact flying was out of the question. Confined to the ground, John spent the morning at his motel making telephone calls to any agency he could find in the yellow pages that he thought might know anything about an abandoned air base in the local area. Notwithstanding his considerable efforts, John Vigilia learned nothing that might have been helpful to his search.

By afternoon the weather had begun clearing, although the clouds were rather low and the visibility still marginal. John, however, had promised his wife faithfully that he would be home later today for her birthday. He decided to abandon his insane quest and try to get back to Elmira. He would risk what pilots called "scud running," flying low and slow under the ragged clouds, in poor visibility, while keeping a watch out for obstacles like radio towers and high tension wires. John would ignore an aviator's maxim that warned: There are older pilots, and there are bolder pilots, but there are no older-bolder pilots.

When John spoke to his wife to confirm his coming, Iris informed him that the weather in Elmira was not very good. She said there had been thunderstorms in the morning, and that if there was any risk, he should stay where he was. His wife confided that she was in bed with severe abdominal cramps, and doubted she would want to go out with him later that day to celebrate her birthday anyway. Iris told John that she loved him, and couldn't wait until he got home, but reminded him yet another time not to take any unnecessary chances. John assured her that he would be careful—as he always was.

Hurriedly packing his two bags, John looked around the room to see if he had forgotten anything. There on the table was yesterday's newspaper, still folded to the article about the divers finding the wreckage of the lost ship *Morgan Sidney*. John picked up the paper and quickly flipped through the remaining pages, then tore out the article about the ship and threw the rest into the wastebasket.

Eight

Spirits, which by mine art
I have from their confines call'd to enact
My present fancies.

Shakespeare *The Tempest IV. i.*

The weather over most of Nova Scotia on the afternoon of May 20, 1927 was a frenzy of contradictions. Thc province happens to be so narrow that no part can be found more than 50 miles from the sea. Yet on that day the southern coast was clear with excellent visibility, while the northern coast had numerous areas of rain with cloudbursts. On Cape Breton Island, farther to the north, there were patches of snow on the ground. As always, spring was slow in coming because of the presence of ice and frozen waters offshore.

Two fishermen sat in their small boat, bobbing in the dense fog that covered Saint Georges Bay. They had been out since dawn and had only caught a few flounder and some sole. The air was damp and cold. They were considering returning to their home dock near Antigonish when they heard an unfamiliar noise.

"So what's that sound there, eh?"

"Think it might be some kind of motor, maybe."

"I reckon it sounds kinda like an airplane, eh"

"There ain't no airplanes round here though."

"None that we might know of, eh."

"Look! I make it out just there . . . see where the fog's be a breaking."

"Seems like it's been painted silver, eh."

"It's a queer looking airplane. Got only one wing. . . ."

"And I see only one motor . . . ."

"It ain't no seaplane then, eh."

"No tain't . . . look at them there big wheels it got."

"Can't hear it no more, eh."

"Me neither. . . ."

"I think maybe it's coming down, eh?"

"Can't be landing . . . ain't no landing fields hereabouts."

"It's landing somewheres . . . over in the farm fields there, maybe."

"Don't see it no more, da you?"

"There tis . . . can't hear its motor though, eh."

"Looks like it's going down behind them there hills, can't be sure though with this here fog, eh. . . ."

"Don't suppose it's in trouble, eh?"

"Maybe it's just flying low cause a the fog. . . ."

"Can't hear it no more . . . kin you?"

"Neh. . . ."

"Probably landed down there in the hay fields, eh."

"Maybe . . . can't imagine where though. Ain't no farm fields big enough that I know of down there, eh."

"Never been down that way myself."

"Not much fish today . . . think maybe it's time we should head in, eh?"

"Maybe we should head over toward where the airplane went down and take a look . . . maybe it came down somewheres on the shore, eh."

"Could be. . . ."

"Ya know it's a shame there's not more airplanes round hereabouts. Ya know flying got started right here in Nova Scotia it did."

"Why ya say that, eh?"

"Well, when I was a kid we lived over there on the Bras d'Or. Mr. Bell, you know the man who invented the telephone . . . well he lived on the other side of the lake, and he was always making all kinds of kites for people to go up in, eh. Then he had that there Curtiss fellow come up from New York State to put motors on 'em. I seen the things fly, eh . . . he used to send them up off the harbor during the Harvest Home Festival."

"Ya don't say . . . ya really seen 'em fly then?"

"I think I hear it again, eh . . . ."

"What's that?"

"The airplane."

"Look there . . . it's just come out from behind them there low hills, eh."

"Ya think it might have gone down then?"

"Dunno. Must be some big fields over that way then."

"There it's gone again, in the fog. . . ."

"No, it's turned. It's over that way."

"Yeah, I see it now . . . so where'd ya think it's going, eh?"

"Can't say . . . ain't nothing out that way but caked ice and Newfoundland, eh."

"Ya think we should go in and report what we seen . . . I mean if it goes down in the ocean they'll be looking for it and all that."

"Ain't no one gonna go lookin' out that way, eh. There's nobody gonna fly over the Atlantic."

"So where d' ya think it's going then?"

"Dunno."

Nine

The fringed
curtains of thine eye advance,
And say what thou seest yond.

Shakespeare *The Tempest I. ii.*

Determined to keep his promise to his wife to be home in time for her birthday, John Vigilia departed from Welland as soon as the fog had lifted a bit. Following the shore of Lake Erie, he pressed on regardless of the low ceiling and poor visibility. After landing to clear customs in Buffalo, John took off again and flew along in a slight drizzle, following the refulgent band of the New York Thruway to Batavia. There he picked up the railroad tracks heading southeasterly that would lead him to Elmira. A scant thirty miles from home, the sky, which had been a low gray overcast, began to darken further. Visibility was down to about a half mile. John felt the temperature of the wind on his face dropping rapidly, the sure sign of an approaching rainstorm. Strong turbulence shook the Bücker, racking him against the seat belts. The previously light rain had increased; becoming so intense that John could no longer see the railroad tracks he was intent on following. Banking steeply, he made a 360 degree turn to try to assess his situation. John hoped that these were only local air mass storms, which he could fly around, even though the weather forecast had told him differently, this was a lengthy front. Seeing no opening in the tumultuous sky surrounding him, John continued into a second clearing turn.

Then vertigo hit him. The instrument panel seemed to melt in front of his eyes. The cabane struts turned from chromoly steel to rubber. John Vigilia shook his head; not exactly clear where he was or what he was doing. The spell lasted but a moment, yet it left him disoriented. Normally John could navigate himself from anywhere to somewhere by pure intuition. But ever since his experience in the clouds over Lake Erie, this power seemed to have deserted him. John was confused, and now the rain had turned to hail. The violent tempest was everywhere around him. A bolt of lightning danced across a row of hills dead ahead of him, illuminating their outline just minutes before he might have run into them. John banked the airplane sharply. Looking up, he saw the better part of a small maple tree, roots and all, come hurtling past him carried on the howling wind.

Forced down to only three hundred feet above the ground, John Vigilia circled a large field. He was seriously considering making an emergency landing as his only alternative. Tall trees, violently lashing to and fro, formed a barrier obstructing all four sides of the field. Also the covering of grass in the center appeared to be uncut and rather high. If John could manage to get the Bücker in it would probably nose over and be damaged. But should he risk continuing on and probably get himself killed? Lightning flashed over the low ridge off to his right. John was about to commit to a landing when another four million volts illuminated the railroad tracks running alongside the field among the trees. The lump stuck in John's throat as he started to pick his way along the trail of thin silver rails heading off to the north. The tracks should lead him back to the town of Batavia, beyond which he knew lay the safety of a small airport.

Bouncing along among those wind-raked hills, John Vigilia felt as if he were flying to the end of the world. The sky was laying bare its total internal construction, electrical discharges, claps of thunder, and roaring winds, all the while pouring down heavy rain, soaking John and collecting in the bottom of the cockpit. Fighting every inch of the way, he was able to make a retreat out of the front and find Batavia, its windsock swinging violently from one side to the other. But he had yet to land his airplane.

Although it had been unhappy in the sky, the Jungmann now was even more reluctant to come to the ground in a raging crosswind. John did not bother to fly a standard traffic pattern, assuming no one else would be up in this weather, but set up for a straight in approach from the direction he was coming. Crabbing down final, he kicked the airplane straight with the rudder just before the wheels touched down, and then danced on the brake pedals as it skidded down the slick, wet runway. He was none too soon as the storm that had been raging behind him overtook the airport with the full force of its fury shortly after John had managed to get the Bücker safely into a hangar.

"Hello Dear! Happy Birthday! . . ." John said into the receiver, trying to project a bright smile in his voice.

"Are you at the airport?" his wife asked cautiously hopeful.

"The airport in Batavia," John said apologetically. "I was only thirty miles from Elmira when the thunderstorms came up and forced me to turn around and land here. I'm sorry, but I won't be able to make it in tonight, the weather is just too bad. I've taken a motel room. Look, I'm only a few hours away by car. This place is rather nice . . . with an indoor pool and sauna. Why don't you pack an overnight bag and drive out here. There's a good Italian restaurant just next door. We'll have a mini-vacation together. You said that you could use a change of scenery."

"It's a sweet idea John, and I would love to do it, but I just can't. My abdominal pains are getting worse. I was going to go to the doctor today, but I can hardly get out of bed."

"Don't worry Iris; remember the doctor said that it was nothing, just a problem of getting older. Okay, you stay in bed and I'll see you tomorrow. I love you."

"I love you too. . . ."

John went to sleep more concerned about the weather then his wife's pains. As he lay there listening to the rain beating on the roof, he was brought back to the time he had spent in the farmhouse sheltering from the rain with the strange old man. He kept hearing his voice, trembling under these new rains, resonantly, and yet lightly asking John to come back and take him to Ireland to help him find his brother.

The next day was clear, as it usually was after a night of thunderstorms. Arriving in Elmira in midmorning after an easy half-hour flight, John put his Bücker in the hangar, and then called his wife. He only got the answering machine, which John took as a good sign. She must be feeling better and gotten out of bed to go shopping, he told himself. John decided he didn't need to rush on home, so he stopped at the maintenance hangar to chat with his friendly mechanic, Al Quest. He told Al the results of the competition, and about the crash of Adrian Sebastian's Jungmann. Al agreed to meet with John at his hangar tomorrow to give the Bücker a thorough going over. Passing through the airport lounge to get to his car, John tried to telephone his wife another time, but still got no answer. Driving home he began to worry.

"Iris! I'm home. . . ." John shouted as he entered the house through the mudroom. His winter supply of firewood, which he had so diligently chopped, still lay scattered about the floor unstacked. "Where are you, Iris? Iris, I'm home!" John hollered again as he came into the front hall.

There was no answer, just a strange stillness in the house that told John his wife was not here. But she must be home; he reassured himself, her car was in the driveway. She must be upstairs sleeping, John supposed, yet vaulted up the steps, a sense of urgency suddenly coming over him. Pushing open the door to the bedroom John found the bed empty, with the covers in disarray. He slowly looked around the room. There, on the night stand was a hastily scribbled note:

John,

It's nine o'clock, and I'm feeling really bad. I've called the hospital. They are sending down an ambulance. I would have called you but I didn't write down where you were staying. Don't worry; everything's going to be okay. In fact I will probably be home before you find this note.

I love you, Iris.

John Vigilia wandered around the second floor, looking into the bathroom and the other rooms as if not believing the message he had just read. John was dialing the hospital from the upstairs telephone when he saw a police car pull into the driveway. He hung up the phone and went downstairs to open the door.

"John Vigilia?"

"Yes."

"I'm Officer Kaminski, would you like to go inside and sit down please. I've something to tell you about your wife."

"Yes, what is it?" John asked stepping back into the house with the officer. "I just got home and found her note. I was about to phone the hospital. . . ."

"I'm terribly sorry to have to tell you this, Mr. Vigilia . . . your wife is dead."

"Dead? . . ."

"Yes sir. All I know is that last night she telephoned for an ambulance, which came right away and took her to the hospital, where she had to have an emergency operation . . . and apparently there were some complications. Something must have gone wrong. I don't have any details. I'm sorry, sir. That's all that I can tell you. I think you had better call the hospital."

Ten

When every grief is entertain'd that's offer'd,
Comes to the entertainer. . . .

Shakespeare *The Tempest II. i.*

Having spent his afternoon tramping the streets of Dingle, John Vigilia had read every poster in the window of every pub in this small seaside town. He was looking for a band that played "Irish Music," which wasn't easy to find here in Ireland. He had spent the previous three evenings since arriving in this country in three different pubs, in three different towns, listening to Elvis Presley imitators. His late wife, Iris, had been Irish. It was from her that John had acquired his taste for Irish Music, the classical old folk songs that were currently heard mostly on public radio in America. John and his wife had come to Ireland together on their honeymoon. Now, he had returned alone, both to remember and to try to forget.

Last month had been a nightmare of tears, and of doctor's reports, accusations and counter accusations, and visits to lawyers. John was still not sure what exactly happened that night he had been stranded in Batavia, and his wife was rushed to the hospital in an ambulance. Had Iris's doctor, a kindly old gentleman still back in the dark ages of medicine, failed to accurately diagnose her ovarian cancer? Had Iris's self-help treatment of Chinese herbs and acupuncture actually compounded her problem? Should she have made a call to the hospital sooner? Had the operation been a success, or a failure? Had the night nurse given Iris an improper dose of medication that caused her to go into a coma? Might Iris have recovered if another nurse hadn't been two hours late in making her rounds? The only thing John knew not subject to conjecture was that his wife was dead.

John Vigilia came to Dingle because, of all the places he had visited with Iris, this was where they had been the happiest together. The town, however, was different now, busier, more prosperous, but then all Ireland was. And you could spot the drug dealers on the streets, even in this picturesque seaside town. Nevertheless, the Bay of Dingle was still there, with its undulating blue waters, and the summer winds chasing cloud shadows across its sparkling surface.

It was the middle of the afternoon. The pub, its walls papered with ads for events which had taken place long ago, and products no longer produced, was full of wrinkled men smoking and staring down at their dark, sweaty pints of stout. The sun slanted through the front windows on the time-worn, mahogany woodwork that suggested the premises dated from the late nineteenth century. A soccer match rerun occupied the television screen, but the sound was a song by some rock group unfamiliar to John, but then he was not too up to date on pop music anyway. He ordered a pint. While they both waited for the tan foam to settle into the dark brown mass, John Vigilia started an idle conversation with the bartender:

"I don't suppose you would know if there's a kind of orphanage, or maybe a home for children run by nuns . . . something like that . . . anywhere around here, do you? I'm trying to find out about an American boy that might have stayed there sometime ago . . . around 1927."

"No, don't know nothin' about no orphanage round these here parts. That's a long time past, 1927 . . . only been here the last six years m'self though," the barman said. He placed John's pint in front of him, nodded his head at the end of the bar and said: "Maybe one a those there gaffers might know of someplace like what yer askin' about . . . they have the look like they must a been round here for a while."

John asked his question several more times, going around the barroom, becoming bolder and louder with each repetition. The old men, their cheeks flushed, and eyes reddened, sucked on their cigarettes, coughed, and listened intently to his query. Nevertheless, one by one, they shook their heads, took a sip from their warm pint to wet their throat, coughed, and answered negatively. John scratched his head, wondering what kind of strange impulse had prompted him to ask the question in the first place.

The third night of John's third day in Dingle found him still making the rounds of the pubs, still inquiring about an orphanage for children where an American boy might have been kept in the late 1920s. John Vigilia could not figure out why he had begun asking the question. Perhaps it was providence, something he remembered from a story heard in a musty farmhouse on a stormy day in Canada. He had gone in search of the abandoned air base, and the farmhouse, but not been able to find them again. Unable to overcome the grief of his wife's death, John Vigilia had convinced himself the whole business in Canada was just a misunderstanding, or perhaps a dream, a dream he might awaken from and find Iris still alive. He felt guilty that he had delayed his return and not been there when his wife needed him in what had become her final hours.

It had not been John's plan to come to Ireland to uncover the truth behind a farfetched tale he had heard from an old man about a boy who had been Lindbergh's copilot on his flight to Paris. He had only come here to try to make step by step progress toward finally shaking from his mind the anguish of his wife's passing.

John Vigilia had taken a leave from his teaching job, and put the Bücker Jungmann up for sale. Ever since Adrian Sebastian's unfortunate crash, he had lost his confidence in the old biplane. Besides, John felt that he had spent too many hours and too much money on the old airplane anyway. He decided that he would use his time to write something, perhaps another novel. Tired of the academic calendar, John would try to live a seasonless life, attuned only to the whimsy of his mind. For one semester, or maybe longer, or maybe for the rest of his life—John had not been rational enough to figure out his finances—he would drift in and out of practical purposes, leaving his care to others and to fate.

As he took another sip from his pint, John's eyes traveled around the murky, smoke-filled front room of a hip pub called McSweeney's. He watched the dense crowd sail by him in the semi-darkness in loud confusion; with the shuffle of sixty feet, and the chatter of thirty mouths, a disorderly migration of spiked hair in pink and green and red, tattoos, nose rings, and black leather; a river flowing full of noise, dark looks, sly winks, chopped up by laughter, and the prodigious babble of local gossip.

"Like, are you the Yank what's looking for the children's orphanage?" a voice next to John asked, taking him by surprise.

The question had come from a young girl—spoken with the scratchy voice of an old woman. She was tiny, and dressed all in black, in clothes that hardly covered her body, most of the naked flesh being decorated with tattoos of red and blue dragons and eagles and a crucifix. Her nose, navel, eyelid, and ears were pierced and inserted with glittery baubles.

"Yeah . . . sort of. You're rather young to know anything about it though, aren't you," John replied a bit nonplussed.

"Give me a cigarette. . . ."

"I don't smoke."

"That's okay I got me own . . . like I just thought you might have had some American cigs." She took a cigarette from a pack and lit it from the end of the butt she was about to discard. The girl coughed slightly, and the overhead light picked up the tiny chrome bolt bisecting her tongue.

"How did you know I was looking for information about an orphanage for children?"

"They just didn't have children there, my grandfather said. Like, he told me to get in touch with you. Like, you talked to him yesterday in a pub. But he couldn't talk to you then, there were people there who knew him to be someone else, if ya know what I mean."

"Someone else? . . ."

"Yeah . . . like he's not really who he's supposed to be."

"So then how do I get in touch with him?"

"Like I can bring you there right now," she said, taking another a drag on her cigarette and coughing again, "but it's gonna cost ya . . . ."

"How much?"

"Twenty American dollars . . . ."

"Why should I pay you that much?"

"Cause, like if you don't pay me, I ain't gonna take you to see me frigggin' grandda."

"And why should I want to meet your grandfather?"

"Cause, he knows somethin' about the boy you're looking for, ya know what I mean. . . ."

"How do you know I'm looking for anyone?"

"Like you've been asking round. . . ."

"And how do I know you're not just scamming me?"

"Look, do you want me to take you there or not?"

"So what's your name?" John asked.

"Brigid. . . ."

"So you were named after the movie star. . . ."

"Hell no . . . not Brigitte. Like I'm Irish. Irish don't name their daughters after no friggin' French film stars.

They name us all after saints. It's spelled B-r-i-g-i-d. Ya know, Brigid is one of the greatest saints in Ireland's history; only she didn't actually do anything. Like, they sort of just made her up in the early days of Christianity to fill in for some other pagan feast or something, if ya know what I mean. So do I get me twenty dollars?. . ."

John Vigilia handed Brigid a crisp U.S. twenty dollar bill, which she promptly folded and tucked down the front of her black tank top, the little bumps of her nipples outlined boldly underneath the thin material. He wondered what was going to keep the bill from falling out of the bottom of her shirt, which ended about three inches above her navel, which was three inches above where her skirt began.

Brigid led him toward the door. As they passed through the crowd John felt that everyone's eyes were on him, that he was being paraded. In this group his normalness made him the freak. Brigid stopped a moment to talk to a huge man, with a shaved head and wearing red suspenders, who she called Eamonn.

"Like I'm taking this here Yank to meet me grandda. If I'm not back in two hours or so you should come looking for me. Will ya?"

"Oh, I'll do that fer ya, luv," Eamonn said, glaring at John and then glancing at his watch.

"Like, I'll see ya then. . . . "

John wondered if all this was some kind of secret code, and that he would soon end up in a Dingle back alley cleaned of the rest of his money and his possessions.

The two stepped out of the smoky pub into the fresh air and a summer night made bright by the illumination of the full moon. An airplane passed silently high overhead. Out of habit, John stopped to watch as its strobe lights disappeared into a sky that spread so far and wide its clouds seemed to have divided and fenced it, breaking it up into a mass of separate worlds.

"Come on . . . we've got a ways to go." Brigid urged him. "Like didn't you hear me tell that big bloke with the red suspenders that if I weren't back in two hours to come and look for me. And he'll do it too. Like he looks after people . . . yes that's what Eamonn does."

Brigid walked ahead, smoking and coughing. John studied her thin white legs, swaying under her short black skirt that seemed to end where the gentle curve of her tiny buttocks began. They were near the waterfront now. Strange dark birds filled the sky, circling and revolving in great crisscrossing arcs, and flapping their wings heavily on the warm sea air.

The girl suddenly ducked into a dark alley. John hesitated, and then followed her, as he didn't know what else to do. She had stopped in a corner and turned around, her cough and the dim glow from her cigarette revealing her presence. John approached cautiously and stopped short in front of her. Abruptly, and without a preamble, Brigid, named for the patron saint of brides, grabbed hold of John Vigilia's hand and slid it between her legs. He could feel the soft, moist folds of her vulva, not surprised that she was not wearing any underpanties. John tried to withdraw his hand, but she held it there, gently frigging herself with his fingers. She took a deep drag from her cigarette, exhaling the smoke through her nostrils like a vamp in an early Hollywood B movie. John coughed and hastily withdrew his hand.

"So do you want to fuck me or what?" Brigid asked, sounding somewhat anxious. "Like we can do it right here, standing up . . . it's okay. Nobody ever comes down this alley at night . . . and I have condoms, if you don't." She lifted up her very short skirt, displaying what she was offering. The fickle clouds chose just that moment to part, the moon revealing the startling whiteness of Brigid's exposed mons pubis, her shaven crotch looking not unlike the first little girl John had ever seen.

"I'm sorry, I don't do it like that. . . ." John said backing away.

"Like what? Oh, I see, you mean you want to sod me up the backside then? Well that's okay by me . . . like I take it that way too," Brigid said quickly turning around. She bent over a garbage pail, hiked up her skirt and spread her thin legs.

"No. You don't understand. I just don't want to have sex. I mean . . . my wife died only recently, and I'm . . . well sort of not in the mood."

"I'm sorry to hear that. Like I can understand," Brigid said, quickly reorganizing her clothes. "I had a boyfriend up north; got in with the IRA and got blown up trying to make a bomb. Then I didn't feel like it for a while. Like I mean I was really down. Even started going to Mass again, and confession and all that, if ya know what I mean. But hell, like at least let me give you a gam."

"A gam?"

"Suck your dick . . . like you did give me twenty dollars."

"Look it's okay. You don't need to do anything for me other than to take me to meet your grandfather, as we agreed."

"Okay, if that's all you want . . . but I do give good head . . . like this here stud in me tongue really turns blokes on . . . gets their pricks standin' at attention in no time. Like I start to twirl it around. . . ."

"Can't we just go already? . . ." John stammered, interrupting her description. He was beginning to regret this now becoming stranger by the minute encounter.

"Well that's hacked. Let's go see me grandda then . . . like if that's all ya want."

Deep inside his own thoughts, John Vigilia followed the girl a short distance down several streets to a dark warehouse that faced on a weathered dock near what he took to be the very end of town. Brigid fumbled with a key in a lock. On her third try the tin-covered door opened. Holding it wide she motioned to John to go on in. His eyes adjusting to the light John saw that he was standing at the bottom of a rather wide stairway.

"Like you just keep going up them there stairs," Brigid advised him. "From here on you're on your own. Like I'm going back to McSweeney's." She started to leave then turned back and added, "Like if you change your mind about wanting to have sex, you can find me there."

"Wait!" John said, putting out his hand to stop her. "What am I supposed to find at the top of these stairs?"

"Like what you paid me twenty dollars for," Brigid explained, "me grandfather." She turned and was quickly gone.

With a dull, suppressed vibration, the heavy door swung shut behind him. John stood in the entryway listening to the tapping of Brigid's tiny heels, and her coughing, as she retreated down the street. The sudden coldness of the building made John Vigilia feel as if he had entered another climate, a different region of the earth, or January in August.

As he slowly climbed up the mold smelling stairway John wondered what he would find at the top. Is this where Eamonn was waiting to knock him out and take his money? Or had Brigid really been honest with him and he would meet the man he was looking for? And why had she offered to have sex with him? Did she go for older men, or was it because he was an American and she hoped he would give her a lot of money. Perhaps she was a nymphomaniac who just wanted to have sex with everyone.

A door opened at the top of the stairs. Someone up there must have noticed John's presence. A voice shouted down: "Well don't just stand there, man . . . will ya come on up now!"

As he climbed the rather creaky, dirty steps, John was preparing himself for filth and squalor, or maybe to be mugged. He was not expecting to arrive in a large, clean and well-lighted art studio.

"So you've come to have a look at me pictures, have ya?" a voice asked in an upbeat tone.

An older man was extending his hand toward John Vigilia. He was short, but well built and trim, economic of gesture, wearing gold wire-rimmed spectacles. John noted furrows of worry on his face. A large window behind the man was opened onto the bay, allowing in a gentle flow of balmy salt air. The room, a spacious loft, was filled with framed oil paintings of boats; ocean liners, steamships, and sailboats. From just a casual glance John could see that the pictures had been executed by someone who was more than an amateur, and who had practiced his craft for what must have been a very long time. An unfinished painting of a nineteenth century sailing vessel running before a storm rested on the large, wooden easel.

"A young lady brought me here . . . she didn't say anything about looking at paintings; although I would be happy to do so . . . I was an artist once myself," John volunteered.

"It seems like everyone's been a dab hand at sometime or other in their life," the old man said resignedly. "I can hardly go anywhere without having to look at somebody's half-baked efforts."

"I'm a . . . writer now," John added somewhat hesitantly.

"And so how many books have you published?"

"Well, er . . . none. I have finished a novel though."

"And you didn't publish it?"

"No. I did have an agent, however, who liked it, and sent it around to publishers for a while. But he couldn't place it. He said that it was a 'hard' book, whatever that means, and that hard books just didn't sell. I guess I used too many big words, or something like that."

"Well, I live by selling these paintings . . . so I guess that makes me a real artist, doesn't it; although there are those who would say otherwise. There is this here fellow down in London, very popular in the art magazines and with the rich and trendy collectors these days, who exhibits cut up cow parts that he floats in formaldehyde . . . what is he then? A butcher? I don't suppose he even cuts up the cows himself. . . ."

"Look, I like your paintings, they're really nicely done," John said, interrupting the man. John Vigilia had no idea why he had been brought here, or what this was all about. He thought now that perhaps Brigid had played a joke on him, and just taken his twenty dollars. He had been studying the oil paintings during the man's screed searching for something to say. "Yes, I like them; although, I wouldn't paint anything like this myself . . . I mean I wouldn't paint boats."

"And what's wrong with boats? Before I made my living from paintings, I made my living *on* boats, as a stoker. I traveled all over the world . . . everywhere but your country."

"My country?"

"Yes."

"America?"

"I can tell by your accent that you're from the United States. I was supposed to go there, but the war was on and I decided not to ship out. I was afraid the boat would be torpedoed by U-boats in the Atlantic. As it was the ship I would have been on made it across safe, but then was lost in a storm on one of your Great Lakes, Lake Erie, I remember it was. I'll never forget the name of the boat either . . . it was the *Morgan Sidney*, out of Liverpool. I thought it was just my good luck . . . so I never took work on any other ship to North America."

"The *Morgan Sidney* . . . out of Liverpool!" John repeated, suddenly seized by a cold chill. "I've got to go." He backed away from the man and turned to leave.

"But wait, boats are not what you came to talk about . . . you want to know about the children's orphanage. The local gossip has it that you're planning to write a book about it."

"Orphanage?" John said, stopping at the door. He was trapped like a dog that had reached the far end of his chain. "What orphanage are you talking about?"

"You asked me about it in the pub . . . but I couldn't talk to you there, you see I was with some of my friends . . . and they don't know who I really am. Anyway, they aren't aware that I grew up in that terrible place. I mean they're devout Catholics, and wouldn't believe it if I told them the tortures we suffered at the hands of those priests and nuns. It wasn't really an orphanage, more accurately it was an insane asylum, a catch all for anybody who didn't fit in anyplace else. Then it was called The Saint Romanus Home. Wouldn't you know that good Saint Romanus is the patron saint of madmen . . . and those who have drowned?"

"Excuse me," John interrupted again, he was feeling a bit faint. "Can I have a glass of water, please?"

"Ya can, but I didn't reach the age I have by drinking water," the bibulous old man replied with a quick wink, magically producing a bottle of stout for each of them. Lifting his bottle to this person he had only just met, he toasted him: "To a long friendship then," adding, "and by the way, my name's Sean. If we're going to be friends I should know yours."

"I'm John . . . John Vigilia," he said raising his bottle too.

After a few sips of the dark liquid John felt somewhat calmer and sat down to listen to the man's story. Now he painted under the name of Patrick Murphy. His real name was Sean Devlin, or so he was called back in The Saint Romanus Home, which was not here in Dingle, he said, but had been up near the town of Tralee, where he was sent for schooling when his father died.

John listened patiently to the man's tales of being beaten by the nuns, and the bigger boys; of being sexually abused by the priest who came to hear his confession; of naked inmates tied to their beds and left to lie in their own excrement.

"And was there a boy at the asylum who had come from America?" John asked all too eagerly.

"Oh . . . Yes there was." Sean confirmed. "I recall him specifically because he was such a strange boy. He came to us in May of 1927. I remember exactly because that was the month of my birthday, I had only been there three months. The boy was older than me, maybe 15. They said he had been found wandering around on the beach near Dingle, near to where I had lived with my sister and mom before my dad died and I was sent away. Nobody around there said that they knew the lad, so the coppers figured he must be a runaway. They thought he was out of his head because he kept telling them he had flown across the ocean in an airplane, and if they would only call his uncle in America he would come and get him. Now I couldn't hardly read . . . and we didn't have newspapers anyway . . . so nobody had any idea what he was talking about. Most of us had never even seen a real airplane, let alone met anyone who had claimed to actually have been up in one.

"For the first three days they put him in the bed next to mine. He said his name was . . . let me think now . . . Ariel. Yes, I remember that clearly because it wasn't a common name . . . but the nuns kept calling him Anthony. He said he had a twin brother Caliban, and that his father, who had worked in an abattoir, named them after some characters in a Shakespeare play. Now could you believe that? I can't ever imagine any meat-cutter that would read Shakespeare.

"And that weren't the wildest of his tales. He told me all kinds of stories about flying in airplanes in America, and flying across the Atlantic with this man who had set him down on a beach . . . so he could go on to Paris alone. But it must have been the wrong beach because no one came to get him . . . and then he was picked up by the authorities and brought to Saint Romanus. I thought he was sorta crazy, and had made up all the stories he told me . . . yet he didn't seem crazy like the others. Then after a few days they took Ariel away . . . put him in a special cell all by himself, although he wasn't chained. It was like a zone of silence had been created around him . . . the nuns said it was for his own protection . . . no one was allowed to talk to him. He lived in a kind of no-man's-land, unaffected by what was going on with any of us around him."

"And what happened to him?" John Vigilia asked, He had taken out his pad and ballpoint pen and was rapidly jotting down notes.

"So you are writing a book like they say. . . ."

"No, not really . . . I mean maybe. You see I don't actually know what I'm doing at the moment. I guess that I'm kind of the young writer of brilliant promise never fulfilled, who just keeps going at it despite himself."

"Well they say that every writer, and artist, harbors a secret dream, which is not about creation, beauty, and truth at all, but only an insatiable desire for their own self-aggrandizement," Sean spat out, adding; "I know this only too well myself."

"That may be so, it may even be true in my case . . . but to make my story short," John continued, "my wife died suddenly, leaving me feeling very much alone. I decided to come to Ireland to get over my grief . . . then I remembered this tale someone had told me at an abandoned airport in Canada. When I found myself in Dingle, I just started asking around the pubs, where you heard about me. So, don't let me interrupt you . . . go on with your story. What eventually happened to the young boy you say was named Ariel?"

"Well, about a week after he was put in the cell by himself, his uncle and another man came for him . . . or so they said. I mean that's what the nuns told us, but I knew it wasn't true, because I saw the two men who came for him, and heard them talking to each other in a strange language. I couldn't tell what they were saying, but I was sure it wasn't either English or Irish. I guessed that the men must have been speaking Spanish or maybe Italian. Also I watched from a window when the men were putting Ariel into the cab . . . they seemed to be hurting him, and I heard him shouting, 'You're not my uncle. My uncle is in America. Where are you taking me?'"

"And did you ever hear from Ariel again?"

"Never. . . ."

"Do you remember his last name?"

The painter Patrick Murphy, formerly the fatherless Sean Devlin, paused to think for a moment: "You know I thought I didn't . . . but it just came back to me . . . I mean I think it was something he must have made up, at Saint Romanus we all had made up names . . . kind of funny names."

"So what was his name?"

"He said his name was Angel Lucy. Really kind of a funny name Angel Lucy . . . don't you think so?"

"Not 'Angel Lucy,'" John said trying to suppress a smile. "I admit it's rather a peculiar name, but Ariel's actual last name, if he is the same person I'm looking for, may have been Angelucci."

"Angelucci? So he was Italian after all. Then maybe that really was his uncle who came for him."

"I doubt it. Ariel's parents apparently were Italian, but had immigrated to the United States, to Chicago. I believe that he was American by birth. And I have it on good account, from his twin brother, that his uncle never found him. In fact the brother believes the uncle came to Ireland looking for Ariel, and either fell, or was pushed, off a train to his death."

"Holy Mother of God! Why on earth would anyone want to do something like that?"

"I don't really know. The man who told me the story seems to have vanished. That is, I went back to look for him and couldn't find the abandoned airfield that he lived near to. It was somewhere in Canada, but no one I asked seemed to have any idea what I was talking about. Several days earlier I had been flying around low in bad weather and just sort of stumbled on this field and landed. An old man took me to his house to get out of the rain and told me the story about his brother Ariel."

"And that's who you're here looking to find? Are you a private detective or some such thing as well as a writer?"

"No, let's just say that I'm someone who's curious about things. . . ."

"Ya' know, I just remembered something that my sister told me just before she died," the artist interrupted. "She said she never told this to anyone except our mother, who told her not to repeat it because people would think she was crazy. When she was a little girl she saw an airplane land on the beach near our house, only then she thought it was a big silver bird, and a boy got out and ran up into the rocks and hid."

Early the next morning, still rather bewildered by what he had learned from Sean Devlin, now known as the artist Patrick Murphy, John Vigilia checked out of his hotel and boarded the bus to Tralee.

Eleven

Now does my project gather to a head:
My charms crack not; my spirits obey, and time
Goes upright with his carriage. How's the day?

Shakespeare *The Tempest V. i.*

John's suitcases seemed to have gained weight since he left Elmira. Wishing he had one of those little pull carts that airline stewardesses always seemed to have he struggled his bags through the side door of Rome's bustling Statione Termini out onto Via Giovanni Giolitti and found a cab. He got in and handed the driver a paper on which he had written the name and address of Count Ferdinand Sperone. The man took a cursory look, then nodded his head and handed John's note back to him. He did not have to be told that Count Ferdinand Sperone lived on the stylish Lungotevere in Augusta. There were many Palazzos in the Eternal City, and the drivers knew them all. But Count Sperone's was one of the most opulent, or so John Vigilia had read in his guide book on the trip down from Ireland.

The massive whiteness of the Vittorio Emanuele II monument passed by on the right. John was not expecting to see it, neither on the right nor the left. Something was out of order. As he traced the route from the station on his visitor's map, there was no need to go past Vittorio Emanuele at all. He was being taken for a ride. John shouted out one of the few Italian words he had memorized while on the train: *Diretto!*

The driver suddenly knew some English, "*Diretto?* You want I should go direct? I am sorry . . . I think perhaps you want-ed to see some of our more famous the monuments. . . ."

"Direct," John repeated. He certainly could not afford an enormous taxi fare. Ever since he had begun this crazy search John's money seemed to be disappearing much faster than he had anticipated.

John Vigilia had come to Rome from Tralee. True to Patrick Murphy's word, he found that The Saint Romanus Home no longer existed. During World War Two it had been converted to a troop hospital, and after the war ended the old building was torn down. A parish priest, thinking John was searching for his Irish roots, had responded to his request for information by directing him to a nearby convent, where an elderly nun who had worked at Saint Romanus was living. John was fortunate to discover from the nun that the Saint Romanus records were stacked in boxes in the basement of the very same residence that they were presently in.

With the patient help of good Sister Dympna, named for the patron saint of the insane and those possessed by the devil, John found the file of a boy, believed to be a runaway, who had been apprehended on Stradbally Strand on 23 May 1927. The texts were written entirely in Gaelic, so he could only take Sister Dympna's word for their meaning as she would not let the records be removed from the storage room. Several things did agree with Sean Devlin's story. The boy's last name was Angelucci, and they had listed the first name as Ariel. And the boy had been diagnosed as being out of his mind, because he kept telling an extravagant story about having flown from America in an airplane.

There were also several letters in Italian in the file, which Sister Dympna, with her knowledge of Latin was able to make a little sense of. For reasons not noted, some important people in Rome had taken an interest in this strange boy. This was apparently why he was isolated from the rest of the inmates. Shortly thereafter two Italian men appeared at Saint Romanus and took the boy away. The records said that the boy was sent to live in Rome with the family of a Count Sperone, a name that John recognized from the early history of Italian aviation. Excited by this discovery, John Vigilia had copied all that he thought relevant into the notebook he was now keeping. Thanking Sister Dympna, John went back to his hotel to make plans for traveling to Rome.

The sister had also pointed out to John, with great awe, that the document authorizing the release of the boy Ariel Angelucci had been signed by none other than the pope at the time, His Holiness Pius XI. Sister Dympna wondered who this child might have been to be the concern of such high personages as a pope and a count. She was very impressed at finding a document signed by Pius XI himself, a man she felt was sure to become a saint some day.

When John Vigilia returned the next afternoon for another look at Ariel's file, carrying Gaelic and Italian dictionaries, he was told by the good Sister Dympna that the Angelucci papers were no longer there. After he had left she had informed her Mother Superior about the pope's letter, who immediately contacted their bishop. John had just missed the bishop's secretary who had come to the convent in a car that morning and removed the entire file.

Placing a call to Rome, John Vigilia had by luck gotten through to the present Count Sperone's secretary, who informed him that the count would be pleased to call him back later. Sensing now that there might have been some kind of conspiracy surrounding the disappearance of Ariel Angelucci, John had not revealed his real reason for calling Count Sperone. John had lied, claiming that he was writing a book on aviation, and would like to get some information on the early Sperone biplanes. These were in themselves quite advanced designs for their day and had at the time set several flying records.

The count had returned John's call almost immediately, which was a surprise as he was not expecting the man to respond at all. Count Sperone, whose family had been among the pioneers of Italian aviation, was a great fan of American air shows, and traveled every year to the largest of these in Oshkosh, Wisconsin, where John Vigilia regularly was a featured performer.

"It is a great honor to speak to you, 'The Stunt Flying Professor,' a man who I have seen flying on several occasions, and whose skills I greatly admire. . . ." Count Sperone gushed into the telephone.

John had been amazed that his name was known to Sperone, and thankful for the count's fine command of English. At the end of their conversation Count Sperone had insisted John do him the honor of staying with him at his palace when he was in Rome. And so here John Vigilia was, in a taxi on his way to the Palazzo Sperone.

Taking John's order of a direct route as an inspiration, or perhaps a challenge, the taxi driver carved his way through Rome's bumper-car traffic with the skill a Grand Prix professional, casually nipping between lanes while changing a cassette in his tape player with one hand while lighting a cigarette with the other. John Vigilia, who was never too comfortable in moving vehicles driven by other people, clung to the seat, his fingers digging into the fabric, hoping that the row of plastic religious icons arrayed along the dashboard attesting to the intrepid drivers considerable faith, protected his passengers as well. Thankfully before John received his call to the afterlife, the taxi turned the corner and immediately screeched to a halt. The driver proudly announced, gesturing with his hand: "There is it the Palazzo Sperone."

Looking out the window John could see a number of picturesque buildings, but nothing that resembled a palazzo. With the longer portion of the block left to go, his cabman seemingly had lost his incentive to continue. Farther along the street John spotted the problem. Near the other end of the block an armored troop carrier and at least a platoon of military personnel dressed in battle gear had closed off the way.

"We cannot to drive-ed any more . . . you must to walk, the entrance will be just there," the driver said pointing.

Alighting from the cab, John had not taken more then a dozen steps in the direction of Palazzo Sperone when he was immediately accosted at gunpoint by three of the armed soldiers. The cab driver, shouting that his passenger was American, backed up and made a u-turn hurriedly driving away. John stood there for several uncomfortable moments while an officer was sought who could speak English.

"Now the Palazzo Sperone is close-ed. There will be not tours for you today," the officer said, presupposing John's purpose. He glared down his moustache at the foreigner. "You must to go away. You can to come back maybe yet next week. . . ."

The normally mild-mannered John Vigilia was becoming miffed by this cavalier treatment, he growled: "I am not here for a tour. I have been invited by the count to be his house guest!"

"You are to be a guest?"

"Yes, Count Ferdinand Sperone has invited me to stay with him," John repeated slowly.

There was a perceptible change in the officer's manner. He dialed up someone on his field radio, spoke into it quickly, and then asked the visitor his name.

"Professor John Vigilia," John replied, supplying his rarely used but entitled to honorific, and pronouncing his name with what he thought was an Italian sound.

"*Professore* Jahn Vee-gel-ee-ah. . . . " the officer repeated into the radio. A brief and one-sided conversation followed, during which time the man mostly listened and repeated: "Si, si, si. . . ." Clicking off his radio, he saluted at John saying: "I am very sorry for the confusion, *professore*. You can to go there now. Just this way please." John Vigilia followed the man to the ornate side entrance of the palazzo where a small elevator waited just inside the lobby.

John rode up alone in the red velvet-lined lift. There was a tiny upholstered seat, almost like a miniature throne, in the corner. John figured it must have been installed there specifically for the count, or other visiting royalty, so did not sit in it, as he was tempted to, but remained standing.

The button the officer had pressed for John Vigilia caused the elevator to stop and open on a modest office. There he was met by a cheerless man wearing tinted wire-rimmed spectacles, perhaps the count's secretary, who told him to sit down and wait. In less than five minutes another man appeared. He was smartly dressed in a dark blue pin-stripped suit of the finest cut. His eyes had the pseudo-honest stare of a New York stockbroker, while his mouth, which appeared only nominal, needed defining by a dark, neatly trimmed mustache. Nattily brushed-back hair disappeared into gray at the temples. He extended his hand, which John noted to be small, but unfaltering, and broke into a smile saying:

"So you are the famous Stunt Flying Professor. I am so pleased to make your acquaintance; I have long since admired your aerobatic skills. I am Count Ferdinand Sperone, at your service."

Trying to recall the Italian phrases John had memorized on the train, John blurted out what he though meant pleased to meet you.

The count smiled back at him, "I see you cannot to speak Italian, no problem; I can to speak the perfect English." Then he said something quickly to his secretary in Italian, and smiled at John again. "This way, come with me please."

"Thank you for seeing me on such short notice," John said, heading in the direction of the count's extended arm.

"It is not a problem . . . the honor is mine," the count replied. He escorted his guest into the next room, and then out into a hall lined with paintings. None of the artists were familiar to John although one appeared as though it might have been by Tintoretto. They descended a short flight of stairs. The count was talking rapidly on the way, trying to explain to John why he was detained. "You must excuse the soldiers; you see several days ago there was an attempt on the prime minister's life."

"Yes, I know. I read about it in the Irish newspapers."

"And so he his presently staying here, not exactly hiding. Just for the time being. So the police and the military have the palazzo surrounded. It is most difficult to come and go. So, although I have invited you . . . you cannot stay here at this time. But it is not a problem. You see, my family owns a fine hotel just off the Piazza del Popolo; I will put you up there. But first we must have something to eat. Are you hungry?"

"Yes," John admitted, only having had the odd serving of train, ferry, and railway station food for the past two days.

Count Sperone led his guest through a massive carved wooden door that opened into a vast and ornate dinning hall. The walls of the room were lined with large paintings, portraits of what must have been the succession of former Count Sperones. John Vigilia could not help observing to himself that the nobles posing so proudly in these elaborately framed pictures looked not unlike like the present Count Sperone might look had he dressed himself in the appropriate costume of the period. In the center of the hall a group of men were already seated at a long and well-set table. The men were deep in conversation. While they nodded and greeted the count, they took little notice of John's arrival.

"I hope you don't mind," the count said, turning to John, "we will be talking politics, and speaking in Italian . . . you are dining with the prime minister and his top advisers."

John had never dined with a prime minister before. As the only other politician he ever sat down to eat with had been a councilman from his ward in Elmira, John Vigilia was quite impressed, even though he was being virtually ignored. And the food far surpassed anything he had ever eaten, although he had to admit that his Italian meals in the recent past had been mostly taken at his local Pizza Hut.

After the meal was finished Count Sperone excused himself, as he and the prime minister needed to attend another meeting. Much to his disappointment, John was being sent away. Sperone ordered his car brought around, and his chauffeur dodged John Vigilia through Rome's traffic to the family's hotel just off the Piazza del Popolo.

When he arrived at the hotel, John found that the count was true to his word, the hotel was indeed of the highest quality. John Vigilia was shown to a splendid room that seemed to have been outfitted in the late nineteenth century. Out of habit John walked up to the large mirror to smooth his hair and was startled by what a frightful figure travel had made of him. His skin was pallid, and there were dark circles under his eyes. All at once the enigma of his journey sprang up and hit him. John wondered why he was here, and when would he get home again. He felt a tension in the contradictory impulses that were driving him on this strange, unknown mission, for if he could not even recognize what he had become, how could he anticipate what he would do in the future?

Tired from his travels, and full from a lunch that had lasted almost three hours, and at which he had drunk more than his usual share of fine Italian wine, John Vigilia decided to take a shower, and then to lie down.

Alone now, John's mind clouded over with thoughts of his dead wife, Iris. His guilt at having failed her in her final hours still had the possibility of overwhelming him. He had not shed a single tear when his father died, but could not prevent himself from crying, even now, when he remembered Iris, and the life they had shared, and all the things they did together. Taking a small note from his wallet, John unfolded the well-worn paper and read what he had written on it the day he learned his wife was dead: "Grown men don't cry." Stretched out on his bed, he stared at the note, trying to heed its command, as he had done so often in the past. Although it was at present only late afternoon John soon fell into a deep, mesmeric sleep. He did not wake up again until late the next morning.

Sunshine filtered between the drapes. As John slowly awoke from his first healthy sleep in several days there began to grow in him a yet unlikely sense of pleasure in everything. He felt as his life had reached a low point, from which he could now only go upward. How long this optimistic feeling might last John chose not to speculate. Still not yet quite back to his senses, a knock summoned him to the door. A man was standing there with a tray holding hot coffee, hot milk, three slices of bread, three pads of butter, and a small pot of jam. John was delighted, but also surprised. He had not called to order this food. How had the man known that he was now awake, and ready to eat?

Having last eaten breakfast at a train station in England, where he had dined on a greasy mix of eggs, sausages, runny tomatoes, and toasted white bread, John had forgotten that Italians did not eat breakfast as he generally knew it to be taken. He thanked the man for the *prima colazione,* and was reaching into his pocket for a tip when the waiter said, with an awkward accent that sounded more eastern European than Italian: "All is taken care of for you by the Count Sperone," and left before John could ask him if he could trade the coffee for a pot of tea. Since John's stomach didn't tolerate coffee he poured the corrosive stuff down the sink, and ate his bread and marmalade with the warm milk. This had left him still a little hungry, so John Vigilia decided to take a short walk around the neighborhood to see what he could find to eat.

The time was getting on to noon. Checking out the pay phones in the coffee shops he passed, John had discovered that none of them took any of the coins he had accumulated. Not sure he would be able to make himself understood in his quest for the correct money; John hurried back to his hotel room to call Count Sperone at exactly twelve o'clock as he had been instructed to do. On the first ring John Vigilia got the count's secretary. He told John that the count was not available, and that he should call back at three and Count Sperone would tell him when to come for dinner. John was encouraged to enjoy the rest of the day seeing the sights of Rome, and if he needed a car and driver there was one at his disposal. John politely thanked the count's secretary, saying that he could use the exercise after the confinement of his long bus, train and boat trips, and would be content to walk wherever he might be going.

At 2:30, after having tried three shops on the way, John Vigilia still did not know the source of the mysterious coins called *guttones* used in Italian public telephones, so he went back to the hotel to call Count Sperone another time. As happened earlier, the count's secretary answered, and again apologized that the count was presently unavailable, and would be dining out this evening. The secretary advised John that the hotel had an excellent restaurant, and that he should eat there, and charge it to his room. He was also told to call back tomorrow at twelve. With several hours to pass until the dining room opened, John decided to go for another walk, this time purposely passing by the palazzo, hoping that perhaps he might run into Count Ferdinand Sperone going in or coming out. Nevertheless, when John finally got near Sperone's residence he found a small army still occupying that portion of the street, so did not walk past the count's palace but turned around at the corner of the block.

For the next three days John Vigilia tramped the streets of Rome, his mind not on the scenery, but on either his dead wife, Iris, or the elusive Count Sperone and his relation to the mysterious Ariel Angelucci. Repeating a routine set on the first day on each subsequent day, John would faithfully call Count Sperone at twelve, only to be told the count was not available, but that he should call again at three; when the count was still not available, however, please call again tomorrow at twelve. John could not say that he was not enjoying himself to a certain extent. More specifically, he was enjoying immensely not having to pay for anything but the odd souvenir, or lunch eaten outside of the hotel.

In spite of all this, John was becoming rather bored with The Eternal City, having walked it from one end to the other and back. Rome had become for him not so much a place, but a compendium of related impressions, with a bust here, and a horse and rider there, a tomb below, or a fountain with some turtles subdued by a fusillade of water, and behind more than one of the elaborately sculptured doors the pious kneeling in semidarkness before a gilded altar, heedless of the fact that the religious images freely surrounding them were also priceless art treasures.

Before John Vigilia had begun his quest for Lindbergh's copilot, a mission that he now fully accepted he was on, John had been content with the intellectual whirligig he had supervised at Elmira. He had occupied his time chasing beauty with truth, telling himself, and his students, that an art without pulchritude and eloquence, even the sumptuous, was not an art at all, but merely a form of recreation. Worrying about art, or its absence, had blinded John to what he had suspected deep down, and what had been revealed by all that he had seen here in Rome: that all artists and writers, like priests, often maintain an unsubstantiated relationship with their deity.

Another thing, of a more mundane nature, had also become obvious to John Vigilia. Apparently he was now being followed everywhere he went. While John was not a professional spy by any stretch of the imagination, he had had some spy-like experience, having spent a month in the Soviet Union several years ago. Through the generosity of the United States Information Agency, John had received a travel grant to lecture there on American writers. He felt honored at being selected out of who knows how many applicants, but figured he had probably gotten the gig because he lived in Elmira and had kind of presented himself as an expert on the work of Mark Twain. Notwithstanding, the Russians found it amusing that an author who had not yet published a single book of his own had been sent to them to talk about American writers. John lied and explained that he was more of a scholar than a creative writer. He hadn't needed to do much research preparing for the trip either, as the USIA sent along boxes of books by contemporary authors for him to hand out as gifts. All John had to do was talk about these books, many of which he hadn't even bothered to read. As his talks were simultaneously translated into Russia, and sometimes from Russian to Lithuanian, or Georgian, John Vigilia had no way of being sure of what he was supposedly saying anyway.

His hosts at The Union of Soviet Writers, however, had been very impressed by the fact that John Vigilia owned and flew his very own airplane, as private aviation virtually did not exist in their country. That he could afford an airplane on a modest professor's salary was also something not to be believed. This apparent incongruity had led the KGB to come to suspect that John was actually a secret agent. Or so he was told. Because of their suspicions John had found himself followed more closely than the usual cultural exchange visitor.

At first it was the people from the embassy who had taken great pride in pointing out to John his various tails: the men in black leather trench coats who sat in the hotel lobby reading newspapers, one of whom invariable got up and followed him out the door; the pimply-faced man who sat next to him and his female translator in a box at the Bolshoi, who never took his coat off, and who tagged along when John went to the men's room. After the first week such characters became easy enough for John to spot on his own. He began to play at eluding these shadowy followers, ducking down alleys and hiding in storefronts, the whole adventure giving him a perverse sense of vicarious excitement. Eventually the embassy took notice of what John was doing and warned him that it was a dangerous game he was playing at, and that he should knock it off before he got himself into real trouble.

In the beginning, John had thought that perhaps his Roman tails were just a coincidence, or maybe even a product of his over-active imagination. How could there be anyone in Rome who would want to have him followed? But there they were. John first spotted his shadower on the afternoon of his second day at the hotel. He had refused the count's offer of a car and decided to walk to the most obvious tourist attraction in the city, the Spanish Steps. Two blocks down the Via del Babuino John had stopped to look in the window of an antique shop. The reflection in the glass revealed a man behind him, the same man who he had seen sitting alone in the hotel lobby when he came down, and who departed at the same time he had, standing across the street apparently watching him. When John moved on the man followed him, keeping pace about twenty yards behind.

John's intuition told him that some sort of sordid drama was being enacted in silence around him. Wanting to test if his instinct was true, he walked briskly for one more block, attempting to put some distance between him and his persistent tail. Suddenly, and without hesitating, John quickly dodged down a side street. Turning onto the Via Margutta, and out of his suspected follower's sight for just a few moments, John Vigilia increased his pace, almost running, and then, in the best motion-picture-spy technique, ducked into a doorway.

The entrance was to a small and unctuous barbershop. The front window was empty except for a plastic man's head wearing a wig, a woman's torso clad in a towel, and a foam foot advertising what John took to be some sort of toe fungus cream. One glance at this strange and rather ghostly tableau was enough to raise his mind to an alarm state of intrigue. Fleeing from his flight of fancy, John turned his gaze back to the sidewalk just in time to watch his tail hurry past. The man walked half way down the block, then stopped and looked around furtively, realizing he had lost his quarry. He looked left and right, but did not think to double back. This caused John to conclude that whoever it was that was having him followed was not using the best professional help.

Arriving at the ever bustling Spanish Steps, John found a vacant place on the stone stairs among the tourists and street vendors and sat down to pass the time of day watching the passersby. He had only spent a few moments in blissful melancholy when he was surprised to see a person who he took to be the same man who had followed him a bit earlier passing through the hurly-burly crowd milling in the Piazza di Spagna. It was the man's plainness that set him apart from the others. He displayed that rather undistinguishing appearance tails are supposed to have; in fact his face looked not unlike the plastic figure that John had just seen in the barbershop window.

He wanted to dismiss the whole situation as being mere chance. After all John told himself, Rome was a small city. But the feeling that he was being followed was very strong. The man had stopped and looked around when John was hiding in the shop entrance. Now he had reappeared, walking at a brisk pace and glancing about as he went. As the strange man passed the fountain, which had been designed by Berenini in the form of a sinking boat, John wondered if he too might be sinking, sucked down into some decades old conspiracy that he would better off not knowing about.

The quick focus of the man's head as he crossed the square revealed to John that his follower had caught sight of him. Back on the scent now the man hastened across the street and started up the stairs headed in John's direction. Arriving abeam of the seated John Vigilia, the man halted, and stood on the step for few seconds. John's heart beat faster. The man was so close his shadow fell over his quarry's feet. John felt that the man was staring at him; however, he did not dare to look up to challenge his gaze, nor did he crane his head around when his stalker finally left, seemingly having accomplished what he had intended to do, which John Vigilia guessed was to intimidate him.

The man's footfalls sounded on the hard stone as he proceeded on up the stairs. Assuming his intrepid follower had taken a place several steps higher, and was watching him, John folded his arms in front of his body and affected the patient, priest-like, pose he often took while fulfilling his required student office hours back in Elmira.

A half-hour went by, a long time sitting on hard stone steps. Although these famous rococo stairs attracted a constant parade of interesting people that one might observe, including young, thin-legged girls in short shorts and miniskirts, John sat there with his head bent down. His mind kept drifting back to his dead wife. To think of her was like to stare at the sun at midday, an abysmal perversity. John could feel a tightness growing in his throat. He recalled how at the train station in Tralee he had, out of habit, ordered two tickets to Dublin. It was not until the ticket seller asked him his wife's name that John realized what he had done.

Tired of sitting, and perhaps eager to confront his stalker, John rose and turned to go up the steps. To his dismay, the tail he was sure had been sitting behind him watching was not there. John Vigilia let his eyes roam over the busy emptiness of this prime tourist attraction, but could not find anyone with even a slight resemblance to his sinister follower. Breathing a sigh of relief, John chalked the experience up to his febrile imagination. If only he were so inventive when he was seated at his computer back home trying to write something, John told himself.

At the top of the stairs the façade of The Church of Trinità dei Monti, with its twin campaniles and the obelisk in front, stood not unlike a great stage. John turned left hoping to perhaps find the Via Gabriele D'Annunzio. D'Annunzio was one of his favorite writers. He had read his novel, *The Flame of Life,* based on his love affair with the actress Eleonora Duse, through several times. Although somewhat flowery, John admired D'Annunzio's imaginative and melodious style. He wished he could write like that, but then no one wrote like that anymore. John also wondered if he might be attracted to D'Annunzio because he was a pilot. Although John was by choice strictly a civilian pilot, he respected D'Annunzio, who had flown in combat in World War One and suffered an accident that had blinded him in one eye and threatened the other.

After some searching, John finally found the sign: Via Gabriele D'Annunzio. A strange silence came over him. John Vigilia stood on the path, lined by a low stone balustrade, and looked out over the vista. The City of Rome spread out below him like an enormous, populated motherland. That he was in the presence of D'Annunzio he was sure, a feeling John had in some way not sensed while sticking around waiting for Mark Twain in his gazebo back in Elmira.

The gathering wind smoothed out the sounds of the traffic below, gradually melding the noise into one gray din that slowly spread out over the sea of tile roofs and spires. In the milky, smoky air of the afternoon John Vigilia could sense a storm was brewing. For no reason, he glanced to his right, toward the green profusion of the Borghese Gardens. To John's shock he saw someone he took to be his dead wife Iris standing against the balustrade bent over, listening to the distant roar of the city. She seemed to be catching an energy from the sounds that was bringing a warm smile to her ashen face.

As John Vigilia watched in disbelief, the woman he saw as Iris began to dance; slowly at first, and then increasing into a wild gypsy fandango. The gusting wind gently lifted her skirt as she twirled around, to the delight of a passing group of small boys, who clapped and turned to look back as they were quickly led away by a scolding, wimpled nun. Out over the city a bolt of lightning flashed. John's eyes darted in that direction for just a moment, waiting for the sound of thunder. When he turned back Iris was not there. In her stead was the man he believed to be following him, again standing and watching. The clap of thunder brought a stab of fear to John Vigilia's heart.

It had begun to rain. His nerves now whipped naked, John spun around and fled down the tree-lined stairway that led to the Piazza del Popolo below, his follower trailing after him as if a participant in some insane procession. Helpless and panic-stricken by the uncertainty of what had just occurred, John ran, like a rabbit down a hole, slipping on the wet steps, not willing to look behind him. At the bottom of the stairs, sure that his pursuer was about to spring on him in this semi-concealed place,

John plunged into the safety of the busy street. Shaking his fist at the sky, he shouted over his shoulder like a child at play: "Catch me if you can!"

The driver of a blue Fiat Uno blew his horn and squealed to a stop as John Vigilia stepped in front of his car. *"Stùpido!"* the motorist screamed, displaying his finger to John in a defiant gesture and shouting some unintelligible words of Italian at him as he roared away.

Recklessly dodging a few more cars and trucks, and even a bus that honked madly, John charged across the busy street. Safely on the other side, he paused to look back. The rain had stopped. It was only a passing summer shower. The sky above the two look-alike churches that defined the piazza had become speckled with rain clouds giving the square an anxious mood. Carefully surveying the route that he had just taken, John concluded that no one had been following him. Nor had Iris danced in the street. Perhaps, he had seen a real gypsy woman; they were everywhere here in Rome. Maybe he *was* stupid, John thought considering the Fiat driver's shouted words, about more things than just crossing a street. Ever since Iris had died it was as if he had taken leave of his senses. What was he doing here? Why was he waiting around to talk to this Count Ferdinand Sperone? The rational thing to do would be to just pack up and go back to Elmira, and his comfortable teaching job, and wait patiently to step into his next stage of mortality; goodbye and better luck next time. John hurried back to his hotel.

When he came down to the lobby the next morning, the plain-looking man John had suspected of tailing him the day before was again sitting at a table by the window drinking a small espresso and reading a newspaper. John Vigilia stopped at the desk to ask if he had received any messages. His action drew the familiar man to his feet and he hurried out before John had received a reply from the clerk. Fight the thing that you fear,

John told himself, and made it a point to walk around the city again for most of the morning. He did not sense that he was being followed. When he went out again in the afternoon, however, John was clearly aware of being tailed, but by a different man from the first, however, just as plain, someone who apparently wanted him to know that he was there.

Despite his repeated telephone calls, always made at exactly the proper time, John Vigilia had been still unable to arrange a meeting with the elusive Count Sperone. And so, with nothing better to do, John continued his tramping about Rome, being followed off and on, or so he thought. Perhaps, like a jungle cat hunting its prey, John's trackers let him see them only when they wanted to be seen. At any rate, John was enjoying the game, while still hoping to get an audience with the count. Naive as he was at the time, he did not feel that his life was in any grave risk. He judged his shadowers to be competent, but not as skilled as the KGB had been. John wondered if, in fact, his watchers might be mistaking him for someone else, or merely using him for practice. In any case, John Vigilia took the precaution of avoiding dark, and empty streets when he was alone, which was all the time. While he had not yet been hit by a lightning bolt John was sure that he was still very much in the center of the storm.

Now in his sixth day in Rome, John Vigilia was lying on his bed, trying not to think of Iris, wondering if his past life had been too small and tight, waiting to put in his regular twelve o'clock call to the count. John had decided to tell Count Sperone today that he could wait around no longer, that he had other things to do, even though he didn't. Then John's telephone rang.

"*Buon Giorno!* Hello, Stunt Flying Professor, I am the Count Sperone calling to you! And how are you today?"

"Oh! . . . Hello, Count?. . ." John was surprised to hear the count's voice, and not sure that it actually was

Count Sperone, as he had spoken to the man only once before over the telephone, and that was by long distance from Ireland.

"*Mi dispiace molto* . . . er, I say I am very sorry. But you know now the problem with the government it is very big . . . but then it is always that way in Italy. Anyway, I have been very busy . . . with many strange things to do. But I have not forgotten about you *professore*. I hope you have been enjoying my hospitality, and have found Rome interesting. I take it you have not been to our beautiful city before."

"Oh, no I haven't . . . but I have been enjoying myself immensely. Thank you again for all you've provided for me. I am finding Rome quite fascinating. But I really must be getting on home . . . so I was hoping we could get together before I leave. After all, it was you I came to see, not the sights of your city."

"Yes, of course, this was why I just called. I was planning we would be able to meet tonight, but I have been called out of town unexpectedly. I must go to Viterbo on business . . . now it is not far, but I am leaving in a few minutes. My calendar also shows I am invited to a party this evening in Bracciano, on the lake; it is the house of Luigi Bosco. Do you know him? He is one of Italy's leading film stars. He made a grand movie some years ago where he played Leonardo da Vinci. It was a big success in your country . . . even shown on television."

"Yes, I have seen it. . . ." John interjected. He thought to add that he had found the film rather entertaining, although not too accurate, but restrained himself.

"So . . . would you like to meet Bosco? He is a dear friend to me. I have call-ed him, and told him I would be coming to his party and perhaps to bring a guest."

"Thank you. That's very kind. And how will I get there? Are you coming to pick me up?"

"No. I am sorry. Viterbo is to the north of Bracciano, I will stop at the party on my return. My driver is taking me so I cannot send him for you. I have arrange-ed for you to have a ride with one of the other guests who will be also coming, a fashion designer named Trinculo Solaria. You have probably not heard of him, but he is quite famous here in southern Italy. In any case, you should stand out on the Lungotevere by the Ponte Margherita, that is the bridge near your hotel, be on the side facing north at six o'clock. *Allora,* watch for a black Mercedes sedan."

"But the Lungotevere will be filled with black Mercedes sedans at that hour. . . ." John protested.

"Trinculo has a sense of humor . . . when I told him you were an American, he said he would tie three balloons, red, white, and blue, to his antennae . . . you should be able to notice that."

"But why can't he just pick me up at my hotel?"

"Trinculo is from outside Rome . . . he hates driving in the city. I had all I can do to get him to drive in on the Lungotevere. So make sure you are there at six. . . ."

"Don't worry, Count . . . I will be on the bridge well before six to be sure. I am looking forward to seeing you again . . . and to meeting Luigi Bosco. Until this evening then. . . ."

"*Ciao, Professore* . . . or, as you Americans say: See you later."

After hanging up the telephone, John stretched out on his bed and breathed a sigh of relief, revolving the strange situation in his head. He was finally to have a meeting, of sorts, with Count Ferdinand Sperone. His usually accurate intuition, however, told him that their meeting would not be pleasant. Despite his attempt at sounding friendly, the count's words had not had that airy vitality of their previous conversations, rather John had detected in his tone a hint of something invidious or perhaps even grim.

No matter, now John had the whole afternoon to kill. He got out his guidebook and began to plan another walk. Then his eyes fell on the hotel stationary stacked on the end table. He decided to write a letter.

John Vigilia's scratchy handwriting rapidly filled three pages with a cursory outline of what he had learned about Ariel Angelucci so far, and what had happened to him since arriving in Europe. John could think of no one that he was close enough with to actually send the letter to, so addressed the envelope to himself at his home in Elmira. Reluctant to leave it with the desk clerk for posting, he decided to take a walk across the river and down the Via del Corso to the Central Post Office in Piazza San Silvestro.

Looking over his shoulder frequently during the rather long, but direct, trek John Vigilia did not observe anyone that he thought might have been following him. Nevertheless, when he got on line at the post office a stranger immediately jumped in behind him and stood unusually close, even for Italy where lines tended to not only be rather casual, but often times rather intimate.

And when John reached across the counter to hand his crème-colored envelope to the postal clerk, it was as if he couldn't detach the letter from his fingers. He stood there, with his arm extended, for a brief moment before the postal clerk finally took it from his hand. For some reason the clerk turned the envelope over and looked at the back, perhaps to see if it was sealed. The man behind John was not quite so subtle as he peered over John's shoulder to catch a glimpse of the address. "Air mail," John Vigilia said, even though he knew the words in Italian.

The clerk told John the cost in Italian. He paid the postage and walked away. The man behind, again a rather plain man, stepped up to the window, although John had clearly observed that he did not have any letters or packages in his hands. Perhaps he was just buying stamps, John thought, although he could not contain his suspicion.

Pausing at the door, John watched as the man spoke to the clerk. The clerk handed him a letter. Although John Vigilia was some distance away, he was sure that it was his letter in its crème colored envelope. No, John told himself, it couldn't be, a postal worker wouldn't do that. He was just being paranoid. If anyone were really after his letter they would not have behaved so obviously. Turning around, John left the post office and started off at a brisk pace in the direction of his hotel. He had a party to go to this evening, not just an ordinary party, but one at the villa of a famous Italian movie star. He was, however, still a bit shaken. This recent incident at the post office had left John Vigilia in a state of anxiety he found hard to contain.

Twelve

There be some sports are painful, and their labor
Delight in them sets off; some kinds of baseness
Are nobly undergone, and most poor matters
Point to rich ends.

Shakespeare *The Tempest III. ii.*

Somewhere a church bell clanged, joined immediately by the ding-dong of another and the ring-ding-ding of a third. Bells of every sound rang everywhere and all the time in Rome; although John Vigilia could hear fewer of them now engulfed as he was in the roar of the heavy traffic on the Lungotevere. It was now approaching seven o'clock. He had been waiting here for over an hour and a half, having arrived at 5:30 to be sure that he didn't miss his six o'clock ride. Countless gleaming, black Mercedes-Benz sedans had whizzed by John, who was stationed there rather like a homeless person, but none displayed the signal red, white, and blue balloons tied to their antennae. Tired of standing, and unsure that his ride was even coming at all; John decided to give up the wait and go back to his hotel.

As he was fumbling to unlock the door to his room, John heard the telephone inside begin to ring. He rushed in and picked up the receiver, but no one was there.

Sitting down on the bed he kicked off his shoes to wait. Perhaps the caller, who must have been his ride Trinculo, as John was expecting no one else, would call back. Realizing he had worked up a sweat, and was covered with grit, from standing in the sun watching cars race by for over an hour John slipped out of his clothes and stepped into the shower.

His wash-up finished, he dried off and stretched out on his bed to rest. As much as John tried to he could not prevent his mind from wandering back to his dead wife. Staring at the ceiling, John watched as the sunlight filtering through the diaphanous curtains suddenly gave form to a complete and unmistakable face, not just any face, but the face of Iris. Before his eyes, the passing clouds moved the shadowy visage from the left of the room to the right. Spontaneously, John bolted upright for a better look; the image was gone, vanished. He wanted it back. If it was indeed Iris's ghost it would not escape from him. John lay back down, hoping the face would return, but as such chance pictures do, it had run away. Disappointed, his fatigue began to overtake him. John had just begun to doze off when he was awakened by a repeated and delicate knocking on his door.

A voice fluttered through the panel: "Ciao! Flyer . . . it's me, Trinculo . . . come to take you to the par-tee!"

After his shower John had fallen asleep without anything on. He quickly wrapped himself in the rather short terry cloth robe the hotel provided, and went to open the door.

"I'm sorry I'm late, my dog was sick. . . . ." The visitor paused. His eyes ran up and down John's body. "Well . . . hello! Like, I wasn't expecting this. I bet you're naked under that robe!"

"Eh, hello, I'm John Vigilia, and who are you?" he said. The man was staring down at John's legs which, for someone ten years ago he would have called an older man, were well formed. John patted at the front of his robe to make sure it was closed and that no part of him was protruding.

"I'm . . . Trinculo," the visitor said, extending his hand and waltzing into the room. "So you're the famous *fly-er.*"

The way he had said the word "flyer" made John think that Trinculo was not asking if he was someone who drove airplanes around the sky. He reluctantly shook his visitor's extended hand, finding it firm, not the fish-like grip John had expected.

Without having been invited to, Trinculo flopped down in the room's only chair. "I'm sorry that you had to wait so long on that ghastly road, but my dog was sick, and I had to take it to a vet. I would have called but my cell phone is dead. God-awful thing is always going out of whack. "

All John could do was stand there in his robe; he had thrown his clothes over the chair, and Trinculo was sitting on them.

"Well . . . are you going to get dressed? Or shall we just have our own party here? . . ." Trinculo said, almost too eagerly.

John Vigilia stepped back. "Well . . . er, I'm not that way . . . errr, I mean I had a wife, but she died recently. . . ."

"You're not what way? . . ."

John Vigilia hesitated, searching for the right word: homo, poof, queer, queen, fag, pansy, tinkerbelle, fairy, something that an Italian would understand, "Tooty-fruity," he finally blurted out.

Trinculo laughed. "Yes, I get what you are trying to say. The correct pronunciation of the phrase is *tutti frutti.* It's Italian for 'all fruits' the slang usage comes from your country where 'fruit' denotes a gay male."

"Oh. . . ." John said surprised at him, a writing professor, being given an English lesson by an Italian.

"I went to school in San Francisco, the Art Institute, that's why my English is not too bad," Trinculo revealed. "I worked construction, so I know all the slang. It's such a stereotype; everyone thinks I'm gay . . . just because I'm a fashion designer, when as a matter of fact I'm AC/DC. I mean I enjoy fucking a beautiful lady just as much as I do a handsome man."

"Look, it's not that," John stammered, feeling totally put down and looking for a way out of this conversation. "It's just that you're sitting on my clothes. If you'll get up I will get dressed and we can go."

"Oh! Well don't let me detain you . . . I'm sorry, I hadn't noticed," Trinculo said laughing and jumping up.

Clutching his clothes, John ducked into the bathroom to change, closing the door tightly behind him. When he emerged fully clothed he observed that Trinculo had a decidedly disappointed look on his face.

"Well. Let's go to the party," Trinculo said.

Double-parked in front of the hotel was a black Mercedes sedan that the factory would surely have been too embarrassed to acknowledge having made. But then they wouldn't have had to, for its distinguishing emblem had already departed from the hood. Three balloons, red, white and blue, were still proudly flying from its antennae. John did not judge the car to be that old, but it appeared as if it must have at one time had the misfortune of being parked in the middle of a riot between the police and striking university students.

"Oh god look! Another dent," Trinculo hissed. "I think I got another goddamn dent just while I was parked out here. Ooooh, I so hate to bring this car into town. Oh well . . . get in *flyer* the door's unlocked."

John Vigilia went to sit down, but there was a black plastic bag containing a cold, stiff, lumpy something taking up the passenger seat. "What's this?" he asked, attempting to move whatever it was.

"Oh, it's just my dog. Put him in the back. . . ."

"Your dog?"

"Yes. Remember I told you I was late because my dog was sick, and I had to take him to a vet. Well he died on the way . . . so I turned around and came straight here. Luckily I had that plastic garbage bag in the trunk to wrap him in."

John Vigilia lifted the package onto the back seat, observing that it must have been a small dog. Trinculo pounced on the gas pedal and they roared off, the sound of the muffler echoing the condition of the rest of the car.

The traffic was still very hectic even at this hour, so Trinculo drove in silence, a study in concentration, only occasionally breaking the quietude to honk his horn, and scream, in two languages, at any driver he felt had willfully impeded his progress: "Multo stupido, asshole!"

They crossed the Ponte Milvio, and then took the right fork, the Via Couch toward Viterbo. Once out of Rome, Trinculo became more relaxed, and started up a conversation:

"So the count tells me you're a famous stunt pilot . . . and that you're also a professor who writes books . . . and that you are now writing a book about Sperone airplanes. . . ."

"Well, not exactly. I'm trying to find out about an orphan boy that the count's family may have taken in back in the 1920s," John said, and then stopped short. Without realizing what he was saying, he had blurted out something he had not intended to say. "I mean, I can't tell you anymore. That's just something, er . . . another matter that I'm looking into for someone else, a friend. Actually, yes, I am writing a book about Sperone Aviation. . . ."

"Well I wouldn't know anything about that . . . I have no interest in airplanes . . . other than that they arrive and depart on time. Say . . . do you know any of the other people staying at your hotel . . . I mean somebody from there who might also be coming to this party?"

"No. Why?"

"There was a black Alfa Romeo sedan parked in front of the hotel. When we were leaving a man got in it and pulled out when we did. And I think he's still behind us . . . it's as if he's following us."

"It must be just a coincidence," John said not too convincingly, trying not to sound paranoid. "There's no one who would want to follow me. Is there anyone who would want to follow you?"

"Not that I know of. . . ." Trinculo said, turning and giving John a quick glance that seemed to say while he was unaware of what was going on, he was taking it all in good humor.

By the time Trinculo and John finally reached Bracciano the sun had set and it had become quite dark. Unlike the streets of Rome, the town of Bracciano's were not well lit. But Trinculo had been here before, and knew the way. Turning halfway around in his seat, John watched as a pair of headlights kept in step with the Mercedes at every corner. They drove along a stone wall, then turned into a gate marked Villa Bosco. The black car that had been following them stopped a discreet distance behind, and put out its lights. In the darkness John could neither clearly distinguish the make of the mysterious car, nor could he read its license plate number.

The villa they had arrived at was of an enormous size. It appeared as if been created from a group of old farm houses that had been redone, and then joined together by a covered walkway. The large courtyard was packed full of cars: Ferraris, Jaguars, Rolls-Royces, Lamborghinis, and several esoteric makes John couldn't even recognize.

Although they had arrived at what John thought was a late hour, the party was actually just beginning. Most people in Rome did not eat until ten o'clock anyway, and famous movie stars and the like were accustomed to dining later than that. In the old kitchen a large pig was roasting on a spit in a huge stone fireplace. When they entered, Trinculo had taken John Vigilia by the arm and was now showing him off as if he were his date. John looked around for Count Sperone, but could not spot him immediately as this was a very large party, with numerous people in many rooms. Trinculo tapped a man on the shoulder and he turned around, displaying his full beard and intense eyes. John had never seen a man who looked more like Leonardo da Vinci. He wanted to sit down with the man and discuss his notebooks, tell him how they had helped him with his own paintings, and how he had made, and successfully flown, from the top of the town water tower, a flying machine based on his design.

"This is our host, Luigi Bosco, he speaks excellent English. In his films none of his lines are dubbed," Trinculo boasted. "Luigi, permit me to present my American friend, The Stunt Flying Professor."

"John Vigilia," John stammered.

"I am pleased to meet you, *professore*. I have heard of you. I am a great fan of aerobatics . . . you know in Italy flying is an art form. Remember we had the Futurists, and D'Annunzio. And Azari. Do you know the work of Fedele Azari?"

"Azari? I can't say I do. . . ."

"He was a Futurist artist and a writer, mostly of poetry. A pilot in the World War One, he proposed that after the war the airplanes be painted bright colors and trailing smoke perform vast dances in the sky, a kind of 'aerial theater' I believe he called it. It was a novel idea; however, there is unfortunately no documentation that he ever accomplished any of this, even on a modest scale."

"That's too bad. When I lived in New York City there was an artist trying to do much the same thing. I even saw a show he had in one of the galleries. He had his actual biplane all painted up and in the gallery, along with drawings for his performances."

"It must have been a huge gallery."

"The gallery was big . . . but the airplane was small, a Pitts Special. It only has a seventeen foot wing span, but he had to take it apart to get it in through the door, and then reassemble it."

"Sort of like a ship in a bottle," Luigi joked. "And whatever became of this artist? What is his name? With such an exhibition as this it is strange that I have never heard of him."

"You know, it's funny, but somehow I can't remember his name either. I seem to recall that it was a Polish sounding name."

"But with such a unique idea as this he should have become world famous, yet I am not aware of him."

"Yeah . . . for some reason the art magazines chose to mostly ignore him. I think it might have been because the gallery he had his show in was not part of the New York art world power clique. I did see some of his drawings in another gallery years later. Then it was like he just disappeared."

"It's too bad, maybe he will reappear," Luigi said, and then changed the subject back to his guest. "Will you be doing any flying while you are here in Italy?"

"I hadn't really thought about it . . . I don't have access to an airplane."

"It is a pity. I would love to have seen you fly . . . but wait a minute! What am I thinking about? Your story of the sky artist has given me the perfect idea." The actor looked around the room. "I don't see him now . . . but I know that he is here. I am sure he has not left, he is always the last to leave . . . usually carried out dead drunk. He is such a great artist. You must meet Hans Hockenheim. And you shall . . . later tonight! He may be able to help you, and you him. But now you must please excuse me, I must attend to the rest of my guests, but when I find Hans I will present you to him. In the meantime enjoy yourself . . . the roast pig will be done shortly, and I personally will carve it up."

"I think he likes you," Trinculo, who had been standing there without speaking, finally said.

"Are you jealous?" John said, trying to sound a bit hissy.

"Jealous of what? . . ." Trinculo asked. His smile went crooked and his eyes gloomy.

"Jealous that I might have found a new boyfriend: you've been parading me around all evening as if I were your date."

"Never in your wildest dreams *flyer.* You're not my type."

Having exceeded the limit of their tension, the atmosphere between Trinculo and John became clear. For Trinculo possibilities had faded and declined into a void. He left his *date* to cruise the party. Freed of his escort, John wandered from room to room, continuing his search for Count Sperone.

The gathering ebbed and flowed in an atmosphere of excessive facility, every whim flew high, every passing excitement grew into an empty parasitic passion; a light gray vegetation of fluffy conversations sprouted forth, crafted from a weightless fabric of gossip and bold noses stuffed with cocaine. Faces over-painted like masks fluttered their colored eyelids, and too red lips whispered voicelessly.

Asking around, John Vigilia learned that Count Sperone had not arrived yet. To provide some distraction until he came, John wandered through the crowd seeking someone who spoke English, hoping to engage in some polite conversation. Except for the host, and Trinculo, who was eying him from a distance like a spurned lover, everyone was talking in Italian. This suited John just fine, he told himself. He was never any good at parties. His late wife Iris had wished he talked more, showed a little more passion for human contact; however, John preferred to cleave to things rather than other beings. Iris reminded him that most people found closed individuals too much to bear, especially those persons who consciously held themselves back, refusing to take the risk of openness. "Smile," she used to urge him, "it's good for your brain."

"Hello. They say-ed to me that you are American. I can be Bianca. I am learn-ed English. I can . . . to speak whiz you. Okay?" A woman said, staring up at John with half-closed eyelids, a sensual smile on her lips.

He studied the woman's face. Its features had had years, and at the same time any sense of expression, removed by a plastic surgeon's knife. Then, as was a man's habit, aware of it or not, John's eyes flashed down to her body. Looking back up, he caught her eyes just returning from a tour of his crotch. She smiled. The woman was wearing a short, fringed leather cowgirl outfit that appeared as if it might have been a costume left over from an early Roy Rodgers and Dale Evans movie.

"*Buon giorno* . . . my name is John," he said lapsing into that sing-song tone Americans use when talking to foreigners, the same tone they use back home with little children. "And I am studying Italian," he said, referring to the time he had spent on the train with his copy of *See It and Say It in Italian.* "We can talk to each other."

"Good. First . . . may I please to correct you, for you are own good, and so you can learn-ed well. You not say *buon giorno* now . . . it is too late for the day. These words is for the . . . morning . . . or afternoon. Now is evening, or maybe night . . . so we use as greeting, *buona sera* . . . say after me, *bwoh-nah seh-rah.*"

"*Bwoh-nah seh-rah. . . .*" John repeated.

Bianca smiled again, and winked at him. He saw that he was wrong; her face did have an expression after all. Someone squeezed passed behind them, and Bianca moved forward to make room. John felt her warm body brush up against his. A brief frisson of excitement passed through him. He was rather surprised. This was the first physical reaction to a woman he had had since his wife died.

Bianca was an actress, but had not worked at her vocation in some time. In halting English she told John the story of her life, as if she were reading it from a tabloid, and as if everyone in the world was waiting to hear it. A young girl of modest talent, but considerable beauty, from the small town of Orbetello, she had been discovered working in a gelato shop in nearby Port' Ercole by an important film director. There was the coaching, and the minor roles, and finally a kind of stardom. Then, after a few less than profitable pictures, the studios stopped calling. The cycle was as predictable as the seasons. Bianca, however, blamed the demise of her career on her refusal to sleep with certain influential moneyed people.

As they talked Bianca moved closer and closer to John, until she was standing much too near. When she spoke, she touched him repeatedly, giving John little pushes, or pulling at his shirt. Now and then she flecked a speck of nothing from his shoulder. It was making him upset, his nerves tense. It was like torture to John, this constant touching by a woman he had only just met. Even his wife had never touched him this much in public.

"I think I'll go in the other room and refill my drink. . . ." John said, making a swirling motion with his empty glass in case he was not understood. Uncomfortable with the situation, he was hoping to make an easy escape. Bianca had now lapsed almost totally into her native tongue and, as best as John could make out, was revealing to him the sexual habits of all the currently popular Italian movie stars.

"*Bere. beh'-reh,* say it," Bianca admonished, poking John yet again with her index finger.

"No, I'm not drinking beer . . . I'm having wine," John corrected her, laughing nervously.

"I not say beer, that is *birra, beer'-rah. Bere* is the word for to drink." Bianca said, taking his arm and steering John Vigilia to the bar. He was hers for the evening, or until someone better showed up. She was secretly hoping to meet the American director who was casting a spaghetti western that he was shooting in Italy, which was why she was wearing her curious little cowgirl outfit.

Their drinks having been topped off, Bianca now guided John around the party, introducing him to people that he had already met with Trinculo. He was being paraded again, or being used as bait. Bianca kept looking around for her director, who John had never heard of but who had an Italian sounding name and who he had been told was world famous. It would certainly be better for Bianca to bump into him with someone on her arm than alone.

"Why do you be here?" Bianca asked, tugging on John's shirt. She must have run out of gossip to spill. Now she would allow him to speak. Or maybe she was genuinely curious.

"In Rome? . . ."

"No at this . . . affair. You are not a cinema person."

"I am here supposedly to meet Count Sperone. . . ."

"That . . . how do you call it?" Bianca hissed, and made a wiggling gesture with her hand.

"Snake?"

"Yes," she said with another jab to John's ribs, "*sèrpe* . . . Sperone is the lowest snake. It is from this Ferdinand that are all the problems in the government come now."

"What do you mean?"

"I tell you . . . whatever you have for your business with Sperone, not to trust him. He is the lowest," she announced, dismissing him with a sweep of her hand.

Before he could question her further, Bianca and John turned the corner and came upon a somewhat intimate and cozy room they had not yet been in. On a couch in the center, surrounded by a small group of people, a tall, and rather handsome man with wild hair and a clipped black beard was boisterously holding forth in German, breaking his screed only occasionally to take a drag on his cigarette, a gulp of his beer, or to slide his tongue into the mouths of one or the other of the two attractive women seated on either side of him. The brunette on the left had her legs across the German's lap, and he had his hand up her abbreviated skirt. On his right, the blonde woman had her blouse half undone, and the loud-talking German was openly fondling her breasts.

"I am make-ed a mistake what I say you," Bianca said, starting to pull John back out of the room. "Sperone is not the lowest . . . this one is the lowest possible of any animal."

At that moment John felt a tap on his shoulder and turned around expecting to see Count Sperone, but it was Luigi Bosco. Luigi glared at Bianca, who clung tightly to John Vigilia's arm.

"Ah, *Professore*, I see you have met Bianca . . . the biggest little bitch in Rome. Don't believe a word she tells you . . . it's all lies. If she made up screen plays instead of gossip . . . she could have that comeback she so badly desires, however not as an actress though . . . for despite what she has probably told you, she never was much of one."

"Thank you for the compliment, Luigi. And thank you also for inviting me to your little party." Bianca parried, giving him a quick poke in the ribs. Fluttering her eyes at John, Bianca went on with such clarity he thought her story about learning English had been just an act to get him to talk to her. "Luigi thinks that by throwing parties he will be remembered, and maybe get a role starring as a great hero, not just the old men he's been playing lately. Look around you, no one of any importance is here . . . not even his good friend the count."

"Oh! Forgive me *Professore* . . ." Luigi sputtered. "I forgot to tell you, Count Sperone called earlier to inform me he would not be coming tonight, and asked me to give you his regrets. He had to go directly back to Rome. He said you should call him tomorrow at noon. And now, if you will excuse us Bianca, it is important that I introduce the *professore* to the artist Hans Hockenheim." Luigi gestured to the loud German on the couch, "Hans!"

Upon hearing the sound of his name the German, who John at first seeing had taken an immediate and intense dislike to, looked up.

"*Ja, Ja, Maestro,* why do you bother me?" Hans replied in English, perhaps because he had overheard Luigi's previous exchange with John. Although he appeared to be drinking heavily, John Vigilia had observed that Hans Hockenheim never seemed to lose contact with what was going on in the room around him. "Can't you see these fine bitches have need of my good stiff cock, and the evening is growing old? I think it's time we are going upstairs to fuck." That said, Hans growled like a dog and the young women laughed, although much too loudly, displaying their well-maintained teeth.

"*Maestro* . . . I have an American I would like for you to meet. . . ." Luigi said dragging John over to the couch as Hans had not bothered to get up.

"*Nein.* I don't want to meet Americans anymore . . . the Berlin Wall is torn down . . . now we Germans have no use for fucking Americans," Hans guffawed, reaching for his mug of beer on the table in front of him. The blonde woman, one of her breasts suddenly uncovered by the removal of the artist's hand, self-consciously tugged her blouse together. "Yes . . . Americans should all go the fuck back to America. . . ." Hans laughed again, retrieving his cigarette and tapping the ash onto the floor.

John was not sure if Hans' comment was meant as a joke, there was a bitter sting in his voice. He smiled nervously.

"But Hans, *this* American can help you . . . he is a pilot."

"A pilot?" Hans was interested now, he wiped his mouth with the back of his left hand; his right hand was still up the brunette's skirt. "An airline pilot?" He put down the cigarette and hastily took a swig his beer.

"No," John answered, "I guess you could call me a stunt pilot . . . I have my own airplane, a biplane . . . a Bücker Jungmann."

"A Jungmann!" Hans jumped up from the couch scattering the two young ladies, his mood instantly changed. "You have a Jungmann. . . . I am the conceptual artist Hans Hockenheim . . . I am pleased to meet you." Hans extended this right hand. John took it and caught the smell of the woman's private parts.

"See, Hans," Luigi beamed, "I told you I would find the perfect man for you."

"Look . . . you two cunts, I am busy now," Hans said chasing the two women off the couch and indicating John should sit down next to him. "We will do some fucking later . . . now you go up and wait for me in the green bedroom . . . the one at the top of the stairs."

Sent away with little pats on their behinds, the two women trudged off like obedient puppies. John looked around for Bianca and Luigi, but they had somehow disappeared.

"So what is your name?" Hans asked.

"John Vigilia."

"But that's not an American name."

"It's Polish . . . both sides of my family were Polish."

"Veeggeylia? It's a kind of festival isn't it? On Christmas Eve people eat special food . . . fish. They do it in many countries. It's a vigil; watching for the Christ child to appear."

"Yes, you are quite correct. My name is pronounced the same, but spelled slightly different."

"So. You know I am not stupid. Some people think that I am an ignorant fool, but you can see that I am very smart. You are half Polish! This is fantastic; it will make my performance even more significant."

"Your performance? . . ."

"*Ja*, I am Germany's most important conceptual artist, and I have been invited to design a piece . . . it's going to be the main event . . . to be executed at the International Performance Art Festival, which is held in three weeks time on the Lago Maggiore at Locarno in Switzerland. It is known as the most important avant-garde festival in all of Europe."

"Well . . . congratulations," John said, coughing and quickly fanning the German's cigarette smoke from his face. "But what does this performance have to do with me?"

"I have designed a piece that includes a stunt airplane, and you my friend," Hans said placing his hand, which still smelled of estrus, on John's shoulder, "are going to fly that airplane. Just think of it! What could be more ironic than an American of Polish background, flying an airplane that was built by Nazis to train their pilots for World War Two? The piece will also have Italian skydivers and a Swiss marching band. . . ."

"But I won't be here in three weeks . . . I have to go home, back to Elmira, New York," John interrupted.

"But why should you go home? Come with me to Locarno. It is on a lake, one of the most beautiful places in the whole world."

John hesitated, and then realized that at the present telling the truth was probably his best possible excuse. "Well the fact is that I'm running out of money."

"So, you are out of money? Well don't worry I have wealthy sponsors who can give us plenty of cash. Just now there is an airplane already and waiting for you to fly in Switzerland. Your expenses will all be paid and you will receive a substantial fee for your efforts. I guarantee it. Where are you going after your visit to Rome?"

"Nowhere . . . as I said, probably back home."

"Look . . . those two bitches are waiting for me upstairs, do you want to screw one of them?" Hans asked, at the same time offering John a cigarette, which he refused with a shake his head. "Have one of the cunts and we can talk in the bedroom while we fuck."

"I, er . . . ." Taken aback by the bluntness of Han's offer John didn't know what to say except: "Well . . . I'd rather not."

"Oh . . . so you are gay?"

"No, it's just that. . . ."

"That's okay. I can handle them both myself. Fucking two is always better than fucking one . . . hah, hah, ha. Here is my card. Call me in three days time, when I will be back in Munich. I will arrange for you to come there, and to study my plans for the performance. If you agree to do it, I put you up in a nice hotel in Locarno, paying for everything of course. And you can see the airplane, and practice with it for a week or so, and be ready for when I come with the rest of my people."

Nonplused by Hans' offer of a job flying an airplane in his performance John Vigilia took his card, telling Germany's self-defined "most important conceptual artist" he would think about the possibility of participating in his event, which at the moment he had no thoughts whatsoever of doing.

"*Ja, ja* . . . you think about it, but don't pass up my offer. You can make a fucking ton of money. Now what about a chick? The blonde one has a tight pussy, and I know she has a thing for Americans."

Eager to get away from what he now thought was a madman, John told Hans that he would pass on the women, but would call him in Munich in three days time with his decision.

The party was slowly breaking up. John filled up a plate with leftover slices of pork and some pasta, and wandered through the rooms looking for Trinculo, his ride home. He found his host Luigi sitting alone by the fireplace, the embers of the wood used to roast the pig still glowing. Cars were pulling out of the courtyard, but a considerable number of people were still dancing in the main room, which had been turned into an impromptu disco.

"Have you seen Trinculo lately?" John asked Luigi, who seemed tired and out-of-sorts. His eyes were bleary. The party had not attracted the crowd of A-list film people that he had been hoping for. He listened to John Vigilia's words without stirring and then answered:

"Yes . . . he left with that bald-headed bastard, the Turkish wrestler."

"He's gone! How am I going to get back to Rome?" John asked, sounding a bit alarmed.

"There are plenty of people going in that way . . . they want to catch the clubs before they close. Trinculo said he thought you would be going back with Bianca, I think his exact words were, 'Let that bitch give him a ride home . . . and then he can give her a drive when they get there.'"

"But I haven't seen Bianca for some time now, have you?

"She said she felt sick . . . she was going upstairs to throw up, and then maybe lie down."

After casually searching through the still buzzing house and not finding Bianca, John went outside on the back porch for some fresh air. He did not expect to discover the actress sitting alone on the steps. Bianca avoided his curious gaze, not saying anything, as she sat there, strangely numb, her face contorted by a spiral of wrinkles on her brow, an apparent maelstrom growing deep inside her.

"I was worried you left. You don't look well. Are you drunk? Unfortunately my ride has gone. Do you have a car?" John said, concerned about her plight as well as his own."

"Yes, I have it a car, but I am too. . . ." Bianca said, making a noise as if she was about to throw up.

"Look, let me drive you home in your car," John said. "I actually haven't had that much to drink."

Bianca didn't answer, just nuzzled up against him, stretching out her hand to tousle John's hair. Their physical contact made, she began to speak, or at least to mumble. "I am so old . . . so ugly . . . nobody wants me. Nobody wants me anymore. The American director didn't even bother to come to the party . . . after he say he would meet me here."

She stood up on her unsteady legs, balanced as if to go somewhere. With her head rigid and with flaming eyes, and her body trembling with internal conflict, John could not help thinking that in her Dale Evans cowgirl outfit, Bianca looked not unlike a child's windup doll in which the internal mechanism had broken.

"Well . . . Count Sperone stood me up too," John empathized. "Here, let me help you . . . where are your car keys?"

"In my bag," she said glancing down at the empty stairs next to her. "Oh, it's not here. It must to be yet upstairs . . . I must have lose-ed it in the toilet when I was sick. Can you go get it for me, a blue bag, small . . . you must to go through the first bedroom at the top of the stairs."

The bedroom door was slightly ajar. John reached in and groped around, but his hand did not find the light switch. He could see clear through to the bathroom, where the light was on, so pushed the door open. On the bed, in the semidarkness, was a grotesque array of forms, chalk figures, a porcelain snake copulating with itself. The pile was moving. Instinctively, he stepped back.

"*Ja*, it's the American pilot. He has come to join us after all . . . take which one you want . . . or maybe you rather have me, ha, ha, hah." It was Hans' voice coming from somewhere deep within the bundle of writhing flesh.

"No, ah, I just wanted to go through to the bathroom."

"So, feel free to use the toilet, we are not shy. . . . Leave the door open and if you want you can watch us while you jerk-off your prick. . . ."

"That's all right I just needed to get this purse. . . ." John Vigilia said, spying the object he had been sent for.

"Oh, your purse . . . I wasn't sure you were like that. . . ."

"It's not mine."

"That's okay, I am how do you say it? AC/DC. . . . Don't forget to call me. I want you to come to Munich. As I said everything will be paid for by my wealthy sponsors."

John didn't answer, but turned and went back downstairs to get Bianca. They stumbled out into the edgy darkness of the courtyard and found her Fiat Uno. He was happy to discover that she had one of the more modest cars still parked there. It was very late, and even if he had not drunk very much John was extremely tired, and not too sure how his response mechanisms would be functioning. If he were going to crash some other person's car at least it happily would not be a Ferrari.

"Let's blow this dump, sweet heart." Bianca said, playfully jabbing at John's ribs, sounding not unlike she had heard the line before in an old Bogart movie.

John slowly helped her around to the passenger side and opened the door. But Bianca was not ready to get in. Throwing her arms around him, she pressed her body to John, and began kissing him on the mouth. Her tongue tasted of gin and salami. Despite this sudden outburst of passion, John Vigilia pried Bianca lose and, with considerable effort considering her small size, piled her into the car. She stretched out on the seat, her little cowgirl skirt riding invitingly up her thighs.

"Take me home now, big guy," Bianca blurted, seemingly on the verge of passing out.

After spending a few moments trying to figure out how everything worked, John got the Fiat's engine started. He was hoping Bianca would stay awake long enough to give him directions on how to get to her apartment. "Which way should I go?" John asked.

"Just to go straight home," Bianca ordered in a curious and strained voice, punching his shoulder.

"You have got to tell me where to turn," John reminded her.

"I didn't say turn, I said to go straight home," she slurred, chortling at her own bad joke.

John Vigilia wished now that he had paid more attention on the way out. He had not been watching the route, believing that he would be driven home by Trinculo. John was sure that he could get them back to Rome some way or other, but had no idea where Bianca lived. At the moment, he was not only tired through and through, but morbid as well as miserable. It was as if John's psyche was running out of gas. And he had not just been making up excuses when he told the artist Hans Hockenheim why he was planning to head back to America. The truth of the matter was that John Vigilia was very close to being completely out of money.

The Fiat lurched as John let out the clutch a bit too fast. He had always owned a car with an automatic transmission ever since marrying Iris, who couldn't drive with a standard shift. Revving the engine, he managed to guide the car out of the courtyard and into the dark street. In the dim moonlight the passing shapes took on a singularly threatening aspect. At that very instant a huge black cat chose to make it its business to vault into the glowing circles of the Fiat's headlights. John slammed on the brakes. Not wearing the seat belts, he and Bianca lurched forward in their seats, and then sat and watched as the slinky feline disappeared down a pitch-black alley.

With his eyes straining into the night in front of him, John cautiously headed the Fiat for Rome. It occurred to him that, despite his best intentions, this trip was not off to a positive start. A black cat crossing your path can never be considered a good omen, John thought, even though he was quite fond of cats. Nonetheless, as he glanced in the rear view mirror, John was pleasantly surprised when he discovered that apparently there were no other car lights following along behind him. Perhaps his shadowers were already in bed, being more tired than he was.

Thirteen

What, all so soon asleep? I wish mine eyes
Would, with themselves, shut up my
thoughts. I find
They are inclined to do so.

Shakespeare *The Tempest II. i.*

Bianca's apartment house was as modest as her automobile, which to John's credit had gotten them there safely, despite its owner having given him several wrong directions. The actress lived in Parioli, a forgotten middle class section of Rome, on the third floor of an older building that had neither an elevator nor a doorman. John Vigilia found a parking place for Bianca's Fiat in the street, which was where she normally left it. After lifting her out of the car, he struggled Bianca down the block, and up the three flights to her apartment. John was happy that the actress was still a woman with a slender figure.

As they clambered up the narrow stairs, Bianca seemed intent on waking the whole building, even though it was now almost dawn. John had to bundle up her arms to prevent her from banging on every door she passed. One of the neighbors on the first floor opened his door, stepped out in his underwear, and shouted something at John's companion in Italian. From his tone John took the man's words to be not exactly a compliment, nor did he imagine was Bianca's equally loud and bellicose reply.

The actress worked her key in the lock, breathing heavily, and repeating to John in English: "I'm so old . . . so ugly . . . nobody loves me." The tumblers clicked. She pushed the door open and stepped inside.

He hesitated at the entrance. "Well . . . *buona sera*," John said.

"You don't say *buona sera* now, it is too late . . . you say *buona notte*, good night."

"*Buona notte*," he repeated.

"But I don't think we should say that just this minute," Bianca said giving John a rather coquettish smile. "Would you like to come inside for a little while?"

It had been a long time since John Vigilia had heard just such an invitation, although he wondered if either one of them was in any condition for sex. He had had a long day. All John wanted to do was sleep. He doubted, however, that he could find a taxi at this time of night, and had no idea how to get back to his hotel from here on foot. John took Bianca's arm to keep her from falling and the two stumbled inside.

The apartment was small, apparently only three rooms, but deeply carpeted, with walls lined with silk hangings and gilded mirrors. It was furnished with what once must have been costly furniture that now showed its age. Tiny, but elegant, crystal chandeliers had been set into the ceiling. The profound stillness of Bianca's rooms seemed filled with the many secret glances exchanged between the mirrors and the gallery of photographs that covered every open space of the walls up to the wide molding. Everywhere John Vigilia looked a younger Bianca smiled back, lifting her eyes to the viewer, black, sibylline, quiet eyes, with a gaze that she could now no longer manage.

"The bedroom is just through there," Bianca said lighting a cigarette. It was the first time all evening that

John had seen her smoke. "Would you like one?" she offered.

"No thank you, I don't smoke . . . never started."

"I shouldn't either," Bianca said. She crushed out her cigarette in a sea shell ashtray, and sat down on her bed. "Undress me John. . . ."

Without saying anything, John Vigilia began to do what he was bidden. First he removed the absurd cowgirl hat, which had been hanging on her back by the chinstrap for most of the evening. Next, he untied the red bandana she had around her neck. Having laid bare the whiteness of Bianca's neck, he instinctively kissed it. When she did not respond, John kissed it a second time, gently grazing his tongue over her flesh. He had been a good lover once and, despite his fatigue, felt these skills surging back into his body. Then he undid the three leather ties to Bianca's fringed buckskin vest. Where Dale Evans would have covered herself wearing a shirt with a yoke and pearl buttons, and a well-padded bra, was only Bianca. John admired the firmness of her breasts. Caressing them softly with his hands, he placed a delicate kiss on each nipple, yet wondering if the fullness was truly hers, or something that had been constructed for her in a doctor's office.

"Oh, John, how can you look at me? I am so old . . . so ugly." She said again, a whiny refrain that had lost any of the meaning it might have had when he first heard it back on the steps at Luigi Bosco's villa.

"No you're not Bianca . . . you still look young and beautiful." John replied, uttering the line that he sensed he was expected to say.

Bianca stretched out her legs, and John pulled off her fringed skirt, at the same time skillfully removing her lace bikini underwear. She lay back on the bed, naked except for the red cowgirl boots. He bent over and kissed her breasts, working his tongue down her well-browned torso to her navel. John's hand had found the covert of her body, and his fingers were exploring the moist, fleshy folds.

"My boots John, you have not taken off my little boots. . . ." Bianca commanded, suddenly becoming alert.

John tugged at the boots and slid off first the right one and then the left, being careful not to let them drop to the floor.

"Suck my toes, John. Would you? No one has sucked my toes in a long, long time. . . ." Bianca said in a tone somewhere between pleading and a direct order.

John hesitated. He wanted to tell Bianca that he had indeed sucked a few toes in his sexual prime; however, her feet, which had been in the cowgirl boots for sometime without benefit of socks, were a bit sweaty and not too clean. In truth, they smelled.

"What is the matter John? Why do you wait, are my feet ugly . . . are my feet old and ugly? Do they repulse you?"

"No, they are beautiful feet, Bianca. It's just that they are a little. . . ."

"Dirty? Yes they are dirty . . . then you should wash them. It is not a problem. The toilet is through there, you can find soap and water," she said, pointing. "We will make a little theatre, you can play Mary Magdalen, and I will be Jesus. No, I should be Mary Magdalen, she is the patron saint of fallen women . . . and I am a fallen woman. But then I must to wash your feet."

John went into the bathroom, while Bianca remained lying on the bed. Looking back at her, she appeared to him to be on the verge of falling asleep.

Running hot water in the sink John glanced up and saw his reflection. And then in the mirror behind him, which Bianca must have arranged so that she might frugally do her own hair, he saw himself again, and again—a chain of John Vigilias stretching back into infinity. What was he doing here? John wondered. These were not his people, these sophisticated and worldly actors and actresses, artists and counts. He was only an English professor from a small college in upstate New York, who had gone off on a wild quest for a boy who was supposed to have flown with Lindbergh. His wife had died, and he had taken time off from teaching, without pay, and spent a good bit of his small savings, and knew no more about anything now than he would have if he had stayed at home.

John moved his face closer to the mirror. The rest of the row of John Vigilias disappeared. He saw that his beard had grown, and there was a pimple on his cheek. No matter how old he got there was always a pimple, a flaw; this was reality for John. He felt that his life was as thin as the paper that he wrote on, and betrayed with each new page its imitative character. At times he had the impression that it was only the small image directly in front of him that filled the picture of his existence, everything else was a masquerade already disintegrating and, unable to sustain itself, crumbling into the dim backstage of an enormous, empty theatre. John realized, however, that for the present at least he was seeing himself, and being himself, more than he ever had since leaving New York City for Elmira many years ago.

"Where did you go? I am fall asleep," Bianca mumbled when John returned with the damp washcloth and towel for her feet.

"I was washing my face. . . ."

"Why are you standing there with all your clothes on when I am just lying here naked? So why don't you take off your clothes?"

Once again, John began doing as he was told, undressing in front of Bianca. He tried to hurry, but he was tired, so the act became slow, almost like a strip tease. Bianca was watching him with interest; her right hand had moved down to that covert triangle between her legs. She was gently stimulating herself.

Naked now, he stood in front of her, waiting for her next command. Sitting up, Bianca took John's penis in her left hand and began rubbing it around her face, stroking it, and kissing it, her other hand still fingering her clitoris. Taking on its own will, his staff was growing in size.

"You are so . . . beautiful . . . John," Bianca slurred, slowly stroking him, while vigorously manipulating herself. "It is not fair, women only get ugly when they get older . . . but men get more beautiful."

"That's not true . . . you are still beautiful, Bianca," John whispered.

Hearing these soft words brought a sense of satisfaction to Bianca. Her whole body trembled. She let go of John and fell back on the bed in the grip of her ecstasy. He heard her slight moan and knew that she was finished.

I am tired John, I go to sleep now," she mumbled. "We can make sex in the morning . . . I must to sleep."

"Then I guess I'll go home . . . its not too far, I can walk." John heard himself say, the sound of whistling in the wind.

"No, John." Bianca opened her eyes wide, "I not want to be alone . . . I am so afraid to be alone . . . stay with me . . . please hold me," she begged. Then her consciousness vanished.

John Vigilia went back into the bathroom and tried to satisfy himself, but the urge had passed, and he could not bring it back. He was just too worn out. When he returned to the bedroom Bianca was snoring loudly. John brushed back her hair, and kissed her lightly on the forehead, as he had done so many times before with his wife Iris. Then he slid in bed next to Bianca and pulled the covers over both of them. Through the bedroom window John could see a golden dawn faintly beginning to creep westward across the treetops defining the Villa Ada.

After a few hours or so of sleep John woke up with a start. It was the same dream that kept recurring to him ever since his wife died:

He saw that Iris was ill, terribly ill, and had been for a long time. He had given up all hope of her recovery. There were horrible moments when he harbored a timid, secret longing deep down inside of him for her to die. Yet the fear of her death filled him with terror. He saw her lying in her bed, and he was watching over her, knowing she would soon be dead. He felt like crying and telling her something tender and comforting. Instead he clung to her, as though seeking protection, and then screamed at her: "Iris, I can't stand it anymore, my strength is gone, For God's sake, why can't you just die!?" And in that moment she did.

The bedroom window was full of sun light. Outside birds were singing amid the sounds of traffic and church bells that defined the city of Rome. John turned and looked over at the sleeping figure next to him. Bianca was still snoring. He got out of bed, put on his clothes and quietly slipped out of the apartment without waking her.

It was after twelve o'clock. John had already missed his call to the count, and it was a beautiful day, so he decided to walk. John Vigilia hoped that the walk would clear his head of the sense of confusion and helplessness that he had begun to feel ever since his strange conversation with the artist Sean Devlin back in Dingle.

Although John did not know what direction to take, he knew that Parioli was on one of Rome's seven hills, so decided his best plan would be to proceed downhill. He hoped that eventually he would come to the Tiber River and be able find his way. John looked around. No one was following him, nor had he been followed last night; that fact alone made driving Bianca home from the party worthwhile. But John knew now that he had had enough of Rome, and of looking for someone, an old man by now if he was still alive, named Ariel Angelucci. He would leave a message for Count Sperone, and, if he could get a flight out, head for home tomorrow.

After ten minutes of walking John, realizing that he had not eaten since last night, stopped at one of the many small cafes that lined the streets of The Eternal City and ordered a cup of tea and a roll. This was one thing about Rome that he would definitely not miss; the slight look of condescension from the waiter whenever he ordered a *"tazza di te."* In Italy real men only drank coffee. Coffee arrived instantly, but the tea never came, and when it did it was weak and tasted of coffee from the cup it was served in. Because of this John had taken to drinking grappa, that foul tasting, clear liquor made from the wasted part of the grape, as his mid afternoon drink. No waiter sneered at John when he ordered grappa, especially when he choked the glassful down in one fiery gulp.

Reaching into his pocket for change, John Vigilia found an unfamiliar piece of paper. Taking it out he saw that it was the address of the boorish German artist he had met last night, Hans Hockenheim. John had all but forgotten about this man and his strange proposition. He had no desire to go to Munich to visit this crude fellow, even if the German had offered to pay all his expenses. John turned the card over in his hand, and then looked around the cafe for a place to discard it. Finding none, he slid it back into his pocket.

Finally arriving back at his hotel after having stumbled through various parts of Rome that he had not discovered on his numerous earlier walks, John Vigilia found three messages waiting for him.

Bianca's message: *I am sorry you leave with not waking me, I was plan to make you breakfast, and after that to have a special treat for you. Call me and we can make plan to do it again some other time.*

Trinculo's message: *I'm sorry I left the party without you. I was sure you were going home with Bianca. I hope you got a ride, and if you did go home with Bianca, that things worked out, if they didn't you would be the first. The Turkish wrestler was a total bore. I have another party tonight at an art dealer's place. If you're interested in going, give me a ring.*

Count Sperone's Message: *I am sorry I missed you at Luigi's party. I hope you had an interesting time. I had to come directly back to Rome for an early meeting. I will be free this afternoon and can meet you at four o'clock at the palazzo.*

John Vigilia looked at his watch; it was already three. The walk back had taken awhile. He telephoned the count's secretary to confirm the meeting was still on, and that he would be there. Then John undressed and headed into the shower. His body still smelled of Bianca's perfume.

When John got to the block that held the Palazzo Sperone he was surprised to find the military guard that had occupied it for the past week was gone. He retraced the steps of his first visit. The only person who questioned him was the old man who watched the gate. Count Sperone was waiting for John as he stepped out of the red-velvet elevator. After what seemed a rather perfunctory greeting, the count escorted him down a different series of hallways, considerably less sumptuous than the ones that they had taken before, to an isolated, apparently unused wing of the building. This inner section, by comparison, seemed almost dingy. The count, who had not said anything on the way, as they had walked briskly almost in a hurry, opened the door to a very small, but cluttered room. Piles of boxes were everywhere, filled with papers which, judging by their musty smell, John guessed be several decades old.

"Sit down please . . . there, that is the more comfortable chair," the count said gesturing.

"Thank you," John Vigilia replied taking the place that he had been directed to. John sensed by the count's demeanor that the man was not in a good humor.

"I am sorry I could not come to Luigi's party. But it is better we talk here . . . you see this room contains many of the early documents of Sperone Aviation that you are supposedly so interested in. Or are you not?"

"Oh . . . I see." John said. He detected a sarcastic tone in the count's voice. This was not the same man who had been so happy to meet The Stunt Flying Professor one week ago.

There was an awkward silence as John stood and shuffled through some of the boxes.

"These are not all of the papers . . . there are hundreds of more boxes at my sister's house in Como . . . they are all open for your inspection," the count added.

"But these are of no use to me . . . they are all in Italian, I can't read Italian," John Vigilia blurted out without thinking.

"Then tell me why do you come here bothering us with your story about writing a book about Sperone Aviation . . . when you cannot even read Italian?" the count said, his tone suddenly becoming severe. "You have not even brought a pencil and paper with you to this interview, which I am only granting you at the expense of my other activities."

Count Sperone gave his visitor a cold stare. This was the same look John had seen on the faces in the large paintings in the hall downstairs when he had first dined here with the prime minister and his group. The paintings had gazed down at them then, Count Sperones from earlier times, long dead but still dominating the proceedings. This current count was a direct descendant of these generations of counts who had tricked and schemed their way through history. Deceiving and seeing through deceit was in their blood. John Vigilia had to admit that, by comparison, at this game he was not even a beginner.

Taken aback by the count's attack John could only stammer, "Well . . . I'm not actually writing about you or your family . . . only about the airplanes."

"Are you sure that is all you are interested in? There is not something else you are trying to find out?" Count Sperone said with a kind of haste, as if he had predetermined agenda, and was eager to get on with it.

"Whatever do you mean by that? All I'm researching is the early airplanes built by Sperone Aviation," John lied, turning his eyes away from the count's face.

The air was becoming stifling in the small, closed space. John was having some difficulty breathing. And then, as if he was becoming bored by the direction the conversation had taken, Count Sperone abruptly changed the subject asking: "And how was our little Bianca last night? Did she suit you? Trinculo was very jealous . . . he thought I had provided you for him."

Someone must have supplied Sperone with the details of John's whole evening. He could feel his heart pounding. Performing a snap-roll on takeoff in his Bücker, the wings just clearing the ground, John had a heart of oak, but here, in this small, musty room that must have been at least 500 years old, he felt fear. John Vigilia had the premonition that there was something going on around him that he was not aware of, and furthermore had no possible way of controlling.

"Trinculo was late to pick me up . . . because his dog died," John said confused by the counts change of direction, but relieved to be on a new subject. He had not expected Sperone would see through his cover story so easily. The men that had been following him off and on must have been in the count's employ. Now Sperone appeared to be leaving him a way out. "I found Bianca to be rather pleasant," John continued, hesitatingly. "She seems to have more intelligence than most people give her credit for."

"That little slut . . . intelligent? I knew her years ago, when she was younger, and still fairly attractive. We were quite close. But she was never intelligent. And she never was much of an actress. All she ever was good at was in bed, and even there she was rather mediocre. I actually got dragged into producing one of her first films. I lost a lot of money too. And as for that pervert Trinculo . . . his poor dog probably died because he had been humping the bitch too much."

Count Sperone had lost his sheen, revealing a totally different person from the one John had first encountered, someone bitter and obscene. It was as if he was reminding his guest that his family had not hesitated at violence to achieve their aims in the past, and he would not be indisposed to do likewise in the future. Realizing that their conversation was going into a spin it needed to be recovered from John asked: "So where are the airplanes?"

"The airplanes? . . ."

"Yes . . . If you recall, I said that I had come to Italy to do research on Sperone airplanes . . . not the Sperone family."

"Then why did you come to Rome? What is left of the airplanes are not here but in Como. We have a large museum there in the old factory. We used to build all the Italian airplanes, fighters and bombers, for two wars. Now all we make is a small transport plane that no one buys except impoverished Third World countries. If you want to see the airplanes you must go to Como, my sister lives there. She takes care of the museum."

"Then I'll go to Como," John Vigilia announced.

The count went quiet. He smiled, accompanying the smile with a peculiar clearing of his throat to break the silence. "Then you shall go to Como. I will arrange for your travel. You will be the guest of my sister, the Contessa Juno Sabatini, at her villa overlooking the lake. It is smaller, but more beautiful than my palazzo. Sometimes I wish I could trade with her . . . not just houses, but our whole lives."

Count Sperone got up and showed John out of the room. On their way through the halls the two men walked hurriedly, limiting their conversation to improvised and desperate raillery. The count was full of gossip about Luigi Bosco and the artist Hans Hockenheim, as well as about Bianca. Waiting for the elevator, however, without warning, the count let his bomb drop.

"So what have you learned about this Angelucci man you are searching for?" he asked trying to sound offhanded.

"What man?" John asked, stunned, not sure that he had heard correctly. What did the count really know about his visit to Rome? John wondered. He had been careful not to tell Sperone his real reason for coming here, and had not mentioned Ariel specifically by name in his slip of the tongue to Trinculo.

"I have heard you are looking for an American man named Ariel Angelucci. Why would you be looking for him here?"

John Vigilia went rigid. He forced a smile, hoping that his face had not revealed too much, "I don't understand what you are referring to. Where did you hear such a story?"

"I have many ears *professore*, some even in the Vatican," the count replied, his expression changing, almost as if he had lifted a mask from his face. "Perhaps they are wrong, but I have been told you came here from Ireland, where you were seeking information about this man. Rest assured *professore,* the Sperone family knows nothing about a former American orphan named Ariel Angelucci. So go to Como *professore*, visit our factory, see our airplanes, and then go home and write your book. You have my best wishes, *Professore* Vigilia. My secretary will make all the arrangements. He will call you later with the schedule. Tomorrow my car will pick you up at your hotel and take you to the train station."

The count pressed the elevator button and the door opened. Taking John Vigilia's elbow, he urged him in. He offered John his hand and he gave the count his. "Thank you for all you've done for me," John said, it was the best that he could come up with at the moment.

"Goodbye, to you my friend *Professore* Vigilia, *arrivederci*. You will enjoy yourself in Como. You have my best wishes for a long life. But you must take care of yourself.

You look tired. We wouldn't want anything to happen to you while you were here in Italy." Smiling at his visitor yet one final time, the count quickly turned on his heels and walked away before the door to the shaft had closed all the way.

With a clatter that betrayed its many years the red velvet-walled elevator plunged down nonstop to the ground floor. Confined within its narrow walls, John experienced a sinking feeling considerably greater than the three stories he was actually dropping. The car halted with a jolt and the door slid open. He passed through the small, marble-lined entrance way and out into the bright Roman sunshine. Tomorrow, at the count's insistence, he would leave for Como. As John Vigilia slowly walked back to his hotel, he thought about one of Count Sperone's parting comments. Perhaps he should take better care of himself; after his wife died he had kind of let himself go.

Fourteen

O, 'twas a din to fright a monster's ear,
To make an earthquake! Sure it was the roar
Of a whole herd of lions.

Shakespeare *The Tempest II. i.*

Mary Devlin played by herself most of the day. Since her father had died three months ago, in March of 1927, her mother had taken work as a cleaning woman for the parish priest. Mary had a brother, but the good father had arranged for him to go to school in Tralee, at the Saint Romanus Home. Mary's mother did not earn much money, and she had to give some of it back to the priest to pay for her son being in school, so Mary stayed at home alone all day, and sometimes played by the bay. Mostly, she liked to just hide up in the rocks and peek out and watch the sea birds circle around.

Today had been a wonderful day for Mary Devlin. She had seen an amazing thing, and couldn't wait for her mother to come home so she could tell her about it.

"Momma . . . do you know what I saw today?" Mary shouted as soon as her mother was in the door.

"No, child . . . pray tell your mother what you saw."

"I was up in the rocks by the strand. . . ." Mary started breathlessly.

"Gracious Mary . . . you went all the way to the strand by yourself. You've got to be careful; I can't be here to look after you."

". . . and I was watching the birds . . . there are lots of them there by the water."

"I can imagine . . . gulls and pigeons and all," her mother said setting her parcels on the kitchen table.

". . . and then there was a real loud noise . . . and all the birds flew away."

"Really, a real loud noise . . . what was it like?"

"It went like this: Rrrrrrrrrrrrrrrrrr . . . real loud, a big roar, like a lion! I covered my ears."

"And then what happened?"

"Then there was a great big black shadow. I thought it was a monster."

"A big black shadow?"

"A shadow that covered the whole beach. . . ."

"And what happened after that?"

"Then a big silver bird came. . . ."

"Silver?"

"Yes . . . like your big Christmas bowl that you shine. . . ."

"As bright as that!"

"Then the silver bird walked on the land for a while . . . and when it stopped walking a door opened . . . and boy came out of it."

"No! A boy got out of the bird," the mother said, taking her apron down from the peg next to the sink.

"Then the bird ran down the beach, real fast . . . and jumped up into the sky and flew away . . . and the boy hid in the rocks. I looked for him, but couldn't find him. . . ."

"Mary Devlin . . . what kind of stories are ya making up to tell your poor mother?" the woman said tying an apron around her waist. "You know it's a sin to tell lies . . . you'll go straight to hell."

"No, I won't go to hell! It's not a lie . . . I saw it! I saw it!"

"I'm sure you did, Mary," the mother said. "Now you come on and help me make our dinner ready. And don't you go tellin' that story to anyone else . . . they might think that you've gone daft."

Fifteen

Fair encounter
Of two most rare affections! Heavens rain grace
On that which breeds between 'em!

Shakespeare *The Tempest III. i.*

At the train station in Como John Vigilia was met by Stefano, the driver for Count Sperone's sister. The man could not speak English, and had held up a sign with "Jon Vegilea" lettered on it. It was midday, when the shops were closed, so John was quickly whisked through the semi-deserted streets toward the contessa's villa. He would have liked to have visited the downtown, of what appeared to be a relatively new city for Italy, but assumed that he would get the chance to come back again. At least he was heading for the villa to meet the contessa, John thought. Hopefully he would not be cooling his heels in a hotel room as he had done in Rome. John sat in silence as they drove along the shore, admiring the clear water, and the sheer mountains covered with lush vegetation that plunged almost vertically into the lake. Then the car turned and started climbing into the hills. John wondered where he was being taken as he had assumed the contessa's residence was somewhere in town. He asked the driver, but all John got was a "not speak

English" reply. The upward climb was only brief, however, and they soon arrived at the Villa Diamante, located just outside of Como, hanging precariously on a high, steep slope, which afforded an excellent view of the city and the immense lake below.

Alighting from the limousine John looked up to take in the elaborate façade of the villa, but his eyes were immediately drawn to the sight of an attractive woman, wearing a trim dark blue business suit, coming down the wide marble stairs to meet him. Not wanting to stare, he glanced down at his luggage, and then peeked up a second time to confirm that her skirt was indeed a little too immodest for the steep steps she was descending.

"Hello . . . I'm Signora Grazia," the woman said, smiling and extending her hand. She had the air about her of someone who was very comfortable dealing with all manner of people,

"And I am John Vigilia . . . I don't speak Italian, do you speak English?" he said slowly and clearly.

"Yes, of course, and American too. I am the contessa's private secretary . . . I can also speak German, French, Spanish and Japanese."

She was of fair complexion, with a high and elegant forehead, eyebrows traced in a long arc, and blue eyes with irises as variegated as agates. Her luxuriant black hair was cut efficiently short, yet seemed unruly, as strands grazed her eyes and the back of her neck. As he bent down to pick up his bags, John's gaze flashed again to the woman's tanned and well-turned legs; his mind missed a beat. "I'm sorry," he said. "I didn't catch your name."

"Grazia."

"Yes . . . thank you too, but what is your name?"

"Grazia. . . ." the woman said smiling. Her eyes sparkled behind her round wire-rimmed glasses. "I understand. It is often confusing to foreigners. Grazie, spelled g-r-a-z-i-e means thank you . . . a word that most people know. My name is Grazia, the same word but ending with an 'a.' The English equivalent would be Grace. My first name is Miranda. My mother was half English. She liked to read Shakespeare so she named me after a character in one of his plays."

"Yes, I know the play, *The Tempest,*" John Vigilia said, and then added, he didn't know why, "and you don't happen to know an Ariel and a Caliban, do you?" She paused and gave him a rather confused look; apparently she had not read the play.

"You can call me Miranda, a lot of people do. In fact the contessa is one of the few people who calls me Signora Grazia."

"Grazie, Signora Grazia," John said. "Then I will call you Miranda, grazie." It sounded a bit lane, but he was pleased when the woman laughed at his feeble attempt at humor.

"Mind the steps, they're quite steep," Miranda said turning, and starting up the stairs. Her entire person shone with the luster of health. John judged her to be in her mid thirties, and still in her full bloom.

"They are steep aren't they," he said, puffing a little, although John would admit that his eyes were not on the stone steps as he followed her trim little figure up to the villa.

"This entire structure dates from the Renaissance," Miranda informed John as they entered the main hall.

"Yes, of course . . . very interesting," he said, not revealing that his knowledge of Italian architecture was based solely on reading several chapters in a thin guide book while passing time in Rome. He was surrounded by walls covered with lavishly decorated frescoes and a collection of smaller paintings. The hall was provided with numerous doors, all closed, and a wide marble stairway to the upper floors. As Count Sperone had indicated, the residence was smaller, but more opulent than his palazzo.

"Stefano will show you to your room," Miranda announced, as a male servant appeared. "Then you should come right down, as we are about to dine. We will be on the terrace, which is out through those glassed doors."

Stefano took John Vigilia upstairs to his room. The large French doors to the balcony were open, letting in the fresh lake breeze. Nevertheless, the interior of the room itself smelled musty, as if it had not been used for some time. He stepped out onto the balcony, which appeared to wrap itself around the entire floor. Then remembering lunch was waiting for him, went back in, quickly washed up, and went downstairs.

"Here we are," Miranda said showing him a big smile as John poked his head out of the door to the terrace. "Come on outside . . . you can sit here. Stefano will bring the wine."

Despite having said "we" when she announced lunch Miranda was sitting alone at a large table under a canvas canopy. A wind blowing off the lake gently rustled the covering's colorful fabric. The secretary was not wearing her glasses, and had changed from her dark business suit into a printed silk shift, which bared her shoulders. She nodded almost imperceptibly, and Stefano began to pour the wine.

"It is the house wine. As you already may know one of Count Sabatini's many enterprises is Diamante Wine, named after this villa. It is sold all over the world," Miranda explained. Then winking at her guest she added: "I suspect the count earns more from his wine than the contessa does from her shares in Sperone Aviation." The secretary raised her glass, "Please allow me to make a toast."

"Shouldn't we wait for the contessa and her husband?" John said pausing with his glass in midair.

"But they are not here . . . they left this morning for his family home in Naples," Miranda said, her tone implying John had forgotten something that he was supposed to have known.

"What? The contessa is not here. . . ."

"Didn't they tell you this in Rome?"

"No! Count Sperone specifically said that I should come to Como and meet his sister," John said a bit angered.

"I didn't know that. She had no plans to go anywhere as far as I knew, and I am her personal secretary who should know . . . then last night I was told they were leaving for Naples the next morning . . . Count Sabatini's mother is very old; maybe she was taken ill. Unfortunately they didn't say anything about the reason for their trip."

"When are they coming back?"

"They didn't tell me that either. The contessa only told me that you were coming to do some research on the early Sperone airplanes. And that you would be staying here . . . and that I should take you to the factory . . . and also let you look around the barn."

"The barn? . . ."

"Yes, behind the house is a large barn . . . it is filled with old airplanes, and motors, and parts . . . and boxes of yellowed papers, and magazines."

"Well," John said, trying to hide his disappointment at hearing the news of the contessa's departure, "if I can't see the contessa then I will have to content myself with seeing her barn."

"And you shall see it . . . tomorrow. In the morning we will first visit the factory, where the museum is also located, and then in the afternoon you can go and see all that is in the barn."

The barn? John thought to himself. He hoped that he would have a somewhat better experience in this barn than he had in the barn he sheltered from the rain in when he landed at the abandoned air force base in Canada.

When they finished eating Miranda said that she had some work to do and would be busy for the rest of the day. She told John they would meet again at dinner, which also would be served on the terrace. Then she showed him to a tiny office on the ground floor and indicated that it was his to use while he was staying here.

Left alone, John blew the dust off the ancient Olivetti typewriter that dominated the desk thinking he might try to write something on it; and then he saw that it had no ribbon. His eyes gazed around the walls, which were lined with bookshelves filled with books from Dante to Manzoni, all volumes with beautiful leather bindings, and all in Italian. Finally John tried the telephone that had been provided for him; there was no dial tone.

He went back up to his room and unpacked. John was tired from the trip and wanted to take a nap, but couldn't sleep. He lay on the bed thinking of his wife, but every now and then a new and disparate image intruded on his thoughts. John could not help thinking about the woman he had just met, Miranda. She had introduced herself as Signora Grazia, the Italian reference for a married woman, yet she wore no wedding ring. He was embarrassed to admit to himself that he had checked for this when he looked at left hand.

His wife Iris had been John Vigilia's first love. They had grown up together. This had been one of those rare silent, shy, and solitary loves which had rather devoured the strength of his inchoate youth. Her reappearance in his life, after his years of debauchery in New York, had been the means of John's recovery. And even after his apparent redemption, Iris's presence had continued to be his strength.

The evening had become listless. A shadowy rank of images ran through John's head, not clear enough to be seen in the gray light that was stalking his somnolent brain as he passed into sleep:

John envisioned himself standing by his wife's open coffin, but trying hard not to cry. After a moment he thought his own eyes had gone mad in the back of his head. A procession was forming behind him. The first person, bubbling with laughter, was clad in a small cowgirl outfit and was twirling two revolvers. Behind her, also laughing, was a stern-faced woman in a trim blue business suit; a women who looked frighteningly similar to the woman he had just recently met. In the meantime it had begun to snow, and he sat down on the coffin and was eating pizza out of the cardboard box. John's fingers felt numb, but not from the cold. Without introducing herself, the cowgirl handed one of her revolvers to the business woman. Still laughing outrageously, the two women pointed their pistols at him. Despite being filled with abject terror, the best he could do was to hold out his hands and offer the two women pieces of pizza with pepperoni and extra cheese. He saw two puffs of smoke, and then two holes appeared in his heart.

Throwing himself upon the freezing, snow-covered ground, John crawled to the casket, opened the lid, and climbed in. Divested of everything but his scream, John Vigilia watched himself carefully nail his own coffin shut; while an unnamable tune, by an unseen musician, had set the two women to wild dancing. The snow turned to rain and quickly washed the previous whiteness from the ground, like shaving cream flushed down the drain.

"We do not know that you have not died in a field," the cowgirl said thoughtfully.

Inside the coffin John heard the hum of insects and the distant song of birds. He could see that the face on his dead body was twisted into a strange kind of tepid smile.

John awoke with a start. Realizing that it was almost time for dinner, he changed and hurried down to the terrace.

Miranda was already there, wearing a different dress from the one that she had worn at lunch, long and black with a very deep décolleté.

"Good evening, Professor Vigilia," she said pouring him a glass of wine. The wine was a red *Sangiovese,* also from the Villa Diamante, to accompany the *Bocconcini alla Fiorentina* that was to come as the second plate. The chauffeur Stefano's wife Ceres was the cook. Stefano and Ceres, along with Miranda, were the only people who stayed in the villa when the Sabatini's were away. There was also a gardener and his wife, but they lived in a separate, small house behind the barn.

Off over the mountains the sun was dropping out of a varicolored sky, the kind of sunset that promised a beautiful day for tomorrow. Miranda leaned toward him and refilled John's wine glass. Perhaps it was just John Vigilia's fantasy, but the woman seemed to bend over more than was necessary, her low-cut dress revealing the fullness of her firm breasts. The candles on the table flickered with the zephyr coming off the lake. Below them the lights of the town glimmered. Stefano brought dish after dish of food, each one excellently prepared, and each more exquisite than the last. John could not imagine that there were people to whom this style of living was a routine. When this meal of many courses was finally over they finished their dining with chilled glasses of *Liquore di Limoni.*

"You must be getting tired," Miranda said, helping to clear the last of the plates, her small concession to the fact that she was indeed an employee at the house.

As she paraded back and forth the deep slit in her long skirt gapped open giving ample display to her well-formed legs. John wondered if Miranda dressed like this when she ate with the count and contessa. Perhaps then she had to eat in the kitchen with Stefano and Ceres, and was only here for his benefit. He had no idea what the contessa looked like, but Miranda was a woman almost all other women would be jealous of. He wondered if Miranda and the count might have something going on between them. Why was he thinking this? What business was it of his anyway? John thought. He should be grieving for his dead wife; a respectable time of mourning had not even passed. But what was the proper period for grief in society these days, a week? a month? a year? Tomorrow he would spend the day pretending to be interested in the Sperone airplanes, and then leave here and head home. John was tired and running out of money. What difference would it make if he ever met up with an old man named Ariel Angelucci, who would probably only laugh at him and say something like: I see that you've been talking to my nutty brother in Canada? John stifled a yawn with his hand. The gesture was caught by Miranda's ever-observant eyes.

"You are exhausted from your trip, I will not keep you any longer," she said. "I am retiring to my own room to read. You have a good night's sleep. I will see you in the morning. Breakfast will be at eight o'clock." Smiling, which John took to be politely, but he hoped otherwise, she turned and went back inside.

John followed her in, attempting to pick up the thread of a conversation. "So is this the end of our lovely evening?" he said standing there awkwardly.

"It is. Good night, Professor Vigilia," Miranda said, stopping and shaking his hand before she began her climb up the stairs, a clear sign that he was not invited to follow her. And she had addressed him as Professor Vigilia, not as John.

"*Buona notte, Miranda. . . .*" John called after her, hoping his Italian sounded convincing. All sorts of possible scenarios teased at his brain as his eyes followed the sway of Miranda's slender body as she ascended the steep marble staircase. Then he turned and went down the hall to find the stairs that led to his own bedroom.

The glowing green hands on the travel alarm indicated that it was past midnight. John Vigilia lay on his bed in the dark room heavy with sleep, yet his mind, floating and undulating with the events of the day, was unwilling to give up its tenuous hold on his consciousness. No light came into the large window from the starless sky. The silence of the villa told John that he alone was awake, wandering mutely through the sing-song memories of what had happened to him since his landing at an abandoned airport in Canada, and then, first his aerobatic pilot friend, and next his wife had died.

Suddenly the stillness of the night was broken by the sound of a car pulling into the gravel courtyard. Perhaps it was the contessa and her husband returning. Rising from his rumpled bed, John stepped noiselessly out onto the balcony, being careful to stay back against the wall out of sight. Below, in the shadows at the side entrance, a small car was parked where none had been earlier. The ornate side door to the villa slammed shut with a loud clang, but no lights came on in the house. John stood there for awhile waiting, but no one came out, so he silently slipped back inside.

He lay awake listening for the car to depart until sleep, which had been so elusive before, quickly overcame him. When John woke up, at first light, he went out on the balcony and checked the side entrance, but the car that he had seen parked there last night was gone. John went back inside to shower, and prepare himself for what he hoped would be an interesting day.

"Good morning, Professor Vigilia. I trust you slept well," Miranda said standing up to greet him as he stepped out onto the terrace. The bright sunlight picked out the sheerness of the thin white silk robe she wore with apparently nothing underneath, the pale rosebuds of her breasts temptingly visible through the delicate weave of the fabric.

"I had a hard time falling asleep . . . I must have eaten too much," John replied to her question. "I'll have to be more moderate today. I was finally about to doze off when that car pulled up to the side of the house."

The look on Miranda's face, if only for an instant, gave a clue she hadn't expected his response. "What car? You heard a car last night?"

"Yes . . . it was well after midnight; I checked my watch. I stepped out onto the balcony and saw it parked next to the house, by the side door. But it was not there when I woke up this morning."

Miranda glanced quickly at Stefano, who had just arrived with the *panini e burro*. "But there couldn't have been a car. No one came to the villa last night . . . we were the only ones here."

"Maybe you were robbed then . . . have you checked?"

Miranda seemed upset. She turned to Stefano, and then said something in Italian, speaking rapidly so that even if John had understood the language he would have had difficulty catching the exchange. Shaking his head, Stefano went back inside.

"Stefano says there was no car here, and we have not been robbed. It was a dark night. You were mistaken." Then, spoken almost as a command, she added, "And now enjoy your *prima colazione* . . . when you are finished we will go to see the factory."

They ate breakfast without speaking another word, Miranda nodding politely while turning an apparently deaf ear to John's questions and entreaties. Under the table her legs were crossed and her elevated foot swung about nervously. Miranda's now pouting silence, quite charming in itself, did not make the difficult task John had taken on of trying to understand her any easier.

During the drive to the factory, with Stefano at the wheel, Miranda still sat quietly, but her eyes shone and her lips had an enchanting smile, as if she wanted to confide something to John, or to reveal a secret. Suddenly she turned to him, stubbornly fixing her face, which he could now see was flushed, and, squinting her sweet eyes, asked: "So just what is it you say your business here in Como is?"

A taken aback John Vigilia was saved from answering the question by a speeding car that hurtled past them on a curve, almost crashing into a truck coming from the other way. Stefano honked his horn loudly, shouted and made an obscene gesture with his finger, while the other driver sped away. The ensuing conversation between Miranda and Stefano, John supposed that it was about the joys and hazards of driving in Italy, took them all the way to the factory. Once, however, when out of terrified boredom he had looked over his shoulder on one of the curves, John had discovered a black Alfa Romeo with a Milan license plate following them close behind. The car looked strangely familiar. He had not noted the plate number, but John clearly remembered it had been a black Alfa Romeo sedan that had followed them the night he had been driven to the party by Trinculo.

The factory was just that, a series of high-ceilinged industrial buildings, whose stark and cold architecture suggested that they might have been constructed during the Fascist era. They lay on prime waterfront space in the downtown of Como, which John thought strange, until he remembered that the early triumphs of Sperone Aviation had been with floatplanes. John was sorry that he had not prepared his cover story more thoroughly. But he was sure he would know all about the Sperone aircraft before he left—or was allowed to leave. After his meeting with Count Sperone John had thought that everything was out in the open, despite the count's goodbye, which was said with a smile that had mingled mystery and circumspection with ribaldry.

Count Sperone had made it clear to John that he was to spend a day or two in Como with his sister. There he would pretend to be doing research for his book, and then go home. Now things had turned strange again. Why, John Vigilia wondered, had the count sent him to Como knowing that his sister would not be there? Or had Sperone telephoned her and told her to leave on a quick vacation. The secretary had seemed confused by the sudden departure of her employers for Naples. And why had

Miranda denied that a car had come to the villa in the middle of the night when John had clearly seen it.

And then there was Miranda herself. Whether the woman was aware of it or not, she had awoken John from the artificial days he had been living since his wife's death. Now he watched her standing there by the lake, bathed in the reflections of the morning sky, his heart filled with desire. With a woman like her, John told himself, he could begin to mend the fragments of the broken vessel that his life had become.

"The lake is so beautiful," Miranda said. "It is a shame they had to build the factory right here on its shore. But then that is the Italian way. And now the buildings are hardly used at all, except for the museum."

She pointed out to him the various structures as they walked along a causeway the city had built that jutted out into the water from a tree-lined park. Miranda, wearing her too short business suit again, had shown John the park, and its outdoor collection of sculptures. He had not told her that he wanted to be a painter once, but somehow she seemed aware of his interest in art. Or perhaps she was just proud of her city of Como and wanted to show him its artistic culture.

Approaching the factory across the parking lot, John realized that the buildings were even larger than they had appeared from the causeway. Sperone Aviation must have had great wealth, and considerable influence to have been able to construct this vast industrial complex on such expensive property in a period when most of the world at the time had been going through a severe depression.

The immense hangar that fronted on the lake had since been converted into a museum. Once inside John saw that the lofty space was filled with what Miranda said were the last remaining examples of most of the early Sperone aircraft. The museum also served as a workshop, with several of the vintage aircraft undergoing restoration right out in the open on the floor next to the static displays. They walked around rather casually looking at the airplanes. Miranda stopped underneath a giant metal seaplane with four engines mounted on a pylon above the wings. The top of the floats alone were as high as John's head.

"This is the Sperone Gabbiano IX," Miranda began, reading from a card. "In 1929 it set the world speed record for a transatlantic flight." And then, making it a point to turn and look John straight in the eye, she added, "But no one cares about that, do they? The only transatlantic flight anyone remembers is Lindbergh's flight from New York to Paris."

"Yes . . . that seems to be so," John Vigilia replied, curious as to why she had brought up the subject of Lindbergh, and worried where she might be going with this question.

"He flew all that way alone. . . ."

"Yes . . . so they say. . . ."

"So, are you interested in Lindbergh, John?"

"No . . . not really," he said trying to sound noncommittal. Nevertheless, he was secretly pleased that she had called him John rather than Professor Vigilia.

"And why are you not interested in Lindbergh? Is it because he became a supporter of Hitler?"

"No . . . I don't think so. I just hadn't really thought about it. I mean I'm not really interested in Lindbergh's flight," John lied, afraid that she was trying to bring him out. "I've got plenty of other more important things in my life to concern myself about."

"But maybe Hitler and the Nazis knew something about him that he did not want the world to know . . . maybe he was being blackmailed."

"Look, I really don't know anything about Lindbergh. I mean what could they have been blackmailing him about?" John asked.

"But they did steal his child."

"I don't remember the story exactly, and I'm not sure the child was kidnapped by Nazis anyway. . . . As I recall, it was someone from New Jersey." Trying to change the subject, John put his hand on the floatplane's ladder: "Wow! Is this how they had to get up into this thing back then? That's pretty high up."

"The cockpit is open to visitors . . . do you want to climb up and take a look at it?"

"Well, okay. If you think you can make it up the ladder. . . . " John said, referring to the short skirt she was wearing.

"Yes," Miranda said, "I had better take my high-heels off."

John wanted to say that wasn't what he meant, but restrained himself.

Now Italian men were generally not reticent about vocalizing their admiration of a woman's assets. At the sight of Miranda's long legs slowly ascending the ladder in her miniskirt, most of the men working on the airplanes stopped what they were doing and stared. Then they let out their whistles and catcalls:

"*Mama mia! . . .*"

"*Ciao bella! . . .*"

Miranda didn't seem to mind, and ignored the men's attention. Or was she enjoying it, John Vigilia wondered? He closed up the space between them on the ladder, attempting to preserve a bit of Miranda's modesty by screening her behind with his body.

Once inside the huge airplane John was surprised to find that the cabin space was quite limited. They had to duck their heads to get through the small door into the cockpit. John and Miranda sat down in the seats, crowded next to each other in an area that, despite the passage of many years still, smelled of worn leather and sweat. As all pilots do by habit when seated in the cockpit of a strange airplane, John studied the rows of instruments. They were not that much different from those in his Bücker Jungmann. John noted that in the years before an airplane's instrument panel became complicated, by being loaded with devices that were supposed to make flying easier for the pilot, just about every airplane had much the same simple instruments in relatively the same position.

John recalled how he had laughed when, at a lecture, he had been shown a slide of the monitor of the first fly-by-wire autopilots. There, on the elaborate video display were graphic images depicting the standard analog instruments. "Why not have the real instruments, instead of this simulacrum?" He had asked. "That way they can fail one at a time . . . if the picture tube goes on this thing everything is gone."

The man doing the presentation had ignored John Vigilia's question as being too dumb to even warrant an answer. In the darkened room someone had quipped, "The display is run by a computer . . . computers never fail." Some people in the audience had laughed, most had not.

"Rrrroooaaaarrrrrr." Miranda was crouched in her seat, playing pilot moving the controls from left to right, watching out the window as the ailerons traveled up and down. Her skirt, which had hiked up when she clambered into the airplane, had not been tugged back down. John wondered if it was by accident or design. Her legs were stretched out on the rudder pedals. John Vigilia stared at the dark triangle peeking between her thighs, wondering if it was her, or just the blackness of her underwear.

Miranda caught his gaze. She smiled, and gave a rather perfunctory downward tug to her skirt.

"Those things are the ailerons," John explained, changing his focus. "They make the airplane bank, and when it banks it turns."

"I know," she said.

"Well. Yes I suppose you should . . . working for Contessa Sperone you would learn a lot about airplanes."

"My husband was a pilot. . . . I flew with him sometimes."

"Was? What does he do now?" John asked, trying not to sound disappointed. Miranda was not wearing a wedding band. But then he had never worn one either.

"He's dead. . . ."

"Oh! I'm sorry to hear that."

"It's okay . . . it was three years ago, I am over it now. We all must die sometime. Only his time was a little too soon."

"How did he die? if you don't mind my asking."

"He was killed in a plane crash." Miranda stopped, but then went on, as if she needed to continue, to close a circle. "He was a test pilot for Sperone. They were developing a new jet, a small plane that only held four people, and that a businessman could fly by himself. It would cost less, but be as fast as a Learjet, maybe faster. The airplane flew very well . . . way beyond the designer's first expectations. Sperone was hoping to make a lot of money, as their business had not been very good lately. The factory was in the last phase of spin testing. I had gone down to the lake with the others to watch the tests. The jet did a one-turn spin and then a two turn, recovering nicely each time. My husband climbed back up for altitude and then started what would be the three-turn spin. The airplane never stopped spinning until it hit the lake. They recovered the airplane, and my husband's body, but they were never able to determine why he didn't bail out. I think it was because he wanted so much for the airplane to be a success that he fought the spin until it was just too late. The airplane was the only prototype . . . when it crashed they never made another one."

"It must have been hard for you to continue working for Sperone after that."

"No. When the crash occurred I was not working for anyone. I was pregnant; we were going to have a family. I ran to the edge of the lake and jumped in to save my husband . . . it was futile. The crash was in the middle of the lake . . . there was no way I could have got to him. The doctors said I went into shock, and had a miscarriage.

When I was recovered the contessa gave me this job. As you can see it is a good job; I don't work too hard. The contessa is the kindest and most generous person . . . I would never do anything to hurt her. They say that when she was little her father took in an orphan boy . . . so that she and her brother would learn what it was like to be poor."

"An orphan boy? . . ."

Miranda's face flushed, she paused, and then recovered her composure, "It was only a rumor . . . kind of like a legend, something that people say. I don't even know if it is true or not."

"You don't remember what year that was supposed to have happened?" John asked, unable to restrain himself.

"Oh, look at me," Miranda said, pulling down her skirt, trying to change the subject. "I'm coming undone."

"But you're sure that there was an orphan boy?" John said. Looking at her face, he thought he saw fear reflected in her eyes.

"I don't know anything . . . not first hand, only stories." Then she asked her own questions: "Tell me Professor Vigilia . . . what is it you are looking for here in Como? And what is it about you that made the contessa and her husband run away?"

John hesitated briefly, pondering his answer. "I don't know. I came here looking for one thing . . . and now I think I have found something else."

"And what is that?"

"You, Miranda. . . ."

He leaned over and placed his arms around her, putting his mouth on her lips. Miranda relaxed, as if she was about to accept his kiss, and then suddenly stiffened and backed away:

"Not now John, not here. . . ."

"Then when? And where?"

"John, I don't even know you . . . you only arrived here yesterday. You say you are writing a book . . . yet we have been here all morning, looked at many airplanes, and yet you haven't taken any notes. . . ."

It was the same observation Count Sperone had made, John realized. He had a notebook back in his bedroom, and had considered bringing it, but it was filled with his notes about Ireland, and Rome, and Ariel Angelucci. John Vigilia was not very skilled when it came down to establishing credibility. He needed another lie.

"Well . . . you see I have already done the research on the Sperone aircraft . . . from books, back home. What I came here for was to see the actual airplanes," John explained, and then he added, later wondering why he had, "What I want to do here is to make some drawings of them . . . for the book. I thought it would be more interesting. I didn't bring any supplies because I planned to get that stuff over here. I didn't want to have to carry it on the airplane. And I figured that things might be cheaper here, especially your fine Italian paper." John looked at Miranda. He couldn't tell if she had bought his hastily concocted story.

"Now we must go back to the villa for lunch," Miranda informed him, jumping up and clambering from the cockpit. "I have things to do in the afternoon. You can look through the barn; maybe you can draw some of the airplanes that are there. We will stop on the way back and get you some materials."

Miranda had not only bought his story but, clever woman that she was, had gone John one better. She was going to put him to a test.

After a brief stop at a shop in town to purchase art supplies, the driver delivered John and Miranda back to the villa. She went somewhere to do something, and he went up to his room to wash up. John's bedroom, like the rest of the villa, had a rich character about it. Nevertheless, it was an atmosphere that he found suffocating. As he was about to lay out his new art materials on the bed, John noticed a slight impression in the freshly made bedspread. This told him that someone had been in his room while he was out. Looking at the top of his dresser, John saw things were not exactly as he had left them. It was a trick he had learned in Moscow.

Whenever he was going to be out for a while, John always carefully put certain objects on his dresser in a relation to others, and committed their positions to memory. Some of his things had been moved around; someone had been here. He went to the closet. His suitcase was still locked, but the hair that he had placed under the left side latch was gone. John opened the case. His money was there, so it had not been a thief. A second hair that he had left in his notebook was still in there, but at the bottom of the third page, not at the top where he had put it. Whoever went through his room was not exactly an amateur, but not as observant as they might have been.

At lunch John noticed Miranda was not as friendly to him as she had been on previous occasions. Also she had put on a prim white blouse underneath her suit jacket, and even seemed to be wearing a bra. When they had first met, and at the museum, there clearly had been nothing under the suit's jacket but her. This had prompted John to recall a comment he had made to his wife once, while thumbing through one of her fashion magazines, that the clothes on display were all fantasy. "What kind of woman," he had asked, "would wear a business suit with such a short skirt, and a jacket with nothing on underneath?" Iris replied that she loved the suit, but would have gotten the skirt much longer, and would certainly have to wear something underneath the jacket. John had glanced down at the price, and quickly turned the page.

"Now we will see the barn," Miranda announced after their lunch was finished, a rather abbreviated affair by yesterday's standard, but much more than what John usually ate. "You should get your materials . . . there are all sorts of airplanes there that you can draw."

They walked over to the barn where Miranda tugged open the huge wooden door. John stood in the doorway like a schoolboy, a drawing pad under his arm and a box of pencils, and an eraser and sharpener in his hands. In front of him, in a vast and semi-dark space, a large array of airplanes in various states of completeness stood together in solemn silence, apparently unvisited by anyone for who knows how many years. Although each may have been lacking a minor component, an aileron here or rudder there, the barn appeared to hold many more airplanes than the museum. Hidden away in this ancient stone barn were the less than impressive products of Sperone Aviation's history: open cockpit biplanes, small two place trainers, utility airplanes, all types that had served well in their capacity, but lacked the panache of the record breaking globe circlers and sleek fighters and bombers housed in the official space down by the lake.

These aeronautical detritus were not displayed in well-lighted rows, or in some absurd diorama supposed to give a sense of the aircraft's history, but rather crowded together, or even piled one top of another. John noticed, however, that while the whole scene seemed chaotic and disorderly every piece, every fuselage and every wing, bore a label. The writing was hand-lettered in Italian and in English.

"Why are the labels also in English?" John asked.

"I don't know . . . I think there was a man who used to work here a long time ago who was supposed to keep things in order . . . who spoke English." Miranda said then stopped abruptly, and corrected herself. "No, that is not the reason. English is the official language of aviation. An Italian pilot landing an Italian airliner at Milan's airport Malpensa has to call the tower in English . . . doesn't he?"

"In theory. As I have never flown into Malpensa, I wouldn't know what actually happens. I have flown into a number of airports in Quebec and heard a lot of pilots speaking French. It does make it hard to know where the other traffic is . . . if you don't speak French."

"And you don't speak French? . . ." Miranda asked.

"No."

"And you don't speak Italian?"

"No . . . I've already told you that. Don't you believe me?"

"Aren't you going to draw something?" she said pointing around the area they were standing in. They had been walking around the barn looking at things, Miranda turning lights off and on as they went.

"Why don't you draw this motor . . . it is very old, and very rare," Miranda said pointing, and sounding almost as if she were getting impatient for John to begin.

"Well, I wasn't planning to draw just motors."

"Why not? It would make an excellent subject; look at the lines and the angles. All the tubes and wires. It would make a fine picture . . . kind of like the Futurists."

John hesitated. He held his pencil up in front of his eye and studied the subject, something he had never actually done, but had seen artists do in the movies, hoping that it would give him a certain bit of credibility.

"Don't you like the Futurists, John? They were Italy's leading modern art movement, a true avant-garde."

"No . . . I don't have anything against the Futurists."

"So what's the matter then? Can't you draw the motor? Is it too hard of a thing for you to do?"

John had taken Miranda's questions as being a challenge, a challenge that someone else had obviously put her up to making. See if he can really draw. Shaking the dust off an empty crate, he dragged it over and positioned it in front of the aircraft engine. The two of them sat down and John Vigilia began making a sketch. He had not drawn anything, at least anything that he had attempted to accurately render, in many years.

In his youth, when he thought he might become an artist, John had been a good draftsman, and practiced a great deal. Leonardo had said that this was what you must do, and he had done it. Drawing was like riding a bicycle; something you never forgot. After a few tentative strokes, John felt his manual skill returning. Fascinated, Miranda watched over his shoulder as the image of the motor began to appear on the page.

"You are a good artist . . . did you ever take any lessons?" Miranda remarked, apparently approving of the result she was seeing.

"No, I taught myself, and I read da Vinci's notebooks," John Vigilia replied, rubbing his hands together. He was getting into his work.

"Well, I must go now," Miranda said, standing up abruptly and brushing the imagined dust off the back of her skirt.

"But don't you want to see me finish this drawing?"

"No . . . I have seen enough. I have other things I must do. You can stay here all afternoon. Look at whatever you like. Stefano will come to tell you when it is time to prepare for dinner."

John stood up and stretched his arms out towards her.

"Goodbye, Professor Vigilia," she said, deftly pushing him away, "I will see you at dinner." Then Miranda turned and walked rapidly from the barn without looking back.

John did a few more drawings; what else could he do. Miranda had made it clear that he should stay here until he was called. Wandering around, he came upon a stairway that seemed to have been added considerably later to the original structure to provide access to a loft, which had been built under the eves. John climbed up and found a door to the loft, but it was stuck shut by the warped floor. Something urged him to go inside.

After considerable effort with his shoulder, John forced the door open, and entered what appeared to have once been a small apartment. Light filtered in from a kind of skylight in the roof above. Some old furniture still stood about in the dank, moldering space, but it was apparent the place had not been inhabited, nor even visited, in quite some time. A large desk contained a neatly kept set of files which, on his inspection, seemed to indicate that the former inhabitant of these rooms had held a position of responsibility for the order of the things stored below.

The apparent bedroom of the rough loft space contained only a single bed, and a nightstand. Stains on the floor indicated that there had been other things in the room once, perhaps a large bureau. The shelf over the bed was half full of books about airplanes and aviators, all in Italian. Then John Vigilia's eyes locked on the one anomaly. There was a battered copy of *Night Flight,* by Antoine Saint-Exupery, and it was an English translation. As he curiously flipped through the pages a card fell to the floor. John picked it up. His hands shook as he read it: "to Ariel, Merry Christmas. . . ." The rest of the card, the part that might have contained the name of the giver and perhaps the date, appeared to have been torn away. There was the name he had been looking for, Ariel, certainly not a common name in Italy. Could this be more than a coincidence?

John slipped the card between the pages and put the book back on the shelf. Imagining that he heard a noise from down below, John stopped to listen, but heard no sounds. Some primitive curiosity caused him to glance under the bed. What is this? he wondered. There, tucked in the shadows, cloaked with dust and cobwebs, was what appeared to be a scrapbook. John slid the large black leather-covered book out and opened it, aware more than ever of the musty, mildewed scent of the room. The yellowed newspaper articles were in Italian, but there was no mistaking the name and the face in the faded photographs. The book was filled with clippings about Charles Lindbergh.

There was a noise again, louder, and a voice:

"Professore Vee-gee-lee-ah! Professore Vee-gee-lee-ah!"

John hurriedly slid the scrapbook back underneath the bed and exited the apartment, pulling the door tightly closed behind him.

Discovering the man he had been seeking at the top of the stairs, Stefano began waving his arms wildly and shouting in Italian, a look of horror on his face. John Vigilia did not understand what the man was saying, except for the one word he kept repeating: *"Proibito! Proibito!"* The servant appeared to be deeply distressed. Carrying on in a nonstop barrage of Italian, Stefano quick marched John back to the house.

At dinner Miranda remained very distant. She had not been waiting for John as usual, but joined him a few minutes after he sat down. She was wearing her usual business suit, but had changed to a beige blouse, which complimented her deep tan. John wondered when she got the time to sunbathe, and where she did it.

"Stefano told me that he found you up in the barn loft. . . ." Miranda said as she sat down. She took the bottle from between them and poured wine for herself, ignoring John's half-empty glass.

"No . . . I wasn't. I mean, I didn't actually go into the loft," John lied. "I was just about to try the door, which was stuck shut . . . when Stefano came for me. . . ."

"But he said it looked to him like you had just come out."

"No . . . Stefano was mistaken, I was just trying the door when he came to get me."

"Well then don't go up there again. It is not allowed," she said rather directly, digging her fork into her *penne.*

"But why not? You said that I could see everything."

"There is nothing up there. Besides, the floor is all rotten . . . it's not safe. You could fall through and be killed."

"Yes . . . I certainly wouldn't want to be killed," John muttered, finishing the last of the wine in his glass.

"Would you like more wine?" Miranda asked, filling John's glass before he could reply. They did not talk again at dinner after that. Her warning to stay out of the loft had been uttered with a firmness that tolerated, but did not allow for contradiction. When they had finished their liquor, Miranda broke the silence and asked:

"Would you like to see the rest of the house now?"

"Yes, if I could," John said, surprised by her unexpected offer.

She led them on a tour of the villa, with its many rooms, ignoring some doors and opening others without explanation for her omissions. In the rooms they did go in Miranda went into elaborate detail about the paintings and the tapestries, and their historical significance. Her manner, and the impersonal tone of her voice, made John feel as if he had merely bought a ticket and was part of a guided tour group. John wondered if perhaps he should apologize to her about what had happened between them at the museum. Had he been too forward with her? Or was she just angry with him for having gone up in the barn loft?

It was clear that she did not believe the story he told about not going into the apartment. And why did she make up that lie about the floorboards? Did anyone know about the Lindbergh scrapbook under the bed, which must have been lying there for decades? And he regretted considerably not pocketing the card with Ariel's name written on it. No one would believe what he had seen there if he told them. In fact he now found it hard to believe himself and was wondering if he just might have imagined the whole incident. John told himself that he would like to return for another look, but he had been specifically forbidden. He was sure that he wouldn't get back into the loft anyway as Stefano had probably put a padlock on the door.

"This is the ballroom!" Miranda said throwing open the doors to a large, and elegant hall. She flipped a switch and the chandeliers, which had been electrified, began to glow with hundreds of tiny, artificial candles.

"Quite impressive," John remarked. "They must have had some parties here in the past." He noticed that Miranda's eyes were sparkling, reflecting the glow of the many lights.

She smiled at him, the first time John had seen her smile since their encounter at the museum this morning.

"Do you dance, John?" she asked unexpectedly.

"Oh . . . I used to be pretty good at disco. . . ."

"I don't mean like that . . . I mean real dancing, like the waltz."

Miranda lifted the lid of an ornate, vintage phonograph and put on a record, an old style 33 1/3. There was a brief, scratchy moment while the needle found the grooves, and then they heard the sounds of Johann Strauss.

"Dance with me, John," Miranda said, removing her business jacket and laying it over a chair. In the coruscating light her diaphanous blouse had become almost transparent.

John took Miranda in his arms and together they began to glide around the floor. Miranda was an excellent dancer, so John Vigilia resigned himself to following her lead. As they came together in close proximity John could feel the heat of Miranda's body, and smell the so sweet attraction of her scent. He was elated.

When the record stopped, Miranda laughed and pulled John to her, giving him a quick kiss on the cheek.

"Thank you so much John, that was wonderful," she said. "I love to dance, and I haven't danced in such a long, long time. Shall we put on another record?"

They danced for what must have been the better part of an hour. John stumbled over his own two feet, but kept going on for the moment when the music stopped, and they would come together, and she would give him a big hug, or a kiss, and smiling at him, squeeze his hand. John was puffing and sweating, and felt awkward, but was happy because Miranda seemed happy too.

"Oh! Look what time it is . . . it's late. You must be very tired," Miranda said. They stopped dancing, and she began to put the records back into the cabinet.

"I'm okay," John said laughing, and trying to hide the fact that he was breathing heavily and his armpits were damp. "I needed the exercise."

Miranda put out the lights and closed the doors to the ballroom. The two stood for a moment in the dim hallway.

"Your room is down that way . . . and mine is this. . . ." Miranda said pointing. "If you go straight down the hallway you will come to the main entrance . . . I am sure you can find your way from there."

"I know the way," he said, pausing, "but I was hoping that you would come with me. . . ."

"Thank you, John . . . you are so kind," Miranda said looking into his eyes as if she held some secret she dare not betray. She patted his hand, and then let go. "I cannot, not now . . . maybe sometime, but not now, I cannot explain it to you. I am very sorry. Good night."

"Why not now?" John asked painfully. He reached out for her.

"Good night", she repeated. Brushing his hands away, Miranda turned and, without another word, disappeared down the hall, her footsteps echoing hollow on the hard floor.

Back in his room, John stretched out on the bed, not yet ready to go to sleep, listening for Miranda's knock on the door, hoping that she would have a change of heart and come to him. Unfortunately, he could not go to her;

she had not shown him where she slept when they had toured the vast warren of rooms that comprised the villa. John was also listening for the sound of a car. The car he had heard last night, and seen, but that Miranda had denied existed. John worried about the car, not that it might belong to someone who had followed him from Rome, but that it might be someone who was Miranda's secret lover. He lay there fitfully, hearing only the wind. For the first time since her death John fell asleep without thinking of his wife Iris, and without tears rolling down his pillow.

The morning sun slid through the window, removing the shadows from the room, and rousing John from his sleep. Despite what was going on around him, he had slept fairly well. Insomnia was never a big problem in John Vigilia's life. He took a shower and dressed. Looking at his watch he realized there was still some time before he had to go down for breakfast, so he walked out onto the balcony to take in the view. Seeing that the balcony disappeared around the side of the house, he could not resist exploring where it went. When he turned the corner, John found a set of stairs that appeared as if they might lead to the roof. He decided to climb them and see where they took him.

Arriving on a flat part of the roof, John was greeted by a view even more magnificent than the one from his room. In front of him the lake stretched all the way to the mountains beyond. John was enjoying the fresh air and this beautiful sight when out of the corner of his eye he caught sight of a head suddenly bob up from behind one of the chimneys. Curious he walked over in that direction. He was delighted to find that the head belonged to Miranda.

"Oh . . . it's you. I thought I heard something," Miranda said. No one else ever comes up here but me," She was sitting down on a chaise lounge, her back to John, only her head visible.

"So this is where you hide out when you're not working," he laughed, walking across the roof toward her.

As John Vigilia came around in front of the chaise he stopped short, his eyes open wide. Miranda was sitting there totally naked, her skin covered with oil, sunning herself. To his surprise, she made no attempt to cover up her exposed body.

"Oh . . . I'm sorry, I didn't know you were up here . . . like this," John said, modestly turning away.

"Oh, you come back," she laughed. "You can't tell me you've never seen a naked woman before."

"No . . . it's just that. . . ."

"That you're an American . . . and Americans have an unhealthy attitude about nude bodies. I am told they can't even show them on television in your country. Is that true?"

"It's the Puritan in us . . . they settled our country you know."

She held up her left leg and began lathering it with oil. Her pubic hairs had been shaven off. John could not help staring at the delicate bud that seemed to be opening just for him. He felt himself growing hard. Miranda handed him the bottle of oil, smiled, and rolled over on her stomach:

"Here . . . do my back. It's a good thing you happened along, I never can do my back properly . . . and I can't very well ask Stefano to do it . . . he knows I sunbathe up here but would never dare come up. He's a devout Catholic . . . if he looked at a naked woman, other than his wife, he is sure he would go straight to Hell."

John eagerly, and deftly, did as he had been instructed, his fingers rubbing the pungent oil into Miranda's soft skin. As he worked his way down her back, the discovery of a small mole just above the cleft of her buttocks gave him an ineffable shock. This brown circle was in the exact same spot as a similar flaw on his late wife's backside. He continued applying the oil, unable to take his eyes off this duplicate marking.

Miranda's body wiggled, responding sensually to his touch. John could feel himself swelling with a lust he had not known in some years. For that moment the memory of his dead wife was abolished, his anxiety about the future was calmed. There was only the present; there was nothing on this earth that John Vigilia wanted now more than to have this woman.

"Do you like my body?" Miranda said peering over her shoulder and smiling at him.

"It's a beautiful body. . . ." John said, working his way slowly down Miranda's legs. He paused for a brief moment, poured more oil on his hands, and then began rubbing her buttocks. He felt her body shudder slightly.

"Does my body excite you, John?"

"Yes. . . ."

"Then take me John. . . ."

"What?"

"Take me here, right now. . . ." Miranda said, rolling over on her back and spreading her legs open wide in an almost obscene gesture.

"But. . . ." John looked around at the sky, the vast empty space around them. He had never had sex in the out-of-doors, and not often in the light of day. Sex for him had always been something done at night, in a closed dark room, with the partners groping blindly at one another.

"What's the matter John? Don't you want me . . . take me now," she said. Her hands began unbuttoning his shirt.

As he had been bid, John made love to Miranda there on the roof, the warm sun on his bare back as he mounted her. His sense of reality had abandoned him. It felt to John as if he were surrounded by some peculiar atmosphere that isolated him from the prying eyes of the rest of the world.

In the heat of their passion John and Miranda had collapsed the folding chaise lounge and fallen off. Laughing, they rolled together naked onto the hot asphalt, not breaking the cadence of their activity until they both came as one.

John stood up and quickly dressed himself, hopping on one leg to put on his shoes. Miranda had re-erected the lounge and was just lying there. She had not gotten dressed as she had no clothes to put on, not even a towel. She must have walked up here nude from her room, John assumed, which must be somewhere nearby.

"Thank you, John . . . that was wonderful," Miranda said with a smile. She seemed relaxed, but was still breathing a bit heavily.

"I enjoyed it too," John added, and then became embarrassed by his apparent casualness. Leaning over, he gave her a kiss on the forehead. "When can we do it again?"

"We can't! There will be no *next time*. That was all . . . the only time," Miranda replied rather firmly.

"Why do you say that? I think I'm in love with you. . . ." John blurted out.

"You're what?"

"I'm in love with you," he repeated. Having said this, John wondered if the character who spoke those words was really him. He had begun the day with no precise goal, except perhaps the desire to return to America. Then he recalled the misery of his dead wife, and realized now that he had found the woman who could make him forget the past.

"You can't be in love with me, John . . . you even don't know me. Besides," she said, her voice taking on an unexpected urgency, "you have got to leave this place immediately."

"What do you mean . . . leave?" John said a bit confused.

"I was going to tell you at breakfast. For your own safety, you must be gone from Como by this afternoon. Don't ask me why. I can't explain. It has nothing to do with us. Perhaps we will meet again under different circumstances. But for now you must just go. I don't know where you will be going, and if you yourself know, please don't tell me. If I am asked I don't want to know."

"Who is going to ask you? And why must I leave today, and in such a hurry?" John pleaded.

"That is all that I can tell you. Now you must go to your room and pack. Bring your bags down with you when you come for breakfast. As soon as you are finished, Stefano will drive you to the station in Como, there are frequent trains to Milano. From there you can get transport to wherever you wish. My advice to you is that you go back to New York, and forget about whatever it is you are looking for."

John felt a chill run through his body. A cold wind off the lake was blowing a bank of low cumulus clouds in over the villa. Miranda felt the cold too and wrapped her arms around her nakedness.

"I don't understand whatever it is you're talking about," John protested, although he had guessed clearly enough what she was referring to.

"There is nothing more for you to understand, John . . . just leave here, go quickly."

As John started down the stairs to his room, he turned and looked back. Miranda was still there, lying naked on the lounge staring up at the sky. He wondered if this would be the last that he would ever see of her. John Vigilia sensed that somehow, without his knowledge, his fate had been decided, and there was nothing he could do to change it.

Sixteen

There's nothing ill can dwell in such a temple:
If the ill spirit have so fair a house,
Good things will strive to dwell with't.

Shakespeare *The Tempest I. ii.*

Having been distracted by an unanticipated meeting as John was leaving Como, he did not reach Milan's Port of Garibaldi Station until late afternoon. Upon arriving, John Vigilia went immediately to a bank of telephones and selected one that took credit cards. He dialed a number in Munich from a piece of paper that he now felt fortunate to have inadvertently not thrown away:

"Ja ... hallo!"

"Hans Hockenheim? This is John Vigilia."

"Goodbye fuck head, whoever you are, I don't speak English language. . . ." the German barked into the telephone.

"Wait! Hans. Don't hang up. You told me to call you . . . we met at Luigi Bosco's party. I am the stunt pilot from America."

"Oh . . .Yes, of course, the stunt pilot. So you call me now to tell me you are coming here, right?"

"Yes. Look . . . I can do that flying thing for you . . . for your performance in Locarno . . . that is if you still need someone."

"*Ja Ja,* I have someone. . . ."

"Oh . . . I'm sorry, I guess I should have called you sooner. . . ." John said a bit taken aback.

"*Ja,* but you are better . . . you are an American, and Polish besides, and now I know you are a famous stunt pilot, it makes my performance even many more times so spectacular."

"But, what about the other pilot? . . ."

"He is not a problem . . . that guy is an asshole . . . a Swiss, a nobody, I blow him off. I don't like him anyway. Too cocky. So when are you coming here to see me here in Munich?"

"I'm at the station in Milan right now . . . there is an overnight train later . . . I'll be in Munich in the morning."

"*Ja Ja.* I know this night train from Milano, I have taken it sometimes myself . . . I have an art dealer in Milano. You know . . . I am one of Germany's most important artists . . . I have galleries all over the world. My work sells for big money. I wait to see you at the station, you can recognize me . . . I will have two beautiful chicks with me, one on each arm . . . blondes, long legs, short skirts, with big tits. Now I have to go . . . there are some cunts here waiting for me to fuck them. I will save one for you. *Auf Wiedersehen.*"

"Don't you want to know the time that the train. . . ." John began to say, and then heard the dial tone.

He went up to a window to buy his ticket. After some difficulty communicating, John was made to understand that trains to Munich did not depart from here, but from a different Milan station. In a bit in a panic, John grabbed a taxi out front. The distance to Central Station was rather sort, however, so he arrived there with plenty of time to spare, although with his nerves further rattled.

He had still not quite gotten over what had happened to him when he was waiting to leave Como.

Having probably overpaid the taxi cab driver, John Vigilia hurried up the wide, stone stairs lugging his suitcases. By now he had learned enough Italian to know to get on line at the windows marked *biglietti,* although he still could not even attempt to pronounce the word properly.

"Andata e ritorno," the ticket agent asked.

"I'm sorry I don't understand. Do you speak English?"

"To go and return. . . . Do you want a round trip ticket? Will you . . . to be coming back to Milano?"

John Vigilia thought a moment, and then responded, "No only one way." Why he made this decision he did not know. John was not quite sure where he would end up.

There were three hours until the train left. John had not eaten since breakfast at the villa, and then had been in no mood to eat much. He was hungry, but not hungry enough to go in search of food. John was mentally, as well as physically, tired, and couldn't face up to the task of forever trying to make himself understood. Maybe there would be a dining car on the train. He realized now that he probably should have gotten a sleeping berth, but did not know how to ask. Perhaps things would be easier in Germany, John thought, we occupied the country for twenty years or more didn't we? Everyone should know English, but maybe they would all be like Hans Hockenheim and refuse to speak it.

Always one who planned ahead when he could, John scouted out the platform his train would depart from and found a convenient place to sit. John Vigilia had been anxiously looking over his shoulder since leaving the Villa Diamante and believed that he had not been followed, or at least not by anyone he had detected. John watched the people passing, wondering if one of them would suddenly pass a note to him, as had happened at the train station in Como.

Recalling the initial contact between himself and a strange man who claimed to have the information that he was seeking, he had come to doubt that it had been a chance encounter. John was beginning to question the truth of all that he had learned since arriving in Rome.

That morning Stefano had deposited him in front of the train station in Como, dropping his bags from the trunk and hurriedly driving off without even so much as a polite *Arrivederci.*

The station had been quite crowded at the time with what John Vigilia took to be commuter passengers. He bought an express ticket to Milan. Told the next train was due in one hour, John sat down on a bench to wait and watch the passengers. A local train arrived. He noticed one of the departing passengers because the man was wearing the blue coverall uniform of the workers at the Sperone Museum. The man slowed as he walked by, almost as if he knew John, and was surprised to see him at the station. He watched the man go to the end of the platform with the group he was with. Patting his pocket as if he was missing something, he let his friends walk on, and then went over to the kiosk and purchased a pack of cigarettes. Although he could not see him clearly, John sensed that the man was standing by the kiosk, smoking a cigarette and watching him.

After a few minutes, the man walked up to where John was sitting and crushed out his cigarette in the nearby receptacle. He saw the man's face, and recognized him as one of the men who had been working in the museum when he and Miranda were there. John and the workman briefly made eye contact. The man walked to the end of the platform, apparently checking to see if his friends had gone. Then he looked at his watch and came back and sat down next to John, lighting another cigarette, but saying nothing. The man glanced at his watch again, as if he were in a hurry, or perhaps late for an appointment. Suddenly, the man in blue coveralls got up and rushed off. Looking after him, John saw that he had left his cigarettes behind. John was about to shout to him, when he noticed a folded piece of paper tucked under the cellophane. His instinct told John Vigilia that this paper must be meant for him. He casually picked up the pack of cigarettes and slipped it into his pocket.

Crouching in one of the toilet stalls, John unfolded the paper tucked in the cigarette pack. He read the note, which was written in English:

I know where is the man you are look for. He is my grandfather. You can to meet me today at Duomo in middle of day. I am in three rows from back at right corner. I tell you then.

John Vigilia had turned the note over in his hand, wondering if it might be some kind of prank. Perhaps the workers heard a rumor that he was looking for someone and decided to play a joke. But then why had Miranda been so secretive, and in such a rush to send him away. John wished that he had his camera with him when he found the scrap book under the bed in the loft, and been able to take some photos of it. He was sure now that he would never see it again. But the book's existence didn't prove anything, except that someone who had worked for the contessa had been fond of collecting articles about Lindbergh; and why not, he was a world-wide hero at the time. But then there also had been the labels, carefully printed in almost a child's hand, in English as well as Italian. And the book in English, with a card inside that said "to Ariel," on a shelf that obviously had held many other books in the past. And why had the contessa suddenly gone off to Naples with her husband before he had arrived, when he had come to Como specifically to meet her?

John Vigilia came out of the toilet just in time to see the last morning train to Milan pulling out of the station. There would be no trains until this afternoon. With more than three hours to pass, John decided to go to the Duomo and wait for the man who had passed him the note to appear, if he did. John could not go back to the museum, or walk around the town; Miranda or Stefano might see him. Perhaps the note was not a joke; perhaps the man who gave it to him would come. John put his bags in a locker and pocketed the key.

Looking it up in his guide book, John learned that the Duomo, like most of the cathedrals in European cities, was located at the heart of the town. Moreover, this Duomo was crowned by an impressive green dome, which he could faintly see towering above the other buildings. He started for the center, staying on the shady side of the street. John reasoned that he would be less noticeable in the shadows, and most people walked on this side anyway to avoid the heat of the midday sun.

The glass panes of the shop windows reflected the hubbub of the city, the center of which was closed to automobiles at this time of day. Above all the massive green dome of the Duomo hovered, leading John to his goal as he remembered the water tower giving direction to his wanderings in the small town where he had grown up. Stopping occasionally to peer in a shop window, John pretended to be looking in at the merchandise, but actually was checking the reflection of the passersby in the street behind him. As far as he could tell it did not appear as if anyone was following him.

The vast interior of the Duomo had been divided into three aisles by immense tapestries hung between the columns. The walls were lined with paintings, and niches containing small chapels with finely carved altars. Brought up a Catholic, out of habit John Vigilia dipped his fingers in the font of Holy Water and blessed himself when he came in. As he was early for his meeting, if the note writer was coming at all, John decided to take a turn around the cathedral and look at the artifacts, mingling with that casual mix of tourists and believers that seemed to occupy every Italian church significant enough to make its way into the guide books.

Eventually arriving at the crypt, John decided to light some candles for the souls of the departed of his family. Digging into his pocket to find coins for the donation slot, John had been surprised to pull out the paper with the German artist's name and telephone number on it, which he thought he had thrown away. Again seeing no place to dispose of it, he had tucked the now rather crumpled paper in his wallet.

After depositing his coins John took the flame from another candle with a waxed straw. He felt the heat as he reached over the glowing bank to light a candle in the middle of the last row. This candle was for his mother. John always lit candles in the back row ever since having watched the nuns blow out the ones in the front before they were completely burned down, and replacing them with new candles to obtain additional revenue. The nuns, with their long-sleeved habits, could not lean over to snuff out the ones in the back. If a person got indulgences only for as long as the candle burned, John Vigilia wanted to be sure his mother's soul got its money's worth.

Using the straw another time, John lit a candle for his wife. They had lighted many candles together when she was alive, in many different churches, and yet he had been never quite sure if she had actually believed in what she was doing. He wondered about her: Was she in Heaven? If such a place existed, she surely should be there. She was a good person, as far as he knew. But had he ever really known her? John was sorry that she had died so relatively young. Was there something more he could have done? He asked himself. Had he been insensitive to her pain? John hoped that she had not suffered too much; all by herself on her last day. He was crying now, but trying to hide it. There was a tightness in his throat. John felt so alone, so used up. He wondered again what he was doing here in Italy on this strange search for someone named Ariel Angelucci. And what difference would it make to him if this man had really been Lindbergh's secret copilot.

John had one more candle to light. All his Italian coins were gone. The money in his wallet was all in big bills, too generous an offering to shove into a candle slot. The donations were on the honor system, so he could easily have lit another without paying. But to cheat the church would probably be a double sin. John had planned to light a candle for his dead father; however, as the senior Vigilia never put much faith in the church anyway, he decided to light this one for himself. Although he wished his father well, wherever he might be, John Vigilia felt that, at the moment, whatever divine help this sacred flame was going to provide he needed it more.

The candles flickered and glowed in neat rows in their clear, red glass holders. Reaching up to the right, John counted down three. The note had said the third row. John lit his last candle. No, he said to himself. The man would be coming into the church from the back, right would be left. He quickly blew out the candle and held the flaming straw to a candle three rows down on the other side. The straw suddenly flared up, burning John's hand. He shuddered, wondering a bit facetiously if this might have been the work of the Devil. Sucking his smarting fingers, John sat down in a nearby pew. For some reason, perhaps because it was what one usually did in a church, he began to pray.

"Holy Mary, Mother of God. . . ." John mumbled, and then stopped. "Mother of God, full of grace. . . ." Grace! That was Miranda's name. Don't go there, John told himself. He tried to begin again, but realized that it had been so long since he prayed that he had forgotten the words. "I don't know what I'm doing here," John continued, making up what he thought to be a prayer as he went along, "but if it's going to cause harm to anyone please don't let it happen . . . and if harm is going to come to me, please don't let that happen either. . . ."

In a chapel next to the crypt a mass was being said in what John Vigilia made out to be Latin. He paused to listen to the familiar sounds he that recalled from his childhood. He never knew exactly what all the words meant, but the chants had had magic, and the power to instill fear in him. Unlike most people John was coward enough to fear the magic, but not quite coward enough to admire it.

John Vigilia stopped going to church around the time they started saying the mass in English, with the priest facing the congregation instead of with his back to them facing the altar, and the choir and organ had been replaced by a folk singer strumming a guitar. But these were not the only reasons why John had stopped going, there many were other things he could not understand; the main thing being that the Catholic Church was so preoccupied with the evil of birth control, when there were so many other, greater evils in the world.

Hearing the priest's words John was surprised. He didn't know that the church allowed the mass to be said in Latin anymore. Then he listened carefully, and realized it was not Latin, but Italian. The words sounded beautiful. If he lived in Italy, John told himself, he might go to mass just to hear them sung.

Suddenly remembering why he was here, John looked at his watch; it was fifteen minutes to twelve. He read the note again. It clearly said "in middle of day". He wished it had been more specific. Obviously the writer knew English, but not well. Yet who was he to complain, he couldn't even read a menu in Italian. John strained his eyes and peered back into the dimness. On the right side of the cathedral, where the light slanted in through the stained-glass windows there was a man sitting alone in the third row from the rear. He had his head bowed as if in prayer.

Assuming this was his man; John walked slowly down the right aisle, purposely passing him by, and went out into the vestibule. He had not looked up, so John could not be sure that this man was the same one who had passed him the note, whose face he had not paid much attention to at the time anyway. Moreover, this person was not wearing the tell-tale blue coveralls of the Sperone Aviation Museum. But then he might have changed out of his work clothes to come to church.

John waited until twelve o'clock and, when no one else had appeared, went back into the main part of the church and slipped into the pew next to the person that he had previously spotted. Apparently intent on saying his rosary, the man looked up, nodded, and then went back to his prayers. This brief glance was enough to tell John that he was not the one who had passed him the note at the station. He decided to wait and see what happened.

The man continued praying, letting the plastic beads slip silently through his fingers. He occasionally turned in John's direction, but gave no sign that he had anything to say to him. Then, out of the corner of his eye, John spied a man wearing blue coveralls come in the right side door. As he walked down the aisle, this man slowed his pace at John's pew. The sight of another person next to John must have confused the man, as he continued walking toward the front of the church. Too late, John realized that this was the man from the station, the one he had been waiting for. He slid out of the pew and started down the aisle after him.

The man in coveralls was kneeling in front of one of the small chapels, the one dedicated to Saint Anthony of Padua; John slide into the same pew. The man did not turn to look at him.

"You left me a note," John whispered, staring up at Anthony, specially invoked by people desiring help in finding lost objects.

"I cannot to talk now . . . you have someone here with you. . . ."

"No, that other man is just a stranger. I arrived early. When I saw him in the third row, I thought it was you . . . so I sat next to him. When he had said nothing after a few minutes, I knew he was the wrong person. Then you came in."

"Did that man see your face?"

"I don't know. Why?"

"I recognize-ed him . . . he works for Sperone sometimes . . . in the office." He spoke with caution, a man apparently unsure of what he was going to say, and why he was going to say it.

"Well, he didn't seem to show any recognition of me. . . ."

"We must to talk quickly. I need to return soon to work. Let us go there, to the Chapel of Saint Francis," he said gesturing with a nod of his head. "From there we can see who is watching at us. I go first and you can come in a little after."

John Vigilia waited until the man had been settled in for a few minutes, and then got up to join him. En route John quickly scanned the back of the church. The person who had been sitting alone in the third row was gone.

"Saint Francis is my patron saint," the man said when John was seated next to him.

"Mine too," John quickly added as an encouragement.

"Your name is Francis?"

"No, my name is John, John Vigilia. My Saint Francis is Francis de Sales. He is the patron saint of authors. I'm a writer."

"I am Francesco Angelucci . . . I was name-ed for a relation of mine, or so I was told, who was a famous stunt flyer in America."

On hearing the name Angelucci, John Vigilia felt a shiver run through his body. His eyes darted around the church. For the first time since arriving in the Duomo, he was aware of the cold and dampness of the vast stone structure and of the smell; the chocking odor of stale incense, candle smoke and burning wax. John struggled to go on, not sure that he wanted to hear what he expected would come next.

"So what is it you want to tell me . . . Francesco? And why is it that I should be interested?" John asked cautiously.

"You are looking for some word of my grandfather, yes . . . Ariel Angelucci. Do you know that he is yet still alive? He lives in Switzerland, in the city of Locarno."

"Locarno!" John exclaimed, making a connection in his head. It was a place he had never even knew existed until three days ago when Hans Hockenheim told him about a performance he was going to do there. John returned to the present, "And what makes you think I am interested in your grandfather, or where he lives?"

"I do not know . . . which is why I want to talk with you. I was just going to write you down a note, but as you can see I can to speak English better than I can to write it. My father taught me."

"Where's your father now?"

"He. . . ." Francesco suddenly stopped talking and stared straight ahead.

"And where's your father now?" John repeated, thinking Francesco must not have heard him.

"He is dead. . . . But I do not have now time to tell you some story of my family. . . . I must to know what it is you are trying to find out of my grandfather."

"Well for one thing . . . why are the Sperones so concerned that I not learn anything about him?"

"Maybe because of what happened between him and the Contessa Sabatini, before she married. . . ." The man broke off again and gazed ahead blankly.

"And what was that?"

"When she. . . ." Francesco stopped once more, and again stared off into space, his eyes glazed over.

Was this man afflicted with some kind of malady that involved momentary fits of rigidity and trance? At present John was not inclined to feel any compassion or concern for him. Was Francesco having a stroke? Or did he fear something so much it was causing him to become cataleptic. John considered that perhaps he should take this opportunity and leave Francesco here in his state. He wished, first and last, to be clear of this decades-old mystery surrounding Lindbergh's supposed copilot. John had collected his thoughts, formulated his plan and was going home. Now here was this Francesco Angelucci dragging him deeper into it. "When the contessa was what? . . ." John Vigilia asked, immediately sorry that he had done so.

"When she was yet a girl," Francesco began, coming out of his stupor. "When she was a girl . . . Ariel made her with a child."

"Pregnant! So how did that happen?" John inquired, moving over a bit closer in the pew. Here was an element of the story that he had not heard before.

"The old count adopt-ed Ariel from an orphanage in Ireland," Francesco said. He paused a moment, but did not go blank. Whatever it was that had come over him must be passing. He went on, "Ariel live-ed with them almost as if he was of the family. When he get older, then the count make Ariel in charge of the airplanes he have stored in his barn at Villa Diamante. Ariel sleeps in his own apartment in barn. The old count used to send his son Ferdinand and daughter Juno to the villa on weekends and in the summer. Although there was some difference in their age Ariel and Juno are very close, like brother and sister. When Juno becomes older she think she in love with Ariel. It not clear who start the affair. My grandfather claim-ed it was her. As a result she becomes with child and he is send to live in Switzerland.

"It could not be known that Juno is having child, so she stay at the Villa Diamante until it was born, and then baby gave up to nuns. The Count Sabatini must not know about this . . . problem from his wife's past or he would not to have married her. The Sabatini family is very religious; one of the sons is even a cardinal at the Vatican.

"Some years later Ariel find where his child is taken, the boy my father, and adopt him. That's all I can to say you . . . I must to go back to work now. If you wish to know more you go to Switzerland, and to speak with my grandfather."

"You say he lives in Locarno. Do you know the address?" John asked, hurriedly pulling out his notepad.

"Yes . . . 33 Via Flaviano. Not so far from the train station. This is the same apartment he have always live-ed in."

With that Francesco got up to leave. He was in a hurry to go, his eyes wide, like a startled deer.

"Wait! I have just one more question," John said. "Did your grandfather ever tell you how he got to Ireland?"

"Ireland? No . . . he never speak-ed about this," Francesco replied, sounding rather equivocal.

"He never said anything to you about this at all?" John asked. He had not gotten up from his place to let Francesco out of the pew. Francesco started to slide to the other side. John Vigilia put his hand on the man's arm. "I can't believe that. . . ."

"He always say me he had come there from America," Francesco answered. "But he never tell to us how. It was almost as if he not want anyone to know. I remember he say it was in 1927 though. He must have to come on a boat, I think. Back in those days no airplanes flew across the Atlantic . . . except for Lindbergh. . . ."

John wanted to ask the man if his grandfather had ever mentioned Lindbergh, but Francesco Angelucci slipped out of the pew and hurried down the aisle, and out of the cathedral. John Vigilia waited several minutes before leaving, the story he had just heard revolving in his mind. During this time he had considered praying, but did not. John felt embarrassed about the little prayer he had made up earlier. A man with his imagination should have done better than that, he told himself.

Exiting the vastness of the Duomo, John began his walk back to the train station, taking the narrow streets of what he had figured out on his map to be the longest route. Only now did he notice the sadness of the enormous masonry that made up the anatomy of the center of the city. The shop fronts were barricaded, and the streets deserted by a population that had gone home for lunch, and perhaps a nap, or other things. Walking alone through this barren landscape, John was submerged deep in his own thoughts. Today had begun beautiful and ethereal. His making love to Miranda on the villa roof, in the brilliant sunshine, had been so perfect that every moment of its brief duration seemed like a miracle extended beyond measure. But now John was left with only a painful memory, and the sad and heavy skies that were gathering before a storm.

By the time he got back to the terminal cold winds had begun to blow the clouds down across Lake Como from the mountains beyond, the sky establishing an enormous gray monotony over the city, giving it a feeling of the north. As John Vigilia sat on the platform shivering, he sensed that here they must have a very early fall.

Seventeen

Thou shalt be as free
As mountain winds; but then exactly do
All points of my command.

Shakespeare *The Tempest I. ii.*

On the night train from Milan to Munich, John had been fortunate to find an empty compartment, so he stretched out on the seat and allowed his tired brain to sleep through some of the most spectacular scenery in Northern Italy. But then it was dark and he would not have seen very much anyway. The train had turned north at Verona, and then left the plain of Venice and followed the Adige River through the valley it carved from the Brenta Mountains, climbing its way into the natural wonder that was the Dolomites. Had the moon been shining, and John put his face to the window at just the right moment, he might even have seen the cluster of rocks that was supposed to have inspired Dante's *Inferno.* As it was he did not break his sound sleep until roused by the banging of the customs inspectors making their invasive rounds through the compartments while it waited on a siding in Brennero/Brenner.

Awake now, and with dawn rising in the East, John stared out the window at the tidy Austrian landscape, wondering what awaited him in Munich. He recalled that he had instinctively taken a dislike to Hans Hockenheim when he had first encountered him. Nevertheless, working on the German artist's project would allow him to replenish his rapidly dwindling money supply, and have a valid reason for being in Locarno, Switzerland. This cover story John hoped would be considerably more convincing than the spurious tale that he had been using about writing a book on the history of Sperone airplanes.

For the past hour, as the train rattled on, John's mind had been going over his meeting with Francesco Angelucci. Was the man really who he said he was? The whole event, from the way he passed John the message in the train station to their hushed conversation in the Duomo, had all been a little too theatrical. It had seemed to him almost as if it were scripted. At the time John had felt like he was acting out a part in a spy movie. He wondered if the story that he had been told about the Sperone family's lying to cover up the fact that the young contessa had had a child by Ariel Angelucci was true. Or had he been set up? Was the story, and the address in Locarno, just a red herring, designed to divert John's attention, a plan to send him off on a futile search that led nowhere.

Then John's brain locked onto a key question that he had not thought to ask Francesco at the time of their meeting: How did he know who he was, and what he was looking for while in Como? John Vigilia remembered clearly that he had not been introduced to the workers, and no one, not even Miranda, had been aware of any reason for his being here other than to look at the Sperone Museum's airplanes. Yet the man's note had begun: *I know where is the man you look for.*

The rattling, clacking, and swaying slowed down, as the train finally slid into Munich station. The journey was long, but they had arrived fifteen minutes early. For some unknown reason a small street band was playing on the platform as John got off. He lingered listening to the band's music until the last of the departing passengers had left, some met by friends, but most alone. John's eyes searched the now empty platform. Despite his promise on the phone, Herr Hockenheim apparently had not come to meet him. Or perhaps he had mistaken Hans' comment about meeting the train. John had taken this to mean the platform. Doubtless Hans was somewhere else; he rationalized, most likely in the bar.

Checking there, John found several look-alikes, but not the genuine, shouting, obnoxious, Hans Hockenheim. As he had not eaten since his breakfast in Como, John found the buffet and bought himself a beer and two bratwursts. He swabbed the brats with mustard, and then sat down at an empty table on the mezzanine overlooking the entrance. Below him was a constant parade of any number of "beautiful blonde chicks, with short skirts and long legs, and big tits" passing by, but none were hanging onto the arm of a tall, bearded artist, with a wild head of hair, and a loud, and especially filthy mouth.

After an hour had passed, considering that he might have missed Hans during the time he was in the toilet washing up and shaving, John went to the information desk and had him paged. There was no response. He waited at the desk another half-hour and then asked directions to Hans' address. The attractive young woman who worked there, and who spoke excellent English, told John Vigilia that Hans' studio was in the Schwabing section of Munich near the university and easily reached by subway. She even wrote the directions for him in his notepad.

Never having been in Munich before, John Vigilia did not know that the subway system had no turnstiles, but worked on the honor system. He had begun down the stairs, assuming he would have to pay somewhere farther on, when suddenly, and without warning, a huge woman accosted him, shouting something in German.

"I'm sorry I don't understand," John pleaded in English.

"You are not from here, zen?" the woman responded. Then, pointing at the ticket kiosk, which John had not noticed, she admonished him, "You must to pay there . . . if you don't pay you go to jail!"

He looked at the woman; she was not in any official uniform or anything. It took him a moment to understand what she was referring to. Embarrassed and intimidated, John retreated to the window and bought a ticket, wondering if one did go to prison for not having a ticket in Munich, but not willing to be a test case.

Having arrived safely at his desired stop, John struggled up the stairs and along the narrow street with his suitcases. Unnoticed to John the tip of his tongue stuck out as he walked along, as it was in the habit of doing when he was deeply concentrating on something. John Vigilia walked past three blocks of houses before coming to the turn the woman had written down for him. There, as promised, he found Blutenstrasse, hardly the "short distance" from the subway stop which he had been told it was. The street was lined with coffee shops and bookstores, the Schwabing district being the artistic and intellectual quarter of the city. The street was also lined with young ladies standing in doorways who, although they conceivably might have been university students, or shop girls on their break, seemed to John as if they were intent on some more carnal activity.

A quiver of expectation ran through him as John finally arrived at Hans' address. Would Hans be as crude as he remembered him to be, or would he be, playing on his home ground, a little more cordial?

The ground floor of building number 99, contained a small art gallery, named appropriately enough Galerie Bluten. Next to the gallery was a side door, which gave access to the floors above. John read the names; then he pressed the buzzer marked Hockenheim, H. There was no answer. He waited a minute and tried again.

Spying a stranger standing outside of his building a smartly dressed man came out of the art gallery and asked: "You are the American, yes?"

"Yes, I am an American. . . ."

"I am Otto Taugen . . . I am the owner of this gallery," the man said extending his hand.

"And I am John Vigilia," John said returning the handshake.

"So, you have been ringing for Herr Hockenheim, who is not there, yes?"

"I rang . . . but there was no answer."

"Then I have a message for you. Hans has telephoned to me to say that he has been in an accident. He has crashed his car on the way to the station to pick up an American . . . which must be you. He was not badly hurt . . . nor were the two young women who were with him. But his car is smashed, and needs to be repaired before it can be operated. That was some hours ago . . . so he should be coming soon. But he may not be, as this is Germany, and as you may know our officials here take paperwork very seriously. I am sure there will be many reports to fill out. So, in the meantime, I am to offer you the hospitality of my shop. Won't you please come in?"

"Thank you," John said, carrying his suitcases into the gallery. What other option had he?

John's eyes surveyed the clean, sterile interior. The shape of the room, and the large, front windows, gave a hint that the space had not originally been intended to be an art gallery, but had probably been a butcher shop or a bakery when this now trendy district had been the crumbling core of the city. The pictures were neatly hung, with what John Vigilia judged to be a balance between art that Herr Taugen really believed to be on the cutting edge, and art that he felt he could sell. It was strange to see fresh made versions of what had been the avant-garde in the nineteen twenties and thirties. Even John, who did not keep up with art fashions, was aware, from an article in TIME magazine, that this recently recycled version of German Expressionism was the current international art world vogue.

"So . . . what do you think of my artists?" Herr Taugen asked, as John put down his bags and began to look around. "Some are well known here in Germany, and perhaps in America, however, others are completely unknown. I have some good bargains. In the back room I have a one-person show by a talented woman artist."

As he did not want to comment on the group of mostly expressionistic paintings, a style John felt gave every opportunity to the heavy handed and less talented just as long as they could display plenty of angst, he sidestepped the question by asking another question: "Do you think that it is important for an artist to know how to draw?

"To draw? . . ." Taugen said seeming puzzled. "You mean like to make sketches."

John didn't know if he was feeling metaphysical, or just annoyed by what passed for art these days; he pressed on. "*To draw* does not mean merely to imitate things from nature. The word draw has many meanings: pull, drag, provoke, bring about, shrink, suck, tighten, take away, disembowel, as well as the artist's term to reproduce something on paper with ink or pencil."

"So you are a philosopher, Mr. . . ."

"Vigilia . . . as in vigil, to watch, and bear witness," John responded, however not revealing that a lecture on the word draw was one of the standards from his class in creative writing.

"And just what is your point Mr. Vigilia?"

"Artists have always taken from other artists that came before them. They admire certain works and this is what inspires them to go on, in a sense to *draw* from these works. But to imitate what they admire is not enough. In order to find their own voice they cannot repeat what has already been done, although the market place can sometimes provide them with a good reward for doing just that. The true artist must respect the past, and yet add his own future to it."

"So do you think my artists are too derivative?"

"It's a difficult problem, Herr Taugen, and one for which I do not have the answer. So I will leave it to you to *draw* your own conclusions." John concluded, feeling a bit satisfied with himself. No matter how much he tried to run from it John Vigilia was a college professor, and professors loved to hear themselves lecture.

"Well, to be fair, most of my artists are very young. I have no masters here."

"Is that why I don't see anything by Hans Hockenheim hanging in your gallery?" John asked somewhat facetiously.

"I have one of his collages in the back. Do you consider Hans to be a *master?* He himself certainly does, as well as being the future of German art. I have never seen any of his early drawings, however, I doubt that he can draw very well, that is in the paper and pencil sense. His work is in my office, I will get it for you. . . ."

The dealer brought out a small, and rather artless collage, in what must have been a rather expensive aluminum frame. Photographic images cut from magazines were pasted about haphazardly on a map: sports cars, motorcycles, yachts, girls in bikinis. There was writing all over the work, and arrows pointing in different directions. The text, in German, appeared to be some kind of instructions, or notations.

"So what do you think? This is a work by Herr Maestro Hockenheim, and for this he wants . . . wait let me figure it for you in dollars . . . would you believe $50,000!"

"And does he get that much?"

"Not here . . . not in my small shop. But he says he has some fancy dealers in Milan and Berlin who can get that price. And next year he has a show in New York . . . there will be no stopping him. Before he was known, Hans supported himself by working with a circus. He was a side show artist . . . a juggling clown . . . now, suddenly elevated to the center ring, his head reels with fame."

"Then you're not his dealer. . . ."

"No. Not now. Once I was the only one who would show his work, and I didn't do it because I liked it. I only felt sorry for him, and because he lived upstairs. Now he hardly even talks to me. Only when he wants a favor, like receiving a package from the mailman. . . ."

". . . or receiving his American friend . . . who is not about to buy anything from you. I'm not a collector, just a poor college teacher," John revealed. "And besides just talking about it, I've done a little artwork myself. . . ."

"Doesn't everyone? That is always the problem. You can hardly go to your doctor or dentist without having to look at the person's art efforts." Herr Taugen said, carrying the Hockenheim collage back into his office. "What do you think of this building?" He asked when he returned. "It's one of the older buildings around still standing, built in 1929. Although we were not hit as badly as Dresden, did you know that most of Munich was destroyed by your bombers during World War Two?"

John was trying to think of a discreet reply to Taugen's obviously leading question when the front door banged open, and a tall bearded man, with a fresh bandage on his forehead, burst into the gallery shouting in German.

"Here is Hans Hockenheim," Otto said turning to John during a brief pause in Hans' soliloquy. "He is announcing that Germany's greatest living artist is not yet dead. By that I assume he means himself, as he is the only one who would give him such a title."

Using a falsetto voice, Hans again shouted something in German. His tone sounded almost coquettish.

Otto translated for John. "He says, 'Oh, how cruel I am to make fun of a poor man with nine stitches in his forehead.'" Turning back to Hans, he said "This is the

American you went to the station for . . . he has found you by himself, now maybe you will speak English so I don't have to keep translating for him."

"*Ja* . . . it is Veg-ghe-yah-la," Hans confirmed, as usual totally mangling the pronunciation of John's last name. "He is America's greatest stunt pilot . . . for him I can to speak the perfect English."

"It's good to see you again Hans," John said, shaking his hand and trying to sound sincere. "It looks like you've got a bad bump on your head. I hope it doesn't hurt you too much."

"*Ja, Ja* . . . not too bad. I suspect his schlockmeister Otto is sorry that I am not dead. Then he could have doubled the price for my collage, which he keeps hidden in his back room."

"I can't possibly sell it at the price I have it now . . . at double that surely no one would buy it."

"It's not the problem of my price . . . it's that you only know cheap collectors. You need to find a better clientele," Hans parried; then he turned to John. "Come Veegayla, we leave this man to his second-rate gallery. We go up to my studio . . . you can put your bags there. Then we will go out to some festive places and drink some beer . . . to kill my pain, and to celebrate the fact that Germany's greatest living artist is still alive."

"Yeah, let's go have a beer," John said laughing.

Whereas in the past John had been extremely aggravated by Hans Hockenheim, today his bizarre antics caused him to laugh. He was reminded of how men involved in the work-a-day world laughed at artists and poets. They didn't do it with an air of superiority, rather as if they were showing affection, the way one laughed at a child, who was proceeding with no notion of life's uncertainty and lack of exactness.

Eighteen

If but one of his pockets could speak, would it not say he lies?

Shakespeare *The Tempest II. i.*

Thus began three days that John Vigilia would not easily forget; although his febrile memory would remain rathcr vaguc about the details of much of what actually did happen.

"You can put your luggage in here," Hans said unlocking the door. This is my studio in town . . . I only use it sometimes when I stay in the city. It is very small because it was my first studio. Now, I have a big studio . . . and a big house in the country. But we cannot go there today . . . my car is smashed. Do you have a credit card Veegayla? Maybe tomorrow you can rent a car for us . . . and we can go to the country. It's very beautiful there, and not too far away from here."

"I brought a bottle of wine for you," John said opening his bag and taking it out.

"Italian wine! I don't drink that cow piss . . . only good German wine. Where did you get his cheap dago stuff, at the train station?"

"Someone gave it to me."

"So you pass it on to me. From Villa Diamante, hah; I know that shit Sabatini. He is rich, and his wife owns half of Sperone Aviation, but they don't spend any money. The cheap bastard came to my exhibition in Milano, and offered to buy three of my drawings if the dealer would give them to him for half price. *'Sconto! sconto!'* he kept saying. I was going to tell him to go fuck himself, but my dealer said not to mess with Count Sabatini, he is from Naples . . . and in with the *Mafiosi."*

"Oh . . . I didn't know that."

"What? That he's a cheap bastard."

"No . . . that he's in with the Mafia." John said, trying not to sound too alarmed. The knowledge was forming a lump in his throat.

"So fuck Sabatini, who gives a shit about him, I have collectors lining up for my work. Come, now we go downstairs and I give this bottle to Otto. He loves Italians . . . and I owe him some favors."

Otto was happy with his bottle of Italian wine and thanked Hans politely.

After walking three blocks, they came to a place that Hans introduced as his neighborhood beer garden. He insisted they stop in; just for a quick drink. A half-hour passed, during which time Hans engaged in a spirited conversation, in German, with the barman. Hans guided his glass of beer slowly along the bar. Then he took John's glass and, careening and sliding it rapidly over the polished wood, crashed it into the side of the first glass, making a loud "bam." John supposed Hans was describing his most recent automobile accident, wondering which of the two glasses had represented Hans' car.

"Have another beer, Vayegahla."

"I don't know if I can . . . we've had two already, and the mugs . . . they're so big . . . maybe we should get something to eat . . . I'm rather hungry; I've only had two brats to eat all day."

"*Ja* . . . I must to have something to eat also . . . and my head is just now feeling better . . . but the food here is not so good . . . we have one more beer, then I take you to a better place to eat. I can tell you that it is the best food in all Germany."

"Of course," John added jokingly, "Germany's best food, for Germany's best artist." The two large beers on an empty stomach had put John into a silly mood.

"Now you have the spirit," Hans said, taking John's comment seriously. He raised his glass. "So we have one more."

"Well, okay . . . just one more," John agreed reluctantly.

When they were finally ready to leave, Hans patted his pockets, and then turned to John saying: "Veegiklia, can you have some marks to pay for these beers? I must have left my money in the studio."

"Yes, I have a few. I didn't change that much money at the station, I didn't think I would need a lot of money. I thought that you said you were going to pay for everything when I got here."

"It is just not a problem," Hans said sidestepping John's question. "Veggleea, tomorrow I will . . . take you to someone who can change money for you at a better rate. Just keep a count of all what you spend and you will be paid back. . . . "

After they had left the bar, and only traveled a half block in the direction of the restaurant, Hans stopped in front of a building that was showing bright lights on the second floor and announced:

"Wait! Here is a gallery. I forgot . . . tonight is the opening of my friend's show. The work is shit . . . but they give good whiskey. Let's go up now for a few minutes."

Standing among the few gallery goers, casually observing the art work on the walls, John Vigilia held a small glass of whiskey to his lips. He was pretending to sip the drink. The truth was John hated Scotch; the taste was too sweet for him. When he lived in New York City John had been a heavy drinker, but with no artists and writers bars to frequent, and no openings or parties, he had cut back his alcohol consumption considerably after moving to Elmira. Swaying a bit, John saw the room begin to blur. He was feeling the effects of the three large beers, each stein holding almost a quart, which he had already consumed not only on an empty stomach, but also while lacking a good night's sleep.

They had arrived at the opening late, the crowd was beginning to thin out. John looked longingly at the empty trays on the table, not even a tiny piece of cheese was left. John snatched up the last remaining carrot stick and wolfed it down. The art works dripped with paint, and angst, larger versions of the Neo-expressionist paintings in Otto's gallery. There must be a qualitative difference, John told himself, but it escaped him. Just as he could not distinguish the sound of one rock group from another, all expressionist paintings, new or old, looked alike.

"Vagalla, this is my friend . . . the artist Herman Zerstreut," Hans announced dragging the man over to John. "He has made this marvelous show . . . and not one fucking picture has been sold. I tell him don't feel bad . . . we are going to take him to drink some beer. He understands perfect English . . . if you would can you tell him how much you like his pictures here."

"Yes . . . I enjoyed your show . . . very interesting work, and nicely framed too," John stammered and then drained down the hated Scotch he was holding, putting the empty glass on a table near the door as they went out. An artist he had known back in New York had once told John about commenting on the frames. If you can't say anything nice about the work, comment on the frames, he had said. The trouble was that every artist John had ever talked to already knew about this dodge.

To John's disappointment, the beer hall that they were heading to was just across the street. He had been hoping for a short walk to clear his head. Despite John Vigilia's protests the group was on its third beer at this new place, making his alcohol consumption for the night, so far, six beers and one Scotch. When they arrived Hans had insisted that the drinks were on him. Nevertheless, John feared that once again he would be asked for money when it was time to pay the bill.

The two artists were singing, and toasting, and hugging one another. "Don't worry Herman, your day will come," Hans said in a tone that implied his day was, without a doubt, already here.

"Back when we were in art school," Herman reminisced, "who could have ever believed that it would be you, the radical outsider, Hans Hockenheim who would be the first among us to be widely recognized?"

"It is because I have seized the moment," Hans boasted. "We have at the present in Germany the *Spassgesellschaft,* the 'fun society' to you Veegelela. After the war our parents made great sacrifices for their children, now these children want to enjoy the fruits of their prosperity . . . not to work hard. In the past Germans were skilled craftsman, more comfortable making things with their hands than dealing with abstractions, but now this is all finished. Workers do not want to work, they want vacations, and to be entertained. We are on the verge of a great recession. That Herman is why no one is buying your paintings. The old art, made by hand, is over. The new art arriving is performance, which is pure entertainment, but on a higher intellectual level."

The painter was about to challenge Hans's statement, when Hans interrupted him. Through the smoky din, Hans had caught sight of someone he recognized coming in the front door.

"Wait. Look who comes here now, that phony Fliegengewicht," Hans said with a snarl. "But the fucker comes alone? Where is his partner, Speichellecker? Their work brings in big money now . . . but it is pure shit. And soon comes the recession. Those assholes will be fucking finished. Wait here, I go over there now to tell him so."

Even John Vigilia had heard, again from reading TIME magazine, about Heiner Fliegengewicht and Sigmund Speichellecker, who were the current superstars of the international art scene. Their paintings were not that different from the work of all the other Neo-expressionist painters that had emerged in Germany in the past few years, with Speichellecker's looking like upside down versions of Fliegengewicht's. What set the two artists apart, in an always fickle scene dominated mainly by manipulation and gimmicks, where actual talent did not much matter, was their appearance.

Heiner and Sigmund looked rather alike, and so had adopted a common veneer. The two had both had their hair cut short and dyed bright pink. They wore matching earrings and nose rings, and had identical tattoos. They had also purchased a similar wardrobe that consisted of black combat boots, tight black pants held up with red suspenders, and sleeveless muscle shirts, that they wore whenever they went out to art world functions, which, looking like twins, they always attended together. This bizarre mishmash could not fail to capture the rapt attention of the trendy magazines, so that photographs of them regularly appeared on their glossy gossip pages, posed in the company of chic fashion models, designers, film stars, and currently in favor politicians.

There were, nevertheless, two main differences between the two, which only served to amplify the peculiar attraction of the pair. Fliegengewicht was short of stature, and had been a flutist before realizing there was more money to be made in art; while Speichellecker, who was almost a six inches taller than his partner, had been a kick boxer before taking up painting.

Hans, speaking in German, accosted the man he had seen come in and sit down at the end of the bar: "Fliegengewicht . . . your fucking paintings are shit. You and your fucking partner are phonies. Your time is finished. Performance art is the art of the future, and now in Germany, I, Hans Hockenheim, am the master. Remember this moment . . . and my name, Hans Hockenheim." Most self-important artists, especially megalomaniacs like Hans, tended to talk like that when they were drunk.

The man stood up. It was obvious from his size that he was not Fliegengewicht the ex-flutist, but Speichellecker the ex-boxer: "Look you fucking little shit, I don't give a fuck who the fuck you are . . . or what the fuck you do. All I want when I come here is to drink my fucking beer in peace. Is that a fucking problem for you? You already have one fucking bandage on your head . . . I can arrange for you to have a fucking few more."

"Oh . . . I am very sorry Herr Speichellecker," Hans said, grasping the folly of his mistake. "I didn't realize it was you . . . I like your work very much. You are so skillful with the . . . paintbrush."

"So leave me the fuck alone, and get the fuck out of here before I smash your fucking face," Speichellecker said, gesturing with his head.

Making a hasty retreat, Hans worked his way through the smoke-filled room and sat back down with John and Herman, unaware that the conversations going on around them had quieted when he had begun his rant, and the two had overheard most of what had been said.

"So what did Fliegengewicht say?" Herman asked a bit provocatively. "Was he impressed by what you had to tell him?"

"It was not the Herr Fliegengewicht but Speichellecker. . . ." Hans went on, like a man talking to himself.

"Sigmund Speichellecker!" Herman mocked. "He is even a worst phony . . . I bet you tell him off good?"

"*Ja. . . .*"

"What did you say?" Herman prodded before Hans could answer. The two were carrying on their conversation in a loose mixture of German and English for John's benefit.

"I told him my name . . . and that I was the master of a new movement that was taking over."

"What did he say then?" John asked, managing to get a word in.

"He said that he had heard of me . . . and seen my work . . . and that it was very original . . . and he admired very much what I was doing . . . and was sure that I would soon be Germany's next greatest living artist."

"*Ja* . . . I think they are all worried. Now comes a new art world order. Maybe I had better quit painting and get with it too," the painter added, nodding to his American friend. John thought he understood, but was not sure if Herman was being serious or not.

"*Ja, Ja*," Hans confirmed. "However, you are too late to be one of the innovators. But to be in the second wave is not that bad . . . better than to be fucking left out completely." Turning to John he said," Now we can go and have something to eat."

They left the bar, after John had paid once again, and walked to the center of the old section. Saying he was tired from his opening, and perhaps afraid that he might be the next to be conned into paying by Hans, Herman wisely decided to go home. At Marienplatz, he said good night to Hans and John and boarded a tram.

"Look there, Vigghyyla," Hans said to John, using yet another badly mangled pronunciation of his name. "That there is the famous old Rathaus. When it's time the Glockenspiel sends out little mechanical people from inside the city hall to ring the bells. I love to see this happen, for me this is the more interesting thing in Munich . . . except for the Englischer Garten."

Hans sat down on the edge of the large fountain in middle of the square and gazed up at the Rathaus. There was a look of excited rapture on his face, an almost child-like anticipation.

"I love to watch all those little people, some days I stop what I am doing, and come here just to wait and see them go out. But we don't see them now, it's not the time. Now is the time we eat . . . here is the restaurant, coming just around the corner."

Hans led John into a large beer hall which, despite the lateness of the hour, by Elmira, New York standards, was still in full swing. The huge room was crowded with large and noisy people, with ruddy faces and thick necks, sitting together at long wooden tables, stuffing great gobs of meat into their mouths, and swilling beer from tall, frothy steins. Smoky, forest green paint covered the walls, which were decorated with the mounted heads of stags and boars, swords, rifles, and shields displaying the blue and white checkered colors of Bavaria.

Over-large, over-heated bodies slide sideways and a place was made at one of the tables for John and Hans. Greetings were politely passed around in German. John Vigilia repeated what had been said to him, nodded his head, and smiled. He must have said the right thing for all the eyes that had been turned on John when he arrived, now turned away, their owners going back to their spirited eating and boisterous conversations. Barely able to containing his severe hunger, John eagerly grabbed at the menu passed to him and made an attempt at reading it.

A lusty waitress, wearing what John assumed was supposed to be Bavarian peasant garb, dropped off two of the six mugs of beer she was carrying, and then returned shortly with her pad and pencil poised. Speaking German, Hans gave his dinner order to the full-bodied, middle-aged woman. Hans explained to the waitress that his American friend could not read German so might need her help with the menu.

"Everything here ist good," she said in English leaning over John's shoulder, and pointing. Her costume, cut low and cinched tightly at the waist, displayed generous amounts of her ample bosoms.

John Vigilia quickly selected the only thing on the menu he recognized: "I'll have the Goulash."

"You eat za pig meat, yes?" the waitress asked using a curious tone.

"Do I eat pig meat?" John questioned.

"*Ja* . . . za Goulash ist made with za pork. . . ."

"That's fine. . . ." he replied."

"But you are an American. . . ."

"So? . . . "

"And we have two more beers." Hans interjected, sending the woman on her way.

"What did she mean by asking me if I ate pig meat?" John asked Hans after the waitress had left with their order.

"She thought you might be a Jew."

"Why would she think that?"

"I told her that you were an American. Most Germans think all Americans must be Yids because of the way your government sucks up to the Israeli Zionists."

Before John could offer a comment the stout man with a flushed face sitting next to him, taking up his place and half of John's, turned and raised his glass, and then said something to him in German. John Vigilia smiled and raised his stein, responding with the only German word he knew: *"Bitte."*

"Good afternoon to you," the German replied, nodding and using probably the only English words he knew.

"Yes, yes . . . good afternoon to you too, old man, only it's night time now" Hans said annoyed.

"Yes, yes . . . good night time to you," the man said smiling, and then turned back to his group.

Hans gazed about the room and made an indiscernible gesture, adding, "The trouble with this fucking place is there are only these old assholes here, no fucking chicks . . . at least not under fifty years old."

"It looks like all Munich is here. . . ." John ventured, observing that the room was filled to capacity.

"No . . . these fuckers are not from Munich. They are tourists, the German bourgeoisie. They come here because this place is famous. It is where Hitler planned the Beer Hall Putsch."

"The Beer Hall Putsch . . . yes, I've heard of that."

"Everyone has." Hans began, raising his voice over the noise in the hall. "It was here in Munich, in 1923, that Hitler and two thousand of his fucking storm troopers marched against the government . . . but the police fired on them and killed, I think, sixteen . . . and Herr Hitler was arrested. Did you know that he was not such a bad artist? Painted mostly landscapes that no one bought. Maybe if he had sold a few pictures the world would be different place today, ha, ha, hah. Anyhow . . . prison was a good thing for him. Although he only served nine months of his five years sentence, it was during these times that he wrote *Mein Kampf.* He didn't like fucking Slavs any more than Yids." Hans paused to take a draft from his mug.

"That's why I want you, Veegeeleeya to fly the Jungmann," he went on, "because you are an American and everyone thinks you are a Jew . . . and a Slav . . . and the Bücker was used to train pilots for the Nazis. Did you know that Lindbergh visited to Hitler to see the Third Reich's air force before the war? The two men became such good friends."

"Yes, I did know that," John replied, wondering why Hans had brought Charles Lindbergh into the conversation. Then he added, "And his trip to Germany caused him a lot trouble when he got back to the United States."

"You know all this information. So tell me, how is the book you are writing about Lindbergh coming along?"

Blindsided by Hans' comment John's beer stuck in his throat, and then found his nose. He coughed. His head was swimming. Despite his drunkenness, and the clamor in the vast hall, John was sure that he had heard the question clearly. Hans had asked him about the book he was writing *about Lindbergh*. But John Vigilia was positive he had not told Hans anything about any Lindbergh project.

John hurriedly thought back to his conversations since leaving Ireland. He had been very careful not to confide his search for the person who was supposed to have been Lindbergh's secret copilot to anyone. It had not been difficult, for in the beginning John was not exactly fixed on what he was doing himself. The most he ever revealed was that he was looking for an American boy named Ariel Angelucci. He had never told anyone why he was looking for Ariel, nor connected him in any way with Charles Lindbergh.

"A book about Lindbergh? Whatever gave you the idea that is what I am doing?" John said, trying to sound as if it were the first time that he had heard of this project.

"Why, eh . . . you told me yourself," Hans said hesitantly, "on the night we first met . . . at Luigi's party. . . ."

John watched as Hans' face began to spin wildly in front of him. Their eyes met, but Hans did not return the gaze. Then the spinning stopped as suddenly as it had begun, and John started to hiccup. His head was nowhere near as lucid as he would have liked it to be, but Hans' comment had abruptly jolted John out of his drunkenness. He hiccupped again. John knew that Hans was lying. Unlike tonight, he had been careful not to drink too much at Luigi Bosco's, and so remembered the evening clearly. He hadn't liked Hans on their first meeting, still didn't, and thus had been reluctant to talk to him at all. They had spoken only briefly, and then Hans had gone upstairs with the two women. John was sure that he certainly would not have told Hans anything of what he was doing other than his cover story about writing a book on Sperone airplanes. Another hiccup! He had seen Hans again, a bit later, in the bedroom, but Hans had been busy sporting with his naked lady friends, and they had only made passing remarks to each other. Hiccup!

"Bam!" Hans shouted pounding John Vigilia on the back.

"What're you doing!" John exclaimed, almost falling off the bench.

"See . . . your fucking hiccups are gone. "Now drink some more beer so they don't come back. I hate it when people make those fucking little noises in their throat. It annoys me."

Carried by the broad arms of their resolute Bavarian waitress, the food arrived, interrupting their conversation. John found that he was no longer hungry. Nevertheless he ate, more or less in silence, picking at his Goulash, which was somewhat greasy and filled with fatty lumps of "pig meat." While they were eating, Hans kept smacking his lips and raving about the quality of his dinner. John could not tell from looking at it what the German had ordered. When they had finally finished the massive portions, Hans insisted that they have one more beer:

"Take another beer, Vahagalla . . . you just can't have beer this fucking good anyplace else on earth. Beer . . . and my performance art . . . are Munich's greatest contribution to the culture of the world," he boasted, snapping his fingers in the air at the waitress.

The woman returned with the drinks, putting the check on the table in front of Hans. He looked at it briefly, made a face, and then slid the bill over in front of his guest.

"You can pay this, Viggeellea," Hans announced. "Just keep track of everything . . . I will pay you back as soon as. . . ." Hans turned his head and coughed. John did not catch the end of the sentence.

When they finally got up to leave John found that he could walk only by staring straight down at the floor and carefully placing one foot in front of the other. Hans could do no better. He put his arm around John Vigilia and the two of them staggered out of the hall like bloated royalty, reveling in the grandiosity of their drunken fervor.

On the way home they stopped one more time in Marienplatz. Hans stood there looking up at the Rathaus, weaving and breathing heavily, as he splashed a yellow stream into the clear water of the fountain.

Rolling and careening, they made their way back to 99 Blutenstrasse with only two more stops. The first of them was to pee.

"It's always the fault of the fucking governments. You see this here line I make there," Hans said defining the side of a wall with his urine. "Below this was all that was left of this fucking building after it was bombed all the way to shit by your fucking countrymen. And for what good reason? There were no Nazis hiding inside, only frightened old people . . . and they were all probably fucking Jews, anyway. Killed by your bombers . . . not the Nazis. So why not make a trial about that!"

The second stop was to throw up.

"Fucking bastards at the hospital . . . gave me some fucking bad pills . . . I never get sick . . . I drink more than this every fucking night . . . fucking bastards . . . trying to kill Germany's greatest living artist. Whoop! Watch out Vegeegela . . . or it goes on your shoes,"

Leaning against the wall in the dark of some public building, the sight of Hans' vomit splattered over the steps, started a chain reaction in John that caused him to add his own partially digested dinner to the fetid display.

A gray dawn was creeping over the Munich skyline when the two men finally staggered up the stairs to Hans' studio. John did not recall their outbound trip taking that long, even with the various stops, but the homeward trip seemed to go on forever. John Vigilia had a good sense of direction. Even drunk and in a strange city he was usually able to find his way. He suspected that Hans might have taken them by a roundabout route on the trip back, in order to give him a late night tour of the city, pointing out each and every major building, and what had been left of it after the merciless allied bombings.

"We can sleep in here. . . ." Hans said turning on a light.

"But there's only one bed. . . ." John remarked looking around the small, rather dingy room.

"*Ja, Ja,* . . . that way we can sleep together. . . ."

"Together?" John said with a choke in his throat.

"Yes. That way you can suck my cock if you like . . . or whatever you want to do. Or I can sleep on my stomach. . . ."

"But . . . I, er, don't do that."

"Then I can suck your cock. . . ."

"Look, I'm not gay . . . is there some place else I can sleep?" John asked stepping back a pace.

"*Ja* . . . Okay, so you're not gay. So go there in the work room," Hans said pointing at a door. "If you don't want to sleep with me, you can sleep on the floor in there, straight guy . . . tomorrow we go in the Englischer Garten and find some dirty chicks for you to fuck. They sit there naked you know, just so you can look at their pussies and pick out which one you want . . . now I am tired . . . don't bother me, I wouldn't want to fuck you anyway . . . your ass is too fucking skinny."

"Well . . . good night then," John managed to say before Hans slammed the door to the bedroom in his face.

The sounds of traffic from the street outside roused John out of a fitful sleep. He had lain half-awake since taking leave of Hans, fearful that the libido-ridden German would come in the room and pounce on him. He wasn't sure why, but John was glad to see the arrival of morning. The light coming in the window seemed to him a completely different light from the light that he had experienced in Italy. The light appeared more radiant, the sky had a glow, yellow, like the light in the pre World War Two German movies he remembered seeing. These films had been made in black and white and yet, watching them, John had marveled that the scenes seemed flooded with a blonde, Aryan light.

For a major city, the air coming in through the open window was surprisingly refreshing and tart. John looked around his space, a bit confused. He did not recall the window being up when he had scoured the room for the pile of cardboard and rags that he had eventually made his bed from. Before he had gone to sleep John Vigilia had taken a Swiss army knife from his traveling kit, and lay down with the blade open next to him.

Fully awake now, John realized he was dressed in clothes that had not been laundered since Elmira. Thinking about it, John Vigilia recalled that he had been traveling in Europe less than two weeks, yet it felt as if he had been away for months. Hans' accommodations, while supposedly costing him nothing, were certainly the worst that he had experienced. John had been spoiled by luxury hotels and palatial villas. This studio was more like the occasional hangar floor that he had slept on when traveling to aerobatic competitions with the Jungmann. But back then John had not felt physically threatened, as he had last night.

Hearing a noise in the kitchen, John decided it was time to get up. He wasn't exactly looking forward to seeing Hans again. John had been taken completely by surprise by Hans' reference to a book that he was supposedly writing about Lindbergh. And John could not help wondering about the homosexual pass Hans had made at him. Had Hans been serious about their sleeping together, or had he just been joking? John certainly couldn't tell last night; there had been laughter in Hans' eyes, but on his face a strange look of lust and anticipation. Hans was so drunk that he probably wouldn't remember very much of the evening anyway, John told himself as he nervously walked into the kitchen, his eyes bleary, and head still pounding from last nights revelry.

It was not "Germany's greatest living artist" he found seated at the table drinking coffee, but a young, rather attractive, black woman wearing only an African print robe not quite completely closed in front.

"Oh, excuse me," John said. "Who are you? Or perhaps I am I still asleep and dreaming?"

"I could ask you the same question and I know I'm wide awake," the woman answered, pulling the halves of her robe together. "Hans doesn't have many male friends that stay over. I noticed you sleeping on the floor in the front room when I went in to open the window."

"So it was you then who opened the window. I wondered how it got that way," the now wide awake John said. "I'm John Vigilia, a pilot from America. I'm supposed to be here planning for some kind of art performance Hans is doing in Locarno."

"Pleased to meet you," the woman said raising her cup. "I'm from American too, Brooklyn. I'm here as an exchange student, studying Goethe at the university. My name is Eva . . . Eva Brown, spelled b-r-o-w-n, an unfortunate name to have here in Germany as it sounds like Eva Braun, Hitler's ex. Would you like some coffee? I'm afraid that's all there is left for breakfast around here."

"No thank you. I drink tea."

"Are you the sponsor, then? . . . "

"Sponsor?"

"Oh, I thought that you might be the sponsor for this performance art thing in Switzerland. Hans has been having a hard time trying to find someone to put up the money. The festival supplies some funding, but Hans always comes up with these grand schemes that end up costing much more than he ever gets. And he has very little money of his own."

"I didn't know that . . . I mean that he didn't have a sponsor," John stammered, a bit confused, but beginning to understand now why Hans kept asking him to pay the bill last night. "So there's no tea?"

"Sorry . . . nobody here drinks tea. There's a bake shop that sells rolls and pastries, and tea also . . . it's just a few blocks down the street. I would go but I have got to leave for my class shortly."

"What are you doing living here . . . I mean with Hans, he didn't say he had a mistress or anything."

"Oh, it's nothing like that," she said laughing. "I have my own room in the back, and I always keep the door locked when I'm sleeping. I pay half the rent, which is still less than I would be paying somewhere else. Munich is as expensive as Manhattan . . . and less friendly to *schwarzes,* as they call us here in Germany. The only thing in this town lower on the social scale than a Turk is a black person. I saw a notice of a room for rent that Hans had pinned up on a bulletin board in a local coffee house and called him. I think he thought I was going to sleep with him, which is why he rented me the room. Although I guess he's pretty hard up for money. He has bought an old house in the country, which he's trying to fix up by himself."

A door slammed in the hall, and then a toilet was flushed. Shortly thereafter Herr Hockenheim appeared, his face clean, but still wearing last night's vomit-splattered clothes.

"Oh, my fucking head . . . first they bandage it, then they poison me . . . I'm fucking sick . . . I'm going back to that fucking hospital and punch the shit out of that fucking doctor."

"Well it's been so nice meeting you John," Eva said getting up, suddenly in a hurry. "I have got to run; maybe I will see you later, although I'm not often here during the daytime."

"So I see you have met my fucking *schwarze* chick tenant" Hans snarled. "One of these days I'm going to get into her hot, black pussy . . . then I can cross her name off my list of unexplored dark places, ha, ha, ha," he said leering at Eva.

Ignoring Hans' crude comment, Eva volunteered, "John, if you want to go to that bakery you can borrow my bicycle, I'm not using it today . . . it's in the storage closet under the stairs."

Smiling at John behind Hans' back, she left the room.

"*Ja*, I have used that fucking bicycle myself . . . many times," Hans gaffed, "to sniff the fucking seat, ha, ha, ha, hah."

"Well I think I'll take Eva up on her offer. . . I'll ride down to the bakery and get some tea and rolls . . . would you like me to get you something?"

Hans yawned. "*Ja, Ja,* You can bring me some strudel . . . now I take a bath, and after I go to the hospital . . . and then to see about getting my car back. Later, in the afternoon, we go in the Englischer Garten and pick up some hot chicks."

"I didn't come here to see the sights of Munich, Hans," John replied, "or to pick up 'chicks.' I was hoping to go over your plans for this event you are having in Locarno . . . and to find out just what is it I am supposed to do . . . and I thought that we could draw up some kind of a contract, and perhaps you could give me some money in advance. . . ."

"A contract! . . ." Hans interrupted. "I don't make contracts . . . my word is good enough. Like I told you . . . keep a record of your expenses. In the end you will get it all paid back . . . and also your fee."

"And what exactly will my fee be?"

"We need yet to decide that . . . it depends on what you will do. The plans are there . . . on the big table. When you come back from the bakery we can study them all you like. Now I go to take my bath."

John had wanted to ask Hans about what happened last night, not so much about his homosexual pass; he would wait to see what that was about. What he really wanted to find out was where Hans had got the information that he was writing a book about, or that he had any interest, in Charles Lindbergh's life. Hearing the water running in the bath, John got up and went downstairs.

The bicycle was under the stairs where Eva said it would be. John Vigilia wheeled it outside and into the street, shaking the fuzzy dust of last night's carousing from his still aching head. He regretted not having consulted a guide book to Munich, as John always liked to plan the route he was taking on even the shortest journey. Eva said the bakery was only a few blocks away, but he had neglected to ask her in which direction. He decided to turn left, which by the sun's position John made to out be west, and plunged off into the labyrinth of streets that was Schwabing.

Six blocks later, apparently having peddled past the inconspicuous store front in his exuberance, John turned around, retraced his route and happily found the bake shop which he had been seeking. It was one of those truly noble stores that seemed as if it had been there from the time when the monks first founded this city. Dimly lit, its dark and solemn interior was redolent with the smell of the varnish coating its woodwork, and the aroma of the many brands of coffee and tea from distant countries, and with the sweet odor of sugar frosting.

The pastries looked rare and exotic lined up in neat rows in the glass cases, each variety carefully arrayed behind a hand-lettered sign, like troops marshaled proud behind their regimental banner. The clientele at the round tables was a mix of bearded bohemians, students, and older women wearing flowered-print dresses, and small, festive, wide-brimmed hats. John's eyes scanned the room looking for an empty place. Although he had eaten a large bowel of goulash last night, he had heaved most of it up in his turn. Now, John could hear his stomach rattling. He was about to sit down and order something to eat when John remembered Hans, and his promise to bring him back a piece of strudel for breakfast.

John Vigilia read the cards as best as he could. One looked like it identified what he was after, carrying the word *Apfelstrudel.* As he stood there rather confused, the woman behind the wide counter barked something at him in German. John pointed at what appeared to be the apple strudel and held up one finger. The clerk took out one section and put it on a piece of tissue on the counter, and then said something else. There, next to a sign that said *Hefekranz,* looked like what John wanted for himself, a ring-shaped coffee cake. Again he pointed and raised one finger.

"Ein?" The woman's tone was that of a question. John smiled, then realizing that he had now learned another German word, made his first German sentence, *"Ja, ein, bitte."* The woman returned his smile, and set the roll down on the counter next to the strudel.

Another clerk was putting a cake in a box at the same counter; John pointed to his two pastries, and to the box, and then made the universal signal for *tie it up*, and pointed to the door. The woman understood completely. Knotting the string, she handed the box to John and said something in German, which he assumed was the price. Digging into his pocked, John pulled out all that was left from the hundred dollar traveler's check that he cashed yesterday at the station, and placed it on the table. The woman carefully counted out a sum of money, and then said, *"Danke."* Repeating, *"Danke,"* John slid the rest of the money back into his pocket. There was not very much left, last night's carousing had been rather expensive.

Passing a book store, John stopped and, leaving Eva's bicycle, with the cake box tied to the handle bars, in the doorway where he could watch it, went in and bought an English/German phrase book. Then he got back on the bike and raced for home, eagerly anticipating reading his new book while eating coffee cake and drinking tea. Halfway there, John suddenly realized, his mind still muddled from last nights drinking, that he had forgotten the main item he had gone out for; tea. No problem, John told himself, he would scoot back to the shop and get some. He was enjoying the trip. Riding a bicycle, which he hadn't done in perhaps twenty years, was the most fun John had had in some time, maybe he would buy one when he got back to Elmira, he thought. First he would drop off the pastries with Hans, who he anticipated would be eagerly awaiting his strudel, and then ride back to get the tea.

Balancing the bike, book, and cake with one hand, John rang the bell to Hans' studio. There was no answer. He tried again, still no answer. He considered that perhaps the bell was broken; as he was sure that Hans was there. John was wheeling the bike out to the curb, planning to shout up to the open studio window, when Otto popped out of his gallery.

"Ah . . . Hans' American friend. I see you go by earlier on Eva's bicycle," Otto said. "And now you are back. But it's no use to ring the bell for Hans is gone."

"Gone?" John said incredulously. "I just went out to get something for our breakfast."

"Hans left shortly after you did. He seemed in quite a hurry. Didn't he give you a key?"

"Unfortunately not. . . ."

"Then you are locked out . . . he didn't stop to tell me where he was going either."

"Well . . . we are supposed to go to some kind of garden at three o'clock. I can't imagine Hans being interested in flowers."

"That would be the Englischer Garten . . . it's not a flower garden, but a public park. It is now the most famous place in Munich, where groups of young people sunbathe nude in the middle of the city, and tourists come there to look at them. Yes, they come from all over the world just to see this. Hans goes there every afternoon to ogle the naked girls."

"All completely naked?"

"*Ja*, there is a large meadow in the center of the park, with a small stream, where it is allowed to swim, and to lie around, without any clothes on. There are often hundreds of naked people there, and hundreds more to look at them, maybe even thousands. It is quite a spectacle."

"I don't believe it. . . ."

"At any rate you shall see it all this afternoon."

"Look, can I leave these pastries with you? I need to go back and get a container of tea."

"Fine. . . . But if it's tea you want you can come into my office . . . I take tea myself. I have just boiled the water, there is enough for two."

"Thank you that would be nice. I'm so hungry. We can have some of this coffee cake I just bought."

"What would you like with your tea . . . sugar?"

"Yes please, and milk, if you have it. The only time plain tea ever tasted good to me was on the trains when I traveled in Russia." John explained, making small talk. "Each car had a coal stove that not only heated the cabins but had a kind of samovar on top for brewing tea. An old woman usually tended the stove and made the tea. Everyone drank it with three or four lumps of sugar, from glass mugs with shiny metal holders."

"And what were you doing traveling on trains in Russia?" Otto asked jokingly. "Are you working for the CIA?"

"Heavens no . . . I'm a writer, well I guess you could say more accurately a college professor. I was there giving lectures on contemporary American books."

"So you are a writer? And how many books have you published?" Otto asked, neatly pouring the tea.

"None, I'm afraid to say," John replied as he sliced the coffee cake.

"Then you are the perfect person to lecture on books; a bit like me. I have never made a picture in my life, yet

I make my living, such as it is, selling artworks. I could not make a drawing of my hand if I was allowed to trace it on a piece of paper. Yet many talented artists come to my gallery with their work, very good work, work I never could have made myself, and I must shake my head no and turn them away, most often merely because I have no more space. And they go off in despair thinking, I am sure, the worst thoughts of me. I wanted to be an artist, but realizing I had no talent for art, I became an art dealer."

"I guess that's what life is all about; you settle on one thing and, if you care for it you stretch it out, and out again," John Vigilia said, amazed at how philosophical he had become.

"This cake is very good. . . ." Otto said with his mouth full.

"Yes it is . . . I bought it at a bake shop down the street."

"I know this here shop; I go there sometimes myself."

"Very nice old ladies. . . ."

"And you have just come from Italy?" Otto asked, dabbing at his lips with a napkin, and abruptly changing the subject.

"Yes . . . why do you say that?" John said not quite ready for this question.

"Yesterday . . . after you and Hans went upstairs, a man came into the shop . . . he spoke excellent German, but I could tell from the way he pronounced some words that he was an Italian. He asked some questions about Hans. Then he asked if Hans had an American friend visiting him today. When I told him I didn't know anything about Hans' visitors he offered me some money to watch for you and tell me what I saw. I told him I only sold pictures, not information.

"That was all . . . he just went away?" John asked, feeling a tightness growing in his throat.

"No, there is a bit more. This morning when I came in to open up the gallery the same man was standing in the doorway across the street. He stayed there until you came out, and when you bicycled away he left. Don't turn around, but now the man is back . . . out front looking in the gallery window. He has been standing there just too long to be looking at the pictures."

"Do you think that he's been following me?"

"I don't know. He is not a man I have seen on this street before. That was why I was not exactly joking when I asked you if you were a spy for the CIA."

"I can't imagine what anyone would want with me, I'm just here to help Hans with his performance," John lied, realizing now that he knew far too little of what was going on around him. He hungered to know more, to turn around and confront this man. Was it someone that he would recognize from Rome? Or Como? His mind obsessively turned over the few facts that he did have, searching them for even fuller implications. Had a whistle been blown somewhere, and a long dormant conspiracy awakened and begun feeding on itself?

"You can turn around to see now . . . but the man is gone," Otto informed him.

"I'm sure he's not looking for me," John said attempting to keep up his cover. He slowly turned and glanced out the window. "It seems like it will be a nice day," he said as if that was all that interested him outside. "Thanks for the tea, Otto. You can have the rest of the cake, but I promised the strudel to Hans. If you see him when he comes back would you give it to him, and tell him that since I couldn't get into the studio, I've decided to take a ride around town on the bicycle, just to take in the sights. Tell him I'll be back around three. See you later!"

"I tell him for you. *Auf Wiedersehen*. . . . and John," Otto called after him, "do be careful and watch out for yourself."

At a quarter to three, after having crisscrossed most of Munich on Eva's bicycle, and discovering that he was very much out of shape physically, John turned exhausted, but relieved, onto Blutenstrasse. He was happy at having found his way out and back without need of a map, but then navigation had always been one of John's Vigilia's strong points. There was Otto's shop, right where he had left it.

He put up his hand, signaling to the car following too close behind him that he was about to stop. As he braked the car accelerated, catching the bicycle's back wheel with its fender, and sending John cartwheeling into the air. In his younger days John had raced motorcycles for a brief period, and while he had never learned to win, he had learned to fall. Relax, John's mind instinctively told him, you are only traveling about three miles per hour, sure the pavement is hard, but when you hit your muscles must be as calm as if you were about to roll into your own bed.

John Vigilia saw the bicycle sliding down the street without him. It wasn't making sparks the way fallen motorcycles usually did, especially noticeable when you dropped one down on at night. The bicycle was probably too light to rub enough to spark. As John fell a vision of a competitor dropping a motorcycle in front of him on a banked oval track in Maryland flashed in his mind. A machine whose exhaust smell betrayed it was not fueled by the required pump gasoline, but some exotic, highly flammable mixture. Once again he saw himself swerving out of the way of the riderless motorcycle just before it burst into flames and exploded.

The first part of John's person to hit the pavement was his hand. That was a mistake, he told himself. The hand, a weak and vulnerable item, should have been tucked up inside his arms. He felt the burn as the asphalt ripped off a layer of his hand's skin, then the wrist collapsed, letting his shoulder hit square, instead of his upper arm. Then his knee folded allowing his ankle to buckle. As he went down, John twisted his neck to avoid hitting his face, and cursed the fact that he was not wearing a helmet. John's head struck the pavement. Still sliding as it made contact, the road took some flesh from the back of John's skull. His clothes saved the rest of his skin, but could not prevent the multiple sprains, and the black and blue marks that would appear shortly.

Traffic stopped. People had gotten out of their cars and were standing over the fallen bicyclist gesturing, and talking in German. John crawled to the curb and tried to get up. Looking up he saw the friendly form of Otto running toward him from the gallery.

"John! Are you all right? Here, let me help you. . . ." Otto said all out of breath, "I was looking out my window . . . and I saw it all. That car behind you just accelerated and hit you on purpose."

"*Ja*," one of the onlookers agreed, "I saw it too . . . the car just hit him for no reason. It was a foreign car; Italian . . . the license number began with MI . . . from Milano."

"A car from Milan?" John said slightly dazed. He began to sit down on the fender of a car parked at the curb.

"Oh! Don't sit down there!" another man shouted, grabbing John by the arm, "that's my Mercedes . . . you can scratch it. This car cost me much money. . . ."

"Oh . . . I'm sorry," John Vigilia said apologized sarcastically, wiping his bleeding hand on his badly torn pants, "I certainly wouldn't want to scratch your Mercedes."

"Come, we go to my gallery, and you can clean yourself off." Otto said taking John's arm and helping his American friend hobble down the street. "Wait . . . I need to speak to the man who told me that he had seen the car had a Milan license plate. . . ." John said looking around, but the onlooker had already left.

The crowd was dispersing, anxious to be gone before the police should arrive and ask for witnesses. Someone had propped Eva's battered bike against the front of Otto's gallery.

"I guess I'll have to buy Eva a new bicycle," John Vigilia volunteered, seeing the thing leaning there all bent and broken. He was holding his right wrist, with his left hand. The whole right side of his body was in extreme pain, and he was limping badly.

"Don't worry about that . . . it is an old bicycle, not worth too much . . . we can bend it back in shape for her. I am sure she will be happy. First we must get you fixed up."

John washed up as best as he could in the cramped water closet in the back of the gallery. When he came out he saw that Otto had produced a small medical kit from somewhere, and laid out the supplies on his desk rather officially. Then he began the task of cleaning John Vigilia's wounds and bandaging them. Finally, the gallery owner wrapped an elastic bandage around John's wrist, and another around his ankle, both of which were clearly sprained, and beginning to swell up painfully.

"Thank you Otto, I'm feeling much better already," John said gratefully. "Where did you learn first aid?"

"When I did my military service I told them I would not want to kill anyone," Otto revealed, "so they made me a medic. . . ."

Freed somewhat from his pain, John now began to try to recreate the sequence of events that had led up to the accident.

"Otto, you said you saw the car that was following behind me speed up . . . and deliberately hit me when I gave a signal I was going to stop."

"*Ja*," Otto replied, "as usual, when there is nothing to do in the gallery I stand in the window and look out at the street. I saw you coming, and you slowed down. The car following you had not been at a proper distance behind . . . suddenly it was very close. And then it hit you . . . it looked to me almost like the driver had done it on purpose."

"And you didn't see the driver . . . or get the license number?"

"No," Otto said then paused and thought for a moment, "but I have seen the car before, it was parked across the street this morning. I noticed it because it was an Alfa Romeo, and you do not see many such Italian cars in Germany."

John leaned over and was rubbing his ankle, when the door flew open, and Hans burst in, interrupting their conversation.

"You big fucking asshole, Veegeielea! What the fuck have you done to Eva's bicycle!? You must to pay for this!" Hans shouted at John, and then he noticed his condition, "And what the fuck have you done to yourself? What has happened? Are you hurt badly? Will you be well enough when the time comes to fly the Jungmann in Locarno?"

"I'm all right," John said, trying to stand up, "and I'll make good on Eva's bicycle . . . even if I have to buy her a new one."

"There was a car following him," Otto interjected. "It seemed as if it speeded up and hit the bicycle on purpose."

"Why the fuck would anyone want to hit you, Veegelaha?" Hans asked, sounding confused. "You are only a stunt pilot from America . . . aren't you? Maybe they mistook you for someone else."

"I have seen a man following John," Otto revealed, "and he came into my gallery asking questions . . . he even offered me money, which I did not take, to report to him on John's activities. He spoke with an Italian accent. . . ." John looked at Otto, as if to tell him to be quiet, that he had said too much already.

"He offered you money . . . and you didn't take it. I don't believe that," Hans countered sarcastically. "A cheap bastard like you would sell your fucking mother for a few marks."

"Look, let's not start an argument," John Vigilia said, attempting to raise his hand, and then sensing the numbness in his wrist. He suddenly felt very isolated. The free and easy banter between the two Germans had caused him to feel distinctly alone. And at this moment John could not bear to be alone. He was much too afraid of the vast confusion of whatever seemed to be going on around him. Although he did not completely trust Hans, John turned to him in his helplessness. He would ask the question that had been gnawing at his mind: "Hans, I need to know something . . . who was it that told you I was researching a book about Charles Lindbergh?"

"Lindbergh? . . . Now who the fuck is Lindbergh? Oh, yes, he was an American flyer, wasn't he? I don't know anything about him." Hans replied dodging the question, and then quickly changed the subject. "Look at your fucking wrist . . . what are you going to do? Tonight you won't even be able to jerk-off your prick. I feel so sorry for you. Come, now we must go to my studio, you can clean yourself up, and put on your other clothes. Then we go to the Englischer Garten and find some chicks that we can fuck. Maybe later you will feel better enough so that you can manage it. I am sure that there will be some bitch there willing to play with your prick for you."

"But that's not what I asked you about," John said angrily, His pain was causing him to be more annoyed with Hans than he wanted to show. "What I need to know is . . . where did you get the idea that I was writing a book on Charles Lindbergh?" With that said he continued: "The only thing I'm working on is a book about Sperone Aviation's early airplanes, and I haven't gotten very far with that as of yet. Do you understand me?"

"Don't you be so angry with me Veegeelee, I don't speak very good English; you must have misunderstand me. I only remember making a joke that you were writing a book about hamburgers, not Lindbergers . . . all Americans love hamburgers. . . . This is all I told you," Germany's self-proclaimed greatest living artist said jokingly. And that was all John could get Hans to say in answer to his question.

They went upstairs without referring to the matter any further. When Hans opened the door to the studio they found Eva standing just inside, an upset look on her face.

"I can't believe this has happened!" Eva shouted. She appeared a bit hysterical.

"I'm sorry about your bicycle," John apologized upon seeing her, "I'll get it fixed, or if it can't be fixed I'll buy you a new one."

"My bicycle?" she said sounding a bit confused.

"Yes, I had a crash . . . and I wrecked it."

"And who wrecked the apartment?" she said, pointing at things that had been dumped out of drawers and strewn all over the floor. "Someone's been here, and they've gone through all my papers, and everything else. It looks like they've gone through your suitcases too."

"Fucking bastards . . . who the fuck would want to do this?" Hans said, picking up his drawings from the floor.

"Do you know why anyone would do this?" John asked.

"I have . . . no fucking idea," Hans replied, shrugging his shoulders.

The vagueness of Hans's reply led John Vigilia to believe he was not speaking the truth, or at least not revealing all he knew.

Without saying anymore the three of them began cleaning up the mess. John picked up the little notepad that he had been keeping his information in and painfully turned through the pages with his bruised hand. To his relief everything, what there was of it, seemed to be there.

Glancing at his image in a mirror leaning in a corner of the studio, John Vigilia barely recognized himself, realizing for the first time the full extent of his injuries.

Maybe his ankle was even broken. It was clear to him that he should probably go to a hospital, or at the least get in bed, and remain there for a few days until he felt better. But Hans hadn't provided him with a proper bed to sleep in, only a pile of newspapers on the floor of his work room. Nevertheless, as he was in no condition right now to go looking for a hotel, John decided that he would stay here tonight, but leave in the morning. He was not sure where he would go, but knew that he didn't want to remain in Munich any longer.

Nineteen

This is a strange response, to be asleep
With eyes wide open; standing, speaking, moving,
And yet so fast asleep,

Shakespeare *The Tempest II.i.*

John Vigilia accelerated his newly rented Volkswagen onto the Autobahn and headed south, in the general direction of Garmish-Partenkirchen. Having carefully studied his BP map of Europe, he had found that there was no direct route between Munich and Locarno. In Germany all the big red and blue roads ran north and south, while only little yellow roads ran east to west. He recalled an incident from a trip he had taken several years ago. Driving the narrow and winding stretch through the forest between Pirmasens and Landau John had encountered many convoys of American and German troops in heavy trucks and tanks. Military personal and their equipment were everywhere, partially concealed in the fields and in the woods. Unaware the area was a popular place for war games, John imagined that he had somehow stumbled on some lost battalions from World War Two, who not knowing the war was over were still battling it out in the forests.

While waiting for a convoy to pass, he had asked the burly sergeant directing traffic why all the narrow roads ran east to west. "Why hell, they planned it that way . . . when them goddamn Commie tanks break through that Iron Curtain," the sergeant said, speaking of the Iron Curtain as if it were an actual physical presence, "we don't want them bastards coming at us hauling ass down no goddamn Autobahn. . . ."

Wincing with pain, John shifted the car's manual transmission into fourth gear. His wrist was still wrapped with an elastic bandage. His whole right side hurt, causing him to keep squirming about in the seat trying to find a comfortable position. John admitted to himself now that he probably should have delayed a day or two, until he was feeling a bit better. Nevertheless, he was glad to be leaving Munich, and Hans Hockenheim, even if he had to stop every half hour to stand up and straighten out his body, and even if he was paying for this car himself, with his nearly maxed-out credit card. Despite his boastful promises, Hans had not yet put up one mark toward John Vigilia's expenses. While he doubted that he would ever regain the small fortune the rental car, and everything else, was costing, for some reason John believed Hans, concluding that anyone so vehement should be believed. In a way John envied Hans. He lacked what Hans had in abundance, tactlessness and a bad temper, which he sheathed in obsequious pleasantries. This, John had concluded, was the reason why Hans more or less thrived, making his way here and there, a blatant self-promoter and rough-tongued arriviste.

In spite of his mental anguish and tremendous physical discomfort, John was smiling, happy to be in control of his own destiny once again. He didn't like being driven, and even more so being flown, by someone other than himself. On his rare airliner flights John Vigilia always felt uncomfortable thinking that some young kid, who was probably still trying to grow a mustache, and more likely with less flying experience than him, was in ultimate command of his fate. If he was going to die in an airplane crash John wanted to be at the controls, personally sure that he had done everything that could possibly be done before giving it all up—not sitting in an aisle seat blindly sipping beer and munching cocktail nuts.

Were all these airline pilots, ordinary mortals sometimes called on to perform god-like feats, continually operating in a state of self denial? John wondered. He had known too many of these pilots over the years to ever be comfortable sitting in the back. And so, John Vigilia, the stunt-flying professor, had to confess that except for when he was at the controls, he was deathly afraid of flying.

John's head ached, and the part of his skull that he had slammed onto the pavement was extremely sore to the touch. Nevertheless, he had not wiped out of his memory his time spent in Munich. Driving along, John tried to return to these events in his mind, catching himself in the act of identifying a specific activity before he had retrieved it, trying to make sense of all that had happened. Thus preoccupied, John had not glanced in his rear view mirror for some time, as he had been doing regularly since leaving the city. He had not previously observed anyone following his rented VW, which was not exactly the fastest thing on the highway.

He was still not clear about what had caused the bicycle accident. During his ride across town, John had not sensed being followed. There was a lot of traffic and he had looked over his shoulder frequently. But two witnesses, Otto who he was inclined to trust, and a man who had quickly disappeared, had told John that the car behind him had speeded up and apparently hit him on purpose.

Although John Vigilia was now on a clear mission, he drove on in a way that he hoped gave the impression of aimless wandering. John had left Munich at a leisurely pace, wanting to appear as a tourist just starting out on a trip with a rather vague goal in mind. He would be what John Vigilia was supposed to be, an American writer working on a book about an Italian aircraft manufacturer, who also happened to be a stunt pilot, and who was on his way to Switzerland to pick up some extra money flying an airplane in an event staged by a German performance artist.

Or was it perhaps too late for that cover story? John asked himself. Were the warning signs already in place? Were there too many people now aware that he was looking for a man named Ariel Angelucci? Or was the Lindbergh copilot story actually only a hoax? Was it all a mistake, or had he perhaps stumbled onto one of the greatest conspiracies of the Twentieth Century?

John checked his rear view mirror. For the first time he noticed a black Alfa Romeo, its right front fender appearing slightly damaged, pacing lazily behind his Volkswagen. Now he knew for sure that he was being followed. Such a powerful car would have passed him quickly and been on its way. As he drove on, however, this following car continued to hang back, never closing nearer than three or four car lengths, its driver visible only indistinctly, never reaching that complete sharpness of outline that might give John cause for alarm. Was this the man, or men, who had so thoroughly ransacked Hans' studio, an act which John felt guilty about probably having been the cause of?

Hans, Eva, and John had gone over the apartment thoroughly, putting things back in place, and checking to see what had been taken. Nothing was declared missing, so they had discounted the possibility that the break in had been a random attempt at burglary. Due to the craziness of the day before, John had forgotten to set the telltales in his bags, not imagining that anyone would go looking through them. He had not needed these discreet lengths of hair, however, to tell him that someone had given his things a complete going over even though everything appeared to be there. Strangely enough, the person who had done this, whoever it was, had gone to the trouble of tearing a blank sheet of paper from the sketch pad John purchased in Como.

The very afternoon after the bicycle accident, when John Vigilia had wanted to rest and let his body, and his life, return to its normal state, Hans had insisted on taking his guest to visit the Englischer Garten. And so, his head floating from the pain pills Hans had given him, or at least what he had said were pain pills, and his imagination piqued by Otto's description of hundreds of people lying about naked in a public park in full view, John, breathing heavily through a slightly bruised lung, had hobbled the short distance from Schwabing to the former sheep meadow.

"Look!" Hans had shouted, waving his arms about when they arrived, "Have you ever seen so many fucking naked tits and pussies displayed out in the open at one time?"

John had wished that his head, and his vision, would stop spinning long enough for him to enjoy the spectacle.

Hans, with his always crude manner, was brushed off by the first two groups of two women he had approached. On their third try, however, John and Hans were invited to share a blanket with two naked English girls who were sunning themselves between the path and the small stream that meandered through the grassy area.

The novelty of sitting on a blanket fully clothed, having a conversation with two not unattractive nude young women, while on the sidewalk less than three feet away dozens of casual people, some wearing clothes and some who were not, constantly walked by, some gawking and some not, had clearly aroused John Vigilia from his drowsiness.

The English girls told them that their names were Mary and Beth, and that they were students on holiday from a small art school in the Midlands, "Luff-bro", as they had pronounced it, then spelling it out, L-o-u-g-h-b-o-r-o-u-g-h. Laughing, they pointed out that Australians often mispronounced the name Loughborough as "Loogabarooga." A rather reasonable mistake John thought. Their British accents were proving too much for Hans, who, having failed to understand much of the conversation was beginning to fall into a sulk.

"Like aren't you guys ever going to sunbathe?" Mary asked.

"Sunbathe? . . ." John said.

"Yeah," Beth added, "like aren't you going to take off your clothes?"

"They want us to take our clothes off, Hans," John explained.

"I know," Hans replied. "The words 'take off your clothes' are words I am very familiar with in many languages."

"Well then . . . like go ahead," Mary giggled. "Or are ya shy?"

"I'm not shy. I just don't take any of my clothes off in public," Hans announced rather haughtily.

"Why? Like yer afraid we'll see that ya got a small wanker, or something?" Beth teased, and the two girls giggled to show the comment was only meant as a joke.

"You know . . . I have a very big fucking 'wanker', really big. And I will show it to you when we go back to my studio."

"Your studio? Like you're an artist, or something?"

"He's not just an artist," John butted in, his voice hinting a bit at sarcasm. "Hans is Germany's greatest living performance artist; he told me so himself."

"Brilliant," Mary said. "Like we're both interested in art . . . I mean like we told you we're art students."

"Good for you . . . the world needs more artists," Hans interjected. "Now we can go to my studio . . . which is not so far away from here, and I will show you the designs for a performance I am planning for a big art festival in Switzerland. I will be the star attraction."

"Yes," John added, speaking rather slowly. "I will also be taking part in this performance . . . and would like to see these designs also."

The strong sun was taking its toll on his damaged head. Only the presence of the two naked English girls was keeping John Vigilia from falling into a drug induced stupor.

"Like we can't go just now," Mary explained. "We aren't done sun tanning . . . like we need to do two hours everyday to get just the right shade, if ya know what I mean . . . like we still have a half-hour yet to go."

"You are already tan enough," Hans protested. "In one half-hour you will both look like *schwarzes*. Let's go now. . . ."

"But like you blokes haven't taken off your clothes yet," Beth reminded them, scratching not too discreetly at her peach-fuzz crotch.

"Okay . . . we take off our shirts . . . and stay for fifteen minutes more," Hans compromised, pulling the surplus German army T-shirt he was wearing off over his head. He was well-built, displaying muscles he must have developed from years as a juggler and metal sculptor before becoming a performance artist. The two girls studied his physique with obvious appreciation.

"Like, what about you?" Mary said, turning to John, who had stretched out on the grass and was on the point of dozing off.

"Hey! . . . Vagahala, don't go to sleep . . . you have got to take off your shirt . . . and your pants too, if you want to. . . ."

"Okay, okay," John said sitting up and unbuttoning his shirt with his left hand. Painfully withdrawing his right arm from the sleeve, he slowly removed his shirt.

"Bloody hell! Like what happened to you?" Beth exclaimed, seeing the black and blue bruise marks that covered John's back and all his right arm. "Like, did ja have an accident . . . or maybe you're into S and M, or something?"

"He had a fall off his bicycle," Hans explained. "He thinks someone in an Italian car hit him on purpose. You look gross Veegeele . . . you are making the girls sick, maybe you had better put your shirt back on now."

These token efforts at nudity seemed to satisfy the English girls so, as agreed, in fifteen minutes the four of them left the park. On the way to Hans's studio, however, the girls announced that they were hungry. They wanted to stop at the Weinerwald on Maximilianstrasse. Mary explained to them that they always ate at a branch of this chain of restaurants, if they could find one, as they knew no German and ordered by pointing at the glossy pictures on the menu. They were disappointed when Hans revealed that Weinerwald meant Vienna Woods, not "hot dog world" as they had assumed. John had followed along in a dizzy agony, just content with the opportunity to sit down and eat in a relatively clean, air-conditioned place.

Mary and Beth ate their food as if they had not eaten in some time, which was probably the case. Everyone, at Hans' insistence, had two large steins of beer. Hans kept the table entertained, or at least entertained himself, with tales of his artistic excellence. He knew every German artist of importance, none of whom, he boasted, were as significant as he was, and kept trying to impress the young ladies by dropping names that unfortunately meant little or nothing to them.

John was feeling no pain, and having trouble focusing his vision. He had observed that Mary and Beth both seemed much less interesting with their clothes back on: Mary looking like she might have been a subject for a painting by Modigliani, and Beth could have sat for Francis Bacon. With a sweep of his hand Hans announced: "I will pay bill," and then turned again to John for money.

John Vigilia motioned to the waitress; a phrase that he had memorized from his new English/German phrase book came to his tired mind: "*Ich mochten gern zahlen.*"

The waitress smiled at him and began totaling the bill.

"What is that stupid German you are trying to say?" Hans barked.

"I asked the waitress for the bill . . . she understood me didn't she. . . ." John said defending himself.

"It is a stupid phrase that no one uses . . . too formal. If you want the bill, you just snap you fingers like this. . . ." Hans said flicking his fingers in the air.

"He spoke very nicely," the waitress said taking John's credit card, "and I see he pays also. . . ."

John's brain left Munich temporarily when at Starnberg the road forked. He would have to make a choice. He slowed the Volkswagen down. Both roads led to the same destination, Garmish-Partenkirchen, but he quickly decided on the one to the right, a red road on his map. The smaller of the two roads, it would fit nicely with his image of a tourist in no hurry taking the more scenic route. In his rearview mirror he saw that the Alfa Romeo, anticipating his quarries need for a decision, had closed up the gap between them. In tandem, the two cars left the main highway.

As Hans, John, and the English girls were about to leave the Weinerwald, the two girls had shouldered their backpacks and announced they were going to head to the train station. "Like it's been a brilliant time, if ya know what I mean . . . but we've got to be on our way."

"But you were supposed to come to my studio to see my new artwork," Hans had protested lamely.

"Like we sure would have loved to see your drawings Hans, but we've got a train to Verona to catch, ya know . . . ." Mary said, not sounding too convincing.

"Like, it was a real pleasure meeting you two," Beth immediately added, almost on cue, "and thanks for treating us to the slap-up lunch . . . if you ever happen to be in Loughborough do look us up, ya know. We're in the phone book. Like we'll take you to The Swan and The Rushes, it's our favorite pub . . . just across from the train station."

"Fucking English cock teasers . . . we should have already bombed their fucking mothers," Hans swore as he stood there watching the two girls hurry away without a backward glance. John had enjoyed the fact that Hans had looked rather comical in his breathless confusion.

"So . . . all you wanted was a free piece of pussy," John quipped even though it was he who again had been stuck with paying the bill.

"All they wanted was a free meal. German girls would have at least given a blow-job; and Russian girls . . . they would have let both of us fuck them together, me on top and you up their ass. . . ."

The two men had then returned to the studio with Hans still in a foul temper at having been rebuffed by "the two fucking little English cunts." Eva was at home and Hans made a pass at her, but she quickly retreated to her room and locked the door. No had one mentioned the earlier attempted robbery. Eva had cleaned up most of the mess.

John asked again to see the drawings for the Locarno project. Reluctantly, Hans opened a file drawer and threw some papers on the studio table. John studied the works, which, even with his limited knowledge of performance art, he judged to be somewhat crudely made and without much substance, unable to make much sense of them, or to determine what part he might play in the performance.

Taking a bottle of Scotch whiskey from a cabinet, Hans filled a water glass to the brim and began drinking it straight, without offering any to John, who would have refused it anyway. The stereo was blasting out loud American jazz. John tried to speak to Hans, but was ignored. Finally he got up from the table and switched off the tape player. "So tell me just what do these drawings mean?" he demanded.

"Look, why do you bother me with this shit . . . can't you see I'm drinking, and I was listening to the fucking music. . . ."

"But if I am going to participate I need to know what you are trying to do? say? accomplish? . . . whatever?"

"If I could *tell* you . . . would I need to make all these fucking drawings," Hans replied. He paused for a brief moment as if gathering his thoughts, then continued; suddenly stone sober as if everything before this had been an act: "Look, I can tell you that my art grows out of my need to make it. I just proceed without a rational basis, and yet at the same time I am trying to transcend my agony and my sorrow . . . my delight and my disasters. Somehow my art lifts me clear of my human situation. I must do it and depend on it for my understanding of who I am."

Hans had said the words simply and clearly, almost as if he were reading them from a text, an answer he had apparently given many times before. The completeness of the statement had taken John aback. It was more profound than what he had been expecting from someone who had previously been so crude. Was the statement original to Hans, or was it something he had read somewhere and then memorized to repeat as needed?

"Go on. . . ." John said, hoping get more out of Hans now that he had begun talking.

"Go on? Where the fuck should I go . . . there is nowhere else. My drawings are my drawings and that's that. I am fucking tired. I want to go to bed now. I see you in the morning." Hans said disappearing into his room, although it was now only early evening, carrying his bottle of whiskey, and slamming the door behind him.

At the sound of Hans' door closing, Eva immediately appeared from her room. Apparently she had been listening to the conversation.

"Look John . . . you're all beat up, physically and mentally, you can't sleep on that pile of cardboard again tonight . . . you can take my bed. I have a sleeping bag and can sleep on the floor. But we both need to be in my room though . . . I won't sleep out here with him prowling around. I can trust you . . . can't I?"

"Thank you Eva, you're so kind . . . I wouldn't have even thought to ask you. But I really do need a good night's sleep. And as for trusting me, I give you my word, and we're both from New York. Besides, with the condition my body is in I couldn't make a move on you even if I wanted too." John reassured her. The two sat at the table talking for the better part of an hour and then decided that they too were both very tired and should retire early.

In spite of his pain, and Eva's snoring coming from the floor where she lay at his feet, John slept rather sagely, keeping his body and mind where directed, curling himself up with the extended smile of a man pushed past his limit, too beaten even to grieve for his dead wife.

He felt a host of hands nudging and easing him, pressing him this way and that, raising or lowering him, prodding him to the left and right, palming his head forward, and with the gentlest of urgings tucking his feet in between themselves.

Bam! Bam! Bam! John Vigilia heard a loud banging, and then someone shouting.

"I know you're in there Vagahalaaa! Come on out you fucking sneaky bastard. I know you are in there screwing with my black bitch!"

The first gray light of dawn was just beginning to filter into the back bedroom, around the corners of the drawn shade. John and Eva had been awakened from their separate sleeps by the sounds of an insane pounding. Hans was hammering on the bedroom door.

"Come out of there you two! I know what the fuck you are up to! Is this the fucking way to treat my hospitality!

I am kind enough to let you stay in my house and you two go at it like fucking rabbits . . . in there screwing away all night. . . ."

With muscles only a little more willing than not, John had inched his way to the door that seemed in imminent danger of being battered down. Always a person of no great conversation, he searched for words to soften the anger and violence in the man now confronting him:

"Hans . . . please calm down. We are not in here doing anything but sleeping . . . or at least we were until you started shouting and beating down the door."

"You are a fucking liar! That fucking *schwarze*. Am I not fucking good enough for her . . . she tells me that she doesn't fuck around . . . and then you come here, and right away she hops in the sack. . . ."

"That's not true . . . she only let me sleep in her bed because I had hurt myself . . . and she slept in her sleeping bag . . . on the floor."

"You expect me to believe that shit? What the fuck do you think I am, a stupid asshole?"

Expecting Hans would come bursting through the door at any moment, Eva had taken up a position behind John, an umbrella in her hand. But reason prevailed, and after no small ceremony Hans was mollified, John's few chaste words healing the tension of the moment, as language often has the power to do if allowed, converting even the worst situation into something understood.

But the damage had been done; John could take no more of Hans, than Hans could of him. Arranging a kind of pact between them, they agreed that John should go on ahead to Switzerland and practice with the Jungmann. Hans would join him there in a few days. After all, Germany's greatest performance artist needed America's greatest stunt flying professor for his event in Locarno.

A badly wounded, both in body and spirit, John Vigilia had spent part of the next morning with Eva scouring

Munich for a replacement for her bicycle, another item he charged to his credit card. Eva thanked him, and said she would use the bike to look for a new apartment. He then had gone to a nearby car rental agency and got the Volkswagen, at what seemed to him an outrageous rate. This was also put his card. John could not remember what his credit limit was as in the past he had never even come close to exceeding it. Now he was just hoping the bank would not max his card out before he got back to Elmira.

"Don't worry about the money," Hans kept saying. "I have a very wealthy sponsor, who gives me plenty of cash. Just keep your receipts and all will be paid."

Now, as he drove along, John wanted very much to believe that everything was going to work out as Hans had promised, although he surely doubted that it would. The route diverged once again at Garmish-Partenkirchen. Instead of staying on the main road to Innsbruck, and then going through the Brenner Pass, John turned right, onto a smaller road that headed in the direction of Imst. In his rearview mirror he watched the Alfa Romeo that had been following him also turn right. Having made his decision, John Vigilia cursed quietly to himself. He did not much like driving in the mountains, and would certainly be easier to follow on these less traveled roads. John trusted that following him was all the Alfa Romeo driver had been hired to do.

Falling between the trees, in alternate patches of light and then shadow, the late afternoon sun was now beginning to sink behind the mountains. To John Vigilia it seemed as if the fleeing sun was not just disappearing from view but descending into some great hole, from which it might never return. Whatever hope he had held out for the day appeared to be passing. Perhaps things would begin to change for the better if and when he got to Locarno.

Twenty

I forget;
But these sweet thoughts do even refresh my labors
Most busy least, when I do it.

Shakespeare *The Tempest III. i.*

Father Thomas Brennan was one of two archivists who had been assigned by the Vatican to catalog the more than three million documents stored in their vaults that related to His Holiness Pope Pius XII. Newly transferred to Rome from Dublin, Father Brennan wondered why he had been chosen for this ponderous task as his knowledge of Italian was minimal at best.

Three years ago, hoping to stem the major controversy surrounding the Catholic Church's alleged complacency toward the Nazi extermination of Jews during World War Two, Pope John Paul II, who had made reconciliation with the Jews a key element of his papacy, had worked with Jewish groups to set up a panel of five scholars charged with studying the documents of Pius XII, the wartime pope. Disagreement over the role played by Pius XII had strained Jewish-Catholic relations for decades. There were even those who believed the archives contained proof that Pius XII was an anti-Semite who had somehow ignored evidence of the massacres, and perhaps had even encouraged the Germans in their work.

The scholars had requested material going all the way back to 1923, during the reign of Pius XI. Father Brennan and his partner Father Leon, who in addition to this search had to attend to their regular archival duties, were presently only up to 1927. It was slow going, especially for Father Brennan, who had taken to only skimming the pages of Italian text that he could hardly read, mainly looking for key phrases about Nazis or Jews.

Upon opening a new folder, Father Brennan's eyes fell on words he knew, and remembered very well: The Saint Romanus Home, Tralee, County Kerry, Ireland. It was where he had spent most of his youth; having been sent to Ireland to live in the orphanage after both of his parents had been killed during a German bombing raid on London. It was the good sisters of Saint Romanus who had brought him up to fear God, and eventually steered him toward his vocation. The letters in the file were written in a kind of Latinized Italian. He could make out the story of an orphan boy who had been adopted by a family in Rome, not just any family, but that of a Count Sperone owner of Sperone Aviation, and one of the richest men in all Italy. Why would the count adopt a poor boy from an orphanage in Ireland? Father Brennan wondered to himself, shuffling through the papers.

And there was yet another letter, from Pope Pius XI, authorizing the adoption. He read the name on the file: Ariel Angelucci. It was a name vaguely familiar. Then he remembered; in the past few days he had received two letters requesting information about Ariel Angelucci. The name was on the long list of materials he needed to look for. Now, quite by accident, he had found the file. The father blessed himself thanking Saint Jude, the patron saint of lost causes, for his good fortune.

His curiosity considerably aroused, Father Brennan went through the papers again, wondering why two people were suddenly seeking information about this person, and what was their connection to him? He found that the first request had come from a lawyer in Canada. Apparently the wreckage of the cargo ship that Ariel Angelucci had been on when it went down in Lake Erie in 1942 had recently been discovered by divers. Refusing to believe Ariel was dead, his aunt, who died three years ago, before the *Morgan Sidney* was found, had left him half of her large farm in Canada, currently worth a sizable sum of money. When his twin brother Caliban who had been left the other half died, if he had no heirs, the full legacy was to pass on to Ariel if he could be found. Papers discovered in a waterproof pouch next to what was believed to be Ariel's remains gave a clue that the long missing brother had resided in Rome for a time, and might have produced an offspring that was still alive.

The second query had come from the local secretary of the United Workers Party. Father Brennan had wondered about this request, as he rarely got letters from political parties looking for people. While he did not keep up with the subtleties of Italian politics, which seemed to change daily, Father Brennan was aware of the fight the United Workers were putting up against the current Count Sperone's appointment to an important government position. Could the request for the Ariel Angelucci file have something to do with this?

"Father Leon, I have just accidentally found one of the files that we have had requests for," Father Brennan announced, "the one on a person named Angelucci."

The ancient face of Father Leon, long used to working in these dim archives, not often seeing the sky for weeks, was not a face given to expression; however, Father Brennan observed a slight break in the mask, if only for an instant, a look of concern.

"Very good, Father Brennan," Father Leon muttered in English, annoyed that his colleague's Italian was so poor that he couldn't even converse in it yet he had been assigned to work on this complicated search with him. "Cardinal Sabatini has informed me that the prime minister's secretary has asked about this file . . . I will see that it gets to him."

Several days later, finished with the year 1927, and wanting to return the papers before going on to 1928, Father Brennan asked Father Leon if the prime minister's secretary was finished with the Ariel Angelucci file he had given him: "I would like to put it back in the vault, after first responding to the two additional people who have written for information."

Father Leon stared straight ahead, peering through his half-glasses at the paper he was reading, and answered only with: "What do you mean, father?"

"Excuse me father, I need to return the file I gave you last week, the one concerning Ariel Angelucci." Father Brennan said, speaking slowly, and wondering if he should restate the question as best he could in Italian.

"You must to be mistaken, father . . . you gave to me no such file."

"But I remember that I did. . . ."

"No . . . you did not."

He knew his superior was lying. He clearly recalled his actions from that day. An unaccustomed feeling of angry confusion rose in Father Brennan's heart. Without saying anything more, he quietly left the room. It was almost time for vespers; his anger would compose itself, and subside with the calming influence of his prayers.

He was sitting in the Sistine Chapel, looking up at the grand masterpiece that surrounded him. Father Brennan liked to come here and watch the groups of tourists lifting their faces to the ceiling, pointing to things with upraised hands. Yet he found something grievously embarrassing about these splendid and triumphal images. He saw something painful and unpleasant in the mural, which even at the summit of its success, Father Brennan felt, threatened to disintegrate into parody.

Father Brennan lowered his eyes. He was only a humble priest who had spent most of his life in Ireland, who was he to criticize the masterwork of an acknowledged genius? Nor was he to criticize the workings of the church. He meant to examine his conscience. Father Leon had lied. He distinctly remembered giving him the Ariel Angelucci file. Why had his partner denied it? Perhaps he had just forgotten about the file. Or was there some other reason?

The good father knew he should not question his superiors, but Ariel Angelucci was one of his own, a boy from The Saint Romanus Home. He decided to contact the attorney from Canada and tell him what information he remembered from his quick reading of the file. As for the other request, the United Workers Party, he was not sure what their motives were so he would tell them nothing.

Father Brennan hesitated; he would write the letter to the Canadian lawyer from his residence, on his own stationary, as a precaution. But first he needed the address. Going alone to the archivists' office, Father Brennan went to the cabinet where he kept the requests, intending to copy down the lawyer's address, but could not find the letter. He was sure he had filed it properly, and made a thorough search of other places it might be. Then he recalled the request from the United Workers Party. Checking the file cabinet again, Father Brennan discovered that letter also was missing.

He walked out of the room and into the dark passage, trying his best, with a tolerant impatience, to understand what had happened.

Twenty-one

Let us be jocund. Will you troll the catch
You taught me but whilere?

Shakespeare *The Tempest III.ii.*

Upon his arriving in Locarno John Vigilia's natural sense of direction, aided by a map that he had picked up on the way, enabled him to quickly find number 33 Via Flaviano, the place where his grandson said Ariel Angelucci was supposed to be living. He parked the VW in the loading zone out front. John did not get out, but sat inside his car, studying the building, considering what he should do next. The once grand stone structure, perhaps built in the 1800's as a residence, now served as a modest hotel called Albergo Flaviano. Could this be the correct place? he wondered. The man John had met in the cathedral in Como had assured him that this was the address of Angelucci's apartment. Had their meeting in the Duomo just been a set up to send him off on a wild goose chase?

As it was already early evening, John decided that it would make sense to go inside the Albergo Flaviano and ask for a room. Unfortunately, out front were three rather steep steps his battered body had to negotiate before entering the small and musty smelling lobby. No one was at the front desk so he rang the bell. After a short wait, John rang again. A rather short man, dressed in a well-tailored dark three piece suit, appearing a bit out of breath, arrived from a room behind the counter:

"Buona sera, signore . . ."

"Excuse me. Do you speak English?" John asked.

"Yes, and American," the man said smiling condescendingly at his visitor, "I also am fluent in German, Spanish, French, Greek and Italian. You are now presently in Ticino, Switzerland's southernmost canton, which borders on Italy. Therefore, you will observe that Italian is the language most commonly used by the local people."

"I understand. Thank you for the information . . . but unfortunately I can't speak Italian."

"I wouldn't expect you to. Americans rarely speak anything other than their own language. It's a kind of superiority complex. I could tell by your accent that you are from the United States, probably New York, the state, not the city; upstate more precisely."

The man stared at John waiting for him to confirm his observation. The desk clerk had hit the nail on the head, but he just couldn't give him the satisfaction of admitting it. The man was being too smug. "I'm from Pennsylvania," John Vigilia said, not a lie; he had actually been born in that state.

"Pennsylvania? Hummm. . . ." the clerk pondered. "Then would you say a few more words, please?"

"I would like a room for tonight, if you have one. And I will probably be staying for another week," John said, purposely trying to sound like someone from nowhere.

"Yes, Pennsylvania . . . most definitely the northeastern part of the state. Perhaps somewhere even near the border with New York . . . say near that place that is famous for its gliders . . . what is its name?"

"Elmira," John said roughly, annoyed at being pegged so accurately by someone he had only just met. "So do you have a room or not?"

"No. I am sorry, sir. There are no rooms available for tonight . . . we are full," the clerk said adjusting his wire-framed glasses with his index finger. "We are also full for all of next week."

"Oh, that's unfortunate," John said, trying to be nice. "Would you perhaps know of anyplace else?"

"I am sorry . . . it will be difficult. You have come at a very bad time, you see. You should have made a reservation. You see, next week is the performance art festival, a very popular event, and all the rooms have been previously booked."

"But I am here to participate in the festival." John Vigilia protested. "That's why I've come to Locarno."

"In that case, you should go to the festival office. They have reserved all the space, and would have a room listed for you there."

"And where is the festival office?"

"It is on the square in the middle of town, in the Congress Center. However, I am afraid you cannot go there now, because it has closed. They will open again tomorrow morning at nine o'clock."

"Then do you know of anyplace I can get a room just for tonight?"

"Not in the center of town. You must go and look for a place outside of Locarno."

"I passed some small hotels out by the airport; do you think I just might find something there?"

"Which airport? There are two."

"Two airports?"

"Yes. One on either side of town. If you came from the east you passed the larger one, on the Piano di Magadino, there is a smaller airport to the west in Ascona."

"I came from Munich."

"Then try the towns of Tenora and Gordola, they are on the way to Magadino but not as far . . . I am sure you can find something there just for tonight."

"Thank you," John said. He started to leave, and then turned back. "I have one more question. . . ."

"Yes?"

"Do you have a guest staying here . . . an elderly man, named Ariel Angelucci?"

The desk clerk looked John in the eyes, and studied him carefully for a few seconds before answering: "Why do you ask me about this man?"

"Oh . . . ," John stammered, searching for a believable lie. "My father told me to look him up . . . they were friends back in America."

"There is no one staying at this hotel by that name . . . ."

Something in the clerks tone made John think the man was lying; he pressed on. "Oh? When I was in Rome, my good friend Count Sperone told me that Ariel Angelucci might be staying here."

The man's eyes, magnified by his spectacles, opened even wider: "You are a friend of the Count Sperone?"

"Yes . . . and he told me Ariel Angelucci would be here," John Vigilia repeated.

"Of course. As I said," the clerk went on in a rather unctuous tone, "there is no one staying at this *hotel* by that name, but that does not mean he is not here. Some years ago this building was converted to a hotel from a villa. All the rooms are now part of the hotel, except for a private apartment on the top floor; in the back, there are some individual rooms attached to that . . . this is where Signore Angelucci lives."

"Oh! The Count didn't tell me that . . . I guess he didn't know."

The clerk frowned and gave his visitor an incredulous look. "But he should know, Signore Angelucci has lived here for many years . . . and the count's family has owned the building for an even longer time. And this apartment is where the count stays when he is in Locarno."

John realized now that he had made a slip. It was one of his faults to always say more than he needed to. The desk clerk regarded him with suspicion.

"Well . . . I'd better be going," John said trying to seem casual. "Hey, but I can't go off without saying hello to my dad's old friend Ariel. Do you think he might be in?"

"Signore Angelucci left sometime earlier this evening. I have not seen him since. He does not keep regular hours, so I have no idea when he will be returning."

"I see . . . can I leave him a message?" John fished a notepad from his pocket and began writing.

"I'm sorry, sir, but I don't believe that Signore Angelucci can read English."

"He can't?"

"Not that I know of, that's why I wondered when you said he had been a friend of your father in America."

"Ariel was born in Chicago. . . ."

"I didn't know that. I have not ever heard him speak English in all the years I have been here,"

"Well then . . . can you give him a note from me, in Italian or whatever language it is that he speaks?"

"Yes," the clerk said, producing his own pen and paper. "Tell me what you want to say,"

"Can you tell him a pilot from America has greetings for him from his brother Caliban in Canada, and that I will be in touch with him tomorrow, when I find out where I am going to be staying? Can you do that for me please?"

"I would be happy to do this for you. And who should I say the message is from?"

"From John," he paused, "ah . . . Sebastian. Yes, tell him John Sebastian is looking for him."

"*Buona notte,* Mister . . . Sebastian," the clerk said smiling, and then nodding curtly.

"Good evening," John said as he turned and began slowly hobbling away on his bad leg.

Stepping smartly out from behind the reception counter, the clerk quickly grabbed the front door and held it open: "Here, let me get that for you, I see that you are limping . . . and your wrist is bandaged. Have you had an accident?"

"I fell off a bicycle. . . ."

"You must be careful, Mister . . . Sebastian, accidents can be quite fatal."

"Yes . . . I will be very careful. Thank you and good night," John said exiting the hotel. He did not like the way the clerk sounded when he had reminded him that accidents could be fatal.

The weather had changed completely during the brief period John had been inside the hotel. A cloudy evening was giving way to a clear night. Every trace of the streaked plumage of a fiery sunset had been swept away. A full moon hung in the empty sky, taking on the appearance of a weaker sun, presenting not the sense of brilliant moonshine, but rather of a paler daylight.

John Vigilia sat in his car for a few moments contemplating what had just transpired in the lobby of the Albergo Flaviano. Why had he given the clerk the fictitious name of Sebastian, the name of his dead pilot friend Adrian, when he had suspected that the clerk was on to his scam? And was he finally going to meet Ariel Angelucci tomorrow? Would he find out if the man had really been Lindbergh's secret copilot? Through the window in the lobby door he could see the desk clerk speaking into the telephone. Was he calling Count Sperone? Relax; John told himself, the clerk was probably only talking to someone who had just called looking for a room. Whatever was going to happen tomorrow would happen. He started the car; pulled into the street, and then headed in what he thought must be the direction for Magadino.

Despite having conducted an exhaustive search, John did not find a room for the night. With no other options, he ended up sleeping a very uncomfortable sleep, his bruised body curled up on the cramped back seat of the rented Volkswagen that he had parked in the street in front of the Congress Center. He wanted to be there as soon as the festival office opened.

At 9:05, after observing a woman go in the door, John went in after her and inquired about his accommodations. To his great relief, John found that his name was indeed on a list in the computer. His reservation had been made. Things were going well, he thought. Then, to his chagrin John Vigilia learned that he had been booked in to share a room with Hans Hockenheim. This, he told himself, would just not do.

"Isn't there anywhere else?" John pleaded.

"I will check it for you," the secretary said, whizzing her mouse across a pad and consulting her computer screen. "Yes, there is left just one room in the whole town . . . in the Grand Hotel Sans Souci . . . the penthouse suite."

"I'll take it!" John said, without asking the price, anything would be better than bunking with that madman Hans.

The woman gave him a reservation slip, and then wrote down the directions on another piece of paper. Thanking her profusely, John Vigilia turned and hurriedly limped out the door.

The Grand Hotel Sans Souci, which had been completed only three years previous, stood on crooked street on a hill overlooking the town. As its name implied it was "grand" and done in a French style. John had, he believed, a rather acute sense of form, and the appearance of the Sans Souci annoyed him greatly. The building was much too massive for the site it was on, and full of unnecessary adornments provided by the architect to ape the many older buildings around it, and its façade was a bit too formidable for the narrow street it fronted on. It looked as if it had been designed for some lido on the Riviera, but the architect had accidentally shipped the plans to the wrong place.

At the front desk John presented his reservation from the festival office. The clerk looked at it and quoted him the price of the room in Swiss francs. Newly arrived in

Switzerland, John was not too familiar with the exchange rate. He did a quick money conversion in his head which, John thought, he must not have done right, since the answer he came up with was a very lot of money. Then John Vigilia recalled telling the clerk that he was staying for a week. John assumed he must have been given the weekly rate, which made the number seem quite reasonable, so he accepted. The desk clerk made an impression of his now hemorrhaging credit card, and handed it back to his newest guest with a smile:

"Thank you, Monsieur Vigilia; I hope that you are to enjoy your staying with us. The boy will show you to your room."

The "Penthouse Suite", was about the size of the entire second floor of John's converted carriage house back in Elmira. It had two bedrooms, with and adjoining bath and Jacuzzi, a small kitchenette, and a large sitting room with two balconies. The front terrace looked out over the town and the Lago Maggiore beyond. A little way up the lake John could make out the airplanes rising from the tarmac at the airport in Magadino, where the Bücker Jungmann that he was to fly was supposed to be hangared. He would go there tomorrow to check it out. From the side terrace he could see Monti della Trinita, and the other mountains of the Alps rising behind it. Tired from his trip, and lack of sleep last night, and not having had a proper bath since Como, he decided to try out the Jacuzzi.

Relaxing in the warm bubbles helped to restore John's wounded body. He felt the best he had since his bicycle accident. Popping his right hand out of the water, John flipped the pages of the Italian phrase book that he had been holding in his left. His damp finger came upon a phrase he decided to memorize. John Vigilia was not sure when he would ever use this phrase, but elected to put it in his mind as the words that best described his present situation. *Non capisco tutto, Non capisco tutto,* he repeated in his mind: I don't understand anything.

The bathroom had a glass door that opened onto the side terrace. He had left the large door open to catch the gentle breeze coming off the lake. Through the door John could see the birds hovering over the town, groups of wanderers beating their wings against the sky, birds that at home he could have identified, but here looked strange in this exotic setting. Circling and revolving in great crisscrossing spirals, their lofty flight described majestic arabesques that filled the silent sky. Some of the birds, probably gulls, floated almost immobile on calmly spread wings. Other smaller, more colorful, birds had to flap their wings mightily to maintain their flight in the currents of descending air. Watching them sweep about John sensed that there must be a fundamental order to this apparent chaos, as the birds, large and small, and some crippled ones too limping through the air in awkward one-winged flight, circled around and around, passing and eluding each other with their elliptical maneuvers, yet never colliding.

John rose up in the tub, put down his phrase book and, shielding his eyes from the glare, began to study these flying things. Where did these birds come from to gather here for such a short time, then to scatter again to all four points of the compass? He wondered. Were some of these avian creatures the distant progeny of a tribe of birds that he, in his biplane, might have raced across the clear sky in another time and another place? He marveled at the instinct of these birds, they were not empty and lifeless inside, devoting all their brain power to their external adornment, nature took care of their plumage. Were they, in their carefree way, aware of their attachment to a god, whom that expelled tribe had implanted in their soul, in order that they might return to their ancient motherland on their last day?

The telephone rang. Dripping water in his nakedness, John Vigilia padded across the room to answer it: "Hello. . . ."

It was the front desk. “Mister Vigilia? There is a telephone call for you; just a moment please . . . I will to put it through.”

“Hello? Hello. . . .” No one answered.

“Hello, Mister Vigilia . . . I am sorry sir, your caller seems to have hung up. Perhaps they will to call back again later.”

“Thank you. . . .” John said, wondering who could have learned so quickly that he was staying at this hotel. The thought made him uncomfortable. Was it his friend in the black Alfa Romeo checking on him?

Trying to put this question from his mind, John went back into the bathroom and capped off his Jacuzzi with a cold shower. Then he wrapped himself in a towel, took a bottle of mineral water and a can of cocktail nuts from the Frigibar and moved out to one of the lounge chairs on his front terrace. Gazing around at the unobstructed view, he realized that his hotel was the highest building around. He looked down on everyone, and no one looked down on him, except for the few houses that hung above him on the mountain sides, which were quite far away. Remembering the sensation of making love to Miranda in the full sun on the roof of the villa in Como, John Vigilia unwrapped his towel and sat there naked.

The sun felt good on his battered and worn body. John wondered why he had never sunbathed nude before. But then he had never spent that many hours sunbathing anyway. The only time he was ever out in the sun he usually was seated in the cockpit of his biplane.

The thought of his biplane opened a whole box of memories that he had tried to put behind him. These now came spilling out: the death of his wife; his dull life at the college in Elmira; the abandoned airport in Canada where he had landed to get out of the storm, but could not find again. John wondered what had led him on this strange quest for a man who was supposed to have been Lindbergh’s secret co-pilot. Moreover, he feared that he might really be in some kind of danger because of it. And who was it that had called him while he was in the Jacuzzi, and then hung up when he answered? He had no way of knowing where his search was taking him, and was afraid because of this. At the moment John Vigilia feared that he was a blind man backing into the future, for better or for worse.

John tried to turn his mind back to the present, the terrace, the view, the fresh air, but the past kept returning. He had been able to shut down each of these old files, as soon as they were opened. But then he opened one that he had been lately pretending did not exist. Nevertheless, it was something that he had thought about every night since leaving Como. Try as he might to not think about her, John Vigilia sat there remembering Miranda.

Sensing that his fatigue was catching up to him, John came in from the terrace and laid down for a nap. He didn't take him long to fall asleep. Not having set his travel alarm John did not wake up until after six o'clock. It was too late to go to the airport as he had planned, so John got dressed and went out to look for a place to eat. Finding himself a bit too early for dinner by Italian standards, and no restaurants open, he decided to go by the Albergo Flaviano, and ask if Ariel Angelucci had responded to the message he left yesterday.

The same clerk that he had talked to last night was on duty again. "Good evening," he said apparently remembering that John was an American.

"*Buona sera,*" John said, rolling the "r" aggressively. If he was not good at mastering the grammar of a language, he did give his all to imitating the sound. "Remember me from last evening?"

"Yes. Mister Sebastian . . . isn't it?"

"No . . . I mean yes. . . ." John had started to say: No it's Vigilia, but then remembered that he had given the clerk a phony name. "Did you give my message to Signore Angelucci?"

"Yes, I gave him your message in Italian . . . exactly what you told me as I wrote it down. . . .."

"And?"

"And he gave me this note for you."

John Vigilia took the note and unfolded it. "But it's in Italian. I can't read it."

"Would you like me to translate it for you?"

"Yes, please . . . if you would."

"It says: 'My dear Mister Sebastian, I do not know who you are. I have no brother in Canada. I do not wish to meet you.' That's all it says. He only signed with his initials, A A. I am sorry Mister Sebastian . . . but that is all there is." The clerk folded the paper and handed it back to John.

"Okay, thanks," John said. "Look, I have got to see Ariel Angelucci. Is he in now? Maybe I can talk to him. . . ."

"But he doesn't speak English, Mister Sebastian."

"You're sure of that. . . ."

"I asked him . . . and he said he did not. That is all I know Mr. Sebastian."

Obviously confused and disappointed, John turned and walked out the door, but with a little less pain in his gait than yesterday. As he headed down the street in search of a restaurant, he secretly wished that he would come upon the gaudy lights of a McDonald's or Burger King. He was tired of things foreign, of struggling with menus that he could barely read, of ordering things he really didn't want. The adventure was wearing out; he just wanted to go back home.

Having satisfied his hunger, John Vigilia returned to his grand suite in the Grand Hotel Sans Souci. Lying in bed staring up at the ceiling, his mind once again mulled over the recent turn of events. He had found Ariel Angelucci, well sort of, but Angelucci didn't want to meet him, nor did he even speak English, and probably didn't have a twin brother living on a farm in Canada.

John decided that was the end of that. This whole business was doubtless a product of his own too vivid imagination, which must have gone into overdrive from not having done anything creative for such a long time. When he got back to Elmira he would start working on a book, John told himself, whether anyone wanted to publish it or not. His search for Lindbergh's alleged copilot was over. He would enjoy the rest of this week in the beautiful lake city of Locarno, fly the Jungmann in Hans Hockenheim's performance event, try to collect the money he was owed, and then he would return to the quiet of upstate New York.

There were enough pieces of his life that he needed to put together back there. School would be just about to start when he returned. Maybe he would still have the possibility to cancel his leave, and bury himself in his job. He would start going to those faculty meetings he had been skipping, and working on those committees that he had been bowing out of. If he sold the Jungmann he could buy a sailboat; Seneca Lake was not that far away. No, John thought reconsidering the idea; a boat would be just like the airplane, a lot of money and time spent for nothing.

Maybe he should take up painting again. He had gotten rather into drawing that airplane motor back in Como, which he now realized Miranda had only watched him draw to see if he really could do what he had said he was going to do. As for Miranda, he had to stop thinking about her, to put her out of his mind. True, they had made love, but she had told him clearly it would be only that one time. John Vigilia was beginning to doze off. That's it, he thought, suddenly coming back wide awake, when he got home he would buy a bicycle. He had had fun riding Eva's bicycle in Munich. They didn't cost that much, and had extremely low maintenance. Then John remembered the tragic ending to his last bicycle ride. If he bought a bicycle, he would also buy a helmet. With that thought fully implanted in his head, John Vigilia finally fell off to sleep.

The morning sun falling on his face awakened John from what had been a fitful night. He took another hot shower to relieve his aches and then dressed and went down for breakfast. The room was much bigger than the breakfast room at his hotel in Rome. John looked around, but did not recognize anyone. Nor did anyone follow him when, after breakfast, he went down to the below ground parking lot to get his car to go to the airport. Based on all the movies he had seen, if anyone was going to take him out this was the sinister place where it would be done. Finding no one down there at the moment but him, John did a quick check of the other cars. To his relief he did not find a black Alfa Romeo with a damaged right front fender parked in any of the spaces.

At the airport in Magadino, John found, as he had been promised, a bright yellow Bücker Jungmann sitting in the main hangar. The biplane was almost identical to his except for the all yellow color paint scheme and the red band with the white cross of Switzerland on the tail. The registration number painted in black on the side of the fuselage was H-BUZZ.

"You have flown a Jungmann before, Mr. Vigilia?" the chief flight instructor asked after John had presented himself. The instructor's name was also Hans, which John did not take as a good omen.

"Yes, unfortunately I don't have my log books with me, they're back in the states . . . but I have over 400 hours."

"In total time?" the man said, sounding impressed.

"No, that's just in Jungmanns. My total hours are closer to 3000."

"Four hundred hours in Jungmanns!"

"Yes, I own a Jungmann, I fly it in competitions and air shows," John Vigilia said, producing a photograph of his airplane from his wallet.

"Of course, I have seen photographs of this very airplane in some aviation magazines from America . . . you are the famous 'Stunt Flying Professor,' yes?"

The chief pilot was further impressed when John produced his Air Transport Pilot license, and a zero foot altitude waiver issued by the FAA.

With credentials such as this, John Vigilia expected that his check out flight would be rather perfunctory. His takeoffs and landings were magnificent, and he had demonstrate the basic aerobatic maneuvers, even putting together a sequence that included a square loop, and a loop with a snap-roll on top, all maneuvers Hans said could not be accomplished in a Jungmann. John was surprised, therefore, when at the conclusion of his check out Hans had not signed him off for solo flight, but had scheduled him for another hour of dual instruction on the next day.

"You have been in some kind of accident, that gives you trouble Mr. Vigilia?" the chief pilot asked, having noticed the bandage on John's wrist, and the fact that he had gotten into the cockpit rather gingerly.

Nonplussed by the man's question, John admitted to himself that while in his mind he had felt that his flying was fine, if a little rusty, his sprained right hand had made handling the control stick difficult, and he had from time to time flown left handed. And his bruised right leg and sprained ankle had made him tentative with the right rudder. Also he kept over-revving the engine, which all competition pilots did with their Lycoming O-360s to get that extra bit of power they needed. The engines were not about to blow up, as Hans expressed his fear back on the ground, but running them beyond their limit voided the warranty, and reduced the time-between-overhaul from 2000 hours to 700. Hans would pull back the throttle every time John Vigilia over-speeded the engine, even if they were in the middle of a maneuver, further destroying his rhythm. All of this had probably not inspired confidence in Hans, the instructor, who was therefore reluctant to let John Vigilia go out alone in their rare old biplane.

In the afternoon John checked out in another airplane, a Piper PA-18, a newer version of the venerable "Cub" with a 150 horsepower engine. The organizers of the festival, upon learning that he was a pilot, had asked John Vigilia if he would be willing to take some photographers up for aerial photographs. The PA-18, with its high wing, was perfect for this, unlike the Jungmann, whose bottom wing blocked most of the view below. The other advantage to the ubiquitous Piper was that it rented for one third the price of Jungmann. Hans had signed him off for solo in the PA-18, an airplane that John had only six previous hours experience in, after a mere three takeoffs and landings. This caused John to wonder if perhaps Hans hadn't scheduled him for another hour in the Jungmann so that he might learn something about aerobatics from him.

On the way back from the airport, John Vigilia stopped by the festival office to turn in the bills for the hour and a half hour of dual instruction and aircraft rentals. At least the people at the airport had expected him, and hadn't asked for him to pay with his credit card. Perhaps everything he had already spent would be reimbursed as Hans Hockenheim had promised.

The festival office also had a message for John. It was from Hans, who had called from Munich to tell him that he would be arriving in Locarno the very next day on the three o'clock train, and that John should be at the station with the car to meet him. This riled John as he was not looking forward to seeing Hans again, and certainly did not intend to become his chauffeur.

With the rest of the day to himself, John Vigilia decided to go back to his hotel and have another soak in the Jacuzzi, and then sit in the sun for a bit before going out to find a place to eat. The way back took him by the Albergo Flaviano. For a brief moment John considered stopping and trying to contact Ariel Angelucci once again, but then reminded himself he had decided last night that his search for the man was over. Angelucci obviously was not the person he was supposed to be, or at any rate he had no interest in meeting with him. John drove on past the hotel.

Turning the corner, John braked hard to avoid an elderly man crossing the street. The man did not acknowledge the close call, but went on walking, with a surprisingly graceful, almost feline gait. John Vigilia stared after the man. There was something familiar about him. It was only when the man disappeared into a shop entrance that he realized the man he had just almost hit was an exact double of the old man he met on the farm when he had made his emergency landing in Canada. His was not a face one easily forgot, with his wild and recalcitrant shocks of gray hair bristling in irregular tufts from his warts and eyebrows, giving him the appearance of a nervous porcupine. John needed to stop—to contact this old man. He looked around for a parking space, but he was in the heart of the downtown now, and there were none to be found.

Finally coming upon a space some two blocks on, he parked his car. Gamely limping on his bad leg, John hurried back to the doorway that he had seen the man enter earlier. Pulling open the heavy glass door, John was surprised to find that it did not lead into a small shop as he had anticipated, but was one of the side entrances to a large department store. John Vigilia was in the women's cosmetic section. A pleasant young woman smiled at him from behind the counter:

"*Posso servirle?*"

"Did you see a rather strange-looking old man come in here a few minutes ago?" John blurted out in the only language he knew.

"I sorry, I do not to speak English . . . Italian? German? French?"

"Never mind," John said rudely, his eyes scanning the milling crowd in front of him. Not seeing the old man, John began searching the vast, crowded, space. After completing a tour of the first floor, and not coming upon his quarry, John took the escalator to the second, and then the third. Forty-five minutes of searching later, John left the store without finding the man he had seen crossing the street. All was not wasted, however, as he did spend some of the time buying a new pair of pants to replace the ones that had been ruined by the Munich bicycle accident. When John finally returned to his car, he found a parking ticket on the window. He was not sure what he had done wrong. But he was sure that the man he had almost run over, and then looked for but not found was the elusive Ariel Angelucci.

Back at his hotel, John tried on the new pants, turning around and studying himself in the mirror. They were nice pants, slightly fuller than what he usually wore, with a little more flair, a kind of European cut. He looked forward to wearing them to faculty meetings when he got back to Elmira. Wouldn't they be surprised by his new look. John had spent three times the amount of money for the pants as he normally would have, and had charged them to his bloated credit card. Perhaps he should give the bill to Hans as part of his expenses; John considered as he slipped out of the pants and stepped into the hot and bubbling Jacuzzi.

Outside the open window the birds were whirling with more than their usual frenzy. John Vigilia could see storm clouds building over the mountain and the sky was beginning to darken. The distant sounds of thunder caused him to hurry with his bath.

Sitting on the balcony to dry off, John could feel the temperature on his naked body dropping. The late afternoon sunshine was being displaced by the dark clouds moving in over the town, coating the maze of houses below with the opaque gray light from the approaching storm. Automobiles rushed to and fro to get where they were going before the arrival of the coming deluge. A sudden gust of wind smoothed down the sounds of the traffic, melding it temporarily into the ominous din now spreading over the sea of tile roofs in the milky air of the departing afternoon. He leaned against the balcony rails, bent to capture the distant roar as the thunder advanced down from the mountains. Then the storm was upon the Sans Souci with all its destructive force. John Vigilia retreated into the safety of his penthouse, happy that he needed only to move backward a step or two to be out of the fury, not circling in his airplane desperately searching for a place to land.

The rain drumming on the balcony quickly turned the deck to a river. John stood naked at the open door, the water splashing at his bare feet. Enormous black clouds formed above the city, their ragged underbelly descending in powerful spirals. The sky was being swept lengthwise by the sweep of wind, cut into vast lines of silvery-white energy tensed to the breaking point. Divided into magnetic fields, and trembling with discharges, the clouds, full of electricity, traced the diagrams of their power on the surface of the lake. The enormous beech trees across from the hotel stood with their arms upraised, howling a warning of coming disaster.

The wind intensified in force and violence. John struggled to shut the sliding door to the balcony. The storm had begun to build a many-storied tower over the lake, a green-black ziggurat, growing relentlessly upward, shooting out long galleries of lightning, which raced amid great claps of thunder, through immense imaginary structures, that emerged only to collapse again into the formless atmosphere.

The penthouse trembled gently, the pictures rattled on the walls, the sliding door shone with the illuminated reflection of the interior. There was something out there.

John Vigilia wiped the mist of his breath off the window, as he had wiped clear the windscreen of his Bücker.

It was something dark and large. Was it the rocks at Long Point? He had never flown over them, so had no idea how high they might be. John was hoping for a sandy beach. Pulling back the power, he approached this darkness slowly. It seemed to be going away. Was it a hallucination? The blackness was gone. John increased the power and slide into the mist, whatever it was he did not want to loose it. Anything was better than the fog and wind, and now it had begun to rain. There it was again, the blackness. Then John saw lights. He pulled back on the power again. He was overtaking it. The shape became clear; it was a ship, a large ship, perhaps a cargo boat. He crept in alongside it. He was barely clear of the water, the biplane actually below the ship's bridge. John Vigilia could see the name and the port: Morgan Sidney, Liverpool.

There were men on deck, pointing at him. He lifted his left hand and waved. The crewman waved back. John remembered the story of Lindbergh shouting from the Spirit of Saint Louis to ask directions of fisherman off the coast of Ireland. "Which way to Long Point?" he yelled through his cupped hand. John could barely make out the response of the crewman over the wind and waves, but he was sure that he heard "Long Point," and they were all pointing toward his tail, behind him. Had he somehow gotten off course and passed Long Point in the fog? Was he now flying down the center of the lake instead of across it? He checked his fuel gauge. He had only a quarter of a tank remaining. John looked at his watch. According to the time that had passed, he should still have half a tank remaining. His mind was muddled. He could not reconcile the difference in the fuel consumption. He had been fighting a head wind, but running at partial throttle for a good bit of the time. One thing John did know was that he needed to find land, and hopefully an airport very soon.

The Morgan Sidney had slipped back into the fog. He looked up. Overhead John saw sunshine, a slight break in the clouds. He pushed the throttle to the stop and started climbing in a tight spiral.

Lightning flashed again, very near to the window. Like a frightened child, instinct made John dive into one of the beds. There he curled up, and pulled the covers over his head. The storm continued, off and on, for most of the night.

The next day John Vigilia awoke to clear skies and brilliant sunshine. He felt rested, and his body was in much less pain. After driving all the way to Magadino, however, John found out that he could not fly at his appointed time of 10 o'clock because the airport, which was built on a flood plain next to the Ticino River, was covered with standing water from last night's storm. He was told the water was expected to be gone by afternoon. There was a time available to fly the Jungmann at three o'clock, but that was when he was supposed to pick up Hans Hockenheim at the railway station. Undecided about what he should do, John went back to the hotel to take another nap.

Twenty-two

Where the bee sucks, there suck I:
In a cowslip's bell I lie;
There I crouch when owls do cry
On the bat's back I do fly. . . .

Shakespeare *The Tempest V.i.*

The train bringing Hans Hockenheim from Munich rolled into the station at Locarno exactly on time. Knowing resistance would be useless, John Vigilia was there waiting on the platform as he had been instructed to be. To the casual observer it must have appeared the two men were old friends, meeting again after a long absence. They had embraced, patted each other on the back, and exchanged the usual questions and the usual answers, nothing out of the ordinary. But the truth of the matter was that John had gone there without wishing to, and was acting against his will, barely able to maintain his civility.

"Veeegailyaaah! It's good to see you again my old friend!" Hans shouted, wrapping his arms around John and giving him a great big hug, a European custom which John was not yet comfortable with, preferring the firmly insincere grip of an American handshake.

John's body, still rather sore from the bicycle accident, flinched at the squeeze. "Good to see you too," he replied patting Hans on the back, trying to pretend they had last parted as best friends.

"What have you been up to you sly bastard?" Hans joked, pounding John on his tender right shoulder. "I bet you have been fucking everything here that walks, ha, ha, ha. . . ."

Hans laughed, and John caught himself laughing too, again infected by the German's convulsed, childishly stupid way of laughing.

"No . . . but I have found the Jungmann, and flown it dual for one hour," John answered, massaging his shoulder.

"*Ja, ja.* So you are all ready now?"

"Well I was supposed to fly today . . . but the field was flooded. I will probably need to take another hour of dual instruction tomorrow. . . ."

"Instructions!" Hans exclaimed as they were getting into the car. "Why should you need instructions . . . that costs extra money doesn't it? I thought you were the master of this airplane. That's why I hired you."

"Well . . . the chief pilot is very thorough. I guess, since he doesn't know me, he wants to be sure I can handle the airplane."

"I know this chief pilot . . . his name is Hans also. He is an asshole. I was going to get him to fly the airplane before you. Now the fucking bastard wants to make more money off me."

"Where are you staying, Hans?" John asked as he pulled away from the station.

"I don't know . . . where are you staying? I am at the same place that you are."

"I'm at the Sans Souci."

"Shit! How did you get put in there? It must have been some mistake. We are supposed to be at the Albergo Flaviano. The Sans Souci is too fucking expensive. . . ."

"No . . . I got a good deal, the man at the desk said one thousand dollars for nine days . . . that only comes to about $112 per day, which is more than I wanted to pay . . . but you should see the place, I've got the whole penthouse, a Jacuzzi and two balconies."

"What! Are you fucking dumb? What language did the fucking desk clerk speak to you in?"

"Well . . . he used some English, but spoke mostly French. . . ."

"And you understood perfectly what he was saying?"

"Well, not exactly." John admitted.

"You are a stupid fucking idiot! The penthouse is not one thousand dollars for nine days . . . the fucking penthouse is one thousand dollars for each day! I don't pay for this . . . you must leave there today. You can pay for those days you have stayed yourself. . . ."

Hans was like this, sometimes subject to spasms of singular common sense that were not otherwise part of his normal character. John Vigilia suddenly understood the huge mistake that he had made. That he had been so stupid caused him to resent this whole undertaking. John felt as if he had fallen into some kind of trap. He wished there was a door somewhere that he could open wide and walk through and be back in Elmira. He had only agreed to work with Hans to earn a little money, and with the plan of coming to Locarno to be able to perhaps find Ariel Angelucci. Now, in addition to the fortune he had already spent, he had had his credit card charged for two thousand dollars for two night's rooms, and also one hundred and ten for the dinner he took in the dining room rather than go out in the rain.

They stopped back at the Sans Souci so John could check out. Only Hans' loud diatribe in fiery German prevented the manager from charging John Vigilia for a third night, as he had returned well after the noon check-out time.

"You will like the Albergo Flaviano, Veegeelah," Hans said, "I stay there every year for this festival; it is very nice . . . and not expensive. The desk clerk knows me."

"I can't go to the Albergo Flaviano!" John exclaimed, suddenly in a panic.

"And why not?"

"The desk clerk knows me too . . . though not as John Vigilia, but as John Sebastian."

"And so how is this fucking confusion come about?"

"I . . . ah, was looking for someone who was supposed to be staying there," John said, grasping for a believable lie. "I mean I had a message to give to him from someone else, a man named Sebastian, from back home."

"So?"

"When I left the message the clerk thought it was from me so he kept calling me Mister Sebastian . . . and I didn't bother to correct him," John explained trying to make it sound as if the clerk had been absentminded.

"And you come back to the Flaviano more than one times?"

"Yes . . . I came back to see if the man had got the message I left . . . and if he had left an answer for me."

"*Ja*, you are always looking for someone . . . and there is always someone looking for you . . . what the fuck are you doing Vagyalaaa . . . are you a fucking spy or something? Maybe you work for the CIA, yes?" Hans said not exactly joking as they pulled up in front of the Albergo Flaviano.

Fortunately, there had been a room cancellation and a single was available for John on the top floor. Hans seemed as happy as John was that they didn't have to share. The desk clerk took John Vigilia's credit card and made an impression. He looked at John's face strangely, however, did not make any comment about the name reading Vigilia and not Sebastian. In fact, the man acted like he did not remember John at all, although he had been there only the day before. Then John Vigilia reminded himself that this was Switzerland where people were known for their ability to be discreet.

John had to carry his suitcases up the stairs. As the Albergo Flaviano had no elevator, no porter, and no air conditioning; his battered body became painfully familiar with the hot summer afternoon. Breathing heavily and his heart pounding rapidly, John stopped at the end of the third floor hall to take in the delightful breeze that was gently blowing in through the open window.

John stood there for several minutes inhaling the cool air, before he walked down the hallway to find his room. Arriving at his door, he noticed that the door across from his, unlike all the others, had no number on it. Lettered on the door, the marks worn as if they had been on the wood for a long time was the name: A. Angelucci. A bit in shock, he read the name a second time. He felt that something must be wrong with his eyes. Sometimes, John reassured himself, even in rather difficult cases, the truth often conceived of as unobtainable, quite frequently believed to be hidden or far away, often emerged as a ripe fruit which one need only reach up and pluck.

At the other end of the hall he could hear the water running in what must be the common shower room. John gently tried the knob to the room marked A. Angelucci. It was not locked. Pushing the door open a crack, he peered into the darkness. No one seemed to be there. The curtains were drawn, the only light coming in from the hallway through the open door. John stared at the ceiling. Dangling down on strings were dozens of model airplanes; biplanes, bombers, fighters, every type from every era. Cautiously, he pushed the door open wider. The walls were covered with photographs of airplanes, and additional model airplanes were parked on every flat surface. Several bookshelves were full of books, also about airplanes. John Vigilia was about to step into the room when he felt a cold chill, the thin veil of a breeze rushed in behind him gently stirring the hanging airplanes. The entire squadron began to sway and pivot, their larger than life shadows dancing across the bed, the single empty space in the entire room. Suddenly John was aware of a silence, the shower had stopped. He quickly backed out of the room and closed the door.

Unlocking his own room, John hefted in his baggage and shut the door behind him. He stood there, listening to the sound of his own breathing, and the patter of steps coming down the hallway from the shower. The feet stopped in front of John's door, someone coughed, and then entered the room across from him and softly closed their door.

Having unpacked, washed up, and rested a bit, John went down to the lobby to meet Hans for dinner. Hans had suggested an Italian restaurant just around the corner. Although John was being smothered by a one-sided conversation from Hans as they left the hotel, he did not fail to notice the black Alfa Romeo with the slightly dented right front fender parked in the street out front.

Hardly had they been seated at the restaurant when Hans became a different person. Speaking fluent Italian, in a modest tone with no hint of his German accent, Hans was discussing the menu and the wine with the waiter. John caught the words, *per piacre*, which he knew meant please, uncharacteristically spill from Hans' lips in almost every sentence.

"In these small trattorias they usually have the only one special menu," Hans explained in an English that had now taken on an Italian accent. "It is best to take this menu. Anyhow, I have also eaten in this restaurant before and the food here is excellent . . . and reasonably priced."

Taking Hans's recommendation John also ordered the "menu of the day." The wine came, a local Valpolicella, which Hans sniffed, then sipped, then accepted saying, "Not bad . . . a little young."

Hans raised his glass to his pilot, and made a toast: "To the success of our collaboration. . . ."

John was surprised, not exactly sure what Hans meant. The artist took another sip and then put his glass down. John had expected Hans to gulp the beverage down with the same race-horse speed as he had drunk the hug steins of beer in Munich. But Hans was no longer acting the brute of a factory worker plucked from his machine to play at art; rather he had become a man of the world, a paragon of intellect, accustomed to the finer things in life. He realized now that Hans was a wind that blew many ways. John had not yet recovered from his ordeal in Munich, a city which he, for the rest of his days, would associate with the smell of beer and vomit. To that extent John's relationship with Hans was marooned in those three unfortunate days, and always would be.

The first course was soup.

"This is delicious," John said. "What is it?"

"*Minestra di Castagne* , it is made from chestnuts," Hans explained.

"Chestnuts . . . I've never had anything like this in Italian restaurants in the States. . . ."

"Having visited your country I can understand why. Except for in New York City, what are popularly called 'Italian Restaurants' are usually a joke . . . serving nothing but pizza . . . with too many toppings on a too thick crust, and gross sandwiches sometimes called submarines, or heroes, or hogies, depending on what part of the country one is in. Oh, yes, I almost forgot . . . I have also heard these sandwiches called grinders, for some local reason or other."

John was surprised to hear that Hans had visited the United States. "You're right on the mark with your analysis," he said, recalling places in Elmira with names like Pizza-A-Roma, and Pizza L'Oven. "Saluti!" John Vigilia added, in a better mood now He tried to raise his wine glass, but the muscles in his shoulder rebelled, putting him through a little seizure, a hot wire running up the back of John's neck, and with strange convulsions in his still bandaged wrist.

"Are you all right?" Hans asked, seeing John's discomfort.

"Yes, I guess so," John Vigilia said swallowing hard. "I thought all the pain from my accident was gone . . . but now something seems to have come back."

"Maybe you have a pinched nerve." Hans said, as the pasta course, *Penne con Fagioli*, was placed in front of them.

His appetite returned, John dug his fork into the tubular noodles, ignoring the pain that had suddenly seized his arm. This dish, made with beans, onion, and garlic was also something that he had never tasted previously.

Hans reached into the folder he had brought along and took out some drawings. John looked up from his food and realized that was going to be a working supper. "These are my plans for your part in the performance . . . will you be able to do all this that I have designed?"

John glanced at the combinations of figures; loops, octagons, and horizontal eights, all strung together by 45 degree and vertical lines, and then he began to laugh.

"What do you now find so humorous about my drawings?" Hans said, taken aback.

"Your drawings are not humorous . . . it's your idea." John explained. "You have not designed an artistic performance . . . but an air show. If I flew this as you designed it . . . it would look no different than the flights performed at hundreds of events at airports all over America during the summer months."

"But I have never seen an air show . . . and did not plan to design one." Hans added defensively. Then he went on. "Your flight is only a small part of the total performance, which includes dancers, and musicians, and parachutists. Ideas must be expressed in the most precise possible way. That is why I include many diverse things. If a dance looks like a race . . . it is not a race, but a dance, because it was the intent of the choreographer to create a dance. If an artist defines a urinal as a work of art, as we know has been done, then it is a work of art . . . as that was the artist's intention. I did not intend to make an air show, so no matter what you may think, your part in the performance, if you agree to do it, will not be an air show."

John smiled at Hans' answer. The stunt pilot, however, knew that there was no doubt that he was right. Whatever his aim had been Hans had, in fact, designed an air show. He looked at Hans' plans, determined to find something specifically wrong with them that he could point out, just to see what would happen when he confronted Germany's greatest performance artist with the fault. He was more than happy to have, if only in this one instance, an apparent advantage over Hans. John would be pleased to rebuke him, make a joke, pull his leg; cause Hans to be as uncomfortable as he made him, if only for a moment. He would rub against him, and Hans would attempt to walk away, but then realize that he was carrying his pilot on his shoulders. Like a parasite John Vigilia would cling to Hans questioning what were his goals, and what were his most secret weaknesses.

Wordlessly, John's empty plate was removed by the waiter, and his *piatti del giorno* was set in front of him. This was what he appreciated about European service, the quiet efficiency, so unlike the overbearing, fake chattiness of American waitpersons hustling for a tip. How many times had he cringed at the meaningless, empty statement: "Is everything okay here?" He sliced off a piece of the rich brown meat and began to chew.

"Delicious!" John said, "What is this?"

"*Filetto di Cavallo.*"

"*Cavallo?*"

"*Cavallo* is horse. . . ."

"Horse meat!" John Vigilia sputtered, using a napkin to remove the offending piece from his mouth. "Americans don't eat horse meat."

"Calm yourself, Vaggeelliaa. Here in Switzerland horse meat is quite popular. I am sure it won't hurt you, and you will not be arrested when you return to the U.S of A. You just said it was delicious. Take some more wine to wash it down."

"But it's horse meat. . . ."

"It's not exactly horse meat," Hans explained, "not like those horses you have in your Western movies. These are small, fat horses; they grow them here to eat, not to ride around on."

"Little horses? That's worse. . . ."

"You wear leather shoes, don't you? These are made from horses. Don't be so excited, Veagealeea. Here, take another glass of wine. We can make a toast"

John saw that Hans was trying to make him relax, and relaxed he was supposed to be agreeable, but the art critic in him had been aroused and was not quite ready to be so easily dissuaded from his earlier aesthetic rant.

"So this is horse meat. You and I and the chef all know it is horse meat, but if you, as an artist, define it as beef does that make it beef? No! Suppose I served you dog meat, and told you it was beef, would you still eat it if you learned it was really dog meat?"

"Must I answer all of your stupid questions now?" Hans complained, not eager to be provoked, "I would rather like to enjoy my meal. We can finish your artistic discussions tomorrow."

"Okay, But I am not yet done with the air show business. It's just that I was so surprised," John said slicing another piece of the horse meat, "I mean, here you are talking about a whole new concept of art . . . and you bring out a design that is nothing more than a good old-fashion Midwestern America air show. . . ."

"The true test of an artist," Hans explained, refilling their wine glasses, "a double test . . . is never to be surprised by anything, and always try to balance opposing ideas without betraying either one. Tomorrow we shall work together to design a performance that is totally unique . . . and one that you will concede is not just an air show. . . ."

"Forget what I said," John apologized, a bit embarrassed by his aggressiveness. "I know nothing about art, nothing about anything really, except flying, which was supposed to be my hobby."

"But you are a writer. . . ."

"And unfortunately I don't know very much about that either."

They finished their meal in relative silence, much to the disappointment of the man who had come in after them and sat down alone at the next table. Out of the corner of his eye John had seen the man reach down and covertly turn on a tape recorder in the brief case that he had set on the floor between the two tables. John wondered why the strange man was there, and whether or not he had found their rather droll conversation the least bit interesting.

Three days had passed since Hans' arrival. The festival was now in full swing. Overnight the town had become populated by performance artists, identifiable by their unkempt, long hair and uniform black attire. John had been checked out in the Jungmann and was practicing in the morning, and attending performances in the afternoons and evenings to see what the rest of the festival was all about. When he lived in New York City, John Vigilia had moved on the fringe of the art world, and had come to understand that contemporary art was painting cartoons, and soup cans, and sewing giant hamburgers made out of vinyl. As Hans had explained to him many times since they met, this "old" art was finished; the "new" mode was performance, at least for this week in the city of Locarno, Switzerland, on the shore of the Lago Maggiore.

The first performance art piece John had ever seen, the opener for the festival, was an apparently well-known Polish artist, who had stripped naked while singing religious hymns, and then beaten himself senseless with a stout wooden board. The audience applauded loudly when, after about an hour of punishing himself, the artist had finally fallen down apparently unconscious. John judged by the bloody bruises on the artist's body, and the way he had to be helped out of the room, that the Pole had not been faking any of it.

While John sat there searching for the metaphor in the act he had just witnessed: was it the Holocaust? Communism? religious persecution? the second performance began. Two young women from Ireland, already naked, one body painted blue and the other orange, pantomimed movements simulating combat, beginning with sticks and stones and working up to AK-47s and land mines. Both of the women had their pubic hairs shaven off, and John, although he tried not to, found himself concentrating visually on this part of their anatomy. He could feel his penis growing hard, but kept telling himself that this was not what the performance was about.

Nevertheless, John Vigilia did wonder why the women had decided to be nude, wearing costume disguises that did not disguise but revealed. He recalled reading that early Celtic warriors painted their bodies blue and charged naked into battle to frighten the Roman legions. Orange was the color of the Ulstermen. He wondered what they would think about this comely young woman prancing around clad only in orange body paint representing their cause. He tried to imagine the nude orange woman leading a grand parade of stern-faced and beribboned Protestant males carrying flags down the main streets of Londonderry.

The more attractive of the two Irish women, the one painted blue, reminded him of Miranda. John's mind vividly recalled the last time he had seen her. He had left her lying naked on the roof of the villa in Como as he walked away. She had told him to go, urged him in fact; for his own safety. He was beginning to understand what she had been talking about. He wondered if Miranda was still working for the contessa and, more than that, he wondered if he would ever see her again. To be sure it was not a long journey from Locarno to Como, only one lake over, however, it was a trip that would take more than the strivings of John's heart. He feared Miranda was as gone from him, that something had been done to her to punish her for her indiscretion. Was she perhaps locked away somewhere in a convent, or had something even worse happened to her?

When the performance ended John Vigilia felt a jab in his ribs. He looked up to discover that the blow had been delivered by the ubiquitous Hans Hockenheim. Since the week had begun Germany's greatest performance artist had been everywhere, shaking hands, schmoozing, and making propaganda for his own piece, which was to be, as he never hesitated to remind everyone, the last event, the highlight of the festival.

"*Ja*, Viggilliia, that was two fucking good looking bitches who we have just seen here . . . and naked too. It makes your dick go hard."

Since the festival had begun John was never sure, from hour to hour, of which Hans Hockenheim would appear, the crude German factory worker, or the sophisticated Italian socialite.

"It seemed to me a very interesting performance." John replied, feeling the need to say something positive, although he had considered the whole thing to be somewhat sophomoric.

"*Ja*.. . . Now comes a good one, some Hungarian artists, I think that they will be naked also."

"I'm too tired to watch any more, I'm going back to the hotel." John announced, not mentioning that he had taken to hanging around the hotel lobby in the evenings hoping to run into Ariel Angelucci. The man never took breakfast downstairs with the rest of the guests, but John had heard him coming and going, oftentimes in the evening. He would lie on his bed reading, listening for the sounds of footsteps in the hall, and then pop out and head for the toilet at the end. John usually ran into the same people, but never Angelucci, who if he was listening must have got the impression that his neighbor just across the hall must have had a very weak bladder.

"*Ja*.. . . I know you, Veegeillaay . . . those two Irish girls have got you turned on . . . now you go back to your hotel room to jerk off your prick . . . I see you tomorrow, for me I want to get some real live pussy."

Elbowing his way out through the crowd, John came upon the two Irish women standing near the back, still naked and apparently unconcerned about their lack of clothes, taking handshakes, and hugs and kisses from a group of their admirers.

Upon returning to Albergo Flaviano, John did not go directly to his room, but sat in the lobby for the better part of an hour, hiding behind an Italian newspaper which he could not read, hopefully waiting for Ariel Angelucci, who never did appear.

Normally, John Vigilia practiced with the Jungmann in the morning. In the afternoon he sometimes flew the Piper PA-18, often taking up photographers at the request of the festival organizers. The Italian actor Luigi Bosco, who was also a parachutist, had arrived on the third day. He was going to lead the group that was to jump as part of Hans' piece. John took Luigi up in the Piper to see the site. Luigi did not remember him, until John reminded the actor that they had met at a party he had attended at Luigi's villa.

"Yes of course, I remember you now," Luigi said. "You are that friend of Bianca. "

"It was Count Ferdinand Sperone who invited me," John informed him.

"Yes, Sperone, he is very busy with the government now, and has no time for artists. . . ." Luigi added.

John was enjoying all the flying time he was getting in at no cost to him. He especially liked flying down the lake, climbing up over the Alps, and then zooming back through the valleys, a landscape rather different from home, where he often flew over the Finger Lakes, but where the mountains were only low hills by comparison.

Having seen a considerable number of the performances, John had now accepted the fact that, while the program of maneuvers he would be flying would essentially be no different than an air show, the total effect of Hans' piece would be completely unlike anything else being done at the festival.

Hans' big event was planned to take place over the lake bordering the downtown, with the parachutists landing on the public beach, and the musicians and dancers situated in the parking lot next to it. As the piece could not be rehearsed on the site, the group met daily in the small hall belonging to the dance group, which was from Locarno, to go over their parts in the performance.

With Hans directing, and holding his stop watch, the musicians played and the dancers danced, taking their key from John who, with arms extended to simulate an airplane, ran back and forth making buzzing sounds, and describing what maneuver was being executed at the moment. The parachutists circled around him, supposedly in an airplane also, until John broke off, then they hopped up on chairs, flapping their arms as if falling, the music still playing and the dancers still dancing. After the amount of time that had been computed it would take them to land, they jumped off the chairs and ran up to the musicians, where they were joined by the dancers. Hans applauded wildly, and they all took a bow, except for John Vigilia. He would not be taking a bow at the curtain call, but would be landing at the airport in Magadino nine miles away.

Hans arrived very late to the third rehearsal, and in a fit of total anger. He had just learned that his performance would not be the last, and by implication the most important, event. The noted Serbian artist Dragan Karazdc had been invited earlier, but had to decline when he was injured by a stray NATO bomb that fell on his studio destroying his life's work. Now he had miraculously recovered from his wounds, and was being released from the hospital in time to come to the festival, if only for the last day. The news of such a popular artist, having survived this tragedy, coming at all would have upstaged Hans' event. But now he had been given the evening after Hans' piece for his performance, a period when nothing had been previously scheduled. Also, the start of the final banquet had been moved back to give Karazdc more time. Everyone would surely be at this event.

Hans was not beaten though; despite his resentment, he had come up with a plan. Something that had become almost a leitmotif of the festival, since the first performance by the Polish artist, was nudity. Just about every piece had had someone undressing, or undressed. The two Irish women who had performed wearing only blue and orange body paint either did not wash, or repainted themselves each day, as paint was all they had worn since appearing for their performance, walking around the festival naked while holding hands. Even the audiences had gotten into the act, with many of the spectators taking off their clothes during events when urged by the performers to do so.

"For my event . . . all the performers will wear no clothes!" Hans announced.

This brought an audible groan from the group. The musicians pointed out that they would be on a parking lot in the middle of downtown, and doubted that they could sit there playing without any clothes on without being in violation some law or other. And, if some waiver could be obtained that allowed nudity at an artistic performance they would not take off their clothes anyway, as many of them made their living as school teachers, and by giving music lessons to local children, it would not do for the parents to see them sitting there with their private parts exposed.

The group of dancers pointed out that although they were not shy, and were proud of their bodies, and as their costumes did not conceal much of anything anyway, they would not mind dancing naked if it were in some concert hall. But they were also from the local area, and were not about to dance nude in an open public space where everyone could stare and gawk at them.

The parachutists conferred, and after only a very brief discussion, decided that as they were from Italy and, except for Luigi, no one here knew them anyway, they would jump out of the airplane naked. Part of the public beach was posted as allowing nude bathing, although it was little used. The parachutists would land there, and then wrap themselves in their chutes before running up to the musicians and dancers for the final bow. In fact the parachutists got so into the spirit of things that thereafter at the rehearsals they would take off all their clothes and stand on the chairs naked, wildly flapping their arms, and various other parts of their body, before jumping down and wrapping themselves in sheets they had apparently pirated from their hotel rooms.

"Very good," Hans had said, accepting the compromise. "The parachutists are naked, and they are the most important element. And you Veegeeylla. . . ."

"Me!" John protested. "I'll be at the airport nine miles away . . . and in the sky. No one will know whether I am dressed or undressed."

"Don't panic. That is not what I was going to say. I have arranged for the important French art critic, Renée Coûteux, to take a flight with you. She is very excited about this and wants you to do the 'loop the loops' with her. She is writing about this festival for New Art International, a most influential magazine. I want that our performance should be the feature of her article. So take good care of her special needs . . . if you know what I mean, ha, ha, ha," Hans said, winking and poking John a little too firmly in the ribs.

What could John do? Refuse Hans? It was enough that he was secretly wallowing in exquisite delight at the great maestro's misfortune at being demoted in importance. He did not want to begin a rebellion in this already edgy troupe. And so John Vigilia agreed to meet the art critic Renée Coûteux the next day and to take her for a flight. Not sure he knew exactly what Hans meant John asked naively: "And just what are her special needs?"

"And so . . . are you fucking stupid?" Hans replied sarcastically. "She needs a taste of that big Polish sausage you carry around in your pants." Several of the people present in the group, standing nearby and overhearing the conversation, were heard to giggle.

"Oh. . . ." was all John could manage to blurt out. He had a strange and indefinable feeling toward Hans, a mixture of revulsion and attraction. It was an evil fascination, very evil, that John Vigilia had for the sanguine and violent German artist.

"And when you do the flight with the chick," Hans went on in a scolding tone, "make sure there are no more violations of the Swiss Aircraft Regulations. I don't want you should lose your pilot's license just before my big event."

It was Hans' way of reminding everyone that John's first solo flight in the Jungmann had not gone without incident. Happy to be rid of the scrutiny, and extra weight of Hans the chief flight instructor, John had held the

Jungmann down on the runway during his take-off to build up speed, and then roared up in a steep, high-performance climb out. After which he had flown east, straight down the valley, until John found a field that he judged to be out of the airport traffic area to practice over. Climbing to a reasonable altitude he had put the airplane through a series of spins: left and right, inverted and upright, one, two, and three turns each. A prudent pilot, although John had spun the airplane with the check pilot in the cockpit, he wanted to see how the Jungmann responded with the front seat completely empty of any weight, which moved the center of gravity further aft, causing the airplane to be more sensitive to the controls.

Satisfied with the spin recovery, John proceeded to put the Jungmann through a program that included all the stunts it was capable of doing. As his right wrist was still in some pain, he used both hands on the stick for the aerobatic maneuvers. Tired after a half an hour, he headed back to the airport. At what John judged to be about six miles from the field he called the tower and, as no other airplanes were in the pattern, asked for a "straight-in landing."

Although the tower was required to communicate in English, the international language of flight, the tower operators' command of that language was apparently as proficient as John Vigilia's was in German, French, or Italian. After a series of garbled transmissions on both sides, John heard what he thought was: "Clear to land." By now he was only a mile from the airport, and could plainly tell from the windsock that the wind had shifted and was presently blowing from the west, straight at him. He kept on the power, and came in fast, landing on the main wheels. No sooner had the aircraft slowed enough to settle down on its tail wheel when John heard the tower operator order:

"The pilot of H-BUZZ, report to tower! The pilot of Jungmann H-BUZZ, report to tower, immediately!"

Now John knew that back in the U.S.A. to be called to the tower after a landing meant that you had apparently done something very wrong, so assumed this was also the case in Switzerland. From past experience he further knew that it was best not to hurry right over there, with your hackles up, but to take your time and let things cool down a bit. He parked the Jungmann in front of the hangar and went into the office to sign the biplane back in. Hans, the chief pilot, was there in a mild state of frenzy. He began yelling at John:

"The tower have called to me . . . they say me to tell you, you must to go there at once!"

"I already know that," John said trying to remain calm.

"They ask-ed me if I have explained the rules to you . . . and I say that I have . . . exactly. They say you have fife violations! Fife!" Hans held out his hand and displayed five fingers to make his point. "You do remember me explaining the rules to you, yes?"

"I guess so. . . ." John stammered, although he couldn't particularly remember what the rules were, or that they had been explained to him.

"In Switzerland the rules are very important," the chief pilot reminded John. "With fife violations in one flight you will probably lose your right to fly in this country for ever. . . ."

Hearing this John decided that he had better first call the festival office and ask for a translator to meet him at the tower, preferably a translator with some legal experience.

The tower chief was waiting for John Vigilia when he arrived at the base of the tower. The chief kept holding up his hand, also displaying five fingers, and shouting: "You have made fife violations! Such as fife violations in one flight is not heard of!"

When it was established that the offending pilot could communicate in no language but English, and the tower chief spoke only German and French, they went into the chief's office to wait for the translator, who arrived within twenty minutes. John recognized the young woman as the person who had been at the desk when he had first gone to the festival office for his reservation, a winsome creature who appeared as if her parents might have been French and Italian, and she had inherited the best characteristics of each.

The tower chief, who had previously appeared rather angry, now became quite charming talking to this attractive young woman. No longer shouting and waving the fingers on his hand, the tower chief courteously explained that this American had violated five Swiss air regulations on his previous flight, regulations which, he confirmed, the chief pilot had thoroughly explained to him before he took the airplane up alone.

"C'est dommage. . . ." the translator, whose name was Celia, had begun as she explained John's violations to him. First, his takeoff had not followed the approved pattern. Second, he had flown aerobatics between the hours of one and three, when a noise abatement ordnance prohibits such flights. Third, the farmer over whose field he had practiced had called and reported him as flying aerobatics too low to the ground. Fourth, he had made an improper entry into the airport's traffic pattern, straight-in approaches not being allowed. And fifth, he had landed without a clearance.

Embarrassed by the situation, John Vigilia admitted to Celia that he probably was guilty of all these infractions, but that they should attempt to plead extenuating circumstances. John explained that on his two previous flights he had taken off to the west, and flown an elaborate pattern to get to the east of the field to practice. Today he had taken off to the east, and gone straight out, not knowing that this was illegal, the same applied to his approach. John also claimed that he did not know about the 1:00 pm to 3:00 pm restriction, as he had previously flown in the morning or evening. Although he did not directly challenge the farmer's observation, John pointed out that he had flown over 400 hours in Bücker Jungmann aircraft, and was well aware of when he was flying too low. As for landing without a clearance, John explained that he had attempted to make radio contact, but the transmissions were somewhat garbled, and he thought that he had heard the words "clear to land." John also told Celia to remind the tower chief there were no other airplanes in the pattern at the time, and that his landing had endangered no one.

Celia agreed that these were all good points and that she would convey them to the tower chief. She suggested to John that she also explain he was not a wealthy American tourist, as the tower staff had come to believe, but someone who was here as part of the International Performance Art Festival, and was practicing to fly this airplane in one of the festival's main events. She also said she would mention the name of her employer, Christen Bonaire, who was one of the prime sponsors of the festival, and the owner of a large chain of super markets, with numerous branches all over Europe, one of the richest men in the entire country, and a good friend of many important persons in the government.

Celia and the tower chief held a brief conversation in German, which John did not understand. However, from watching the look on the tower chief's face whenever Celia mentioned Christen Bonaire, he got the impression that the Bonaire name had carried more weight than all his feeble explanations.

Turning back to John, she explained, "The tower chief says that he is sorry for the problem, and if you promise to carefully obey the rules on your next flights, we can leave."

John promised, and Celia relayed his words to the chief, who pumped John's hand vigorously, while saying something to him in German.

"He says," Celia translated, "that he has watched you fly through his binoculars, and that you truly are a magnificent pilot, and a master of your aircraft. And he recommends that when you fly in the future, you go down the lake a little to where it turns, for there it is in Italy, and they have no rules and you can do whatever you like."

Yes, just down the lake was Italy, John mused as they left the tower. And the next lake over was Lake Como, not very far by airplane. At the south end of that lake was Miranda. He glanced at the attractive young woman walking next to him. Why did she not arouse the same desire in him that Miranda had? Then he wondered; had his brief affair with Miranda been simply a reaction to the death of his wife, no more than a fermentation of his carnal desires, which had been prematurely aroused in him and therefore insincere and empty? John told himself that this was not the case. In a moment of what he mistook for lucidity a whim entered John's head. He would fly down to Como in the Jungmann and then, finding Miranda sunning naked on the roof of the villa he would, like some great yellow bird, perform an aerial courting dance for her.

Twenty-three

I cannot too much muse
Such shapes, such gesture, and such sound, expressing
(Although they want the use of tongue) a kind
Of excellent dumb discourse.

Shakespeare *The Tempest III. iii.*

Every morning, but not too early, the artists in town for the festival, crowds of artists, invaded the downtown. The locals watched them wander here and there, in many and various places at once. They clogged the streets, a black-clad gaggle, rushing to and fro to restaurants and coffee shops seeking their friends and their breakfast. Having filled every table around the center square, they chatted heatedly about obscure artistic things in every language, smiling and showing their perfect white teeth to each other. Then, after about an hour or so of this intense activity they disappeared just as mysteriously as they had arrived; not into thin air but into the auditorium of the Congress Center.

John finished his tea and went to see if his Volkswagen was still on the street where he had left it, as the Albergo Flaviano had no parking garage. Today he was to take the French art critic, Renée Coûteux, for her flight. Never having taken a French art critic, or any other art critic for that matter, aloft John did not know what to expect. Renée Coûteux was staying at the Hotel Sans Souci, so he did know where to meet her. He had not been told what she looked like, only the time to be out front.

At the precise moment they were supposed to meet an elegant, dark-haired woman of incredible beauty, clad in an embroidered peasant blouse and a full length skirt stepped from the hotel. The sun shinning on the thin white fabric of her top caused it to become almost transparent, the decorative flower patterns on the front alone supplying a modicum of decency. The top three buttons, apparently left undone on purpose, revealed the deep valley between the woman's ample breasts. As was currently fashionable, the blouse ended about six inches above where the skirt began, allowing a trim and well-tanned stomach to be displayed along with her neatly tied naval. The dark fabric skirt, though reaching to the woman's ankles, had a slit in front that rose to immodest heights. Her feet were shod in the most delicate of leather sandals. This was hardly the costume of a person planning to go flying in an open cockpit biplane. She was not the person he was waiting for, John assumed. Nevertheless, upon seeing him standing there this very fine and splendid woman smiled and spoke:

"Hello, you must be John, the pilot . . . I am Renée Coûteux," she said extending her hand. "I am sorry . . . I didn't mean to be familiar; I have your family name written down here, but I did not want to take the risk of mispronouncing it."

"John Vigilia," John said taking her hand.

"Vigilia. . . ." Renée Coûteux said, referring to her paper. She had pronounced it correctly on her very first try. "I am pleased to meet you, Mr. Vigilia." Giving him a another smile, she ever so slowly withdrew her hand from John's, and added, "You may call me Renée. . . ."

"And you may call me John . . . or the pilot."

Renée laughed, which, for unknown some reason pleased John immensely.

"Vigilia . . . is that a Polish name?" Renée asked as he held the door to the Volkswagen open for her.

"Yes . . . but I am a third generation American."

"Do you speak Polish?"

"No . . . Like most Americans I can only speak English . . . although I did have to study a bit of French in college," John apologized.

"So, would you like to try out your college French on me then?"

"No . . . that was years ago, you are doing just fine in English."

"Yes, I have to write all my articles and reviews in English, so I get a lot of practice. My grandfather on my mother's side was Polish. He came to France to escape from the Nazis during World War Two. When the Germans took over the country he joined the Resistance."

"Your grandfather sounds like a most interesting man." John said. He had just navigated the now familiar narrow streets of the downtown, and was turning onto the small highway that led to the airport.

"Do you know that we are being followed?" Renée asked somewhat casually.

"We are?" John said, trying to sound unconcerned. Despite all the indications of his recent past, John still could not accept the fact that there was some kind of intrigue going on around him. "It must only be your imagination . . . why would anyone want to follow us?"

"No, we are definitely being followed by a black Alfa Romeo with a Milan number plate," Renée said, and then she elaborated: "When I was a child, my father was the French ambassador to Romania. Our family was always being trailed by the secret police, for no reason other than just to keep tabs on us. When we were alone, my sister and I made a game of spotting our tails, and trying to lose them. We actually became quite good at it," she related, and then added, "I will tell you what to do. Slow down . . . see that turn-around up there, pull in without signaling, then make a fast u-turn, and head back the way we came."

"Are you crazy?"

"No. Just do as I say. . . ."

They were knocked about in their seats as John suddenly pulled over and turned the Volkswagen around 180 degrees. "How am I doing?" he shouted.

"Now pull back out and let's see what happens. . . ."

The black Alfa was facing them now, slowing down as if to also make a turn. John pulled out in front of him. As the two cars passed the Alfa Romeo driver shifted his head away, but John caught a glimpse of him and seemed to recall seeing the man before. The car was similar to the one that had hit him when he was on the bicycle in Munich, and that had followed him here. Watching in his rear view mirror, John Vigilia saw the black car pull over, make a u-turn, and come after him. He felt as if he was in Moscow all over again.

"Now quick, make a turn in there," Renée said, pointing out a small side street that they were rapidly approaching. She had suddenly become quite animated, and seemed to be enjoying what she must be taking as a great game of spies.

Following her orders, John slammed on the brakes, and let the back end of the VW slide out. He hadn't needed to brake so hard, but thought that he would add some motion picture drama to the chase.

"Oh . . . that was exciting!" Renée exclaimed. "Just like in the movies, do it again at the next corner . . . he's still after us."

As John down-shifted he felt his hand graze bare flesh, which caused him to shoot a quick glance over at Renée. Turned sideways in her seat to watch the car behind them, the slit in her skirt had opened so wide that it appeared as if she wasn't wearing any. His eyes momentarily distracted, John missed the turn Renée had indicated. "Oh, no!" he exclaimed seeing the sign at the last moment. "We're heading down a dead end street. . . ."

"That's not a problem," Renée advised him. "It's a good tactic . . . stop in front of that garage."

John Vigilia pulled over. "Now what?" he asked as the Alfa cruised by them on the narrow street.

"Quick, back in there. . . ." Renée said pointing to the driveway. "Now let's get out of here."

As he sped away John could see in his rearview mirror that the Alfa Romeo had nowhere to turn around, and had to either back all the way to the driveway they had used, or go all the way to the end of the street. Having turned the corner, John could not see which choice the other driver had taken, but his maneuver had given them the time that they needed to shake their pursuer. Renée was flushed with delighted.

"I think we've lost them," John said, using a tone he hoped gave the impression that he too thought it was a great game.

"See, I told you I knew some clever tricks . . . only our drivers were always Romanian, and no matter how fast we told them to go, they always seemed to slow down so the tail could catch up with us again."

"Well I don't mean to slow down now, but this is the turn for the airport," he announced

"So tell me, John, why was that car following us?"

"I don't know," he said, "maybe they were just playing a game . . . like us. . . ." Looking over at Renée, John noticed she had not bothered to tug the folds of her skirt together around her, but was sitting there allowing the sun coming through the windshield to fall on her well-tanned legs.

When they arrived at airport they found the Jungmann ready and waiting for them in front of the hangar. Heeding John's advice Renée had deposited her dangling earrings and many bracelets in the glove compartment of the car, but kept wearing the small crucifix she had on a gold chain around her neck. "Just for good luck," she said.

Lifting up her skirt, higher than John thought necessary, Renée stepped over the fuselage side and slid down into the front seat. Crouched down behind the windscreen, she seemed small and vulnerable. In the full sunlight, John noticed the lines in her face for the first time. He had no idea of her age, but guessed that Renée was somewhat older than she acted. He told her to buckle herself in, and then realized the awkwardness of his remark. Not only did she not know what to do but, dressed the way she was, in a long, and flowing skirt, it was near impossible.

"I'm sorry," John said, "I forgot about the parachutes, which we have to wear for an aerobatic flight. I should have told you to wear trousers."

"But why?"

"Well you see, the straps on this back pack go around your shoulders, and these straps . . . well they have got to hookup to those straps . . . which go between your legs. But you're wearing a skirt . . . so it won't work. If you want to we can go back to your hotel and you can get a pair of pants . . . or we can just go up and not do any aerobatics. If we merely fly around straight and level then we don't need to wear parachutes."

"No . . . I want to do the acrobatics. I was looking forward to it; I have never done the loop the loops. . . ."

"Then we had better return to the hotel and you can get a pair of trousers."

"We can't. I didn't bring any with me. I don't like to wear pants . . . I think that they do not look dignified on women. . . ."

"So what do you want to do?"

"I will just take off my skirt . . . if you don't mind."

He blushed, and looked away at the tower, as Renée wiggled out of her skirt. "No I don't mind. You can fold your skirt, and tuck it under you on the seat," John said.

"There, now how does this here parachute go on?" Renée asked, her voice filled with a brave enthusiasm.

When he looked back down at her in the cockpit, John saw that Renée was sitting there in the briefest black lace thong, her legs spread open to clear the control stick, her sandaled feet tucked up into the rudder stirrups. Slightly embarrassed, he reached over the side and began to work the olive drab straps around his passenger's legs, trying carefully to avoid touching her bare skin.

Although Renée seemed unconcerned about her state of undress, John Vigilia could feel himself reaching a state of erection. His heart was pounding, his head hot. Sensing his nervousness, Renée took the two leg straps and slid them between her crotch, and then handed the snap ends to John. He hitched them in place and tightened the buckles.

Next, he hooked Renée into the three inch wide safety belt, which went across her lap, providing her with a bit of decency. Finally she was wrapped in the two inch seat belt system, which included a shoulder harness and a crotch belt. John gingerly tightened the shoulder harness, trying to decide whether the straps should go on the inside or the outside of Renée's breasts. Deciding on the outside, he cinched the straps down, his hands gently grazing her soft mounds. Renée smiled at his touch. She seemed to deriving an immense pleasure from this whole buckling in procedure.

John pointed to the loose end of the strap between her legs and told Renée to "just snug it down." She gave it a too hard yank, and he saw the strap pull up into the folds of her crotch. She shuddered and then moaned slightly. She was breathing heavily, her breasts rising and falling, her hardened nipples projecting through the thin fabric of her blouse. "What more is there left to do?" she asked, smiling.

"Only your flight helmet, with the headset and goggles," John said. As tugged it on to Renée's head he noticed the crucifix hanging around her neck. "I though I told you that you had better remove your necklace it might come off when we're flying upside down. . . ."

"But I wear it for good luck. . . ." Renée protested.

"But if it happens to fall out of the airplane when we are upside down, then it's gone, and that will be bad luck. . . ."

"Then you take it off, I can't move my hands all strapped in like this," she said sounding as if she was getting a kind of sadomasochistic sensation from the many belts and straps restraining her body.

As John bent over to remove the little necklace, Renée leaned forward and kissed him softly on the cheek. "For good luck," she said.

"I'll put the necklace in my pocket. It won't fall out, and will still be in the airplane and hopefully bring us luck, if we should need it."

Climbing into the rear cockpit, John repeated the strapping in process on himself. His helmet on, he plugged in the intercom jack, and the radio jack. Next, he visually checked the area in front of the propeller, locked his toes on the brakes, shouted "clear the prop," and pushed the starter button. The four-cylinder Lycoming turned over tentatively for a few revolutions, and then burst into life. John reached outside the cockpit and disconnected the external power source. The Jungmann carried no battery, so if they should accidentally lose power in the air he was not about to restart the engine.

Switching to the intercom John asked Renée if she could hear him. She replied with a startled "Yes", and he told her that they were ready to go. John darted his eyes across the control panel, making sure all the instruments were functioning properly, and then contacted the tower for a clearance to taxi. S-turning slowly away from the main hangar, the way tail-wheel airplanes needed to do, John Vigilia saw the black Alfa Romeo parked by the fence. A man was leaning on the dented front fender smoking a cigarette watching them depart. Farther down the fence, at the end of the parking lot, the lone old man who John had observed was always there was standing in his usual place.

Without saying anything more to his passenger, as he had no idea what he was supposed to say to her, pitch Hans' program perhaps, John took off and flew out to the practice area. There he began to go through his maneuvers. He did not explain very much, but went about practicing his normal routine. The flight for him was rather like work; however, he sensed Renée was rather enjoying herself immensely. The art critic did not ask any questions either, but sat in the front seat alternately screaming loudly and laughing convulsively, as if she were on some wild ride at an amusement park.

"It was a wonderful flight," Renée said later as they were headed back to the Sans Souci in the Volkswagen. "However, I still don't understand why we had to go up to the control tower after we landed, although it was nice of them to want to give me a tour."

John had done everything right, followed all the rules to the letter, even gone down the Lago Maggiore to the Italian side, but on landing had heard the fatal words: "The pilot of Jungmann H-BUZZ, report to the control tower." This time John took Renée with him as his translator, which he soon realized was the person who the tower personnel really wanted to see anyway.

"They want to know if you have a flight instructor's license." Renée had said, translating the tower chief's question.

"Tell him I don't." John answered, not understanding the reason why he was being asked this.

John Vigilia had every possible rating the FAA gave out but that one. He once had bought a textbook to study for the flight instructor's written test, however found himself disagreeing with almost all of the answers to questions that had to do with teaching theory and motivation. I wouldn't do it that way, he kept saying to himself. Although John hated teaching, he was considered, at least his student evaluations said so, an excellent teacher. Thus, rather than memorize a bunch of answers he disagreed with just to pass the written test, John had abandoned the whole project and never gotten a flight instructor's rating.

"The chief says to tell you then that you have a violation . . . as in Switzerland you must have an instructor's license in order to be allowed to take up a passenger for an acrobatic flight."

"Ask them if an Air Transport Pilot's license will do. . . ." John said fishing his license from his wallet and displaying it to the tower chief.

The tower chief briefly studied the paper, made a frown, said something, and then smiled.

"The chief says to tell you he is sorry to have bothered you . . . he did not know you had such a license, and that with this license you could take up a whole 747 full of passengers for an acrobatic flight. He asks me if I would like a tour of the control tower. I told him that if we had time, I would enjoy seeing his facility."

Taking Renée by the arm the tower chief led her up to the observation deck, with John trailing along as if he were not there. Previously strict and official the man had become a sunny day in January, which always has more charm than a sunny day in summertime because it is unexpected, and you know it won't last. John didn't know if the rule about the qualification of his license was correct, so he took Renée's presence as a windfall, an unexpected piece of good fortune.

The tower chief showed Renée every piece of equipment in the room, going into especially lengthy explanations of things like the radar scope, which she had to bend over closely to observe. John couldn't help noticing that Renée seemed to enjoy exposing as much of her breasts as the moment allowed. Word about the comely female visitor must have circulated, for when the tour was over, and Renée, having lifted up her skirt high enough to avoid tripping on it, but not seeming able to hold it so as to keep the slit from opening, finally descended the open, iron circular stairway, everyone with any business at all in the tower was waiting at the bottom.

"Nothing was wrong . . . the tower boys must have been watching us through their binoculars . . . and wanted to see you close up," John remarked as he pulled the car out onto the highway.

"Why would anyone want to look at an old thing like me?" Renée laughed.

He could not tell if Renée was joking, or feigning modesty, or perhaps fishing for a compliment, so John said nothing. He was, he hoped, finally learning when to keep silent.

"Well . . . no one's following us this time," Renée remarked, peering over her shoulder. She sounded almost like she was disappointed.

"I know," John said. "The man in the Alfa Romeo was not there when we landed."

"He got in his car and left as we were taxing out, I looked back and saw him go," Renée said, confirming that she had seen him too.

"But the lone old man was still there; he always is . . . always in the same place. He must be very interested in airplanes."

"So you have observed that old man watching before. Do you know who he is?"

"He has been here every day I have flown, and I think I may have seen him downtown; however, I have no idea who he might be," John lied.

When they pulled up in front of the Sans Souci, John Vigilia started to get out to go around and open the door for Renée, but she put her hand on his arm to restrain him.

"There is a garage underneath the hotel . . . you can park your car there. I would like you to come up to my room for a little while . . . I want to do an interview with you about what your part in the performance will be . . . I think it might make a good separate article."

"About me?" he said. Her unexpected comment had astonished and overwhelmed John. The distinguished French art critic Renée Coûteux, wanted to do an article about him? Familiar with the garage from his own very brief stay at this same hotel, John headed the Volkswagen down the steep ramp.

As the car slid down into the dark tunnel, for some unknown reason John had a premonition of disaster. He thought about Hans' admonishment to, "Take care of her special needs." Renée was certainly an attractive woman, and John would have been happy to bed her under different circumstances, but Hans' statement had tainted things. It was as if he were part of the deal, thrown in to insure a favorable review. Did Renée just want him to sleep with her, or had she actually found him to be an interesting person she wanted to write an article about?

"You are such a very fascinating man, John," Renée said, responding to John's unasked question as if she had been reading his mind. "I think that I might write something about you."

Renée indicated a place where he should park the car. She looked at John and smiled a calm, assured smile. In the dim light of the parking garage her face seemed harder and more irascible than he recalled it being earlier in the day.

At first John had not understood the art critic's statement, or did not believe it; but his heart leapt to his throat at the idea. Since his wife's death John had been at an emotional crossroads, unsatisfied with what he had become, convinced that he had ruined his life through too many careless decisions, like flying airplanes instead of working on his serious writing. But now he was to have an article written about him, for an important international art magazine.

Renée's room was on the floor below the penthouse where John had previously stayed. It was roughly one third the size of the penthouse, with only one bed, one balcony, and a smaller bath with no Jacuzzi. John figured it probably cost about one third the price, which was still more than he could afford to pay. He wondered if the magazine was paying for the room, or if Renée might be independently wealthy and just wrote for various art magazines to have something to do with her time. After all, she had told him that her father had been an ambassador.

Renée mixed them both a drink from the Frigibar, and suggested that they sit out on the balcony, as the sky, which had clouded over during their flight, was now showing some patches of sun. They settled into the lounge chairs. Renée kicked off her sandals and leaned back, crossing her legs and letting the slit in her skirt gap open wide. Turning her notepad to a blank page, she raised her glass to John as in a toast, smiled and said:

"So, tell me about yourself. . . ."

"Tell you what?" John Vigilia replied, taking a sip of his gin and tonic. "You're the interviewer, aren't you supposed to ask me questions?"

"Who says so?" Renée answered. She was idly rubbing her bare right foot, up and down her left ankle.

"I do for one . . . and I'm a college professor. Although I am supposed to teach literature, I work for a small school where you have to teach everything . . . so I occasionally teach a course in journalism, and all the textbooks say. . . ."

"So you are a professor, I wouldn't have guessed that, but let's throw away the textbooks for the moment, John," Renée interrupted. "Just talk, and don't stop talking . . . say whatever you want to say." Her tone had become almost that of a hypnotist.

Lulled by the sound of Renée's voice, the warm sun, and the gin and tonic that he had just finished, John began to tell his story. He was one of those persons who had never learned to be silent, all too eager to repeat those superfluous things that memory makes a fetish of, and treasures so piously, but reason does not discourage one from forgetting soon enough. This was especially a danger to someone like John Vigilia whose mind was perpetually open to the innumerable anonymous emotions conveyed by such things as the wind, the sky, and clouds.

After about fifteen minutes of mostly rambling, John became aware that he had begun much too far back; building model airplanes using sticks and glue in his parent's basement had not caught Renée's interest. Even the tale of the flight that he had made by leaping from the top of the town water tower with his modified Leonardo wings had only produced a sigh, and a bored, "You must have been very naïve," from the person who had so eagerly encouraged him to talk.

Skipping forward, John Vigilia went off to college; then to his first art class; his move to New York City, where he gave up the visual arts and devoted his time to trying to be a writer. As he talked John became more metaphysical. He spoke of his belief in: ". . . never losing hope, of trying to keep alive what has inspired me until it has completed its mysterious journey through my total being." John paused a moment. "I am always searching for something," he concluded, thinking that he had finally rung the bell.

"And are you searching for something now?" Renée asked, shaking her head and catching the sound bite that John had unconsciously given her. She had been listening to him, but not very carefully and he had not noticed her writing down very much, despite all that he had said.

His mind grew cautious at the art critic's question. John was reminded that even now he was on what was probably a futile search. Was this quest for Lindbergh's copilot only a continuation of a life spent searching for things he knew that he could never find? John told himself that if a man was to be condemned for searching for something, then the only innocent men left were those who had never lacked for anything. John wanted to say all this, and more, but: "What do you mean by that?" was all he could manage as a response.

"Well are you?"

"Am I what?"

"Searching for something?"

"I'm sorry . . . I was thinking of something else," he replied.

For a moment John considered telling Renée Coûteux the Lindbergh copilot story. What harm could it do? he thought. She would doubtless find it fascinating. But she was a journalist, who knows to whom she might repeat his strange tale.

"So what were you thinking of?"

"Well . . . I originally made this trip to find out things for a book I'm writing on Sperone aircraft. . . ."

"Oh . . . Count Sperone, I have met him several times . . . the dear man is a great patron of the arts. So you write books about airplanes. . . ."

John Vigilia was forced to reveal that this was his first attempt at writing about airplanes. He explained that while he had begun and then abandoned a number of other books over the years, nothing he had ever written had found a publisher.

"I do not think that my task in life is merely to divert my readers." John went on being a bit pompously defensive. "Books are for me not mere toys, but things of weight and meaning by which I will stand or fall as fortune dictates. I have, however, painfully discovered that the market rules, and that my skills, so dearly learned, must be put to other uses if I am to earn a decent living." Although his one person audience did not seen too interested in what he had to say he plunged on dramatically. "I find that I have too frequently been compelled to do other things, which I never had in mind. What I would like from my life, unless it's already too late, would be to work hard, and amass hundreds of pages of text, so that I might produce a book that would transcend my own being."

"Yes, yes . . . wouldn't we all," Renée said, displaying a surprising hauteur. She rose from her lounge chair. "Would you like another drink? It was a gin and tonic . . . wasn't it."

Renée went back inside to check the contents of the Frigibar. Stealing a glance at the open notepad she had left behind, John was surprised to discover that, notwithstanding all the earnest talking he had been doing, the art critic had not written anything down. Hurriedly flipping through the pages he had found that there was not one word of text, only scribbles and doodles.

"There is a small bottle of gin left, but no tonic . . . John, come inside and look and see what you want from what's left here."

He surveyed the choices and opened a can of orange soda, and then poured it over the remains of the ice in his glass.

"You've told me so very much about yourself that you have made me tired," Renée said, stretching and yawning, actions that John could not tell were genuine or faked. "I think now that we must stop. We can finish the interview tomorrow."

"Okay . . . I'm kind of tired too. I'll be going then," John said hastily gulping down the contents of his glass.

"That was not what I meant," Renée said, slipping off her blouse and letting her breasts fall free. "I meant that now it's time for us to go to bed, but not to sleep, just to relax . . . and to have a little sex."

"Oh? . . ."

"Look. Don't you find me attractive?" she asked sliding out of her skirt and tong at the same time. Renée stood in front of John, her legs spread wide. Her pubic hairs had been shaven off, except for a patch at the top of her crack that had been carefully trimmed into the shape of a heart. She ran her hand over her mons pubis as if confirming its smoothness. "Do you like my heart? It's something new . . . I did it myself this morning. You're lucky; you are the first person to see me this way. . . ."

John Vigilia stared at the little furry love symbol not knowing whether to take her comment as being serious or a joke.

"Well are you just going to sit there? Take off your clothes . . . or do you want me to have to do it for you?" she asked rather sarcastically.

Renée's rapid undressing, and then presenting her crotch to him like a clipped poodle at a dog show, had done little to arouse his passion. John liked slow, drawn-out foreplay, with even a bit of theatre when his wife had agreed to it. "You'll have to catch me first," he said, running around the room, and then out onto the balcony.

"Yes! Yes!" That's a good idea! You can't get away from me!" Renée exclaimed, getting in the spirit of the game. Still naked herself, she caught John in the corner of the balcony and began tearing of his clothes. The two rolled around on the floor, laughing and shouting. "I've got you now!" she screamed as John let her pull off his pants, while at the same time pretending to be holding on to them.

"You are the little devil, Vigilia," she shouted.

"And I've come to punish you for your sins. . . ." John said, biting her neck, feeling his passion rising.

"Hurt me, John! Make me suffer. . . ."

An elderly German man, hearing the noise from the room next door, came out on his balcony to see what was happening. Looking over at the adjacent balcony he spied the two naked bodies cavorting on the tile floor.

"*Verruckt!*" he quietly muttered, and then turned to go back inside.

This was a German word she knew to mean "crazy." They weren't acting crazy. Renée looked over her shoulder and smiled; a smile that clearly said: Why don't you stay and enjoy the show.

Twenty-four

Flout 'em and scout 'em
And scout 'em and flout 'em
Thought is free.

Shakespeare *The Tempest III. ii.*

The last event of the day was already half over when John Vigilia arrived late to the evening performances. He would have been content to miss these events completely, but felt an obligation to show up to lend support to the other artists as the only audience that ever seemed to come were the participants of the next and previous performances, and the reviewers. Although there was no admission charged, the residents of Locarno were not exactly flocking to the International Performance Art Festival, despite the fact that colorful banners advertising its presence fluttered from every lamppost in the downtown. Nor did it seem that it had attracted many of the much anticipated tourists.

John wondered what the purpose of the festival actually was. The sponsors had obviously spent a great deal of money on its expenses, which they could never possibly recover. Skimming articles in old magazines about the festivals of former years, he concluded that either this year's was not as good as the previous ones, or that the performances appeared more interesting in print than they actually were in reality. Socializing, or more accurately schmoozing, seemed to be a major activity of the gathering, with a large cocktail party being held in the Congress Hall every evening after the last performance.

Tonight's final event had a male and female artist, both naked except for red and black body paint, having intercourse, while a person dressed in the robes of a bishop read something in Spanish from an oversized book. Something else may have happened before he got there, but John saw only the last fifteen minutes. And the sex did not look as if it was being faked. From the brief program notes, which were printed in four languages, he learned that the piece had something to do with the Spanish government's harsh response to ETA, the Basque separatist movement. The thing ended, John applauded politely and moved over to the bar, keeping his eyes open for Renée Coûteux. When he had left her apartment earlier, they had agreed to meet here this evening. As he lifted his drink, someone pounded John's shoulder causing him to spill most of his red wine. Turning around John saw an all too familiar face.

"*Ja,* so you have finally arrived Vaggayyllaa . . . so how did it go this afternoon? Bam, bam? . . ." Hans asked, pounding his right fist on his left palm making the classic obscene gesture.

"With the flight? . . ." John asked. That he should be vague to Hans about the details of his afternoon with Renée Coûteux was uppermost in his mind. John wanted to enjoy seeing Hans' annoyance at his reluctance to reveal the full, and lurid, details. This he also hoped would be a clear sign to Hans that despite having what he took as not a totally unpleasant experience, he was annoyed that it had actually been assigned to him as one of his errands.

"Who gives a shit about your flight, we see it when the time comes, and it had better be good. I mean what the fuck happened with the hot French art critic?"

"You want me to tell you if it was good?"

"I know it was good . . . I have fucked her a few times myself; she is better than most professionals."

"I'm meeting her here tonight. . . ."

"You are? If so then what's that shit about?" Hans said gesturing to the other side of the hall where Renée Coûteux was working the room with the two German art stars, Heiner Fliegengewicht and Sigmund Speichellecker, one on each arm. "Look how they suck up to her . . . one blows in her left ear while the other in the right. . . ."

"They're probably just old friends."

"Hah! You are the 'old friends' now, Veegeehlee," Hans added sarcastically.

John's face flushed. The afternoon had not been all that bad, he thought. True, technically he had sort of failed, but John Vigilia believed the rest had more than made up for his sexual misfire. Renée had enjoyed the flight, and the excitement of the car chase, or whatever it was. Back at her hotel room she appeared to have really gotten into their "game." She had seemed delighted when, naked herself, she had just struggled John's underpants down off of his ankles when some old fart of a German tourist popped out on to the next balcony and caught them at it.

Ever shy John had ducked down on his hands and knees to hide his private parts. Renée, seeing this as part of the game, had straddled him like a horse and, slapping John's bare ass with her hand, ridden him back inside. There they both collapsed on the floor, where Renée began pulling on his member. In heat now they mounted one another and performed "the beast with two backs," until they were both sweaty and about to come.

At that point Renée had skillfully maneuvered around and on top of John and, seemingly without any interruption, removed his penis from her mouth and inserted it in her vagina. Now she began to ride his front side with the same gusto as she had ridden him in from the balcony, sweat pouring from her body, slapping John with her hand, and giving out great war-whoops in French.

It must have been Renée's shouts. John did not understand what she was saying, and could only assume they were shouts of pleasure. But John Vigilia's memory had tricks that it played on his mind when it was not in complete harmony with the present. He heard his wife, her cries of pain whenever he tried to penetrate her during her final year: "I'm sorry, I have pains again . . . I can't go on. We have got to stop."

With that notion taking hold of his head, John felt his penis shrinking. He was losing his erection, as he had on so many other nights with his wife Iris. Feeling her partner's organ diminishing, Renée began to gallop faster and faster. She took John's hands and crushed them into her breasts. She sucked on his neck drawing blood, but she was losing the battle. The game was over.

"I'm sorry," John said. "It's something I can't control. It has nothing to do with you. I just sort of happens to me; I don't know why."

"You will finish me. . . ." Renée commanded, annoyed and not ready to accept his apology. Sliding up his body, she presented her vulva to John Vigilia's mouth saying: "I hope that your tongue has not lost its ability too."

John manipulated her clitoris with his tongue and forefinger until Renée shuddered and let out a loud gasp. Then she rolled over on the floor next to him, panting and moaning.

Renée had not then offered to "finish" John, but gotten up quickly and, without looking at him, announced that he should leave as she would like to take a shower and nap before going to this evening's performances. As she closed the door to her bathroom she had shouted casually over her shoulder, ". . . see you later." At the time John had taken her words as a promise of a meeting between them that evening at the festival.

John began dressing without a word, in an almost timid manner, listening to the water running in her shower. He was worried by the thought that Renée might have changed her opinion of him. She obviously had been angered by what had happened between them and neither his attempts to caress her, nor his kind words had done any good. All of this, of course, John did not reveal to Hans.

"Look, she sees us now, and comes over here . . . with those two fucking German con-artists on her arm," Hans scowled.

Renée Coûteux was heading toward them, accompanied by a short man and a tall man, both dressed identically in black combat boots, tight black pants held up by red suspenders and matching yellow muscle shirts, their almost-shaved-off hair was dyed the same shade of pink.

When Renée arrived John Vigilia gave her a big smile and hello, and then leaned forward to kiss her cheeks, aping the European style mostly for Hans' benefit, a hint of what might have happened between them. But Renée Coûteux did not respond and stepped back, merely blowing John an empty air-kiss.

Her introduction of Hans and John was very brief. Hans was "one of the artists who is giving a performance here later in the week." John was not even acknowledged with a name, just, "the pilot who will fly the airplane for Hans' performance."

The pilot? A bit confused by the way Renée had dismissed him, John could only manage a polite nod.

For the matching pair of painters the art critic's introduction was epic: "I would like you to meet Germany's two most famous living artists . . . ." John imagined a drum roll in the background.

"*Ja, Ja,* we have met before. . . ." Hans said, not offering a handshake, but waving his hand in the air in a friendly, yet dismissive gesture.

"Pleased to meet you. . . ." John Vigilia said, still trying to be in the game, shaking hands with first one and then the other of the German artists.

"And now the really exciting news," Renée went on almost foaming over with enthusiasm. "These two great artists, painters, the two major figures of the Neo-expressionist movement, which has taken over the entire international art world, and is in all the magazines, have agreed to become, just for this special event, performance artists."

"Ja, ja," Hans said with a smirk, "I have had a conversation just recently with Herr Speichellecker in a bar in Munich about just this subject."

"I don't remember this conversation you speak of, . . ." Speichellecker responded rather coldly.

"Well never mind. The most exciting part is that they are here . . . and Christen Bonaire has invited them to participate . . . they will be the final event. They are going to do it at the banquet. Isn't that just too wonderful! Their first ever performance . . . here! And I am going to write about it for my magazine. It will be the main topic of my article. . . ."

"Fucking shit!" Hans muttered under his breath.

"Well, come along boys, we've got to go and tell everyone this exciting news. . . ."

"Auf Wiedersehen,." said Heiner Fliegengewicht, nodding his pink head.

"Auf Wiedersehen," said Sigmund Speichellecker, also nodding his also pink head.

"Oh, eh . . . you, the pilot," Renée said turning back to John Vigilia with what must have been an afterthought. "I have looked over the notes I took during our interview . . . on reading them again I don't think it will make such an interesting story after all. I am sorry for this. Goodbye."

John felt the room suddenly become much too bright, and despite all the milling people, suspiciously quiet.

"Fucking bitch . . . she is only sucking up to those two because they are media stars . . . it's a disgrace, all these real, dedicated performance artists working all these years to gain a place, and now these two pimps come and cash in . . . the best spot given over to those two *arrivistes.* I hope you didn't give her a good fuck . . . it's a real screwing she deserves. Now we only get a small mention . . . or maybe nothing; so let's go and have something to drink. It's all you will be getting Viigilliee; you are not interesting enough, hah, hah, hah. . . ."

Hans had laughed at him. John could not forgive him this, one of the many times he had laughed at him. John Vigilia found it no small thing to be made fun of by someone he considered lower, but stronger, than him. That was what it was about Hans that tried his nerves, it was the German's self-assurance combined with his acute sense of noncommittal cruelty.

As the two men headed for the bar, Hans began to work the room, walking along, shaking hands with the artists he knew. Ambiguous phrases betraying the only thing stronger than Hans' ambition, his sexual appetite, peppered his greetings. John lagged behind. Every now and then a loud, long laugh would arise from the man Hans was talking to, probably a response to some course comment he had made about a woman that they both happened to have in their field of vision. John wished that he could disappear. He was feeling an almost oppressive melancholy. A large quantity of obscure, confused thoughts was swelling through his recently humiliated ego.

"Hans!" A loud and lusty voice bellowed from behind them.

They turned around to be greeted by Luigi Bosco, who had a woman on his arm who appeared to be wearing the costume of an American Indian, followed by two men and another woman, all three wearing nothing but parachutes. John's eyes fell first on the naked parachutists.

Then he realized that the woman in the faux Indian costume, her face disguised by what he assumed to be war paint, was the actress who he had taken home from Luigi's party, Bianca Stella. Bianca was looking hard at him as if trying to place John's face.

"Hans . . . how do you like it," Luigi said, lining the nude people up to get the maestro's approval. "These three will be going everywhere at the festival like this, naked . . . wearing only parachutes and boots. Don't you think that it will make good propaganda for our performance?"

"We will need more than nudes now," Hans moaned, with an indescribable look of gloom on his face. "I think I will make no performance,"

"No performance! So why do you say such a thing? . . ."

"They have brought here the two biggest art world pimps, Fliegengewicht and Speichellecker to do a performance . . . and at the final banquet."

"But they are not performance artists . . . they will make fools of themselves."

"No . . . they are fucking media stars. They could stand there sucking each others dicks, which I am sure they are most skilled at, and the critics would rave. Did Hans Hockenheim pose for a fashion shoot in *Vogue Magazine*? No . . . but Heiner and Sigmund did. Was Hans Hockenheim on the cover of *Vanity Fair* wearing pink hair and red suspenders? No . . . but Heiner and Sigmund were."

John had heard this screed before, his mind wandered off. He was intent on taking in the naked woman parachutist without obviously staring at her crotch. She was a very attractive female, maybe in her middle to late twenties, with full but firm breasts. The girl had long dark hair on her head, and a carefully trimmed patch the same color between her legs. The overall brown color of her skin made it clear that she regularly went out in the sun with no clothes on. John Vigilia wondered how she could stand there naked in a public place with dozens of people gawking at her and yet seem so unselfconscious. The woman parachutist caught John's eyes surveying her pudendum. He blushed; she smiled.

"Oh . . . I know you!" A voice suddenly rose up from under a feathered headband. A finger poked at John. "You're that American stunt flying pilot."

Beneath the war paint was a face he recognized. "Why it's Bianca . . . what are you doing in an Indian costume? The last time I saw you, you were dressed as a cowgirl. . . ."

"But who is paying to bring those bastards here? Heiner and Sigmund don't come arround for nothing." Hans said glaring at John and Bianca. He didn't like aside conversations when he was talking.

"Sperone!" Bianca blurted out, as if she were on a quiz show, and thrilled to have the correct answer to a million dollar question.

"Count Sperone?" Hans said incredulously.

"Yes, I saw him last week . . . he told me he was going to sponsor two German artists to do a performance at Locarno . . . he said it would be quite different because they were normally painters. He also told me he would be coming up to see it himself, although at that time he didn't know what day it would be."

"So now he comes for the banquet. That fucking bastard . . . I went all the way to Rome to beg him for money for my piece and he turned me down. He said he didn't give money for performance art, even if it had an airplane in it. 'Besides,' he said, 'you are not even using a Sperone made aircraft, so this means nothing to me.'"

"Did you tell him I was flying the airplane?" John asked.

"Yes . . . he said he had met you. He thought you must be crazy, coming to Rome to find about an American pilot that flew across the Atlantic. What was his name? ah, Lindbergh. He couldn't understand why you hadn't gone to Paris instead.

"Also, he told me to watch out for you," Hans continued, rattling on with the speed of a machine gun. "He told me that he didn't think your fucking mind was all there. He was afraid that something might happen to you; maybe you would have an accident with the airplane. I said that you seemed to me to be okay. I thought then that Sperone was just making up reasons for not giving me any fucking money."

"So did Sperone tell you how he knew I was researching Lindbergh?" John asked.

"Excuse me," a young woman holding a notepad butted in. "You are Hans Hockenheim? I am from *Art World Digest*. Do you mind if my photographer takes a picture of you and your people for my magazine? Then I would like to ask you some questions, if I may?"

"Yes, I am Hockenheim. You can have all the photographs, and questions, you want. It is about time the media took some notice of my revolutionary event. . . ."

Hans introduced the group, with the art reporter carefully recording everyone's name in her notepad. The photographer arranged the persons several times for the supposedly spontaneous shots, each time making sure that the naked parachutists were in front, facing the camera and not blocked by anyone. Despite being fairly short, John Vigilia ended up in the back row, with Bianca crowding up against him, enjoying their fleeting contact.

"I am Germany's leading performance artist, a true innovator, the pioneer of the movement. . . ." Hans began.

Having heard this all before, and knowing his unanswered question to Hans about how Count Sperone had learned of his interest in Lindbergh would have to wait for some other time, John Vigilia quietly slipped away from the group and exited the hall through the back door.

Twenty-five

Bear with my weakness; my old brain is troubled.
Be not be disturb'd with my infirmity.
. . . a turn or two I'll walk, to still my beating mind.

Shakespeare *The Tempest IV. i.*

The Congress Hall was actually located not that far from the Albergo Flaviano, if one snaked their way through the narrow side streets. Rather than drive his rental car, which was still a big expense even when he wasn't using it, John had taken to walking back and forth. The exercise was good for his body which was mostly recovered from the bicycle accident in Munich. He had discovered several ways to go, usually taking the longest, but most picturesque, along the lake in the day when he had more time. Tonight, being rather tired from what had been a very full day, John started back by what he judged to be the shortest route, although he had never been this way before, and even though it passed through some rather dark and deserted areas.

After walking a few blocks, John suddenly realized that he had not gone the way he had intended. Perhaps it was an unconscious desire to find a shortcut, to use a quicker but unfamiliar route, which had misled his mind, creating in it an illusory map of the apparently familiar streets. In the semi-obscurity of the darkness the streets had seemed to multiply, becoming somewhat confused and interchangable. John thought to turn back, to retrace his steps, however considered that this would be an unnecessary waste of time. He would have liked to ask someone directions, but at this hour none of the shops that lined the street were open, and John had not encountered another pedestrian since beginning his wayward journey.

Then John Vigilia spied a shop that he thought looked familiar. According to his calculations he ought to turn into a narrow lane, and then pass two or three more side streets in order to reach the street his hotel was on. Coming onto a street he knew, John began to run, as if anxious not to lose his way again. Then he caught the sound of running feet behind him. He had sensed that he was being followed, but lately had grown tired of the game. Someone always seemed to be behind him, but for no apparent reason. If they, whoever they were, wanted to harm him they could have done it sometime ago, John told himself. He wondered now if even the incident in Munich might have been a genuine accident. The car following close behind him had probably accelerated when the driver saw Otto standing in front of his shop, and knew he would be recognized. John Vigilia was tired of it all. He stopped running and ducked into a doorway. He would wait to confront his stalker. If nothing else John could try to ask this person, using his few Italian words, directions back to the Albergo Flaviano.

Too intimidated to go any farther on John hesitated in the shadows, his hands shaking slightly. He could make out the form of a man gradually coming down the street toward him. As he watched the figure seemed to slither along the dark walls like some insubstantial thing. He could hear the person grumbling and wheezing beneath its breath. Then John saw what he made out to be an elderly man, huffing and puffing along on a rather unsteady gait. He was relieved. How could he feel threatened by such a frail form? John Vigilia stepped out from the doorway and the man bumped into him.

"Aspetti! Wait!" the man cried excitedly as he grabbed John by the arms. This man was vaguely familiar, reminding him of the old man who always stood by the airport fence watching the airplanes come and go. As John retreated a few steps into a circle of lamplight, the strange man followed him automatically, at the same time gasping for breath. *"Mi scusi,"* he said removing his cap and slowly raising his head, looking up and breathing his sour breath into John Vigilia's anxious face.

In the diffused light of the street lamp John opened his eyes wide, like a traveler sleeping on a train suddenly awoken to find he had just now arrived at his destination. He recognized the face, the same wild and recalcitrant shocks of gray hair, bristling in irregular tufts, not only from the man's scalp, but from his warts, his eyebrows, and the openings of his nostrils and ears, giving him the appearance of a nervous porcupine, an exact double of a man he had once met on a stormy afternoon in a barn near an abandoned airport in Canada.

"Mi scusi," the man repeated, wiping his sweaty right hand on his trousers before extending it toward John. *"Mi chiamo Ariel Angelucci."*

A chill went through John's body. Unable to believe his ears, he anxiously shook the man's hand. *"Mi chiamo John Vigilia,"* was the most that he could manage in Italian. "Do you speak English?"

"Yes," the old man said hesitatingly. "I learned it as a child . . . in Chicago. But have not spoken to anyone in English for a long, long time."

"But why were you following me?"

"I know you are looking for me," Ariel replied. "My grandson sent me word you would be coming."

"So you are Ariel Angelucci," John said, a delighted tone in his voice. "But I left you a message, and you indicated that you didn't want to see me."

"I got no such message from you," Ariel said, pronouncing his words clearly, and with drawled the speech pattern of a Midwestern schoolboy.

"I left it with the desk clerk at the Albergo Flaviano . . . I know you live there . . . he said he gave it to you, and gave me your answer."

"The only message I have received recently was from some person named John Sebastian. . . ."

"That was me," John explained. "I stupidly gave the clerk a false name; I thought I was being followed."

"And you are . . . I have seen him. He always is in a black Alfa Romeo, with a Milan license plate, and a damaged right front fender. They used to watch me all the time too, years ago, but no one has bothered with me for a long while. That's how I noticed they were following you. They mean you no harm though, as long as you don't step over the line. . . ."

"Step over the line . . . what line?"

"There are things you can and cannot do. Only no one ever tells you until you've done something you weren't supposed to do. That's why they follow you."

"Are we being followed now?" John asked.

"Not as far as I can tell . . . the man in the Alfa went away this afternoon when you took that lady up in the biplane, and I haven't seen him since."

"So you're the one who stands by the fence at the airport all the time. . . ."

"Yes, I love airplanes . . . I flew a biplane once, but that was a really long time ago. But I must talk to you, and we can't do it here, on a street corner. We must go someplace."

"Where then? Back to the hotel?"

"No. We can't go there together. The person who is keeping an eye on you is staying in the room next to you. He may come back. I know a quiet place down by the lake. . . ."

"Then I'll follow you," John said smiling, confused, almost embarrassed by what just had happened, his search ended, with all the ease and absurdity of a dream.

His guide started off down the dark street. Their short pause must have refreshed him for he was now setting a fast pace, as John discovered struggling to keep up. Ariel Angelucci, if that was really his name, though there was no doubting the resemblance, struck him as being a reasonable man. For the moment John would let himself be diverted by the amenities of the walk and settle into idle conversation. He had questions to ask about this whole strange affair, but wondered whether he, as the questioner, was entitled to receive the truth. Not knowing what to do with it, John felt that perhaps he did not deserve it, and the man's giving it to him would amount to a severe disservice. Learning Ariel Angelucci's true story, John Vigilia considered, if it was what it was supposed to be, also might put him in more danger than he wanted to be in.

The two men walked in silence for a while, always heading downhill, sometimes by a labyrinth of narrow stone stairs that led between rows of houses like a dark tunnel. John could smell the freshness of the lake above the mustiness of the street. Off in the distance he heard the sound of thunder. Numerous anvil-shaped clouds rose over the mountains to the west and embraced the sky, which seemed to have been deserted by the night birds. But he sensed the weather would not be coming here anytime soon. Directly above them the dense clouds parted, revealing a single star. John Vigilia was afraid, and could not stifle his fear. He felt as if an ominous presence was surrounding him.

Suddenly, perhaps animated by his walk and now eager to begin, Ariel started talking, his words coming in short, rapid breaths that kept pace with his quick, but unsteady, step.

His story was not that different from the one John had heard told by this man's exact double in the farmhouse in Canada. Was it too close? he wondered. The words sounded almost as though they had been rehearsed, repeated from a script, a strange coincidence from two men who supposedly had not seen each other in sixty-some years. As they passed a street light John stole a glance at Ariel's face, trying to match it to the words, a face to be tabulated and deciphered for subtler meanings. His visage was that of some ancient aviator, smiling justifiably after some historic flight. There was laughter in his eyes; and in his mouth, honor and sorrow.

They reached a small, and relatively deserted, square. Ariel said that this was not their destination, but that he needed to stop and rest for a moment. He chose to sit down on the low stone wall of the central fountain and John took a place next to him. The old man continued to chatter on, breathing irregularly and mopping sweat from his brow, even though the evening was rather cool. Regrettably, Ariel had become rather garrulous. His story was becoming circular, repeating things he had already told John. He had just arrived at the point in the narrative where he and his uncle were standing in a field in Nova Scotia waiting for Lindbergh to fly in and pick him up when he broke off:

"There's a cafe," Ariel said pointing across the square to a glass window with red curtains that glowed brightly from the light within. "Shall we have a little drink together? Let's stop here for a while before going on."

"A good idea," John agreed.

"I'll take grappa," Ariel said, sitting down in a chair at one of the empty tables out front, the reddish reflection from inside playing on his weathered face. John went into the bar. When he returned, carrying a glass of grappa for each of them, the old man started to rummage through his pockets as if to take out some money.

"It's on me," John said. Raising his glass, he added, "Here's to our new found friendship.

"Brothers in flight," Ariel said, tossing down his drink in one decisive gulp. Shaking like a cataleptic, he laughed and banged his glass down on the table. "They don't give me much money anymore. I haven't had a drink in three days." Then his breathing slowed, and color came back to his porcupine face.

Eager to have Ariel get on with his tale, John took a small sip of his drink, put the glass down, and confronted the storyteller. "But why have you kept silent about this all these years?" he asked.

Ariel looked at John and smiled, a cautious smile that made his lower lip tremble. "I did not reveal my part in Lindbergh's flight at first because my life was threatened, and later because I thought no one would believe me. History had already been written."

"So what exactly was your part in the flight?" John asked, speaking carefully, as if he were walking on wet cobblestones. Above the square the night seemed full of mystery, of a grim silence that betrayed the distant, incomprehensible sounds of a waiting to be born thunderstorm.

"I flew with Lindbergh during the most difficult leg . . . across the Atlantic, through the ice and fog."

"And he supposedly landed in Nova Scotia and picked you up?"

"Yes. The airplane had a wicker seat, which was designed far back for his long legs . . . but in reality it was modified that way so he could slide it forward and make a place for me behind him. I was only fifteen, and small for my age, but I had already been flying with my uncle for three years."

"So why do you want to make all this known now?"

"The sixty-third anniversary of the flight was last May. Lindbergh has been dead for a long time. My story cannot hurt him now. I am not a young man, on my next birthday I will be seventy-nine. And while I feel I have a few more years to live yet ahead of me, I do not want to die as someone not remembered for anything.

"I read some years later that at his first press conference in Paris Lindbergh slipped up and used the word 'we' when talking about his flight. The American ambassador immediately jumped in and explained that when Lindbergh said 'we' he meant the airplane and himself. You notice he kept saying 'we' all the time. He even wrote a book with that name. I believe that Lindbergh was a decent fellow, and had confessed to the ambassador just what had really happened, but at that moment in history America needed a world-class hero. I don't know how the ambassador got in touch with Count Sperone; I believe it was through the pope at the time. And I could never figure out why Sperone got involved in the scheme, I think maybe the old count was trying to get the United States Navy to buy some of his seaplanes."

Finished with his grappa now, John waved his finger over the empty glasses in front of them. Ariel nodded, and John went back inside for two more. Standing at the bar, he thought about his incredible luck at finally meeting with Ariel Angelucci, finding something refreshing in the idea that he could perhaps impose an ending to the mystery surrounding him.

Since the death of his wife, and his involvement in this search for Lindbergh's alleged copilot, John Vigilia had become sullenly hostile to most of the world. He felt isolated. He hated being silent, but his inability to communicate what he was doing to other people had left John feeling distinctly alone, and he was a man who secretly could not bear to carry on by himself. He was much too apprehensive of the vast confusion of life surrounding him, of which he was helpless. At present, John simply mistrusted everyone.

"I remember standing in an open field somewhere in Canada. I was with my Uncle Francis," Ariel began when his new friend had returned with their second glasses of grappa. He seemed to have lost the thread of what he was saying when John had left. "We were waiting for

Lindbergh to arrive in his airplane. I was still not exactly sure where I was . . . or why I was there.

"We had been flying around light rain showers off and on ever since we reached Nova Scotia. My uncle was good at dodging them. I didn't know how Francis was navigating, since we had never been here before . . . and the chart looked a bit different from the ones I knew from back home. But he seemed to know where he was. As for me I was having difficulty just keeping my finger on the map.

"Francis had said we couldn't get lost because we would be flying over an island and that there should be water on one side or the other. I was supposed to be watching for a bay, and then a river, but my uncle must have spotted it first . . . because he peeled-off and dived down and dragged a field that I thought was surely too small for the Jenny . . . let alone Lindbergh's new airplane, which I hadn't seen but heard it needed a lot of runway. Well Francis didn't let me land . . . which I was glad for, but he came around and set that Jenny down in the field on the very first try. Now with the wet ground and high grass we didn't roll that far . . . and I wondered how he was gonna get it out again, even with the weight of me not in it.

"The morning before we had gotten up at dawn, and flown up from my aunt's farm somewhere on the Canadian side of Lake Erie. I should have been in school . . . but three days ago my uncle had said we had to go on a trip, and that he would give my teacher a note. He said we were going to stop to see my twin brother, Caliban . . . who I never saw because it cost a lot of money to go there, which we didn't have. From there we were going on to Nova Scotia, where I was going to meet up with Lindbergh and help him fly his airplane to Paris. . . only no one was supposed to know, so we had to be kinda sneaky about it. It's a good thing he told me the night before so I could look up Nova Scotia and Paris in my geography book, as

I had no idea where I was going because I'd never been east of Chicago.

"Well when we got to the farm my uncle told my aunt we were going to Nova Scotia, but didn't say anything about me going on to Paris. But I did tell Caliban . . . after all it was almost like he and I were the same person. The next day we flew to an airport in Maine that had a telegraph office . . . and slept in the hangar. That evening we received a telegram signed 'Slim' that read only: *Maybe tomorrow.*

"When we woke up at dawn it was cloudy with a light rain . . . and we didn't think we were going to fly. But after about an hour or so the clouds stated to clear out. At 7:30 the telegraph operator handed us another message from 'Slim', looking at us rather strangely. This one read: *Will be off by 08:00 stop you go now.* We took off immediately . . . having a shorter distance to fly to the rendezvous field, but a slower airplane.

"So there we were standing in the mud in a field somewhere in Nova Scotia waiting . . . and a kind of fog rolled in. I asked my uncle if he was sure that this was the field . . . and all he could say was 'pretty sure.' My uncle had wanted someone to meet us there so we could know we were in the right place . . . but Lindbergh had said no. He said that the less people who knew about what we were doing the better . . . and besides he didn't have enough money to pay anyone to meet us.

"As you know Lindbergh was fixing to fly from New York to Paris non-stop and win the Orteig Prize. Since he was not as famous as some of the other pilots who were trying, he was having trouble raising money, until he came up with the idea of doing it solo. After that he had no trouble getting his money and an airplane.

"If you remember ten days before his transatlantic flight Lindbergh had set a record for flying from San Diego to New York. But he stopped in Saint Louis for a break . . . and that flight was only 21 hours. At the airport he ran into my uncle and mentioned how he got tired on the flight, and how he didn't think he could make it across the Atlantic without falling asleep. And so my uncle had said: Why don't you do what I do, take the kid along to help you fly. And Lindbergh said that his was only a single place airplane, and besides he was supposed to be doing it solo. My uncle looked into the cockpit and pointed out that if he moved his seat forward there would be plenty of room for a small person . . . and that no one need know. He could pick up his copilot in Nova Scotia and drop him off in Ireland. So they agreed to have me go along, and, if we got there, Lindbergh and my uncle would split the prize, and I would get half of my uncle's share. Now back in 1927, even half of half of $25,000 was a whole lot of money.

"Well the fog opened up and in a few minutes we saw a silver monoplane and my uncle said: 'There he is.' But the airplane flew right on by . . . and we thought that we must be in the wrong field. Then a few minutes later it swooped in low and saw us . . . and took a look at the field but didn't land. It circled three more times . . . and finally came in bouncing and skidding in the mud. It was a good thing the airplane had such big wheels. Lindbergh cut the engine as soon as the plane touched down.

"The plane rolled to a stop and we ran over to it as Slim hopped out. He didn't want to waste any time, or gas, so the three of us pushed and tugged that airplane over to the very edge of the field, as he was going to need every inch of it to get back out again. Fortunately it was fairly cold, and a good wind had come up. So I crawled in behind the seat. There wasn't much space there . . . and Lindbergh was all hunkered up in front. I looked over his shoulder, and was surprised to see there wasn't any window forward because of the huge gas tank. I asked Lindbergh how we were gonna see out and he showed me the little periscope he had installed. He laughed and said once we got out over the Atlantic he didn't think we would be in danger of running into anybody coming from the other direction.

"Now I had never flown in anything but our old Jenny with its eight cylinder, liquid-cooled, inline OX-5 engine which put out only at best 90 horsepower. The throbbing of that Wright Whirlwind air-cooled radial . . . which I had heard put out over 200 horsepower . . . was real exciting. Lindbergh didn't waste any time. He pushed the throttle in and the airplane started to move forward. I was surprised at how slow we were rolling, considering all that power up front. Then I realized that although he had flown all the way up from New York, he still had over three quarters of his fuel supply on board. I think it was a good thing we didn't have a view out front, for when we finally broke ground we were climbing at a snails pace, and I wouldn't want to have been looking at those trees that were coming up in front of us.

"Watching out the side window it seemed like we cleared the tree tops by only about a foot. And I was sure that I heard branches slapping at the landing gear. I thought we were going to go back over the field and wave to my uncle . . . but Lindbergh didn't say anything, just turned the airplane to the northeast, and in a little while we were out over water. I realized then that I was sitting on a bunch of stuff . . . flashlights, balls of string, a hunting knife, cans of rations, a bundle of flares wrapped in bicycle inner tubing, and a life raft with an air pump. Two aluminum canteens of water hung on the side of the wicker seat. There was also a bag of sandwiches. I remember looking inside to see what we were going to eat. We had two ham sandwiches, two roast beef, and one hard-boiled egg."

Staring out across the empty square, John Vigilia sat at the table and sipped his grappa, mesmerized by the man's words. He was listening wide awake, lucid, and above all rational, to Ariel's recounting of his past.

Who was he to say if the story was true or just make-believe? Then John remembered his tape recorder back at the hotel. He didn't even have his notepad with him. He had not anticipated running into Ariel Angelucci tonight, and was not like most writers who always carried a pencil and paper with them. He couldn't tell the man to stop, hold on, wait until he went back to his room and got his stuff.

Ariel had been leading them along to somewhere else, he said a place by the lake, but he had stopped here, and begun his story. He wanted to tell it now; who knew how long he had been waiting to tell this story. Perhaps tomorrow he wouldn't want to repeat it, or might even deny ever having told it to this stranger, or that it even ever happened. John would have to rely on his memory to recreate the text, as astonishing as it was elusive, its threads infinitely woven and complicated. John Vigilia's mind, already loaded with the many events of the past days, and clouded by the two grappas that he had just consumed, would have to make intelligible tomorrow the tangle of tonight's experience.

"I squirmed around in the cockpit to get a bit more comfortable," Ariel continued, "and found that Lindbergh had brought along two air cushions for me. Down below I could see that the ocean was covered with caked ice. After a while the ice disappeared and I saw a ship now and then. But as we flew along I could see great banks of thick fog rolling in from the ocean. The temperature was dropping steadily . . . and little needles of ice were forming on the fuselage and struts.

"We were still over water . . . but off in the distance I could see that we were coming to another large island. The fog was coming in thicker than ever . . . and we flew low to keep out of it. At the end of the island, which Lindbergh shouted to me was Newfoundland, a brisk wind was tearing the fog into mist and piling it up into what looked like huge mountains.

"Dusk was falling when we finally flew over a fairly large town, Lindbergh told me it was St. Johns . . . and headed for the last tip of land on the continent. Lindbergh carefully circled the stark cliffs that projected out into the Atlantic . . . making sure this was the correct location he had selected as the jumping-off place.

"I looked at my watch when we left the coast. I remember clearly that it was 7:15. Lindbergh turned around. He said that he had been flying for almost eleven and a half hours . . . and that I should try to get some sleep. He said he would get us on course, and try to go on for a few more hours . . . but that I should be ready when he needed me. Then we headed into the thick of the fog.

"The weather bureau back in Maine had predicted it was going to clear up and there was going to be good flying weather . . . but that had not happened. But then they weren't very accurate back in those days."

"They're not that accurate these days either, even with their weather satellites, and Doppler radar, and all the other hi-tech stuff they have," John quipped.

They paused to look up and watch an airliner pass noiselessly overhead, its strobe lights flashing in and out of the cloudy sky. Then Ariel went on. His dialogue had become as grim as the distant sounds of thunder John could now hear creeping across the mountains.

"Soon we were flying in the most dangerous kind of weather I had ever flown in. Thick clouds pressed down almost to the surface of the ocean . . . so cold that they could have at any moment turned into a sleet storm. I was glad we were flying in an enclosed cabin and not an open cockpit like the Jenny. Lindbergh had on a huge fur-lined flying suit and seemed snug. But I was starting to feel the cold through my leather flight jacket . . . even though I had on three sweaters, and a flannel shirt underneath it.

"Then the sleet hit us in earnest. Ice began to form on the wing's leading edge, the struts and the propeller.

Now I don't have to tell you what that means. Despite all the power of the Wright, the airplane began to struggle just to hold its altitude. Lindbergh shouted to me asking if I though we should turn back. He said we could make a safe landing at St. Johns. He would put it down gently in the shallow water near the shore and we would use the life raft to get to land. Now having grown up in the Midwest I had never learned to swim, so was not too keen on the idea. So I told him that, but I also said whatever he wanted to do was all right by me . . . figuring that we would probably end up in the water somewhere anyways.

"Lindbergh was looking all around through his periscope. Out the side window I could see the sleet was coming down faster than ever. Then Lindbergh made up his mind: 'We're going to fight it out,' he said, 'we're going to Paris as planned.' He banked the airplane and shot downward until we emerged beneath the cloud bank . . . scarcely a few hundred feet from the cold, dark crashing waves. Then he leveled off to steady his compass, and headed eastward. Meanwhile I had been getting everything off of the life raft . . . and working it up to the top of the pile of stuff I was sitting on.

"It was a bit warmer down low, and I could see the ice beginning to melt off the struts as we were forced to go lower and lower to get beneath the fog. Now we were so low that the waves seemed to be splashing on the landing gear. Through his periscope Lindbergh could see that directly ahead of us the fog and the sea met as one great solid gray wall. 'We're trapped,' I remember hearing him shout, 'we have got to go back on up there.' This was our only chance. We had to climb up through the fog and sleet and find the clear air on top.

"Lindbergh pushed the throttle to the firewall and the airplane, lightened a bit by the fuel that had been used coming from New York began to stagger upward. Awhile later I looked over his shoulder at the altimeter.

We were at 5000 feet . . . and surrounded by the fog and sleet. At 8000 feet we were still in the clouds. The wings were now one broad sheet of ice . . . but I was beginning to see faint patches of sky. Then at 10,000 feet we broke out on top of the clouds.

"The ice began to shred and fall off in chunks. Every now and then the engine over-revved as the propeller threw off some of its frozen covering. It had been a slow and painful climb of almost two miles. The cloud bank below us looked like the gently rolling hills back home . . . where I secretly wished I was. I wondered why I had let my uncle talk me into this trip . . . and if I would ever see him or his biplane again.

"On top of the clouds now, Lindbergh made a couple of shallow turns and then headed off on a course. I shouted at him, asking how we were navigating . . . as my uncle and I always followed rivers and railroad tracks wherever we were going. Lindbergh replied that he was using his compass for 'dead-reckoning' . . . but that he was flying the 'Great Circle Route', and could not fly in just a straight line. Every hour . . . he was assuming a ground speed of 100 miles per hour . . . he took up a new heading, based on what he had calculated on his charts.

"By now the sky was pitch black . . . with no moon and only a few stars. I caught Lindbergh yawning sleepily. Now that the tension and excitement of the sleet and fog had passed, fatigue seemed to be taking its toll on him. I'll admit that I didn't feel too fresh myself. I leaned forward and yelled in his ear that I was ready to take over whenever he needed me. He shouted back that although he had only three hours of sleep the night before he felt he could go on for a few more hours. I won't deny that I was glad to hear this as I had flown very little at night . . . and never when I couldn't see the ground. Also I couldn't figure how we were going to change positions in that tiny cockpit.

"I wondered why we had started out in the face of such unsure weather rather than wait a few days . . . but then I remembered my uncle telling me that there were other pilots on the ground in New York waiting to take off with better and faster airplanes. Lindbergh had to be the first to Paris; there was no money for second place. I don't know how well you know your aviation history. . . ." Ariel said, indicating to John that his glass was again empty.

John Vigilia went inside and came back out holding two more glasses of grappa. "I think the man at the bar said these are our last," he informed Ariel. "They're closing up in a few more minutes."

"I don't know how well you know your aviation history," Ariel repeated after taking a sip of his drink, "and I didn't know that much myself back then . . . but I have had a lot of time to study it since." The old man was nursing his drink, making it last now that he knew it was the last one. "When I worked at the Sperone Museum in Como the name of Lindbergh sometimes came up. Well most people, especially Americans, seem to have the idea that Lindbergh was the first person to fly across the Atlantic, and that he had done it alone. Now I couldn't tell them that I knew for a fact that he had someone with him . . . at least on the leg from Newfoundland to Ireland. But they were always surprised when I told them that before Lindbergh's flight there had been twelve other crossings starting as far back as 1919."

"Yes," John interjected, eager to show his knowledge of the history of flight. "Wasn't the first crossing by a group of U. S. Navy pilots . . . flying Curtis seaplanes, the NC series or something like that?"

"You're right," Ariel replied with a smile, "which shows me you know more about aviation history than most people. But that was a crossing of the Southern Atlantic. And it was assisted by a whole fleet of Navy ships that lined the way. As it was only one airplane out of the entire group, piloted by a Lieutenant Commander Albert C. Read, actually completed the trip.

"The first non-stop crossing of the North Atlantic was also made in 1919, a month later by two Englishmen . . . John Alcock and Arthur Brown in a Vickers Vimy. Unfortunately they crash landed their airplane shortly after making landfall."

"How do you know so much about aviation history?" John asked, and then regretted his question, realizing that they were straying away from the real story he wanted to hear, the details of Ariel's supposed flight with Charles Lindbergh.

"I love airplanes and flying. As a boy my twin brother and I were left orphans. We were in school the day my father, who worked in a slaughterhouse, went crazy. For reasons no one understood, maybe because he couldn't stand his job, he had been a professor back in Italy, he killed my mother, and set fire to our apartment before taking his own life. I was sent to live with my uncle Francis, who was a barnstormer in the Midwest, my brother Caliban was sent to an aunt who had a farm in Canada. I always thought that I got the better deal as I learned to fly, while he had to work on her farm almost like a slave."

John wanted to tell Ariel that he had been to that farm and met his brother Caliban, who had told him the story about the death of their parents, but restrained himself; "So, why don't you continue with the Lindbergh flight. . . ."

"You want me to tell you every detail of the flight . . . hour by hour?" Ariel asked.

"Please. If you would," John said, trying not to sound like he was nudging the old man along.

"Do you know that that flight, with Lindbergh in 1927, was the last time I was ever in an airplane . . . I have had to content myself with building models, and reading books about airplanes. That's how I know so much of the history. I have a huge library of aviation materials in my room. I go to the airport almost every day to watch the airplanes take off and land . . . that's how I knew it was you who was flying the biplane. There are other pilots who fly it, but no one from around here flies it like you do. I would love to fly in an open cockpit biplane again . . . if only for one more time before I die," Ariel revealed, paused and then went on. "I have a favor to ask of you."

Up until that moment they had been alone in the cafe, no one was out here or inside. Then a man came in from the dark streets, a man with an ambiguous look, plain, appearing as if he might be a school teacher, or a clerk. The only thing that distinguished his unmemorable face was his pale, blotchy skin. Ariel seemed to know him, or at least he stopped talking when the man walked past. The stranger went in and got himself a drink, then came back out and sat down at the one table opposite John and Ariel. Purposely catching their gaze, he nodded and smiled a kind of malicious smile, then raised his glass to them saying: "To your health."

John was very surprised by the man having made the toast in English. They exchanged glances, and then all three men lifted their glasses, and nodded, without saying anything. The stranger continued to stare at them with whitish eyes that froze John's flesh. He felt a chill running through his spine. Ariel muttered something in Italian that John did not understand, and stopped talking completely. Taking his cue, John Vigilia did not say another word, but sat there studying his empty glass. Off in the mountains he could hear the rumbling of a storm that seemed to be passing south of the city in the direction of Como. Suddenly, as happened more often these days, thoughts of Miranda came into John's head. He tried to push the memories away, but, in the forced silence surrendered to the passion and thrill of that day on the villa roof in Como.

After a short time the man finished his drink and got up to leave. He nodded to John and Ariel without saying anything. Ariel put his chin down on his chest and assumed an evasive and nasty look. When the man had disappeared back into the darkness, Ariel laughed.

"Do you know him?" John asked.

"I have seen him around," was all Ariel would volunteer. He laughed again, and went on laughing without explanation. John was dying of curiosity to know not only what the man's connection to Ariel was, but also to hear the rest of the Lindbergh story. Then the old man spat on the floor, saying something in Italian John took to be a curse. Turning again to his new found friend Ariel Angelucci continued rather reluctantly: "Just before that man came in I was going to ask you for a favor."

"Yes, yes, I remember . . . go ahead. If it's something I can do I will be glad to do it for you."

"Would you please take me up for a flight in the Jungmann?" Ariel said. His words were filled with a kind of timidity and awkwardness that belied the urgency of his request.

John realized now that he had been afforded a kind of leverage over this old man. He actually had something that Ariel wanted, which was perhaps why he had decided to confide in John and tell him his story. He had probably not known that John was allowed to take up passengers until he had seen him fly with Renée Coûteux. John decided that he would press his advantage and get the whole story, maybe even get Ariel to repeat it into his tape recorder. "I'd be honored to take you up, Ariel," John answered. "We can probably go tomorrow. I usually practice in the morning, as you have seen. I'll make the arrangements."

"Thank you," the old man said, his eyes sparkling like galaxies. "You cannot know how happy this makes me . . . to fly again, after all these many years."

"So now tell me, Ariel," John asked, prompting him back to his tale. "Did you ever get to actually take the controls of the *Spirit of Saint Louis?*"

"Oh yes, yes, of course . . . my story of the flight." Ariel paused to wipe his brow, the wind had died down and the air in the square had become hot, almost oppressive. "We were on top of the cloud bank, which seemed to go on forever. The motor was beating smoothly, and gave us a bit of confidence. Lindbergh told me to open the package of sandwiches. I asked him what kind did he want and he said whatever is on top. So I took off the oiled paper covering it and handed him a ham sandwich. I ate half of the other ham sandwich and gave the rest to him which he finished. Then we both took a swig of water from the one of the two canteens hanging on the back of the seat. I remember how cold the water tasted, and how curious and lonesome our meal had seemed.

"After each hour passed Lindbergh faithfully recorded another hundred miles and corrected the heading on his compass. These hundred-mile sections of his progress seemed to be keeping him awake. Every time he made a new compass change he explained the procedure to me again . . . telling me that if I took over I would have to do it exactly as he had been doing it. He realized that there was no way I was going to be able to sleep in my little cramped space . . . so it had become a situation of carrying on a conversation, each keeping the other from dozing off.

"Lindbergh told me the night would be very short. We were flying directly toward the sun, and at that latitude dawn came at about four in the morning. He said he had calculated that our ground speed of 100 miles-per-hour should cut about two hours from the darkness so that the night would last only four hours.

"Out the side window it had not been all blackness. Shortly after we had climbed above the clouds, the moon had appeared through the misty sky and flooded the upper surface of the cloud bank with a strange and beautiful glow. Lindbergh said he was happy to see the moon as it made the flying a bit less complicated. Below us through the fog I occasionally spotted a blur of light . . . that must have been a ship.

"The fog bank finally lowered and we descended with it. Then the clouds thinned and Lindbergh slid down through them to where it was warmer. We were flying only about a hundred feet above the water, sometimes as low as ten feet. Lindbergh explained he liked to fly low to take advantage of that cushion of air near to the surface of the water. He was also able to determine the wind drift more easily closer to the water. He showed me how to watch for white caps on the waves. When one of these formed the foam would be blown off, allowing him to estimate the wind's direction and approximate velocity. This foam remained on the water long enough for him to get a good idea of our drift.

"We flew along at a low altitude for some time until we came to a hailstorm and had to climb back up. But there was no getting above the clouds this time. I don't remember how high we went, but I do know we reached a point where the airplane just would not climb anymore. We were still in the dense gray clouds. There was nothing to do but fly on blind. Now I've seen photos and sat in cockpits of later airplanes, their panels loaded with instruments for flying in bad weather; artificial horizons, directional gyros, automatic pilots, and all. I can tell you for sure that the *Spirit of Saint Louis* had none of these.

"If I close my eyes, I can still see the instrument board, as they called it in those days. There were only two rows. On the top . . . starting from the left was an oil pressure gauge, oil temperature gauge, then a turn and bank indicator, and the airspeed indicator. The bottom row had a tachometer, three switches for lights, a big leveling compass right in the middle, the altimeter . . . and finally the ignition switch.

"Well I had never ever flown an airplane by instruments so just sat there fascinated. I'd get the feeling in my head that we were turning, or maybe diving, and I'd look over Lindbergh's shoulder and the instruments would be all straight and level; the turn needle straight up, the bank ball in the center, and the altimeter needle, it had only a single needle altimeter, right on. Lindbergh told me that this was what you had to watch out for . . . that when you couldn't see the ground your inner ear gave you false sensations. He said you had to ignore what you were feeling and believe the instruments . . . otherwise you might get into what was called a 'dead man's spiral' and crash. I told him I didn't think I could do this . . . so he said he would keep on flying until we were in the clear.

"I must have dozed off a bit. When I woke up suddenly, it sounded like the engine was over-speeding, and that we were in a steep descending spiral. I laughed to myself and leaned over to tell Lindbergh that my inner ear was playing tricks on me again. Then I saw the instrument board. The turn needle was all the way to the left, with the ball skewed all the way to the right, the airspeed was at 130 and accelerating, and the altimeter was unwinding like a broken clock. It wasn't my inner ear this time . . . we were in a spiral ... Lindbergh must have also fallen asleep while I had also been sleeping.

"I shook him by the shoulder, yelling 'Wake up! Wake up!' He was in a deep sleep and slow to come around. I didn't know what to do, but figured pulling back the throttle was a good idea. It must have been the change in the engine's sound that brought him back. Careful not to overstress the still heavy aircraft, Lindbergh took the controls and, leveling the wings, began gradually pulling out of the dive. As it was we broke out of the fog only a few hundred feet above the water . . . but as I said he rather liked flying down low anyway.

"That was as close to touching the controls as I ever got. Lindbergh's brief nap seemed to have revived him completely. Dawn was beginning to appear. As the light increased the mist started to lift from the surface of the sea. Lindbergh took a look through his periscope and said that the weather was clearing up ahead. We flew along . . . and in awhile I saw white gulls drifting along outside the window. The fog had shredded to nothingness, and it looked like it was going to turn into a nice day. Lindy watched the sun rise through his periscope and then turned to me and said: 'This is what flying is all about.' He was real happy, and kept shouting: 'Come on Ireland!' I asked him how he was going to know Ireland when he saw it, and he replied: 'Ireland is green and mountainous. I'll be sure to know it when I see it.'

"Then, about noon, a strange thing happened. Lindbergh said that through his periscope he could see a shoreline. It was too soon he thought . . . but he said he saw it first low and rather gray, and now it had assumed form, green and high. He changed course slightly, and banked the airplane so that I could see it out the side window. I remember that I too saw cliffs and valleys and distant mountains. Lindbergh resumed course and began to study his maps and calculations. Then he banked the airplane again so we could take another look, but nothing was there. It had only been a mirage . . . but we both had seen it.

"After a little while more we saw a fishing boat. We were sure this was a mirage too . . . but as we got closer we saw it was a real fishing boat. In fact there was not just one boat but several, all grouped within a few miles of each other. We flew over the first boat without seeing any signs of life. But as we circled the second, several men appeared from a cabin door. Lindbergh decided to try to get the fishermen to point towards land. He pulled back the throttle and circled low shouting at the boatmen through his open window. Since I wasn't supposed to be there he told me to keep my head down. Now I couldn't help trying to see what was going on . . . I saw one of the men who had come out on deck standing near the stern, which means he probably saw me, although it was rather dark in the cockpit.

"All these years I've kept hoping that the man who saw me in the back, if for only an instant, might recognize the *Spirit of Saint Louis* from pictures in the newspaper, and come forward and say that he saw two heads in the small window of the strange airplane that circled his boat on that May morning.

"Apparently no one on board could hear Lindbergh shouting: 'Which way is Ireland?' as he circled just a few feet above the boat. Or perhaps they heard but did not speak English, as they gave no sign of recognition. He circled again, then realizing that it was useless, and he was just wasting fuel, pushed in the throttle and we climbed back up on course.

"Less than an hour after we had circled the fishing boats, a rugged and semi-mountainous coastline appeared off to our left. We were only ten or fifteen miles away. The air had been fairly hazy and there were clouds from a few local storms . . . so we had not seen it earlier. The coastline came down from the north and curved over towards the east. Lindbergh was sure it was the southwestern most end of Ireland, and changed his course towards the nearest point of land. This was Dingle Bay; the place where I was to get dropped off."

A man in an apron, who seemed to be the proprietor of the small cafe came out, picked up John and Ariel's empty glasses, and then said something in Italian. Ariel translated, saying that the man was sorry, but he must close now.

Ariel first, followed by, John, got up from the table and started walking toward the lake. As the lights of the cafe blinked out behind them, John heard the clatter of a car on the cobbled pavement, the only car he had observed on this dark and narrow street since they had come down it. He pulled Ariel into a doorway. The car bounced by and kept on going. It wasn't a black Alfa Romeo, but a dark blue Fiat Uno. There were two men in it. John Vigilia gave it no notice until it pulled over and parked some distance farther down the street and the driver turned off the headlights. He waited for the men to get out. In the darkness John could see a number of flashes and gleams, lightning bolts from the mountains across the lake. His mind again filled itself with the strange and disconnected thoughts of his dead wife, and of Miranda.

He was just about to step back out into the street when Ariel put his hand on John's arm, restraining him.

"Wait. . . ." he whispered.

They could hear noise coming from inside the car, the sound of laughter. John moved farther back into the shadows. A kind of vague, mysterious terror was condensing in his brain, some unknowable thing growing, little by little in his consciousness. John felt as if he were standing on the edge, looking into a deep, dark well.

A beam of light slanted down from a tiny window overhead, and just as quickly as it came, it went away. The two men remained crouching in the doorway in a silence so deep it seemed a suspension of time itself.

Then the car started up and drove slowly away. John gently shoved Ariel into a side alley.

"Let's go this way," he said softly.

"But I forget where this street goes." Ariel replied. He was breathing heavily, and walking slowly on the uneven stones.

"It doesn't matter. I think I might know where it comes out," John said, trying to sound reassuring.

After a time they made their way back to the Albergo Flaviano by a devious and tiring route. Ariel said little during the walk back, having to stop frequently to get his breath. He confirmed that Lindbergh had landed on a beach near Dingle and let him off, and that it was the wrong beach. John was just questioning him further about the orphanage when they turned a corner and found themselves back at their hotel.

"You go in through the lobby," Ariel said stopping short of the entrance. "I'll use the rear door . . . that's how I always go in anyway. It's best if the desk clerk doesn't see us talking together."

"So when am I going to hear the rest of your story? I mean what happened to you after you were left on the wrong beach?"

"I will tell you tomorrow."

"When can we meet . . . sometime in the evening?"

"You said you would take me up in the biplane. . . ."

"That I did," John said, remembering his promise, which Ariel had not forgotten. "Okay. We can go up tomorrow morning; the weather is supposed to be good. I am signed up to fly at 10:00. Do you want me to come by for you around 9:00?"

"No. It's better if we are not seen together here at the hotel at all. I can get to the airport by myself; I always take the bus. I will be in my usual place . . . by the fence. Look for me there. Until tomorrow morning then . . . good night," Ariel said, shaking John's hand.

"Good night," John replied. He could feel the cold and damp perspiration on the old man's palm.

"Oh," Ariel said turning back, "you never told me how you learned my secret."

"Your brother Caliban told me."

"My brother, Caliban?" Ariel said, a pained expression coming over his face. It was as if John had suddenly entered some illegal zone of the conversation.

"Yes, I met him almost three months ago, when I landed at an abandoned airport near his farm in Canada. . . ."

"Then it's a lie!"

"What's a lie? I tell you I did meet him."

"It's a lie that he's dead. Years ago, when I had some trouble with the count's daughter, they told me that I was going to be sent away. I asked them if I could go back to America. They said I couldn't, that everyone in my family had died. I said I had a twin brother Caliban, and that he was too young to be dead. They told me that he had joined the merchant marines, and that the boat he was working on went down in Lake Erie in 1942. They even told me the name of the boat, the *Morgan Sidney,* a British boat, from Liverpool."

"The boat he was on was named the *Morgan Sidney!"* John exclaimed, exhaling deeply, the last remnants of anything cohesive having been sucked from him. "You're sure of that name?"

"Yes, I wrote it down, and carried the name around with me for years. I was planning to look it up in a ship registry if I ever got the chance. But now you tell me Caliban is still alive." Ariel turned to John; his eyebrows working wildly, "This is such good news. How did he look? Was he well?"

"He looked rather, ah . . . like you," John replied, too spooked to think of anything else. Ariel's story had corroborated what he had been told by the artist in Dingle, and read in several newspapers back in the U.S.A., the *Morgan Sidney* had sunk in 1942. Then what was the ship that he had he seen in the fog? And who was the person had he met on the farm? "Caliban seemed to be doing well," John said, not sure of what exactly to say at the moment. "Look, it's late. I'm tired and we've both had enough excitement for one night. I'll tell you all about your brother when I see you tomorrow."

"You're right, I'm very tired too; until tomorrow then," he whispered, shaking John's hand again. Turning around, Ariel quickly disappeared into nothingness down the dark walk that led to the back door of the hotel.

As John Vigilia climbed the steps to the lobby, he noticed a black Alfa Romeo parked in the loading zone out front. The damaged right front fender appeared to have been repaired, but he recognized the Milan license plate.

"There is a message for you, Professor Vigilia," the night clerk said handing John a note when he stopped by the desk to pick up his key.

He wondered about the clerk addressing him as 'Professor Vigilia.' He could not recall telling anyone at the hotel that he was a professor. He had certainly not checked in as Professor John Vigilia. John turned the paper over in his hand and studied its quality. Then he unfolded the note and read it. It had been hand written and was from Count Ferdinand Sperone. The message read:

> *Dear Professor Vigilia,*
>
> *I have come to Locarno to attend the performance art festival. While I am here I would like to talk to you about the progress you are making on your book. Can you meet me in the lobby of the hotel tomorrow afternoon at 15:00? Leave a message for me at the front desk.*
>
> *—Your friend, Ferdinand Sperone*

John read the note, and read it once again, wondering just what its implications might be. It was then that the realization hit him; a vision of what must have happened so many years ago, the omnipotence of the old Count Sperone shutting Ariel's life off as if he were in a prison, and his son willing to continue the sentence for no other reason than that he could. John Vigilia was from a time, and a country, where authority was still somewhat controlled, but he saw that there were uncounted varieties of existence in the world that he had yet to be faced with. Despite his attempt at sounding friendly, John did not take count's message to be one of good tidings.

Twenty-six

. . . So full of valor that they smote the air
For breathing in their faces; beat the ground
For kissing of their feet; yet always bending
Towards their project.

Shakespeare *The Tempest IV. i.*

Thc dim light from John Vigilia's desk lamp turned the stale night into a microcosm of shadows as he sat up late transcribing Ariel's story into his notebook. He was tired, and the fatigue was causing the arm that he had injured in his bicycle accident to begin hurting him again, making it difficult to write. John wanted to sleep, but needed to finish his notes. The story was still incomplete, he realized, lacking an ending. This would come tomorrow, John hoped. Would this conclusion also give him some clue to his own fate? He wondered what Count Sperone really wanted to see him about. John feared that the story's ending might be something threatening to him. He saw Ariel telling his tale, but could not always remember what he had been saying. Ariel's face became strange to John, as he had also become strange to himself. He felt empty. It was not an easy emptiness. It was as if something had left him that now was trying to make its own way in the world. With each passing day,

John's doubt of the story he was seeking had become more acute, more insistent, more goading. And every day he had fed on this doubt with a greater intensity until, in the long moments of this night's conversation, it had become for John a kind of incurable illness, and, confronted by the events irremediableness, he had been overcome by an immense feeling of futility. Unable to understand his frustrations, he let his soporific mind be dragged along by the unknown. John's brain began to shut off. His head nodded and eyes blinked, as he drifted in and out of sleep.

The next morning dawned clear, and with fresh breezes blowing down from the Alps. When John Vigilia arrived at the airport, Ariel was there waiting at the fence as he promised. John had stayed in bed rather late, and skipped breakfast, partially because he did not want to run into Hans, or any of the other festival people, but mainly because he did not feel well. John had drunk too much last night, several glasses of grappa on top of the wine at the festival, and he had not gotten enough rest having stayed up most of the night transcribing Ariel's story. Despite his tiredness, John had slept little, and it had been an anxious sleep. His head throbbed; his stomach was upset; and his right wrist was in pain. John felt worn out, as if he could not trust his own bodily machinery. Under any other circumstances he would have readily canceled today's flight, but he had made a promise to Ariel Angelucci.

He had gone across the hall early in the morning to explain his poor condition to Ariel, but his knock on the door had elicited no response. Assuming that the old man had already left for the airport, John went there intending to find Ariel and tell him that the flight was off. On the way to Magadino, however, John's head had begun to clear somewhat, and he woke up again to the world outside of him. Fearing that Ariel might get some wrong notion at being told that they were not going to fly today, John Vigilia decided to go ahead with the flight. Also, he had come up with the idea that the flight, to some extent, might be a way he could test the veracity of Ariel's story.

John's plan would be to offer to let Ariel take the controls at some point during their flight. Flying was like bicycling or swimming in that once learned it was not easily forgotten. Last year he had taken up someone who had been a fighter pilot in World War Two. The man had not flown an airplane since 1945, but the moment he took the stick John could sense the feeling returning to his hands. Within a few minutes the aging aviator was in command of the airplane, flying as if only a few days had passed since he had last flown his P-47 over Germany. Ariel would certainly be out of practice after a lay-off of some sixty-three years; however, John truly believed that he would be able to tell if this man had ever flown an airplane sometime in his life.

"You are a little late!" Ariel shouted, running from his place by the fence. He was breathing heavily and clutching at his left side. "I was afraid you weren't coming. I have been here for three hours already. Someone flew the biplane earlier this morning. I was worried that it was you going up without me . . . but now it's back."

"I'm sorry, I guess I am a bit late," John Vigilia said looking at his watch. "After we parted I stayed up until the wee hours writing down the story you told me. Then I overslept."

"You . . . you wrote down my story?" Ariel said, sounding somewhat concerned, perhaps even frightened.

"Yes, you said that you wanted it to be known."

"But now Count Sperone has come to Locarno." Ariel revealed, not knowing that he was telling John something he already knew. "He is at the hotel. He has a special suite they keep just for him. He owns the Flaviano you know. It used to be their private residence. They lived here sometime after the war, when Italy was in ruins."

"I know he's here . . . he left me a note saying that he wanted to see me later today."

"To see you! What does he want to see you about?" Ariel asked. His voice had become equivocal, his face showing a look of concern.

"When I saw him in Rome I told him I was writing a book on Sperone aircraft . . . he says that he just wants to ask me how the work is progressing?"

"Maybe so, . . ." Ariel said, but John could tell he thought otherwise. "Be careful with the count, do not play with him. He is a man of extremely great power, and has little tolerance if he thinks that he is being crossed."

"I'm aware of this and I'll watch my step," John said, realizing to himself that, he was coward enough to fear great power, but not quite cowardly enough to admit it.

Ariel hunched along behind John as they made their way into the cluttered flight operations office. To John, the old man seemed to be having more difficulty walking this morning than he did last night. John Vigilia signed the flight book and turned to leave. Hans, the chief pilot, spun the book around on the desk, took one look at it and stopped him.

"Just one moment, Professor Vigilia . . . I see today that you have yet another passenger?"

"Yes," John responded. "I showed the tower chief my Air Transport Pilot's license yesterday and he told me it was okay for me to take up passengers. . . ."

"It's not about your license . . . you didn't put your passenger's name in the book. He must to sign here also, just next to yours."

John handed the pen to Ariel who slowly, and carefully wrote in his name. The chief pilot turned the book back around and looked at it.

"Ariel? A strange name," the chief pilot said. "Is it your real name? Do you know it is the name of an airy spirit in Shakespeare's play *The Tempest,* although in the play the part is sometimes taken by a woman?"

"Yes, I know this fact," Ariel answered patiently, as if he had heard this pointed out to him so many times before in his long life. "It can be a man's name. My father was very fond of reading Shakespeare, even though he only worked as a butcher."

"So, aren't you that old man who stands by the fence and watches the airplanes takeoff and land? I have often seen you standing there . . . over many years." The chief pilot said. Then he turned to John and asked, "And how does a foreigner come to know this local man?"

"I met him long ago . . . in Como, before he came here." John lied, and then changed the subject, asking: "How much fuel is in the Jungmann?"

"It has been filled this morning . . . and was only flown for one hour since. So you should have enough for your flight, although you should check the tank just to be sure."

"I will . . . I always do," John Vigilia said over his shoulder as they headed for the door.

"And mind the step," the chief pilot called after them.

"What's that?"

"The step . . . the rubber has become loose. I wouldn't want that you should trip over it and to have an accident."

"No. I certainly wouldn't want to have an accident," John replied somewhat wryly.

Ariel's face glowed as they headed toward the bright yellow biplane parked out front. Puffing heavily, he clambered up onto the wing walk without being instructed and made his decades-straddling step over the side of the fuselage into the front cockpit. Perhaps it was only the excitement, but it seemed to John that Ariel's breathing was rather labored and irregular. The old man clutched at his left side occasionally, but then, John reminded himself that the man was nearly eighty years old.

Settled in the front cockpit, Ariel immediately took the stick in his hand and rocked it from side to side, checking the freedom of the controls. He watched as the ailerons move up and down. Then he turned half around in his seat and pulled the stick back and forth checking the movement of the elevator, at the same time doing a small dance on the pedals to make the rudder swing from left to right and back again. Ariel smiled. He did not need to say anything; John knew instantly that this man had been in an airplane before, and more than likely had flown it.

John buckled Ariel in with none of the fuss encountered with Renée Coûteux. This made him think of Renée and of the events of yesterday. It was only yesterday, he marveled, but for some reason it seemed like so long ago. Had he actually been so naive as to believe that Renée was interested in him, and been excited by the thought of her featuring him in a magazine article? Why had it mattered so much? Had he become vainglorious like Hans? Or was he more like Ariel in that he was someone who did not want to die not remembered?

"Hello Ariel . . . this is John here in the back." he said into the intercom. "Press that switch I showed you and tell me if you can hear me."

"Yes . . . I can hear you," Ariel replied, talking into the microphone attached to his headset. "This is amazing . . . we didn't have such things back in '27. . . ."

John called the tower and received his clearance, and then began to taxi out. As the biplane passed the parking lot he saw the black Alfa Romeo parked there once again. A man was standing at the fence watching him through binoculars. Presently in high spirits John waved. The man did not wave back.

Having made a proper takeoff, John climbed out and turned on course. He didn't want any more infractions. John thought to fly down the lake to Italian airspace as the tower chief had suggested, but rejected that idea as taking up too much time. Besides, it gave a certain boost to John's ego to know that in the approved practice zone the tower personnel could watch him through binoculars, and that they appreciated his aerobatic flying skills.

Despite all its inherent danger, air show pilots typically were not paid that much, at least when compared to other summertime entertainers like rock stars, pro golfers, and baseball players. For most pilots it was only their love of the activity, and their ego, that kept them going. And John's casual wave to the Alfa Romeo man had had a little of the air show pilots "keep your eyes on me" swagger to it. He knew that the strange man would be watching and wanted to give him a good performance.

"Follow me through on the clearing turns," John said into the intercom as he put the airplane through a series of shallow banked turns to check the area for other airplanes before beginning the aerobatic maneuvers. He could feel an increase in resistance to the controls as Ariel put his hand on the stick. Today, John's previously injured wrist was paining him ever so slightly.

Ariel turned, a big smile on his face, and shouted something at John, but the words blew away, lost in the slipstream.

"Use your microphone," John said into the intercom.

"Oh . . . Ariel replied, finally making the thing work. "I said I see that this is a very smooth airplane . . . much more responsive than the old Jenny. . . ."

"I've never flown a Jenny," John said, "so I guess I'll just have to take your word for it."

"I wouldn't lie to you about something like that," Ariel answered, forgetting to leave go of the transmit button. John could hear the old man's breath gasping in his earphones.

Rocking the stick back and forth got his passenger's attention and Ariel took his thumb off the radio button allowing John to transmit. "Want to do some aerobatics?" he asked.

"Yes . . . that's what I came along for . . . let's do some stunts . . . acrobatics!"

John smiled at Ariel's use of the old term, acrobatics, a word used by gymnasts and the like. It had only become aerobatics a few years ago when someone, he didn't know who, had replaced acro with aero, and coined the new word.

"Let's start first with a slow-roll, that should be easy," John announced. "Hang on!"

"Okay. . . ." Ariel responded without hesitation.

A white spot on the mountain across the valley, apparently someone's expensive hideaway, would be John's reference point. Lining up with the house, he advanced the throttle to full power, and then put the aircraft into a shallow dive to gain an airspeed 10 or 15 miles above level cruise. When he reached the desired speed, he applied back pressure to the stick, and put the airplane in a shallow climb, at the same time applying ailerons and rudder as if he were starting a steep turn. The rate of roll established, John began applying top rudder to stop the turning effect. As the airplane responded, and the bank approached the 45-degree position, he continued the same rate of roll, applying more top rudder to keep the Jungmann's nose positioned on the chosen mountain retreat. He wondered if the people in the elegant house were watching. Were they sitting on their deck sipping drinks, waiting for a repeat of yesterday's air show? Or were they annoyed by his antics, and wished that this crazy flyer would take his airplane and go someplace else?

With the wings now in the 90-degree position in reference to the ground, John had to apply forward pressure and more top rudder to keep the aircraft's nose on point. The plane was about to go upside-down. He hoped Ariel's safety belts were tight as they would be hanging by them for a few brief, but critical seconds. With the airplane now in the inverted position the controls were reversed; up was down and down was up, so John had to hold the stick well forward to keep the nose from falling through the horizon. Rolling past inverted he eased the rudder in the opposite direction to again become top rudder, keeping the ailerons on full to continue the roll. Back in level flight John neutralized all the controls, ending the roll at the same altitude and on the same point that he had begun it.

"Very nice," Ariel said excitedly into the intercom without having been asked. Memories must have been filling his head. "And the engine didn't ever sputter and cut out when we were upside down . . . like it used to do in the Jenny."

"No it doesn't . . . this airplane has an inverted fuel system." John explained through the intercom. "Would you like to try a loop?"

"Let's do it." Ariel replied breathlessly.

John lined the nose of the biplane up with a road, and then pushed in the throttle. Since this maneuver was executed in the vertical plane the road was necessary to be able to check for any drift from a crosswind. Diving slightly, he watched for 140 mph on the airspeed indicator. For some reason this old biplane had been retrofitted with new American instruments that read in miles not kilometers, so John did not need to convert anything, but could use the same entry speeds that he had used for his own Jungmann back home.

He listened to the wind screaming through the wing struts. John had flown Jungmanns long enough to know the sound the taut steel flying wires made at various speeds. On the panel; the airspeed indicator now showed 140. He pulled back on the stick and the nose of the biplane rose above the horizon in a graceful arc, keeping the wings level, and the track straight with just a bit of right rudder to offset the torque of the engine.

The airplane was inverted now. John released the back pressure on the stick ever so slightly so that the loop would not have an egg-shaped top. Relieved of the restraints of gravity, Ariel and John hung against their safety belts for a brief moment. Throwing back his head to pick up the land, John saw that he was still lined up with the road. Inverted on the horizon, he added back pressure, and he and his passenger settled into their seats again, as the airplane started down the back side of the loop, gathering speed. When the nose came down, still lined up with the road, John eased the throttle off smoothly and added more back pressure to maintain the arc of the loop. They felt a bump as the airplane passed through its own wake turbulence, always a good sign; an indication that the pilot had ended the loop at the exact same altitude that he had begun it, which was the way it was supposed to be done.

"Wow! You're one heck of a smooth flyer," Ariel shouted into his microphone.

"It's not me, just the airplane," John replied, "things have changed a great deal since 1927. I don't think I would have done very well in your old Jenny. Do you want to try it?"

"Yes, sir! Please . . . If I can?"

John helped Ariel through a few of the more simple maneuvers: a chandelle, an Immelman, a barrel-roll. Ariel seemed to be enjoying himself, displaying an aptitude for flying that could only have been gained from having done it sometime before, if ever so long ago.

Wagging the stick to show that he was now taking back the controls, John announced to Ariel that he would demonstrate a free sequence, a group of maneuvers, each one flowing into the other with no breaks in between just like in competition flying, except he had no set program drawn out on a card in front of him. Instead, he would improvise; just executing whatever maneuver came into his head based on the airspeed that he had left from the last maneuver.

John slowly spiraled upward to gain additional altitude before starting his sequence. With a heavy, and underpowered airplane like the Bücker Jungmann it was always necessary to trade altitude for airspeed, so he wanted to start with a good bit of distance between him and the ground.

It was during these aerobatic free sequences that John often experienced such an exhilaration that he came close to becoming what early adherents of the gospel of flight called the "alti-man." Lifted from the restraints of gravity, feeling the rush of power that an aviator gets soaring above the earth, one of the select few, the unassailable, the crowded landscape laid beneath him, the empty sky above, and he sailing between them, John sometimes felt as if he had become a new life form, able to conquer all the limitations of the world and, for the moment, dwelled in the realm of the gods.

Coming out of a snap-roll on a 45-degree down line, John found himself with 145 mph on the airspeed indicator, a little more than he needed for the loop he had planned, but not enough for a square loop. In an instant John made his decision. Lined up with a road he pulled the nose above the horizon. Pressing the intercom button with his thumb John Vigilia announced: "This loop is for you Ariel . . . something a Jenny couldn't do a loop with a snap-roll on top."

"Go to it!" Ariel shouted excitedly.

Just a brief moment before the wings reached inverted, John racked the control stick back into his stomach and all the way over to the left, simultaneously applying left rudder. If there was one thing a Bücker did well it was to snap-roll. The airplane came around nicely. As the wings reached the level inverted position, completing the snap-roll, John attempted to neutralize the controls, but they appeared to be locked in place. He jerked on the stick, feeling a sharp pain in his right wrist. The airplane snap-rolled one more time on its own loosing airspeed, then lazily fell off into a spin.

John quickly pulled back the power to keep the spin from going flat. He could recover from an ordinary spin, but a flat spin, where the power kept the nose up above the horizon, was another problem. He tugged on the stick with both hands trying to release the back pressure; and to further compound his problem, the rudder was also locked over to the left.

"Ariel! Ariel! Let go of the control stick!" John shouted into the intercom.

There was no answer. Looking forward he could see that Ariel was slumped over in his seat, not moving.

The landscape in front of John Vigilia had turned into a whirling blur as the spin wound up tighter, the airspeed increasing as the airplane descended at a violent rate.

"Ariel! Are you there? Sit up you're jamming the controls!"

Tugging at the stick with both hands, John fought to regain control of the Jungmann, but the weight of Ariel's body had the controls locked in place. Ariel must have passed out, John reasoned. Then fear struck him: the old man might be dead, probably from a heart attack. His only hope was to abandon the airplane. Automatically, John pulled out the mixture control knob and cut the engine. He did not want to jump free only to be torn to pieces by the whirling propeller blades. Then, he turned off the ignition switch and set the fuel selector to "off." If he couldn't get out in time, and went in with the airplane, he might still survive if it didn't catch fire.

Grabbing at his seat belts, John struggled to undo the buckles. The ground was coming up very fast. This was his final opportunity to bail out, a few more seconds and he would be too low for the parachute to open. Out of the safety harness John tried to stand up to push himself free of the spinning airplane. His left foot caught in the rudder stirrup. He fell back into the cockpit.

In that moment, John Vigilia saw himself back home in Elmira. He was sawing wood for his fireplace with a chain saw. He loved sawing wood, and used to approach the mundane chore as almost a sacramental function, both symbolic and dignified. Cutting wood was an act as old as the human race, a task that he could work at for many hours, standing in the golden shavings, holding the vibrating saw, his back bent. In that bright gap of a memory, in that brief hiatus, time turned into a descending yellow eternity. John braced his arms against the instrument panel as the Jungmann became a screaming creature, attempting to bury itself deeper and deeper into the soft ground.

Twenty-seven

Confin'd together
In the same fashion as you gave in charge;
Just as you left them: all prisoners, sir
In the line-grove which weather-fends your cell;
They cannot budge till your release.

Shakespeare *The Tempest V. i.*

Doctor Prospero's clinic, where John Vigilia awoke to find himself confined, was located on the smaller of the two islands of Brissago in Lago Maggiore, 1 kilometer southeast of Porto Ronco and 3 kilometers southwest of the resort town of Ascona. It was the kind of place where special people went for special treatments. One might find an aging actress recovering from having sections of skin removed from her face and stomach to make her look younger, or a teen-age actress who had lumps of foam inserted in her breasts to make her look sexier. Several of the patients were wives of prominent politicians, or dictators, suffering from the overuse of alcohol or cocaine, or perhaps their husbands, having found other interests, were just tired of having them around. There were also permanent residents, usually the offspring of some wealthy couple who had managed, through some embarrassing flaw in their genes, to produce a child that did not quite measure up, and so the monster was kept hidden away from the world here on the island.

Through the partially open window pleasant lake breezes filtered into John's private room, filling it with a whisper of the nearby mountains. For a moment the colors seen at a distance stayed in the air, but not for long. The lucid images soon dispersed, dissolving into blue shadows on the gray walls, tender and gentle. Unable to hold on to it, the flood of reality receded a little; the waters of the patient's imagination became quiet and abated.

"Doctor, he was awake . . . if just for a moment. I saw his eye blink." John heard someone say close by.

"Professor Vigilia, I am Dr. Prospero. Can you hear me now?" a voice said. An unknown person, who called himself a doctor, was lifting John's left eyelid and shining a tiny flashlight into the pupil.

A happy fanfare of crimson marched into the room. Red flags fluttered on the red walls. A platoon of nurses, wearing bright red uniforms, arrayed themselves around his bed. A procession of clergymen wearing cardinal red cassocks paraded in from the hall, while the air filled with a flock of chirping red finches.

John reached for his tube of paint. Was it cobalt blue? The reflection of the lake fell on the windows and slid into the room. The walls trembled as the azure washed away the fire of the red. The curtains waved the alert as a joyful draft entered from the empty garden below. It was as if someone long lost had appeared from the other side of the wide and blue lake, and was now approaching, bearing good tidings, announced by a flight of swallows, and mile after mile of spreading high cirrus clouds.

"Hello, hello, Professor Vigilia. I am Dr. Prospero. You have been in a bad accident. You crashed an airplane. Do you remember that? You are in my clinic on an island near Ascona. You have been in a coma for three days.

Can you understand me? If you can speak tell me. If not just blink your eye; you should have your ability to speak back shortly."

John formed a sentence in his mind: What has happened to Ariel Angelucci? but nothing came from his mouth. Roving his eye downward, John caught sight of a tube that appeared to be extending into his nose. Looking up he saw the glare of light on the one who called himself Dr. Prospero's spectacles, and the blur of the man's face. John's eye tried to focus. Where was his other eye? The doctor was silent. His eyes were wide open, the color of a wintry sea. His mouth wore a fixed, and very small, smile. Like a cat nodding off, John's eye closed involuntarily.

The doctor took this eye movement to be the blink he had asked for. "Good . . . you are responding," he said and then turned and whispered something to the nurse standing next to him. He poked back at John. "Don't worry Professor Vigilia, my clinic is one of the finest in the world . . . you are receiving the very best treatment."

One of the finest in the world, John thought, wondering if his health insurance, a HMO policy taken out through the college in Elmira, was going to pay for this. Even if it did, the co-payment would probably be more than he could afford. With that thought clogging his mind, John Vigilia fell back into unconsciousness.

The next day he was able to manage a painful smile, and to hold his head up and take soup from a spoon fed by a nurse. Both of John's arms were broken, as was his left leg, and all were in traction. He had not been shown his face, but could see a bandage and stitches out of the corner of his working eye. Despite the drugs he was on, John had a terrible pain in his groin. The male nurse that brought his bed pan, the one who spoke English, told him that one of his testicles had been knocked back up inside his body. John was only able to make simple sounds with his mouth, and to smile. His wife had always encouraged him to smile; she said that it helped to relieve the tension in his brain.

By the sixth day of his confinement, John Vigilia was sitting up in bed, and able to distinguish things in the room. He had also recovered his speech somewhat.

"Wha, wha, what has happened to Ariel Angelucci? . . ." were the first words he slowly muttered, repeating the question three times, each time becoming a little more coherent.

"Ariel Angelucci?" the nurse repeated, finally understanding that he was trying to ask a question. She went and got someone who spoke English.

"Wha, what, what has happened to Ariel Angelucci?" John said again, to the person who had come.

"Who is Ariel Angelucci?" the person who spoke English asked.

"He is . . . the man who was in the airplane with me when it crashed. He was in the front seat . . . a very old man."

"I do not know anything about this," the woman, whoever she was, explained. "I was here when they brought you into the clinic. There was no one else with you. You were alone. There is no patient presently here named Ariel Angelucci. . . ."

Asking the same question of the male nurse who looked in on him later, John received a similar vague and guarded reply.

In the afternoon Dr. Prospero came to check on his patient. He listened to John's heart, took his pulse and read the displays on the machines that John was hooked up to. John Vigilia watched the doctor begin to write something on his chart.

"Dr. Prospero," John said, speaking with great effort, slowly, and as clearly as he was able to at the moment, "Can you tell me . . . what has happened to my friend Ariel Angelucci?"

"I know nothing about anyone named Ariel Angelucci? . . ." the doctor mumbled, looking up from the chart.

"Ariel was the man if the front cockpit of the airplane when it crashed . . . do you know what has happened to him?"

"I do not know anything about anyone named Ariel Angelucci." Prospero replied, adjusting his glasses and looking back down at John's chart.

"Damn it! Why won't anyone answer my question?" John shouted out with a sudden strength, and anger that surprised the doctor. His query had a hint of fear beneath it.

Whether or not Dr. Prospero knew the answer he did not speak. John stared back at the stiff mask-like face. John's first though was that Prospero might be playing a game with him; however, his second notion was more frightful. After all what, if anything, did he know about this strange doctor, and his clinic, who had been engaged to look after him? And why had he been brought to this obviously expensive private clinic rather than a public hospital?

Dr. Prospero started to leave, then stopped at the door of the room and turned back. "There was a copy of the accident report attached to your file when you arrived here," he explained, "and as I recall, it stated that you were alone in the airplane when they found you."

"Are you sure of this?" John said, trying to lift himself into a sitting position for emphasis. "I am positive that there was a passenger in the front seat of the airplane when I crashed it, a very old man. I had only recently met him, but the name he gave me was Ariel Angelucci."

"Yes, I remember the accident report said clearly that no one else was in the airplane with you. Maybe something has happened to your memory. You had a nasty bump on your head. You almost lost an eye. We took X-rays when you first arrived, and they showed no brain damage. Maybe we need to take a few more."

The impact of Dr. Prospero's quick response, and the cold, positive manner in which he had delivered it sent a shiver of fear through John's body. He slid back down in the bed.

Another question formed in John's febrile brain: "Is this clinic expensive?" he asked.

The doctor smiled. "As I told you previously, my clinic is one of the finest in the world . . . and as can be expected, such treatment does not come for a small price."

"So who is paying for it then? Why am I in your expensive private clinic, not just in a regular hospital?"

"You are fortunate to have a good friend in the Count Sperone. It was he who arranged for you to be brought here. Do not worry; he is taking care of everything. . . ."

Such largess from a man he had only recently met, and with whom he had not parted on the best of terms, gave John cause for concern. The only thing that he could think of to say at the moment was: "Will the count be coming to see me sometime soon? I would like very much to thank him personally."

"That remains to be seen," Prospero replied. "As you must know, Count Sperone is a very important man in the Italian government just now; he is very busy working with the prime minister on some new programs. But he does call me from time to time to see how you are doing."

"Can I please talk to him the next time he calls?"

Doctor Prospero gave John a hard look. "I will tell the count that you wish to speak with him," he said as he left the room.

What did John Vigilia know, except that he had been in a crash, and been told that he was in the airplane alone, when he knew that he was not. How improbable was it that he might have imagined there was someone else in the cockpit with him? Was Prospero's silence a way of warning him that he must be silent also? Was the doctor's adamantine stare after all only the cold, awful sneer of someone party to a conspiracy long concealed that had recently come on the threshold of being revealed?

With such expensive treatment, and nothing else to do, John was healing rapidly. He was soon allowed to be wheeled out into the well-landscaped grounds, which extended all the way to the shore of the lake. He observed that although they went outside together, few of the patients ever talked to one another, seeming almost afraid of making contact. In fact at times it appeared as if the nurses and attendants were there specifically to prevent any conversations. On one occasion John did notice two patients who were apparently communicating with each other by tracing letters in the layer of dust that covered a table top. In general, however, the tables were kept too well polished for much of this. Nevertheless, there appeared to be an elite group of patients who gathered nightly in the lounge to make small talk. At least he assumed their conversation was casual. They spoke mostly in German or Italian, so John had no way of knowing what they were saying; although, he had noticed that his arrival in the room usually prompted an abrupt pause in their chattering.

John could not complain about the quality of the medical care that he was receiving, and the meals were excellent, the kind of gourmet food that one might expect to receive at a luxury hotel. He was concerned though. John Vigilia had had no contact with anyone from the outside world since he arrived at the clinic. If someone had come during those first three days when he was in a coma he had not been told about it. When he asked to use a telephone to get in touch with people back in America concerning his whereabouts he was told that there was no need to do this as "everything was being taken care of by Count Sperone." Yet when John asked to speak to the elusive count, he was always informed that at present the man was just too busy.

Most of John Vigilia's day was spent in his room, which had become his own private, although totally fragmented, world. Sometimes he composed letters. As his hands were still in casts, John dictated them to a member of the staff who typed them up and said she posted them; however, answers never seemed to come.

Six weeks had passed since John regained consciousness, during which time he still had not been in touch with anyone from outside the clinic. John now had the distinct suspicion that he was being kept at this facility not just as a patient, but as prisoner.

He had observed that like his, none of the other rooms had television sets. Also, the one large set in a downstairs lounge was rarely turned on. Nor were the clients of the clinic provided with newspapers. John wondered what had happened in the world during the previous weeks he had been closeted here at Dr. Prospero's clinic. There was a library in the main building, but few of the books were in English, one of them being a large, and elaborately illustrated Bible. For days John wandered the desert with the Israelites, or floated on an ark with Noah. He even made the familiar trip to Bethlehem with Joseph and the pregnant Mary to register for Emperor Augustus' tax.

With all this time, and nothing to do, John would have liked to been able to work on some drawings. He had gotten an urge for the activity again when he made the sketch of the motor for Miranda back at the barn in Como. Both his arms were still in plaster casts that partially covered his hands; however, they had recently cut away the section that went around his elbow. To amuse himself, and pass the time, John had taken to sitting in bed blowing soap bubbles through a straw, watching them float into space and then burst; their colors hanging in the still air.

A nurse came and wheeled John downstairs. She said, as best as he could comprehend, that his casts were to be completely removed. The first time the doctor's intern had come at him with the stainless steel rotary saw used to cut up casts, John had been convinced that it was the end for his arms. Despite what he had been told, in broken English, John could not believe that the whirring blade had the sense to cut plaster but not flesh. Nevertheless, it had worked. So he sat there happily as the intern made vertical cuts on all three casts, his two arms and a leg and skillfully removed them. The intern said that John would probably need a week or two of physical therapy to regain the use of his limbs, and then he could probably leave. The intern's statement had done a great deal to calm John Vigilia's anxiety about what was happening to him here.

The casts now removed, Dr. Prospero came in and looked over his patient's appendages. John's arms and leg had little movement. The doctor flexed them through their available range to check the extent of the atrophy. Prospero seemed especially interested in John's right arm. A nurse was sent to bring a wheelchair, and John was trundled downstairs for another X-ray.

When he arrived back in his room John's spirits had risen by 1000 percent. He recalled the intern's statement that he only needed a week or two of physical therapy. The thought that he might actually be leaving this place, and going back to Elmira, filled him with an unimaginable joy. Impatient for action, John Vigilia worked his newly released arms and right leg, devising his own exercises to restore their movement.

That evening Antonio, the male nurse who spoke English, came to John's room with his regular dose of pills. He quaffed them down and handed the water glass back to the nurse.

"Okay, now roll over," Antonio said displaying a little too much enthusiasm, "you have got to have an enema."

"An enema! Why?" John protested. "My bowel movements have been perfectly normal. I don't need an enema."

"They never tell me why about anything, I just have it on my list to give you an enema."

Sure that a mistake must have been made, John demanded to see the head nurse.

The large German woman arrived at John's room almost immediately. "What is your trouble?" she asked in German, communicating through Antonio.

"I want to know why I am scheduled to have an enema." John replied, by translation.

"Because tomorrow morning you go to the operating room," the head nurse informed him, now speaking English. "So you shouldn't make a mess on the table."

"The operating room! But why?"

"It is because of your right arm, it is not healed properly . . . the doctor must to break it, and then to reset it again. . . ."

"And will it be in a cast for another six weeks?"

"*Ja,* that is about normal . . . it takes six weeks time to heal."

"Can I leave here if only one of my arms is in a cast, and my other arm and my legs are all right?"

The head nurse looked carefully at John's chart and shook her head. "You are a very special case Professor Vigilia . . . very important. I can say you nothing. Only Doctor Prospero knows when you will be good to leave us." That said the woman turned and quickly left the room.

Feeling confused, and perhaps a little threatened, John asked Antonio just what he thought the head nurse meant by her statement that he was "a very special case."

Antonio just shrugged his shoulders. "I am sorry I cannot to speak English very much good," he replied.

Twenty-eight

Sit then and talk with her; she is thine own.

Shakespeare *The Tempest IV. i.*

"Professor Vigilia! Professor Vigilia! Hello! Where are you? You have a visitor!" one of the attendants shouted out from the back porch.

John heard the woman's call over the sound of the wind, but told himself that he was just imagining what he was hearing. He had, long ago, given up expecting anyone. Since he had regained the use of his legs John Vigilia had taken to spending his days at the eastern end of the island where a stone pier jutted out into Lago Maggiore. He could see the lake and the mountains beyond, but access to the water was denied him by a chain-link fence obviously installed many years after the pier had been built. The rest of the facility was surrounded by a high concrete wall which, like the clinic housed in what had been an old villa, probably dated from the nineteenth century.

John's arm had been broken again and reset six weeks ago. As if tempting him with hope, Dr. Prospero had for the past week almost daily ordered an inch wide section of the cast removed, until it now covered mainly John's wrist. Blessed with this freedom of movement, he had gotten back to drawing. Although he had asked the nurses for materials none had been provided, some excuse being made that there was no art supply store in Porto Ronco and he would need to wait until someone from the staff made a trip to Ascona.

Using the back of the large bible from the library as his drawing board, John had taken to spending the day sitting by the lake sketching the landscape on clinic stationary, using ballpoint pens filched from the nurses' station. He also had an ulterior motive for sitting on the pier. Having reconnoitered the grounds carefully, after realizing that he was indeed being held here as a prisoner, John had come to the conclusion that his only possible means of escape would be from this pier.

Sitting on a bench in the warm sun, John studied his latest drawing. He noted that the pictures had all become rather alike. He had lost any interest in the detail of what was presenting itself, but had grown concerned only with the form and volume of what he saw. The lake and the sky above it had become small and incidental, with the mass of the mountain across the way totally dominating the center of the composition. Nor was there any perspective, all his forms being rendered with a flatness that kept them firmly anchored to their place on the page.

John Vigilia took out his latest three drawings and placed them next to each other on the bench, holding them with his hand, to keep the gentle breeze from blowing them away. He was surprised by the similarity, which he had not strived for, and had never managed to achieve in the work he had made when he was younger, and when he had thought to become an artist. Was he developing a style? Or was it that this limited view of the world was all he had available to him at the present time.

John pondered why he had given up the pursuit of art, which he remembered as having given him such great pleasure in the past. Had it been Leonardo's notebooks that distracted him? Going there to find knowledge about art, he had instead discovered flight, and the idea for the hang-glider that had almost killed him. And more recently a complicated version of a flying machine had nearly taken his life. While he was not yet dead was it his fate to be kept here in this clinic as a prisoner until he finally did die?

What instinct had taken John back to drawing? He could use his hands now, he could write. Were these drawings merely the reciprocal of what he should be doing? He was after all supposed to be a writer. John had found his story and begun writing it. What had happened to those notes he made that night after talking to Ariel Angelucci? Would he ever see this material again? Would he ever learn what happened to the old man? No matter what he had been told, John knew that he was not out of his mind. Ariel had been with him in the Jungmann when it crashed.

Closing his eyes John Vigilia could clearly see the spinning earth, and Ariel slumped over in the front cockpit. The old man apparently must have had a heart attack. He remembered the hollow ring of Ariel's labored breathing over the intercom, his clutching at his left side as he got into the cockpit. Had he killed him? Was the excitement of the flight too much for this ancient aviator? John asked himself. And was Ariel really who he said he was, or someone he made up many years ago, a story that had become real by its retelling? Nevertheless, shouldn't he be writing this all down, while it was relatively fresh in his memory, even if he had to hide the papers from Prospero, and whoever else was responsible for his being held here? The whole thing was like finding a loose end in a sweater; the more he pulled at it the more it unraveled. Had he pulled too much and was now left with only a ball of yarn?

"Oh there you are Professor Vigilia, I should have known I would find you down here," the attendant said coming up behind him. "You are lucky today . . . you have a visitor."

John covered up his drawings with a blank page and turned around. Then he stood up in shocked surprise. The visitor was Contessa Sabatini's secretary from Como, Miranda Grazia; the woman he had once thought about constantly, but since the accident someone that he had forced completely from his mind.

"I'll leave you two here, but don't forget to come back to the main house in a little while . . . it's almost tea time."

As far as John had observed no one at the clinic was English, yet tea was served religiously every afternoon. He was glad the attendant was leaving them, but he had a subtle warning that they must come back to the main house very soon. John and Miranda stared at each other, but did not speak until the attendant was well out of hearing.

"What are you doing here? I thought I would never see you again." John said, trying to contain his excitement. Miranda was wearing the same dark blue suit with a too-short skirt that she had on when they had first met. John remembered the last time they had been together. In his mind's eye John saw her lying naked on the chaise lounge as he had walked down the stairs the day he had left the villa. It seemed as if it had been such a long, long time ago.

"Oh, John! I was so happy to learn that you were alive. . . ." Miranda said. They had been standing there awkwardly regarding each other when, to John's surprise, she put her arms around him and pulled his body to her, kissing him on the lips.

"So, did they send you here to find out how I am doing?" John said, pushing Miranda away and sitting back down on the bench.

"Who?"

"The count and his sister. . . ."

No . . . not exactly," she replied, still standing.

"Not exactly? What do you mean by that?"

"John, you must forgive me. I am partially involved in the trouble you are in . . . but I work for the Sperone and Sabatini families, and must do what they want me to do. They are very good to me, as you know . . . because of my husband's death. I have come here partially because of them . . . but mainly on my own."

"To spy on me? . . ."

"No John," Miranda said, picking up the large bible containing John's drawings from the bench and sitting down next to him. "I'm not here to spy on you . . . it's because I love you."

"You love me!?"

"Yes John, after you left me in Como I realized that I had fallen in love with you. I know our time together was very short, but somehow I was very happy with you there . . . the first time I had been happy since my husband died. I had been so alone. And I understood that you were alone too. After you left I thought about you all the time . . . although I was sure I would never see you again."

"Is this something Count Sperone has put you up to? Look, I'm not exactly sure what's going on here. I do know that I am being held as a prisoner at this clinic. They keep breaking my bones so I can't get out. I'm not allowed to telephone. I write letters that they say are mailed, but I never get any answers. They say I was in the airplane by myself, and I know I wasn't. And now you show up telling me you love me. Maybe you can tell me what this is supposed to be all about?" John said angrily, snatching the book and his drawings from Miranda's hands. She stood back up.

"John, I swear to you I do not know all of what is going on around you. I can only tell you what I do know, and that is . . . I love you. I can't expect you to love me in return, or to even believe me, but if you will listen to me I will tell you everything that I know."

"Well to start with, tell me what has happened to Ariel Angelucci?"

"Ariel Angelucci? How do you know that man?

"He was a friend of mine. . . ."

"It's funny that you should mention his name. The contessa just recently told me about him. He used to work for the Sperones in Como a long, long time ago. It was he that had the apartment in the barn; where no one was allowed to go for some reason. She had not heard from Angelucci in many years, and then had learned from her brother that he had died from a heart attack here in Locarno."

"No, he didn't. He was in the airplane with me when it crashed. Ariel was sitting in the front cockpit and was killed."

"But, but . . . that's not what I heard. And why would Angelucci be flying in an airplane with you?"

"He lived in the hotel I was staying at. I had just met him, and he asked me to take him for a ride," John said, reluctant to reveal anymore of the story.

"So, do you just take everyone you meet up for a ride?"

"No." John hesitated. "But Ariel was special. He had been a pilot once . . . many years ago."

"The contessa didn't tell me that he was a pilot. She only said that he had worked for the family keeping track of things in the barn."

"He was in the airplane with me. Then something happened to him. Maybe it was a heart attack. He slumped over in his seat, and his body jammed up against the stick. That's why I couldn't move the controls when I tried to recover the airplane from the spin it had gone into. . . ."

"That's not at all the story I heard, John; they told me that he was found dead in his bed in his room at the Albergo Flaviano. He had apparently been there for three days without anyone noticing he had gone missing. It seems he had his own private little room on the top floor which the housekeepers didn't bother with."

"Who told you this?" John asked, a sense of fear gripping at his throat. "It's a lie! He was in the airplane with me when it crashed. I know he was in the front seat; I remember this clearly. He could not have survived the crash, and simply gone back to his hotel and died, even if he hadn't had a heart attack. I've asked the people at the clinic about Ariel and they keep telling me the accident report said that I was alone in the airplane. But I am positive Ariel was with me. Despite what the doctors here seem to think, or are trying to convince me . . . I have not gone crazy. And now you tell me this. I don't know what to believe. . . ."

"What I told you was what it said in his obituary in the newspaper. Her brother sent a copy to the contessa; I read it myself. It was very short; Angelucci was no one of any importance. It is a wonder he got mentioned at all. This was also the story the desk clerk at the Flaviano told me when I went there to pick up your things."

"You have my things from the hotel?" John said, startled.

"Yes, they had them packed up and in storage. I have everything in my car; I can get it for you later."

"And just who told you where I had been staying, and to go and pick up my stuff?"

"The contessa, she learned this from her brother, who had been in Locarno for the festival when you crashed. It was she who suggested that I come to see you. They think of me as someone they can trust. I don't think they know how I feel about you, or maybe they do. At least they have never said anything that would cause me to think otherwise."

Miranda sat back down next to John and put her hands on his. He did not move them away. Their bodies pressed together on the narrow bench, Miranda's lean brown legs revealed by her short skirt. She bent forward and John could see that, just as he remembered, she wore no blouse under her jacket. While John Vigilia was not sure that he could trust Miranda, or that she really did love him, he knew now that in his mind he was lusting after her.

"And what else do you know that I don't?" John asked, a little too sharply. "Perhaps you know when I will be getting out of here?"

Miranda hesitated. He heard her take a deep breath before answering. "The one thing I do know is that while *you* may get out of here, the man named John Vigilia never will. . . ."

"What do you mean by that?"

"The article in the newspaper about your airplane accident said that you died in the crash."

"I'm supposed to be dead? . . ." John's body shook with fear at the revelation.

Miranda sensed his shudder. "Your hands are like ice; the tea must be ready in the main house, let's go back inside."

Twenty-nine

Hear a little further,
And then I'll bring thee to the present business
Which now's upon us; without the which this story
Were most impertinent.

Shakespeare *The Tempest I. ii.*

A west wind blew briskly across the lake, kicking up foaming white caps and giving the water an illuminated appearance. The sky, swelling out in all directions, looked almost artificial, its clouds filled with the powerful breath of pathos and of great gestures. John sat alone on the clinic's pier waiting for Miranda. He still could not believe she had come here yesterday. She was the last person he had expected to see, not that John Vigilia had expected to see anyone from his past ever again.

John had spent the previous evening going through the papers Miranda brought from his room at the Flaviano. The task had not taken him long as there were not many things left there. Someone had obviously gone through all his papers and removed anything that could have connected him with Ariel Angelucci, including the notes John made after their conversation during which Ariel had described to him the vivid details of his transatlantic flight with Lindbergh. After that John sunk into bed without putting out the light; afraid to close his eyes, woefully pondering the new information Miranda had relayed to him about the newspaper article announcing that he had died in the airplane crash. Could it have just been a mistake? John found it hard to believe that among the few friends he did have he might now be spoken of in the past tense.

Notwithstanding the freshness of the day, John was tired. His brain, confused by the enormous tangle of events surrounding him, longed for sleep. Out on the lake sailboats darted to and fro, white papers blown before the wind as if the game were to see who would survive the longest before dissolving once again into motionlessness. Farther out, sleek hydrofoils skimmed by, speeding passengers between the various towns lining the shore of the Lago Maggiore but, as much as he wished it to happen, none of them ever stopped at the clinic's dock for him.

"Hello, hello, John! Where are you?" Miranda shouted, waving as she arrived from the land end of the pier. She was running and slightly out of breath.

"Hello, I'm here!" John responded, standing up and putting his drawings away. Despite his tiredness, John had shaved carefully this morning, something he had not been doing since regaining the use of his hands and having to shave himself. Observing his face in the mirror he had even trimmed the rather wild hairs that were growing from his nostrils. John Vigilia caught himself worrying that Miranda might have been repelled by his unkempt appearance yesterday and might not return.

"They said I would find you down here; that you always sit on the dock," Miranda said putting her arms around him. She smiled and placed a kiss on John's lips. He did not turn away as he had done yesterday, but returned the kiss, glad that he had shaved so closely.

They sat down on the bench, carefully inching their bodies together. John asked the first question:

"How long are you going to stay?"

"You mean today?"

"No, I mean in Locarno . . . three days, a week?"

"I don't know. The contessa said for me to come and see you for 'a few days' she was not more specific. But she and her husband have gone away for a week, so I don't suppose I'll be missed."

"And when you go back . . . will they question you about me?"

"I imagine so. . . ."

"And what will you tell them?"

"I don't know, John . . . I really don't know."

"Will you tell them that you told me you were in love with me?"

"That's only between you and me."

"But won't they suspect something if you keep coming to see me?

"I would imagine so. . . ."

"You will come back to see me won't you?"

"I will John, as often as I can . . . Como is not very far away from here you know."

"Why do you think they are keeping me here . . . if it has been announced to the world I am dead? Wouldn't it be easier to just kill me and be done with it? I might even prefer that to being kept in this place for the rest of my life."

"Don't say that, even as a joke. I would miss you so much if you were dead," Miranda said. She clutched at John's hands. "When my husband died I cried every day for a year. I think I would cry as much for you . . . even though we have only known each other for such a very short time."

"So why have I not been killed? Why are they keeping me here? It would be cheaper if I were dead as this place must cost a lot of money."

"I don't know, John. They didn't kill Ariel did they? They let him live to almost eighty years. Count Sperone and his sister are not evil people . . . I mean they don't just have people killed, not that I know of anyway."

"Miranda, do you believe in heaven?" John asked; not exactly clear to himself why he had just said what he did. Perhaps John was wondering what would happen to him if he ran into both his wife Iris and Miranda in the afterlife.

"What a strange question."

"Well . . . do you?"

"I suppose I do. I'm a Catholic, like almost everyone else in Italy. That's what we believe . . . if you're good; when you die your soul goes to heaven."

"Did Ariel Angelucci have a soul?" John said, getting back to the person that was really on his mind.

"I guess . . . doesn't everyone?"

"And will Ariel's soul go to heaven?"

"I would think so . . . I mean as far as I know he wasn't an evil man. Maybe he will have to stay in purgatory for awhile."

"Don't you think he has served his time in purgatory?"

"What do you mean by that, John?"

"I mean all those years living with his secret . . . wasn't that a kind of purgatory?"

"His secret? What was his secret?"

"Don't you know? Has no one told you what this business is all about? For over sixty years there has been an elaborate conspiracy, which apparently the Sperone family is involved in, to conceal the fact that Ariel Angelucci was in the airplane when Lindbergh supposedly flew across the Atlantic alone . . . Ariel was let out on a beach in Ireland, and Lindbergh went on to Paris, and history, by himself."

"I don't believe it. Who told you such a story?" Miranda said laughing out loud.

"Ariel did. We had a long conversation the night before our flight. Unfortunately, we drank a lot of grappa. I feel guilty. I suppose I was a little hung over and shouldn't have flown. My reactions were slow, and my arm still hurt from a bicycle accident I had in Munich. Perhaps under different circumstances I could have easily brought the Jungmann out of that spin. God knows I have recovered from plenty of other spins in my flying career.

"But I had promised the old man I would take him for a flight. And I didn't want to back out for fear that he might think something was wrong. He had told me a story about flying with his uncle as a boy . . . and then about flying with Lindbergh. I wanted to see if he really did know anything about flying, or had just made up the whole thing."

"And did he know how to fly? . . ."

"Well he didn't fly the airplane all by himself, I helped him a little bit on the controls, but he seemed like he knew what he was doing . . . only a shade rusty, as he would be after sixty some years. Everything was going well until the loop with a snap."

"A loop with a snap?. . ."

"I sort of got fancy. I did a bunch of maneuvers, and then was going to do a loop with a snap-roll on top. I called him on the intercom and said this was special for him. During that maneuver is when he must have had his heart attack."

"If Ariel was with you in the airplane when it crashed why did the newspapers say that you were alone? And why did Ariel's obituary say that he died of a heart attack in his hotel room?" Miranda asked incredulously, still apparently unable to grasp the plausibility of what John was telling her.

"I am not sure . . . I'm not sure of anything, but I suspect it all goes back to covering up Ariel's part in the Lindbergh flight."

"But that's what I don't understand. What does Sperone have to do with the Lindbergh flight? I mean Lindbergh was an American, and he flew to Paris, not Rome. The rumor I heard was that the old Count Sperone had kept Angelucci hidden in Switzerland all these years because he had sent him away after he made his daughter pregnant. And that Angelucci had outlived him so the present count just continued the arrangement. No one has ever mentioned anything to me about Ariel having been in the airplane with Lindbergh when he flew across the Atlantic."

"Then how did Ariel get from the United States to a beach in Ireland, where he ended up being caught by the police and put in an orphanage? And why did the old count adopt this strange American boy from an orphanage in Ireland. I am sure that at the time there were plenty of other orphans in Italy."

"I don't know. I didn't know Ariel was an American. He did have an Italian name . . . actually a rather funny first name for an Italian, actually the name of a character from Shakespeare's play *The Tempest*.

"The name of a character from a play by Shakespeare . . . yes, that's it!" John exclaimed, a memory suddenly filling his head. "That's what the chief pilot said when Ariel signed his name in the flight book. I remember him remarking about Ariel's name. You've got to go to the airport and check that book . . . Ariel's name should be there, I remember he wrote it himself . . . if they haven't taken the book away. Maybe they didn't realize that Ariel had signed the flight book. If his signature is there it will at least prove to you that I'm not crazy. And maybe you will believe me when I say that there is some kind of cover-up going on."

"I believe you, John. I don't need any proof; I love you."

"But I do need proof! I need proof of my own sanity. I need you to go there and check that flight book, and to tell me that Ariel Angelucci was in that airplane with me when it crashed . . . please, for my sake."

"I will, John. I'll go right now. I know where the airport is. I'm not sure how long it will take me, but I'll hurry back. I want to spend my time with you. I don't suppose I can just go there and ask to see the flight book without possibly arousing someone's suspicion. I'll think of a plan. I hope Ariel's signature is there, I want it to be so. I love you, John."

"I love you too."

They embraced, holding each other for a long while. John felt the warmth of Miranda's body against his, and his own heart beating faster.

"Okay," Miranda said breaking away from John, her face already showing a look of emptiness. "Now I had better go and find Ariel's name in that book. Wish me luck."

"Buona fortuna!" John shouted after her.

Hearing his words Miranda stopped and turned around, "So why are you suddenly learning Italian?" she joked.

John smiled. Although he was not sure why he did it, John had spent an hour last night studying the Italian phrase book that was among the things Miranda had brought back from the Albergo Flaviano.

He watched Miranda retreat down the pier. John Vigilia was not yet ready to give up in spite of the fate that seemed to be confronting him. She reached the end of the dock and turned to wave. He waved back, wishing that Miranda and he had met at some other time, in some other place.

John did not have long to wait. A few hours later, Miranda returned from the airport with the tangible proof that Ariel Angelucci was in the airplane with John when it crashed. She glowed with the excitement of her discovery, proud to have provided the evidence that the man she had proclaimed her love for was not out of his mind and on a quest for some fantasy person.

She had also done some checking on her own and found that the undertaker who had supposedly handled "John Vigilia's" funeral arrangements claimed to have sent the body by train to Zurich, where it was put on an airplane to New York. Inquiring at the train station, however, she had been unable find any record of a casket having been shipped out to Zurich, or any other airport, for delivery to the United States around the date that John's accident had occurred.

Miranda was not sure of what to make of her two discoveries. Nevertheless, she now agreed with John's suspicion that he was probably going to be kept at the clinic for the rest of his life. This was especially true in view of the fact that Count Sperone had no doubt learned that John had no wife or family, or anyone else who might come searching for him. Ariel Angelucci was dead, but John Vigilia would take his place. Miranda decided that the sooner he left the clinic the better would be his chances. With her customary thoroughness, she had made a plan. He would depart that very might.

First, as Miranda revealed to John later, she had decided to test their love, or renew it, whichever the case might be. She wondered if their lovemaking on the roof of the contessa's villa in Como had just been a fluke, more wonderful in memory than it had actually been. Or was it just the circumstances?

She had not been with anyone since her husband died, and there she was on the roof sunning herself naked, when this man who she knew only casually had come and taken her, out there in the open air. They had made love so intensely that they had actually collapsed the lounge they were on, and fallen to the floor without interrupting their love making. Then she had watched John go away, knowing that she would probably never see him again. Nevertheless, some strange fate had now brought them back together again.

When she returned from the airport, Miranda first looked up the gardener. She had seen him standing at the end of the pier throwing bread scraps to the seagulls with the iron gate open, so she knew that he must have a key. Her offer to him of the sum of what amounted to a week's pay was sufficient inducement to cause the man to forget to snap the lock on the chain closing the pier gate when he left for the day.

Miranda's second task had even been easier, and cost her less money, but then the favor she needed if discovered carried lesser consequences. Speaking to the desk nurse on John's floor, she inquired about the times John took his medication. The preoccupied nurse, aware that Miranda was in the employ of Count Sperone in some way or the other, had merely handed her his folder. Good, she thought, John only got medication in the morning, so her plan should work as intended, since he had already had his daily doses.

Handing back the file to the nurse, Miranda had included among the papers the equivalent of twenty dollars, saying: "Professor Vigilia and I will be in his room for the rest of the afternoon. We do not want to be disturbed. Do you understand?"

Miranda then went and found John sitting down by the pier. She walked with him to the pier's edge before reveling that she had uncovered the page with Ariel Angelucci's signature on it.

"Ariel's name was there John, just like you said it would be. I didn't doubt you word, but I found it . . . what you asked me to do. It's here," she said, showing him a photocopy she had managed to make of the page.

"That's great . . . at least it proves I'm not crazy," John said in mock relief. "So what's our next move?"

"I am taking you out of here, tonight."

"Tonight!? Just how is that going to happen?"

A flock of seagulls circled overhead chattering noisily to each other in the fresh breeze. Blown by the wind, lake water splashed at the feet of the two people standing near the end of the pier looking out through the fence. Miranda moved closer to John and, in an excited whisper, revealed her plan. She told him about the two staff members that she had already bribed. She had arranged to borrow a boat from someone she knew and would be coming for him in it as soon as it got dark. Miranda explained the details of her plan, and what he would have to do. Then she made John repeat what she had said so she was sure he remembered. When he was finished, she told him that they were going back to his room. Miranda suspected that John's room might be bugged, so from the moment they got there they were not to speak a word to each other, and would not speak again until they met on the boat later that night.

The nurse at the floor station did not look up as they walked past. Once inside John's room Miranda put a finger to her lips, a sign reminding him of the need for silence. He watched as she checked the telephone, the closet, and inside the various drawers, but discovered nothing. Miranda, however, would have been the first to admit that she was a total amateur at this, not knowing what a bug would look like if she saw one.

Sitting down on the bed next to John, Miranda began removing her clothes, starting first with her shoes. She told him later she had thought to say she was glad to be out of these, that her feet were tired from all the running around she had done today. Realizing that this was a comment an old married woman might make, and not very romantic, she had been thankful for their enforced silence. She slowly unbuttoned her jacket and slid it off her arms, revealing her naked breasts. Her eyes were on John Vigilia's face, watching for his response.

John sat there silent and motionless as Miranda unzipped her short skirt and wiggled out of it, drawing down her panties at the same time. As far back as he could remember John had always been frightened of things sexual. A sickly child, he had grown up very much alone, often staying home from school in the company of his mother. Later on this woman had given him grave warnings about having sex with someone you did not want to marry. "They can trick you," she had warned her son in a mother's way. "They let you get them pregnant, and then you have to marry them." John often wondered if that was how he had been conceived.

Miranda stood in front of him naked now, immobile and trembling slightly. John had made no move to undress, so she bent over and untied the belt to his hospital robe. Kissing him on the forehead, she slid the robe off his arms. Unbuttoning John's pajama top she removed it, gently running her tongue around his neck and shoulders. He stretched out his legs and Miranda pulled off his slippers. Picking apart the double knot that he had tied, Miranda undid the string to John's pajama bottoms. Then, taking hold of the waist band, she slowly worked the pants down, and pulled them off his ankles.

They remained motionless, their eyes locked on one another, both of them equally overwhelmed by the possibilities of the coming events, not just the activity of the moment, but the escape planned for this evening. The smell of the lake blew in through the open window, mixing with the odor of fresh linen and the scent of their naked bodies. In the sky the dark masses of high cumulus clouds that signaled the approach of a thunderstorm were beginning to form.

Thirty

All torment, trouble, wonder, and amazement
Inhabits here. Some heavenly power guide us
Out of this fearful country!

Shakespeare *The Tempest V. i.*

Leaving all the lights off in his room, John Vigilia dressed to go out. He put on some of the clothes that Miranda had brought from the Albergo Flaviano. He had to tear the right sleeve of his shirt slightly to get the small cast that he still wore on his wrist through the opening. Although they were John's clothes, garments he had worn many times before, they felt strange and unfamiliar. It was the first time since coming here that he had worn anything but the regulation patient's garments that the clinic provided. Then, suddenly realizing he could not walk past the nurses' station in street clothes without arousing suspicion, John redressed, putting his pajamas and robe back on.

Next John stuffed his regular clothes and the few papers he had that he thought to be of any value in a pillow case. He was concerned that Miranda hadn't found his passport among his things. Whoever had arranged for "John Vigilia" to appear to be dead had probably collected it from the hotel and turned it in to wherever such things were required to be filed. He tied the pillow end closed with the string from his spare pajama bottoms. To that John attached the belt from his robe, and a rolled-up sheet. A fresh breeze entered the room as he quietly opened the window. Leaning over as far as he could, John lowered his parcel to the end of its tether, and then let it drop into the yard below. The sound of its landing was louder than he had anticipated. John waited a few minutes, looking at his watch, listening for some sign that his stuffed-full pillowcase had been discovered. Ten minutes passed. The sun was already behind the mountains. It would be dark soon; when Miranda had said she would come. His baggage pillow lay in the shrubbery. Apparently the drop had gone unnoticed. John checked his watch again. It was time for him to go.

With his heart racing, the shuffling of his slippers making him acutely aware of his own presence, John moved slowly down the dimly lit hallway toward the nurses' station. He was hoping no one was there; however, the desk was manned, by Hannah a rather large and slow-witted woman who spoke little to no English.

"Me," John said pointing at himself, "go watch television." He made a little walking figure with his fingers, then pointed at his eyes, repeated the word "television", and gestured toward the stairs.

"*Ja, Ja,* television go," Hannah said, and then turned back to the papers nurses seemed to be constantly filling out.

John started slowly down the steps. He had already taken his medications. No one would be coming to his room to look for him until tomorrow morning.

The clinic recently had had a satellite television disc installed. Since then, a good number of the patients had gotten into the habit of hanging around in the lounge all evening watching reruns of American sitcoms like *Frazier* and *Friends.*

"Good evening," John said, finding a place and sitting down among the group. He assumed, since they were all watching the program in English, that they spoke the language; however, no one acknowledged his greeting with so much as a grunt. The scene on the screen echoed the one in the room. Frazier, his brother, father, producer, and father's health care provider were all sitting around a room watching television. Although John's wife had been a regular fan of the program he had only found it mildly amusing, even less so when seeing an episode for the third or fourth time. Someone said something in German and everyone in the room laughed, John assumed it was at the comment that had been made and not the program.

"You like this here character . . . Frazier?" the man sitting next to John asked, tapping him on the arm. It was a Mr. Hessman, a stockbroker from Geneva, at the clinic for a drinking problem, or so John had learned from a conversation that he had overheard. The man had never spoken to him before.

"Oh . . . I guess he's amusing sometime. . . ." John answered, surprised at being addressed by one of the other clients.

"I see that you had a visitor here yesterday, and again this afternoon, a very attractive woman. Does she come back some more times?"

John now understood the reason Mr. Hessman had begun the conversation; visitors were a rare occurrence at Dr. Prospero's Clinic. He sensed that everyone in the room had their ears cocked, waiting for his answer. "I don't know. I don't think so . . . she's very busy with her work these days," he lied.

The heavyset man across the room made another comment in German, and everyone laughed again. John did not know if the man was translating the story, or providing his own running commentary, but he was glad for the interruption. He looked at his watch.

"What time does football come on?" John asked to no one in particular. "I thought there was a Jets game on tonight, I'm a big fan of the New York Jets."

"And why is that so Professor Vigilia?"

John was startled to hear his name spoken. Yes, it did say John Vigilia on his chart, and the doctors and nurses all called him Professor Vigilia. Yet Miranda had said that there had been an article in the paper saying John Vigilia had died in an airplane crash, and that he had been in the airplane alone. But she hadn't actually shown him the article had she? She wouldn't lie to him, would she? Hadn't she returned with a photocopy of the page from the flight book with Ariel Angelucci's signature on it, proof that the two of them had been in the airplane, contrary to what the doctor, and everyone else, kept insisting.

Miranda's story about just going to the airport office, and finding no one there, and photocopying the page on their own copy machine, and then walking out without being discovered, had made it seem all too easy. Was she merely doing what the Sperones had told her to do? He had to trust her. They were going away together on a boat this very night, weren't they? He was to meet her in thirty minutes at the end of the pier.

Miranda said that she had bribed a gardener to leave the gate unlocked. She was going to borrow a boat from a friend she knew in Brissago and pick him up on the end the pier. John suddenly had the horrible thought that this might just be a plot to get rid of him. Could it be that there would be other people on the boat, and that they were planning to take him out onto the lake and then dump him overboard? No, Miranda wouldn't do that. Hadn't she told him that she loved him? And they had made love together in his room that very afternoon. She couldn't have been faking that; could she?

"I asked you why you are a Jets fan, Professor Vigilia . . . I, myself, prefer the Dallas Cowboys. They are 'America's Team' are they not?" Herr Hessman said, interrupting John's private thoughts, eager to display his knowledge of American football. "The Jets do not seem to win very often. I believe it was only in 1969 when they won the Super Bowl. It was the time of the Broadway quarterback . . . what's his name? Joe . . . Joe Namath. Am I not correct?"

"You are right," John answered. He had been going to say that he was a Jets fan because he was a pilot from New York, but refrained. John didn't want to give out any more information on himself, especially since just now he wasn't too sure who he was supposed to be, or who he was talking to. "You're right," he repeated, "the Jets are losers, that's why I support them . . . I'm a loser too." After he said this John wondered why he had.

"A very strange idea, Professor Vigilia; and so why do you consider yourself to be a loser?"

"Oh . . . I was just joking," John said, realizing that he had gotten a little carried away with his reply.

"Anyway there is only night football on your Monday night, which does not come here until Tuesday."

"Oh, that's right, how stupid of me, I forgot what day it is."

"It is easy to do so in such a place like this. . . ."

"Well . . . I think I'll go outside and have a cigarette then," John said, looking at his watch and patting his pocket.

"But I haven't seen you smoke ever before, professor. . . ."

"No I don't . . . only sometimes. . . ." John Vigilia lied, standing up as if to go.

"But you have no cigarettes," Herr Hessman remarked.

"I don't. . . ."

"I see you reach to your pocket just now . . . but your pocket is empty."

"Oh . . . it's a habit. I just assumed they were there . . . I have some in my room. I'll go get one."

"No need to go to all the way back there; I have a pack here . . . I will join you on the terrace for a smoke."

"Ah. No thank you, I shouldn't . . . I am trying to quit." John said, realizing that he was trapped, his need for a cigarette being only an excuse to go outside so that he could get his things from the bushes, and sneak down to the pier. What was up with this Herr Hessman, he wondered; why was he suddenly so interested in him? John had only smoked three cigarettes in his entire life, the last one being twenty years ago. He would have a coughing fit if he smoked a cigarette. Herr Hessman would be sure to know that John was faking something, and perhaps wonder why.

"Oh, no, no, no. . . . I am so sorry professor, look here I have left only one cigarette myself, but you must to take it . . . I have smoked too many today already and one won't hurt you. Besides, I stay here, now comes my favorite program, *Third Rock from the Sun*. I love to watch that Sally, she is a real woman, tall, blonde, strong, and with a good chest."

"Oh, okay then, thank you for the cigarette. . . ."

"When you come back we will finish our conversation about American football."

"No, not tonight, I am tired. After my smoke I think I'll go back to my room and retire . . . I'll return your cigarette tomorrow."

"So we will see you here again tomorrow then?"

"Yes . . . I'll be here, I may sleep late," John said hoping no one would come looking for him until he was far away, "but I should be around later in the day."

John walked out onto the terrace. He stood there for a moment, checking to see if anyone was following him. Seeing no one, he retrieved his pillowcase from where he had lowered it. Then John Vigilia ducked into the bushes and quickly changed into his street clothes. Even though it was quite dark, as the moon was covered by clouds, he felt more secure in the deep blues and browns of his normal wardrobe. He tucked his papers under his shirt, and balled up the hospital's garments, shoving them and the pillowcase back under the shrubbery.

The night was completely black as he groped his way among the trees that lined the edge of the clinic's grounds. John walked blindly along the carpet of soft needles, regretting that he had never gone this way before, but always used the path down the center. Where the trees thinned out his feet felt the gravel that ran along the concrete wall. Behind him, through the outline of the tree branches, he could see the many lights glowing in the windows of the main building. The glass door to the terrace John had come out of was still closed; apparently he had not yet been missed.

His footfalls resounded on the flat stones leading to the pier. Staying against the metal fence John made his way to the end. He stopped for a moment and took in the scent of the air. A fresh breeze was blowing from the northwest. Although the sky was totally obscured, his pilot's sense of weather told him that a storm was coming. Feeling along the fence he found the gate, and fumbled his hands around the chain that restrained it until he found the padlock. As Miranda had promised it had been left undone. John undid the chain and tugged at the gate, which startled him when it moved with a loud creaking sound. Looking back at the clinic, he could see that no more lights had come on. No one must have had heard the noise made by the gate.

John checked the luminous dial of his watch. He had almost delayed too long in the TV lounge. Miranda should be arriving any minute now. John had hoped that she would be there waiting for him. Inch by inch he slowly, and noiselessly, worked the heavy and rusty gate open enough to allow him to slip through to the other side. Standing on the wet stone steps that led down to the water, John forced the gate closed behind him and rewrapped the chain as he had found it. Then John Vigilia sat down on the steps to wait, out of sight of the main building, with the cold water lapping at his feet.

The new moon had peeked its not-much-to-see face from behind the clouds, revealing the lake to be a restless ebony. Even the white caps churned up by the increasing wind gave no contrast as they splashed on the slippery stone steps that were John's damp hiding place. The whole landscape had taken on an unnatural luminosity, like the disastrous twilight of the first stages of an eclipse, a scene which only reinforced John's fantasy that he was on some other, and emptier planet that circled around a sadder star. But the more he felt this shimmering abandonment, the more his own grandiose lunacy glowed like a great bonfire. If he should survive this escapade John did not believe that he could write it down, even the most modern fantasies depended on an older and simpler thesis. While the adventures could be mad, the adventurer must always appear to be sane.

After a short time the lower half of John's pants became soaked through by the splashing waves, but he dared not move to a drier place. He stretched his neck and looked back at the main house. John still saw no signs that he was being missed. Checking his watch yet another time, as he had done almost every five minutes since arriving, he saw that Miranda was now almost forty-five minutes overdue. Off to the west, the direction she would be coming from, he could see the faint flash of lightning behind the mountains. John had not seen any boats, not even the large hydrofoil ferries, on the lake since he had taken up his stealthy position. An especially aggressive wave crashed up on the dock, wetting his right arm. He felt the water dribble down into his cast. John wondered if he really needed this cumbersome thing, or was it just Prospero's way of keeping him here tied to the clinic.

Five more minutes passed. Out of boredom and frustration John Vigilia began to beat his cast against the stone pier. Although the plaster was quite waterlogged it still refused to give way. Then out of the corner of his eye, John suddenly, became aware of a ghostly presence approaching him from the lake. He strained to focus his eyes in the darkness. The monster came closer, riding the crest of the waves. Squinting into the spray, he saw that the great white thing was actually a sailboat, maybe twenty feet in length, showing no lights, and carrying full sail, running before a wind that now was beginning to howl like a banshee. On its present course the boat was headed directly for the dock. John's instinct was to shout a warning. Instead he hesitated, being reluctant to give up his concealment. Then he realized that, with the wind and waves, he would not be heard by the occupants of the boat anyway. The boat continued on its collision course. John could see a single sailor at the rear of the cockpit manning the tiller.

As he scrambled up the steps to avoid the crash, the boat smartly came about into the wind, luffing the sails. But the current was still drifting the boat toward the pier. John made ready with his legs to repel the boat, but then thought better of it. He heard the bow crunch against the dock. Looking down, he saw the rough stones tear a gash through the boat's carefully lettered name: *Morgan Sidney*. A chill shot through John Vigilia's already cold body.

"John! John! . . . Get on board quick! There is a storm coming!" a voice shouted from the cockpit.

"Miranda . . . is that you?"

The sailboat was drifting backwards along the pier, away from the step he was standing on. John grasped for the bow pulpit, but it was already beyond his reach. Miranda was holding the tiller all the way over, unable to let go lest the boat fall off onto the wind.

"Jump into the water and swim out!" she shouted.

"I can't!" John yelled back. He was not a strong swimmer, and with a cast on his wrist he would have no chance at all.

For a brief moment the wind seemed to die. The boat was drifting into the pier farther down, almost to the concrete wall. Miranda grabbed a boat hook from off the cockpit floor. Attaching it to the chain link fence, she held the boat fast. John was working his way toward her on the narrow ledge between the fence and the end of the pier. The space was just three inches wide, and slippery, and he could only hold on with one hand.

The wind had picked up again. John could feel it drying the water on his face. He lacked only three feet to the bow of the *Morgan Sidney*, but it was three feet that would give itself up grudgingly. He inched his way along, hanging onto the fence. Looking back at the main house, John thought that he saw the light come on in what he guessed might be his room, but he wasn't sure. He took another step along the ledge, then paused and looked up again and counted the windows. One, two, three; the light was still on. It was his room, on the third floor, the third window from the end on the east side. Someone must have discovered that he was gone. John Vigilia's already pounding heart missed a beat. He tried to speed up his progress along the ledge and lost his balance. Grabbing at the fence with his right hand, John felt a sharp pain under the cast. He regained his footing. Miranda was holding the boat steady. One more step and he would be there.

A sudden shift of wind momentarily filled the sails. The bow hit the dock, swinging the stern outward. Miranda tried to hold on to the boat hook, but was pulled overboard into the water. John heard her faint cry for help. She was trying to swim, but the boat hook seemed to be caught on her clothes and was dragging her down. He shot a quick glance at the main building; lights were going on all over now. Giving himself a great heave, John leaped for the bow as it moved away from the dock.

The weight of his body brought the bow of the boat down. Water washed over the deck, John was on, but sliding off. He grabbed for the headstay, but the fluttering jib tore it from his hand. His left foot caught in the lifelines. John was on board, but was afraid to move, lest he might slip back off. He peered into the dark, churning water for Miranda, but was not able to see where she was.

The wind had momentarily calmed again. Having freed his foot, John began to crawl down the slippery deck to the stern. He tumbled into the cockpit and took hold of the tiller. John had been on a sailboat perhaps three times in his life. Several summers ago one of his colleagues at Elmira had taken him for a sail and explained the basics. He rapidly searched his mind for that rudimentary knowledge. The boat had drifted a considerable distance away from the dock, and Miranda was nowhere to be seen. He tilted the rudder to the left and then to the right, but the boat had a mind of its own. Each time John moved the tiller the boom swung wildly from one side to the other, just missing his head.

John Vigilia was about to give up. Then he blinked his eyes. A mermaid was climbing up the boat's swimming ladder. She swung herself on board. John was not quite ready for this and jumped forward, his hand leaving go of the tiller. The mermaid immediately took charge, seizing the abandoned tiller, while letting out the mainsheet and setting the boat on a close reach. John ducked as the boom came around, and shifted to the windward side, as he remembered once being told to do. And then he recognized the mermaid.

"Miranda!"

"John, I am sorry I am so late," was all the mermaid could say at the moment, intent on her sailing.

He was surprised to see that she was topless. She was wearing green jogging pants, and her hair was hair a mass of tangled seaweed, which completed the mermaid look. Miranda pointed the boat farther into the wind and close hauled the mainsail. The boat leaned over and pounded into the waves. John slid aft on the seat, and tried to say something, but his words were carried away by the wind. Despite the apparent gravity of their situation John could not take his eyes off Miranda's naked breasts, dripping with water, as she struggled with the tiller to retain control of the sailboat.

"When I saw you go into the water, I thought you were a goner," John shouted above the roaring wind. "I tried to turn the boat back, but I couldn't. I don't know how to sail."

"The boat hook got tangled in my shirt, I couldn't get it untangled. It was pulling me down so I had to take it off," she explained.

John could see Miranda was shivering, as the night air had become very cold with the approaching storm. He began to remove his jacket to give to her, and then realized that it too was soaked with water and that he was shivering also.

"Well don't just sit there staring at my titties as if you have never see them before," Miranda yelled. "Go down in the cabin and have a look around. I think there may be some rain gear stored in a locker down there that we can put on."

John hadn't noticed the cabin door. His paranoia returned. Were they waiting for him down there? Was this the plot to get him out on the lake and then throw him overboard? If so it sure was a very elaborate plan. And no one had come out when Miranda had risked her life to get the boat into the dock. Nevertheless, John Vigilia hesitated.

"Just lift up that hatch . . . there should be some rain stuff in the forward locker. There's a light down there, but don't turn it on they might see us from the windows of the clinic."

John went below. To his relief here was no one down there. He found the rain suits, bright yellow hooded-parkas and matching bib-overalls, and carried them back up on deck. Sliding next to Miranda on the seat he held a parka open for her to put on. The wind whipped at the garment and almost snatched it from John's hand.

"It's no use." Miranda said. "It's too windy. You'll have to hold this heading while I go below to change. Can you do that?

"I'll try . . . but like I said, I'm no sailor. . . ."

He grasped the tiller and took up the heading. John was surprised at the force necessary to hold the course, amazed at Miranda's strength. The boat kept pounding into the wind, although the waves seemed not as violent as they had been in close to shore. Unwilling to leave him alone at the helm, Miranda had not descended completely into the cabin but stood in the open hatchway on the top step. John watched her wiggle out of her wet jogging pants and then bend over and remove her underpanties. She had no shoes, probably having lost them in the water. Miranda stood up for a moment to regain her balance, her head and shoulders above the open hatch. The fickle moon chose that moment to smile on them, if only for an instant, illuminating her naked body. The boat lurched, and then headed into the wind, its sails luffing wildly. Miranda sprang from the hatch in her nakedness and seized control of the tiller.

"John! What's happening?"

"Nothing . . . I was just so distracted by seeing you standing there naked that . . . well I lost my concentration."

"John, John, my poor strange John," Miranda said, letting the boat fall off until the sails filled again. "Now hold this heading while I put my rain suit on."

John took hold of the tiller and Miranda rewarded him with a long kiss, her soft tongue subtly exploring the inside of his now dry mouth.

Miranda returned in her rain suit, and then John went down into the cabin and changed into the other one. Back on deck John remarked how professional they looked in their yellow slickers. He joked, and said that they seemed like an advertisement for Gorton's frozen fish fillets. Miranda laughed and said she had no idea what he meant. And John was going to try to explain, and then though it best not to at the moment.

They both had their hands on the tiller now, although John only used his left hand, keeping his right hand, with its soggy wrist cast on his lap. The wind had died down considerably. As the boat rocked to and fro they passed kisses back and forth to each other having become, for the time, not fleeing fugitives, but two lovers out on a midnight cruise.

Miranda trimmed the mainsail flatter and the boat pounded its way into the darkness. Lightning flashed over the steep mountain off to their right. John looked at his watch. They had been sailing for over half an hour and hadn't seemed to have gone anywhere in relation to the lights that John could see on the shore.

"Where are we heading?" he asked.

"The town of Brissago."

"Why Brissago?"

"Because that's where I got the boat . . . I borrowed it from a friend of mine whose husband is an airline pilot. They keep it in a marina there. That's where my car is."

Lightning flashed again off to their right, followed in a few seconds by a clap of thunder, the exordium of a storm aching to be born. John looked around trying to orient himself. The lights of Ascona were behind him, the lights on the opposite shore seemed closer. To his left and far down the blackness of the lake the rotating beacon from the airport at Magadino flashed its intermittent signal at the gathering clouds.

"But Brissago is that way," he said, pointing off the starboard bow.

"And this is a sailboat . . . we can't just head there, we are going into the wind, we have to tack. When we get near the other shore we can come about. I think we can make it in three or four tacks."

"How far is it?"

"About 3 kilometers . . . by car."

An image of a summer sail came back into John's mind. He recalled tacking into a brisk wind in friend's boat of similar size on Cayuga Lake, and watching the bicyclists going up a hill on the lake shore road as they outran the sailer.

"At this rate we won't get to Brissago until morning; that is if the storm doesn't hit us first. Why did you come for me in a sailboat?"

"It was the only boat I could borrow. And besides, I thought it would make less noise than a powerboat."

"I think we are going to have to make a change of plan. Prospero must know by now that I have gone missing. As I was getting on the boat I saw lights being turned on all over the building. They have probably found the open gate and realized that I have gone by boat. They will doubtless be checking with all the marinas. This is probably the only boat out tonight because of the approaching storm. Someone will notice your car, and put two and two together. Dr. Prospero will have his security goons waiting for us when we arrive at the dock."

"But you don't know for sure that they have discovered you're missing."

"Well, I am only guessing, but when I looked back at the main house there was a light on in my room, and I had purposely left it dark. And the terrace, which had been dark when I left, was all lit up.

"Oh John, I'm so frightened. I didn't think they would find out you were gone until we were far away. What should we do now?"

"I don't know. But I do know that I'm not going to go back. . . ."

Pale moonlight filtered briefly through the clouds. John Vigilia saw that they were lower than before, moving faster. The wind was picking up. A flash of lightning arched across the dark sky. The storm, its progress temporarily impeded by the surrounding mountains and hills, was struggling to spill over onto the lake.

"Does this thing work?" John asked pointing to the small outboard motor bolted to the transom.

"I don't know. There's a can of petrol down in the cockpit, and a tube to hook it up with."

John went below and found the gas can. He struggled it on deck, and attached the hose. Then he stood up and attempted to pivot the engine into the water. A gust of wind hit, leaning the boat on its side. John braced himself against the seat to avoid being knocked overboard.

"Shall I lower the sails now?" Miranda shouted.

"No, not just yet," John replied. "Wait until I see if I can get this motor started . . . if it does. Just head her into the wind and hold it steady while I mess around with this thing."

John had started enough gasoline-powered engines in his life to know that each one had its own personality. Only the correct sequence of events would awaken it from its sleep. Too much prime, and too little throttle, and you might flood the engine, fouling the sparkplug. Then you could grind the starter, flip the propeller, or pull the rope for hours, all in vain. Taking a guess, he gave the outboard three quick shots from the primer, and then advanced the throttle one third. John stood up again, scuffing his feet to make a dry spot on the wet deck.

While he had never thought much about it before, John now noticed that all of these small engines seemed to have their pull cords set up for right handed people. Holding on to the backstay with his left hand for balance, he grasped the cord handle with his right. The weight of the soggy plaster cast on this wrist severely restricted his mobility. With a grunt he gave the rope a tug. There was too much resistance; for some reason the engine refused to turn over. Leaning over the stern pulpit, his fingers groped for the drive selector. He found a lever and blindly moved it from one detent to another, hoping that he had put the engine in neutral. John stood back up and pulled the starter rope a second time. The engine turned over freely, but did not start. He pondered the response the engine had given. It had seemed sluggish and overloaded. John twisted the throttle handle to two-thirds open and gave the rope a more enthusiastic third pull. The engine burst into life.

At that first pop from the engine Miranda jumped up and began lowering the sails. She dropped the jib and stuffed it in the bow pulpit, securing it with a few lengths of rope. Then she dropped the mainsail, which came crashing down on John's, head almost burying him. Brushing the canvas out of his face, he used the engine to turn the boat around and head up the lake. With the wind behind them now, Miranda uncovered the rest of John, and then made a valiant attempt at flaking the mainsail to the boom. But the wind was too strong and she had to settle for bunching it up with a few tie ropes.

"So where are we going?" Miranda asked, finally settling down beside John. Their heads bumped together when they tried to kiss and they both smiled, ignoring for the moment the danger they were facing.

"See that flashing beacon up there . . . that's the airport I've been flying the Jungmann out of," John explained pointing off the bow. "That's where we're heading."

Thirty-one

Let them be hunted soundly. At this hour
Lie at my mercy all mine enemies
Shortly shall all my labors end, and thou
Shalt have the air at freedom. For a little,
Follow, and do me service.

Shakespeare *The Tempest IV, i.*

Shivering with the cold, and fear, John and Miranda crouched in the shadow of the main hangar at the airport in Magadino. The PA-18 was tied down on the ramp exactly where it should be, briskly rocking in the gusty wind that signaled the approaching storm. John knew the lock on the cockpit door could easily be pried open with a screwdriver, which Miranda had found in a tool kit on the boat. He also knew that this airplane, like most Piper Super Cubs, had no ignition key only an on/off switch. He had been checked out in it, and flown it several times while taking up the photographers for the festival. He guessed that the fuel tank would be full as the airplane was usually topped-off after every flight.

John and Miranda had motored to the northeast end of the lake and up the Ticino River until they had come abeam of the rotating beacon. There they had ditched the sailboat, running it aground, and made their way across the wetlands to the airport. Finding a hole dug by animals, they had crawled under the security fence and, staying in the shadows, worked their way around to the main hangar. The two had changed out of their yellow rain gear and back into their still wet clothes in order to be less visible. Miranda was wearing John's jacket in place of her lost shirt, with oversized rubber boots from the cabin for her shoes.

The airport had no commercial traffic, so was little used at night. John knew that the control tower closed at sunset, so no one would be there, but was not aware if anyone else stayed around for security purposes. Hunkered down in the darkness, John and Miranda waited, watching for any sign of life. The eager wind rattled the hangar doors.

High above them the rotating beacon maintained its constant parade of white and green, sending its beams dancing across the lowering clouds. John stared at this self-conscious apparatus as it sent out its mysterious signals into the fickle night. These seemingly hopeless monosyllables, once freed of the beacon, seemed to achieve a life of their own. John felt as if the airport beacon had become merely the point of convergence for certain impulses of matter that used its ingenuity for its own secret purpose. He realized that it was fate that willed and worked, and that they were nothing more than seedpods blown here or there. Transfixed, John's eyes followed the wandering electrical currents that repeated in endless lethargy.

"What are you thinking about, John?" Miranda whispered in his ear, seeing him staring at the beacon. She took hold of his arm. They had not said much since John had announced that they were heading for the airport. She was still not clear what they were doing, or where they were going; and she was not sure that he knew either.

"What made your friend name his boat the *Morgan Sidney?"* John asked, not knowing why the question had come to him just then.

"*Morgan Sidney?"* Miranda said, a bit confused. "Whatever gave you the idea that was the name of the boat?"

"That's what was lettered on the bow. I noticed it when you first ran into the dock . . . the stone steps put a big gash right across the name."

"There's no name written on the bow . . . the name is lettered on the stern, and the boat is called the *Bello Uccello,* in English it means the Beautiful Bird."

John Vigilia was about to swear that he had clearly seen *Morgan Sidney* lettered on the bow, but suddenly he was not sure. Perhaps he had imagined it. John turned his gaze to the windsock, which was standing straight out. The wind had become quite strong. He felt extremely cold in his damp clothes.

"I haven't seen anybody around," John said, moving away from the subject of the boat's name, although it was still very much on his mind at the moment. "Have you?"

"No, there seems to be nobody watching this airport at night. It's rather desolate here," Miranda added.

"Then I think we should get started with our plan. I'll run out and untie the airplane and unlock the cockpit door. You stay here. Then if anyone does come you can sneak away in the shadows."

John hesitated for a moment rapidly collecting his thoughts. It was apparent to him that the safety and sociability of their day before had inadvertently fallen away. Crouching there in the cold air and danger, John felt a great trust and loyalty towards his companion, but was it, he wondered, the trust between two lovers, or more the trust of two condemned persons about to share the same scaffold.

"So are you going to take off without me?" Miranda whispered a hint of fear in her question.

John suddenly realized that he had not discussed the plan that he had worked out in his mind, and was about to put into play, with Miranda. He had just assumed that they would be going away together. But now things had become considerably more complicated, as they were about to become actual lawless fugitives. He had wrecked a borrowed boat, and was about to steal an airplane, and he didn't even know where he was going. Maybe Miranda didn't want to go away with him, John thought. Maybe her plan was just to get him out of the clinic and send him on his way back to America. What had been a perhaps insane, yet solid, decision earlier on his part may not have even occurred to her at all.

The storm had picked up speed and was rapidly approaching them. The whole landscape had taken on a luminous and unnatural discoloration, reinforcing John's impression that he might have stepped off the boat and out onto a different planet.

"So are you coming with me?" John asked. He had to act now and had no time to explain things.

"Did I say I wasn't? I haven't fallen in love with anyone in a long time John, and I'm not going to let you get away. . . ."

"Then let's get on with it," he said taking Miranda's hand. "Keep your head down. Maybe we should consider this an elopement."

"I like the idea," she said smiling at him.

Together they scampered across the ramp, John slightly ahead and Miranda clomping behind in the oversized rubber boots that she had scavenged from the boat. The airport was lit, but not very brightly. They crouched down, huddling in the shadows under the wing of the Piper.

"You untie those ropes . . . I'll work on opening the door," John instructed her.

The screwdriver undid the latch faster than he could tell about it. Locks on old airplanes were notoriously flimsy, perhaps in the interest of saving weight, or perhaps back when this Piper Super Cub was built aircraft theft was not much of a problem.

"I've untied the wings. . . ." Miranda confirmed.

"Did you undo the tail?"

"No . . . . you didn't tell me anything about the tail, you only pointed to the wing."

"Never mind, I'll get it. You climb in . . . in the back," John said giving her a boost into the rear seat in the two place tandem cockpit.

He kicked the chocks out from under the main wheels. As was his habit, John walked around the airplane before getting in. Standing behind the airplane to untie the tail wheel, he caught sight of a gust lock on the rudder and quickly removed it. He felt fortunate to have spotted it, as the lock hadn't been on the rudder the previous times that he had done his pre-flight inspection. Someone must have thought the Cub would need it to keep the rudder from blowing around tied down in the storm. John knew that if he had taken off without noticing it he could have flown the airplane with the gust lock in place, but he would have had no rudder control, which would have made things quite difficult; especially in the heavy winds that would be battering the airplane during his takeoff.

John briefly considered checking the oil using the flashlight that they had found on the boat, but realized he had no oil to add anyway if the engine did need some. Off to the west, the lightning flashes were getting closer, the sound of thunder coming only scant seconds later. His mind told John that he was stalling, not knowing where to go, perhaps unconsciously waiting for someone to come and find them. John Vigilia knew, however, that he did not want to spend the rest of his life in Dr. Prospero's clinic. And moreover, if he was caught and taken back, after what happened tonight, they would surely never let Miranda come to see him ever again.

John poked his head into the back of the cockpit and checked Miranda's seat belt. She was sitting there with a look of excited anticipation on her face, appearing almost like a child about to go on a ride she had never been on before at an amusement park. He leaned in to give her a kiss.

Miranda put her arms around him and returned the kiss. "I love you, John," she said. "I'm ready to go anywhere with you."

"I love you too," he replied, squeezing her shoulder. John gave her seat belt an extra tug. His heart was pounding: he wanted to make love to her then and there. They were going away together, and she did not even care where.

John swung himself into the front seat, buckled on his seat belt, and closed the split door. He moved the mixture control to the full-rich position, gave the engine three strokes of the primer, put his feet on the brakes, turned the master switch to ON and the ignition switch to LEFT, as he had been trained. For reasons unknown to John, Lycoming engines were always started on the left magneto and then switched to BOTH after they were running. Leaning forward, he looked over the cowl to be sure no one was standing in front of the propeller.

It was then that John saw the lights of a car pulling into the parking lot. He pressed the starter button. The Lycoming turned over two tentative revolutions then came to life. With no time to waste warming up the engine, he immediately began to taxi, and without turning on the aircraft's lights. Squinting into the darkness, John s-turned between the rows of thin blue lights that defined the taxiway, performing the magneto check as he went along. John did not taxi the airplane all the way to the end, but upon reaching the midfield turn-off advanced the throttle and rolled out onto the runway.

"Are you ready? Here we go," he shouted over his shoulder.

Lined up with the centerline, John Vigilia applied full power. With the cold, brisk wind the Piper required only a few hundred feet to lift off. Once free of the ground, he held the airplane close to the runway to gather airspeed. Then John pulled the Piper up and away in a steep climbing turn and headed in the only direction that he could go, east, down the valley, and away from the approaching storm.

"That was a magnificent takeoff," Miranda shouted, pounding softly on John's shoulder. "I've never experienced anything quite like that before. They said you were a real stunt pilot." Then she added: "Did you see them? There were three cars in the parking lot when we left. . . ."

"Three? I only saw one. . . ."

"I looked behind us. Two more cars pulled in when you were doing your turn."

"Well I don't think that we'll be going back down there anytime soon," John said, maneuvering the airplane in and out of the lower level of clouds. He was searching to find a hole of clear sky where he could climb for the altitude he knew they needed to get over the mountains that surrounded the Lago Maggiore on all sides.

"So just exactly where are we going?" Miranda shouted, continuing their high volume conversation in the noisy cockpit made louder by a door that no longer shut properly, because John had broken the lock, letting the wind come roaring in.

"We've got to head east," John yelled back, leveling the airplane briefly to allow the wet compass to settle. "As you can see there are thunderstorms coming from the west. It looks like a front, not just something local that we can fly around. Unfortunately, the gas tanks aren't full; I estimate we only have about two hours of fuel left. This means that we are going to run out of gas before it gets light. The Alps and the Dolomites are all around us . . . so it's nothing but mountains until we get over them and find the Plain of Venice, but we'll still be in Italy, and I am sure in some place within easy reach of the Sperone family's influence. With this tail wind we might be able to make it all the way to Austria or Yugoslavia, if we can continue to cruise between the cloud levels like we are."

John leaned the mixture a bit more for economy, realizing then that he had been flying with his left hand most of the time, and in the excitement hadn't even noticed. Trying to reach into the map pocket with his right hand he found that his cast prevented him. So he turned and asked Miranda. "Can you fly an airplane?"

"I flew with my husband quite a few times while he was alive, and he let me take the controls. I think I can probably fly an airplane better than you can sail a boat."

"I'm not joking. The charts should be in the side pocket. You hold her steady for a minute and I'll try and see if I can find someplace that we might safely get to with the fuel we have."

John felt the pressure of Miranda's hand on the rear control stick, the airplane stayed level and held its course. He shined the flashlight down into the pocket. There was a flight manual, a discarded tissue, and an airsickness bag. A shiver of disappointment shook him. John waggled the stick, signaling that he was taking back the controls.

"That was quick . . . what's the matter?" Miranda asked.

"There are no charts. . . ."

"No charts! So what do we do now?"

"We just continue going the way we're going . . . keep your eyes open for some lights, something, anything, on the ground."

Rallying what was left of her energy, Miranda straightened up in her seat and pressed her face to the window, her breath fogging the cold plastic. She wiped a hole in the moisture. Down below, through the occasional gap in the clouds, she could see nothing but total blackness.

The darkness out in front of him had a solid appearance. With no lights below for ground reference, and no moon or stars above, John Vigilia was forced to fly by instruments. The Piper having no artificial horizon or directional gyro was not making the task easier. Nor did he have the luxury of that instrument flyer's silent friend, the automatic pilot. John had only himself and a turn and bank indicator to keep the wings level. The turbulence, and the sodden cast on his right wrist were making holding a heading using the only the compass all but impossible.

Scanning the panel John realized that the PA-18, although fifty years newer, was equipped with the same instruments, and from a photograph that he remembered almost in the same position, as Lindbergh's *Spirit of Saint Louis.* He thought of Miranda crouching behind him, not unlike Ariel in his tale of his supposed Atlantic crossing with Lindbergh, not sure where they were going, or even if the flight might have a successful conclusion.

The temperature in the cabin had now dropped considerably. John pulled the cabin heat knob all the way out; however, this did little to offset the cold wind coming in through the broken door. He turned on the airplane's landing light. The beam shot out into the murky darkness revealing a whirling wall of moisture. Leaning forward, John shined his flashlight on the wing's leading edge. His eyes caught the whiteness of the thin layer of ice beginning to collect there. Checking the row of switches, John found, as he had expected, that the PA-18 had no pitot heat. When the pitot tube iced over he would lose the use of the altimeter and airspeed indicator. Reaching forward he pulled the carburetor heat knob all the way out to keep the carburetor's air intake from icing over, and pushed in the throttle to full. They were in the clouds and in icing conditions. John's only hope was to climb out to the clear air on top. Unlike Lindbergh, he was not over a level ocean but the rugged Dolomite Mountains. He could not descend to 100 feet and fly under the clouds. If it were daylight he might find a valley he could slip down. But this was not going to happen; John Vigilia knew that his fuel would be gone long before the sun rose.

The airplane continued to crawl painfully upward. They were already at 6000 feet, and the Piper was struggling to maintain a climb of 300 feet-per-minute, or at least that figure was what John roughly calculated it to be as the panel did not have a vertical speed indicator. This airplane had been equipped only for daytime sight-seeing flights around the lake on sunny days, not for fleeing over the mountains, in the dark and clouds, running before an approaching cold front.

Their climb was almost nonexistent now; the PA-18 seemed to be hanging on its propeller. They were at 9000 feet and still in the clouds, although John sensed that the temperature was getting warmer. It sometimes happened that way. A pilot could often get out of the freezing level by going to a higher altitude and finding a layer of warm air sandwiched somewhere in the middle of the clouds. But the Piper also lacked an outside air temperature gauge so John did not dare level off to wait and see if somehow the thin layer of ice on the leading edge would begin to melt and break away.

"I can't see anything at all out there now," Miranda shouted over his shoulder.

"We're still flying in the clouds," John answered as the PA-18 staggered on up to 10,000 feet.

"It's terribly cold . . . doesn't this airplane have a heater?"

Despite the roar, John could hear a tremor in Miranda's voice. He wasn't sure if it was the cold or her fear, or perhaps both.

"The heaters on full, I'm sorry to say . . . I'd give you my jacket but you're already wearing it."

"You must be cold too. Do you want it back?"

"No . . . you keep it; you need it more than I do. . . ."

As he had as a child, when thinking about the girl that he was in love with at the moment, John gave himself up to impure fantasies. The vision of Miranda climbing up the boat ladder topless, water dripping from her breasts and hair, flashed in his mind. He could not believe that in his panic he had actually imagined that he was being visited by a mermaid. John smiled, as the thought unconsciously warmed him a little. Then, for an all to brief instant, the glowing moon peered through the clouds and returned his smile.

"I saw it John! Over there . . . just for a moment, the moon. Did you see it?"

"Yes I saw it too. We must be getting near the top." John cried, feeling his body quiver with the anticipation. Five minutes passed, then ten, but their aircraft was still cloaked in the frosty vapors.

At 10,500 feet the Piper appeared to be standing motionless. It had taken them fifteen minutes to climb 500 feet. The battle now had become not to climb higher, but rather not to lose what altitude they had gained. They would painfully ascend a hundred feet only to have a gust knock them down two hundred. One consolation was that the airplane no longer seemed to be taking on anymore ice; although none of the ice it had was disappearing.

Without warning the engine began to vibrate, shaking the entire aircraft. John quickly pulled out the throttle and pushed it in again.

"What's happening, John!?" Miranda gave a worried shout.

"It's nothing . . . actually good news. It's the ice melting and being thrown off the propeller . . . it puts the prop out of balance and the engine starts to shake."

"Oh . . . I thought we were going down."

"No, not yet . . . we still have enough gas for a little while more, but I don't think it will last until daylight, climbing like we have been doing uses more fuel . . . but we had to get up here. We're still in the clouds, but at least at a warmer altitude; I guess we should stay here for a while," John Vigilia said, leveling off the airplane and leaning the mixture a bit more.

"You must be so tired . . . I know I am. I wish we were together in a warm soft bed. We will be soon . . . won't we John?"

"Yes, Miranda . . . in a little while," John said, his voice betraying a certain anxiety, wondering if they would ever see the ground safely again before they found themselves being smacked down into it.

John reached behind his seat and affectionately squeezed Miranda's knee. She responded with a kiss on the back of his neck, and her hands began massaging his shoulders. "I love you," she whispered in John's ear.

At that moment the airplane broke free of the cold vapor that had been holding them, and popped out into a palely illuminated cloudscape. The faint light, filtered through a thin upper layer of haze, gave not the sense of moonshine, but rather of an abandoned daylight. Only a few hundred feet below, the ragged cloud tops threatened to drag the airplane back into them, but at least for the moment they were in clear air.

Their interlude of happiness quickly passed as they were plunged headlong into the clouds yet again. But there was no ice starting to form, so John decided to stay at the altitude that he was at rather than consume more fuel climbing. Even out of the clouds the darkness of the night had given John Vigilia little reference to fly by, so he clung to the information provided by his sparsely equipped panel to keep the wings level and the airplane on course.

The extreme tedium of the flight, concentrating intently on the luminous dials of the instruments bathed in the dim red of the cockpit light, and the thin oxygen at this altitude, was beginning to bring on fatigue. John kept shaking his head. Despite the precariousness of their present situation he caught himself nodding off. He was tired. The day had been filled with more physical exertion than the total of all the previous days John had spent at Prospero's clinic. Slowly John's head began to drop. His eyes turned inward.

The white room opened up around him, the diffuse rays of the late afternoon sun filtering in through the slanted window blinds. John was in his bed, but not asleep. Miranda was in the bed with him. This was the clinic, though not confined, but rather expansive. Time passed unnoticed. They held one other close, groping together as children do when exploring another person's sex for the first time. John could feel the warm blood flowing in his veins as it had not done in a long while. In the forced silence of this clinic room they were like secretive young lovers, on the couch in the basement game room, exploring the limits they dared go to while parents watched television in the living room directly overhead.

In no hurry to copulate, they teased and played, exploring each other's body, communicating only by the expression on their faces. A splendid new life had begun for Miranda and John, a love intimate and driven. He understood now that his feelings for Miranda were the same as the feelings she had professed for him, but that he had had such difficulty accepting.

John lay there as Miranda mounted on top of him. She had become unusually beautiful and natural. There was something heartbreaking in her manner, and in her eyes. But on a sensual level, she so bluntly craved his thrusts that the faintest call from her body gave her a look directly suggestive of all things carnal as she rode his rampant staff.

An eternity seemed to pass, a lifetime spent together in a moment. John felt her mute and absolute spasm, but Miranda did not calm until she felt his own orgasm flooding her. Untroubled by conscious thoughts, their hearts exalted by pure emotion itself, they lay down next to each other without stirring.

The absence of the steady hum of the engine that had lulled them both to sleep caused Miranda to awaken first.

"John! John! Wake up! Please!" she yelled, shaking the drowsiness from her head while frantically pounding him on his back. "I can't hear it anymore. I can't hear the motor. I think it has stopped!"

"What? What is it?" John groaned, startled from his own deep slumber. He felt as he had the only other time John had fallen asleep in a moving airplane, the time that he had blacked out during an aerobatic maneuver; disoriented, not sure where he was. Then John Vigilia became aware of the ominous silence, broken only by the rush of the wind whistling in the struts. The turn and bank needle was pointing all the way to the left, the ball slid all the way to the right. The altimeter was unwinding rapidly. The airplane had fallen off into a descending left turn, a maneuver the instrument flight manuals referred to as "dead man's spiral."

Instinctively, John retarded the throttle, even though the engine was already stopped. He leveled the wings and at the same time turned the fuel selector to the reserve position. The air speed indicator showed the airplane was nearing its never exceed speed. He gingerly pulled back on the control stick.

"Are we going to crash!?" Miranda cried, an abrupt violent sob choking her voice as the stark vision of her husband's airplane spinning into the lake flashed before her eyes. They were both being crushed into their seats by the G-forces, their eyeballs driven back into their heads, as John slowly pulled the Piper out of the dive.

"Well . . . maybe not just yet!" John shouted, as the airplane leveled off and the air speed returned to normal. He pushed the starter button and the engine coughed back to life.

"Oh, thank God . . . we must have both fallen asleep. But now what are we going to do?" Miranda asked, seeing that they had descended back down into the thick clouds.

John shined his flashlight at the wing. The weak beam generated by the failing batteries could barely penetrate the dense vapors, but it was strong enough for him to see that there was no ice forming on the leading edge. Also, the temperature in the cockpit felt considerably warmer. Perhaps they were beyond the mountains, at least the taller ones. John glanced over his shoulder at Miranda. In the dull red light of the cockpit, her face showed a look of childlike innocence that belied her age. She trusted him completely; he must not fail her now.

"I think we may be past the mountains," John said. "As long as we've descended this low, let's take her down and see if we can get under this stuff. Maybe we can find a place to land while we still have a little gas left in the tank."

With the engine set at idle, John glided the airplane down. Their world was silent again, except for the sound of the rushing wind. It was an extraordinary silence, so fragile that a mere breath might have put it out of order. As the aircraft slipped through the billowing clouds, they did not dare budge lest their slightest movement disturb the unreal immobility.

John's mind was reeling with some kind of exhausted vertigo. He had climbed the water tower again, and again jumped off without being sure what the outcome would be. His gaze ricocheted from out the window to the panel and back out the window. John Vigilia's greatest danger at the moment was to not see the ground before the airplane made abrupt, and violent, contact with it.

They sat there watching the darkness as the altimeter unwound at a slow rate. John had put the airplane into shallow descent, with the engine turning over just enough to keep the carburetor intake from icing over, and to reduce the drag of the propeller. This would help extend their range, and save the fuel that they might need later on lower down. And if the airplane was going to hit something, hopefully trees and not rocks, it would be better to hit whatever it was at the slowest possible airspeed.

John leaned forward in his seat, his damp forehead almost pressed against the roundness of the windscreen, his eyes staring straight up. Through the thinning clouds above him, John could see the Milky Way, that astral slash at the summit of the sky, shinning in its immensity. Then the clouds below suddenly parted to reveal dark, symmetrical rows of trees, tree tops stretching forward to infinity.

As John Vigilia struggled to focus his eyes, a dark row of what appeared to be tall pines loomed up at them out of the night. Pushing in the throttle, he pulled back on the control stick. Miranda and John were immediately forced down into their seats as he banked the airplane steeply to avoid the trees.

"Oh, John . . . we're out of the clouds . . . we're saved!" Miranda shouted, when he had leveled off again. Patting him on the shoulder, she leaned forward and planted a kiss on the back of his neck.

"We're not out of the woods just yet," John replied, blushing at his bad pun. If one of his writing students had had a character use that line at just that moment in a story, he would have suggested they change it. But at present John Vigilia was too busy banking and maneuvering the airplane to avoid hitting the trees that kept appearing in front of them to worry about making an original comment.

Before the sky above them closed up again, and he lost what little light there was, John had been able to hurriedly assess their situation. They had been fortunate enough to break out of the clouds in a narrow valley. On either side of them the mountain tops were still shrouded in fog. If, by chance, their descent had been a mile or so either left or right of the course John had taken they would have doubtlessly come down directly into the trees.

John climbed the Piper until they were just skimming the base of the clouds. The valley seemed to be widening and descending. Here and there he could see small open spots that appeared to have been made by loggers or farmers. None were anywhere near large enough to land the PA-18, even though the airplane was known for its ability to get in to and out of very small fields. Besides, in the darkness, he had no way of telling if these fields were plowed or littered with low stumps. Nevertheless, John Vigilia would have to make a decision soon, as he estimated that they had only a few minutes of fuel remaining. It would be better to risk slipping into one of these small spaces while they still had power, than to take a chance at whatever might be under them when the engine finally did quit.

"Look! Look! John! Over there, to the right, that dark space . . . it's a big field, or maybe an empty farm!" Miranda exclaimed pounding on his shoulder, and pointing.

Although John had not revealed to her that they were in their final minutes of flight, Miranda must have sensed that this was the case. The clouds above them had again parted slightly, the frail moon faintly illuminating the dense forest. Where she had indicated there was indeed a clearing somewhat larger than any that they had flown over so far.

"So, let's go and have a look. I hope it's big enough," John said, banking the airplane and heading for the rift in the row after row of trees. The tone of his voice indicated that if there were any possibility of putting the airplane down in this space he was going to take it.

Approaching the field from the north, John had no way of knowing the wind direction at ground level, but assumed it would be from the west as they had experienced a tail wind most of the way. Slipping the airplane in low, he flew over the open space, his landing light revealing that the field was clear and relatively free of stones. It appeared as if it might have been farmed once. Unfortunately, like most fields that had been plowed before the invention of tractors, a large shade tree had been left exactly in the middle for the farmer to stop and rest his horse.

Completing his flyover, John started to climb. He would perform a standard landing pattern, coming around to land into the wind. Then, without warning, the engine quit. Pilots are taught never to try to turn back to the field with a dead engine, always to land straight ahead, no matter what the terrain. Banking the airplane increased the stall speed, which could lead to a spin, with not enough altitude available for recovery. But ahead of John Vigilia was nothing but a tall, stout forest. He would have to break the rule and risk turning back.

He dove the airplane at the trees to gain speed, and then pulled up and around in a power-off chandelle. His direction reversed, John crossed the controls and began slipping the airplane in for a downwind landing. The wheels touched; he felt them bouncing on the soft ground. With the tail wind he had landed too fast, and too far down the field. John's feet danced on the rudder pedals and brakes, fighting to keep the aircraft under control. They were heading for the lone tree.

The Piper hit the trunk with its right wing, tearing it off, and sending the airplane pivoting. The aircraft came up on its nose, hesitated for a second and then fell over on its back. Fortunately there was no fuel left in the tanks to burst into flame and explode.

Miranda and John hung upside down in their seat belts. The only sounds that they could hear were the faint ping of the engine cooling down, and the rustle of the wind rocking the tree branches.

"Let's try to get down," John said.

"We can't get down," Miranda said, light-heartedly correcting him. "The way we are presently positioned down is up."

Laughing, John had to agree with her, having the sensation that at the moment the entire cosmos was turned upside down. All the trees were growing downward and all the morning stars were under their feet. Then an opposite certainty came into John's mind. Ever since his wife Iris had died the cosmos really had been upside down, but now the capsized universe had been righted again. The myth which he had been chasing, and which had turned on him, was only a myth in his own heart, which now stood at the base of the large, solitary tree laughing at him.

He did not, for the present, ask his heart any questions or details. Perhaps he had found Lindbergh's secret copilot, or perhaps not. But Ariel Angelucci was dead, and that was the end of the story. The happy fact was that John now realized this search, which he had pursued with such an intolerable obsession, was only the shadow of him trying to catch up with himself. John knew that he was simultaneously a fool and a new man, as any recovery from morbidity must be accompanied by a certain healthy humility. John Vigilia undid his seatbelt and, obeying the law of gravity, tumbled onto the ceiling of the cockpit.

Hanging in such a ridiculous state herself, Miranda could not suppress her laughter.

Tears were in John's eyes as he reached up for her. "Here, let me help you down . . . or up," he said.

Dawn was breaking over everything in the field at once, at the same time fresh and timid. John Vigilia had no idea where they were, but felt an unnatural buoyancy in his body, and a clearness in his mind that he had not experienced for sometime. Taking Miranda's hand, he held it hard. A gentle breeze blew through the tree, so fresh and clear that one might think it came not from the sky, but from an open crack in the universe.

John strode off toward the edge of the field with a new energy, the sleeve that he had torn to get his shirt over the cast flapping in the wind. Miranda followed along at his side, treading in a more cautious and foot-sore manner.

Across the square of the meadow, they made out a tall man, walking with a long stick as if it were a scepter, advancing toward them out of the morning mist. As he came nearer the two could see that he was clad in what they took to be the Alpine style, a fine, but old-fashioned suit with pants that ended at his knees, its color the green of the woodland. At this distance John and Miranda could not tell if he was a civilian or some kind of official person.

He arrived in front of them without speaking. His glance was strong, but quiet. But for the bright maroon hat on his head, covered with strange medals which caught the emerging sunlight, he might have passed for one of the shadows he had recently emerged from.

"Do you speak English?" John Vigilia asked respectfully, forgetting that Miranda, who was standing next to him, spoke fluently the three languages common to this part of the world.

"Hello," the man said with a curious smile, "I saw your airplane come down. You are all right?

"We're fine," John said. "I banged my head a little when we hit the tree, but otherwise we're okay."

"Good. We have been expecting you. I have a car waiting on the road nearby."

Then he turned to walk away, and they began to follow him.

Thirty-two

My master through his art foresees the danger
That you, his friend, are in, and sends me forth
(For else his project dies) to keep them living.

Shakespeare *The Tempest II, i.*

Beyond the large window the streets of the Eternal City were relatively quiet. Out on the highway, however, cars and trucks were backed up as far as the airport Leonardo da Vinci at Fiumicino some twenty miles away. In an effort to curb pollution in the city all nonessential traffic was being banned from the center until 10:00 in the morning. In another hour vehicular hell would break loose on all the roads that led to Rome. Count Ferdinand Sperone looked up from his desk as his secretary entered.

"There is a Signore Vigilia to see you, count," the man said.

"Vigilia. Yes, I have been expecting him. Send him in."

The count recognized the man's face, familiar, but a visage from another era, long ago, before he ever knew this person.

"I'm John Vigilia," the newcomer said, extending his hand. He gave a textbook handshake, whether he knew it or not. It wasn't something they taught to art history majors in college, perhaps in the business school. His wrist slightly bent at an angle, he grasped the count's hand thumb joint to thumb joint, his fingers wrapped firmly, but not too tight. After gently pumping three times, Vigilia let go.

"I am Count Ferdinand Sperone, at your service," the count said. "Sit down please." He studied the face on the young man opposite him. "Amazing, you look so much like the man who is your uncle. If I would have passed you in the street, I would have stopped you to ask if you were related to one of America's most famous stunt pilots."

"Is my uncle? You said 'is your uncle' . . . so you know him to be alive then?"

"I didn't say that. You must excuse me, please, John. May I call you John? While my English is adequate for most conversations, I have not yet grasped all the subtleties of your grammar. I sometimes misstate things."

"But you just said, 'is your uncle,' present tense, this would imply that he *is* alive. If you said he *was* my uncle, past tense, this would imply that he was dead."

"But if I said, 'Your uncle *is* dead' . . . wouldn't that be present tense?" Sperone said, secretly pleased at his own cleverness.

"It would, but that's not the point," the young man replied, rather annoyed with himself that he had let the conversation get off track. "I'm not here to give an English lesson. I'm just trying to find out exactly what you may, or may not, know about my uncle's disappearance."

"Now wait just a moment, Mr. John Vigilia, Jr. . . . . ."

"I'm not *junior*, the John Vigilia you knew was not my father; my father's name is Joseph."

"Joseph? . . . So why is it you, and not your father, who is here searching for his missing brother?"

"The two didn't get along very well . . . besides, my father has Parkinson's disease; so doesn't travel much anymore."

"I'm very sorry to hear that," Count Sperone said. Nonplused, he tried to change the subject. "So you are a student?"

"I was. I graduated last year . . . with a degree in art history."

"And now you are teaching at some major university, and writing articles for prestigious magazines?"

"No. It's difficult to get a job these days, at least in art history. That's why I'm trying to find my uncle."

"So he can get you a job?" The count knew this was not the case, but couldn't resist what he though was a witty riposte.

"No, not really," John Vigilia replied wryly. He was feeling very uncomfortable. He was here to get information, but the count was cleverly taking control of the conversation, and moving it in another direction.

"Would you like a cup of coffee? I'll ring for my man," Count Sperone offered, reaching for the intercom.

"No thank you . . . I mean I didn't come all this way to see you just to chat. It took me a lot of time, and money, get here from Ireland."

"You came from Ireland? . . ."

"Yes . . . there were some things there that I had to check out first."

"So you come from America, by way of Ireland, to interrogate me when you have no job; how do you pay for your travels?"

"That's why I'm here. You see my uncle left a will, not a real will exactly, but a holographic will. . . ."

"Like a hologram, a three dimensional picture in space," Sperone joked again.

"No, the word has a different, legal meaning: a document written entirely in the handwriting of the person above whose name it appears. My uncle wrote out a will, but it was never witnessed."

"Very interesting, but what does this have to do with you?"

"As my uncle's wife is dead, and he has only one brother, my father, who he was not too fond of, he left his entire estate to me. It's not much; his house, car and airplane, a small insurance policy, and his retirement fund."

"You are a very fortunate person."

"But I don't inherit anything until it's proven he's dead."

"I see now the main reason for your inquiry." the count said, leaning back in his chair. Count Sperone had wondered at this opening up of a matter he though was finished some years ago. In his letter the young John Vigilia had not explained his financial interest in the matter of his uncle's disappearance.

"Don't get me wrong, I would be more than happy to discover that my uncle is alive, but if he is dead, I need to find proof of it, to know how and where he died . . . and most importantly, to obtain a death certificate." The nephew's voice had a tone of hopelessness, perhaps even regret.

"So why have you come to me? I knew your uncle only briefly. As I recall we only actually met . . . maybe once or twice." The count paused, cleared his throat. "He said he was writing a book about our family's airplanes, so I sent him off to Como to see my sister who runs our airplane museum there. But why haven't you gone to the authorities? Surely they are more prepared to mount a search for your missing uncle than you are."

"There was a search, but not very thorough, that turned up nothing. The FBI found out my uncle had taken a flight to Ireland; that was the last lead they had. They didn't follow up on it for some reason."

"But his story must have been on television and in the newspapers, his photograph prominently displayed. Surely someone must have come forward with information."

"Thousands of people go missing in America every year who are never found. The only ones who get their faces on TV, and have massive hunts organized for them are cute little kids, or pretty teenaged girls."

"I see. So, why do you think I should know something about your uncle that no one else does?"

"I have been living in my uncle's house . . . cleaning up, taking care of things. I am the executor of his will as well as the beneficiary. Among his mail I found several letters he sent home to himself from Europe."

"To himself?" the count said, affecting an air of incredulity.

"My Uncle John was a kind of loner; he didn't have any close friends, at least none he could write letters to and, as I said, his wife was dead."

"I see that's too bad. So no one really missed him. . . ."

"Not to change the subject . . . but you are mentioned rather prominently in these letters."

"I am mentioned! That is strange. In what possible context?"

"He seemed to think you were hiding something from him, some information that he wanted to know."

"But what could I have been hiding from your uncle? I hardly even knew the man."

"He wasn't quite sure. . . ." John's voice betrayed the uncertainty of someone who had traveled down several roads that hadn't led anywhere, and who was now reluctant to reveal his true destination.

"Would you like a cigarette?" Count Sperone asked, fishing a pack out of a drawer in his desk.

"No thank you . . . I don't smoke. However, I would like some answers."

"But so far you haven't asked me any questions. . . ."

John regrouped, realizing he had let his thoughts get ahead of him, his flights of fancy. "Well . . . in your opinion, just why did my uncle come all the way to Rome to talk to you?"

"I told you . . . he said he was writing a book about the Sperone airplanes."

Rain began to splatter on the window behind the count. With a flutter of wings the pigeons that had been cooing on the ledge made a hasty departure. Although the sky had darkened considerably, John still could not clearly make out the count's face, back-lit by the glare from outside, a placement that he had assumed was by no means accidental.

"Then why did he go to Ireland first?" the nephew asked.

"Your uncle came here from Ireland? I didn't know that. I thought he had come directly from America." the count said, pausing to light his cigarette. He exhaled and then waved his hand, thoughtfully blowing his smoke away from John's face.

"But you did know he came from Ireland," John interjected, sensing that he had discovered a flaw in the count's story.

"I did?. . . "

"In one of his letters he mentions he called you from Ireland. And earlier I said the FBI had traced him to Ireland. And I also remarked that I had just come from Ireland. Where, by the way I have been able to recreate his movements up until the time he left for Rome to see you."

"Yes, you did mention that you had come from Ireland. It must have slipped my mind. Your uncle must have taken a little pleasure trip there before coming here. As far as I know we have never sold any of our airplanes to the Irish, but perhaps there are some there."

"He wasn't writing a history book about Sperone airplanes."

"But that's what he told me. . . ."

"That was just his cover story. He was really looking for an old man named Ariel Angelucci, a very old man, an American."

"And why was he looking for this old man . . . Angelucci?" The count asked. He took another drag on his cigarette, and turned aside to blow his smoke, a gesture designed to face himself away from the young man's gaze, to make himself even more ephemeral.

"That's precisely what I was hoping you would tell me." John said, surprised at his own growing boldness.

"Yes . . . I remember now that he had mentioned something about this man Angelucci. But I forget what it was. It has been quite awhile since your uncle came to see me, and I have so many other things on my mind. Are you aware that I am an adviser to the prime minister. . ."

"A Count Sperone, who I guess must have been your father, adopted Ariel as a young boy from an orphanage in Ireland."

"My father was a very generous man."

"That may be true. But why go all the way to Ireland to adopt someone? I am sure there were plenty of orphans here in Italy."

"*Ha ragione*. You are right. My father was a strange person. I certainly cannot explain his actions. It happened a long time ago. I am sure if he were alive today he would be happy to give his reasons to you." A little smile came across the count's face, observable even to John. "Perhaps he had heard of this boy with an Italian name in an orphanage in Ireland and wanted to save him from eating boiled potatoes instead of pasta all his life," the count said chuckling at his own joke.

John did not laugh. "I believe one of the questions that my uncle was trying to answer was: How did Ariel Angelucci get to Ireland?"

"So how does any young boy get anywhere?" the count said rhetorically, snuffing out his cigarette. "He must have had some problems with his parents and ran away from home. . . ."

"But Ireland is a long way to go. Ariel was an American."

"Or so he had said. . . ." The count paused, realizing that he made a slip. The rain was hammering at the window now, unrelenting.

"He had said? . . ." John repeated, a cold dryness forming in his throat. "So you knew Ariel Angelucci?"

"Well . . . I didn't actually know him personally. I mean he lived at our place in Como, so I only saw him occasionally . . . when I was a child and the family went there on holidays. He was a bit older than us. But everyone had heard his story about how he had come from America. It was some fantasy he must have made up."

"And how did he say that he had he gotten to Ireland from America?"

"If he did come . . . I suppose it would have been on a boat. In those days there was no other way," the count volunteered, only too eagerly.

"He never said anything about coming in an airplane?"

"No, nothing that I remember," Count Sperone replied, and then added somewhat unconvincingly, "Besides, you must recall that there were no transatlantic flights back then."

"There were a few. . . ."

"Not regular flights; only those made by daredevils trying to prove something . . . mostly to get some prize money. . . ."

"So what about the flight by Charles Lindbergh?" John said, throwing out the name like he was playing his trump card.

"What about him? I cannot recall any of their names, but I remember there were several transatlantic flyers before him."

"If so, just why is Lindbergh's flight so famous then? Is it because he did it all alone?"

"More likely, I suspect, it was because you Americans needed a world hero at that precise moment in history."

"But suppose he wasn't alone . . . would his flight have captured the public's imagination the way it did?"

"I have no idea; perhaps not. I was only a child at the time. I never read the newspapers. I didn't even learn about his flight until years later. Why are you bothering me with this speculation? I have no interest in Charles Lindbergh. You said you came here to ask me about your uncle."

"My uncle believed Lindbergh was not alone, that he had had someone with him, a copilot. He believed that there had been a grand conspiracy to cover up this fact."

"A muddled notion, I would certainly say." The count dug out another cigarette and lit it.

"And why would you say that? . . ."

"It is quite obvious. Lindbergh made his flight many years ago. There has been considerable research into the matter since then. Numerous volumes have been written, I dare say hundreds, about the flight, and now comes your uncle, with no background in historical methods, and his silly idea. It was pure self-delusion."

"If you thought his idea was so 'muddled' as you put it, why did you have my uncle followed?"

"Who had him followed?" The count swung around angrily in his chair and took a deep drag on his cigarette.

"You had him followed. . . ."

"And where did you get that notion?"

"My uncle wrote it in his letters. . . ."

"He was only fooling himself."

"Someone tried to knock him off a bicycle when he was in Munich, a car with a Milan license plate."

"So . . . I live in Rome, all my cars have Rome license plates. What was your uncle doing in Munich anyway? perhaps checking up on Lindbergh's close ties with Hitler. He was a great admirer of the Nazi's you know . . . at least in the beginning."

"My uncle went to Munich to meet a friend of yours, a German performance artist. My uncle was running out of money, he agreed to go to Switzerland to fly a biplane in an art event this man was staging."

"Yes, that would have been Hans Hockenheim. Have you been to Munich to see him? Perhaps he knows something that could be of use to you, or if he doesn't, he will make up whatever you want. That's the kind of fellow Hans is."

"No, I haven't been to Munich," John said. He tried to remain detached, but it was apparent he was becoming annoyed with the count's banter. "However, I have been to Locarno."

"A very pretty town on a lake . . . but a little bit out of the way if you were coming from Ireland. Why on earth did you go there?" His tone was a little too theatrical. He sensed that the nephew knew he was bluffing.

"Because that's where my uncle finally met up with Ariel Angelucci, the man that my uncle was convinced had been Lindbergh's secret copilot. They apparently had a conversation."

"Not our Ariel Angelucci . . . he would only have been a boy when Lindbergh made his solo flight."

"That was the point. Ariel was small, but he knew how to fly, his uncle had taught him . . . so he fit in behind the seat."

"What a creative mind your uncle must have had; such an idea. He should have written novels."

"He did a lot of writing, but very little of it was ever published . . . that was why he was teaching."

"And I thought he was just a stunt pilot," the count added, once again sending the conversation off on a different track. "Oh, I shouldn't say 'just a stunt pilot.' John Vigilia was one of the greatest. I saw him fly in the big air show at Oshkosh, in Wisconsin, several times. I thought that 'The Stunt Flying Professor' was just a sobriquet."

"He was a professor at a small college in Elmira . . . but that's not what I came to talk to you about. Let's get back to Ariel Angelucci. Apparently he had confided to my uncle that he had flown across the Atlantic with Lindbergh . . . as his secret copilot. He said that he had been picked up in Nova Scotia and dropped off in Ireland. But he was set down on the wrong beach, and when no one came for him he was apprehended by the authorities and taken to an orphanage in Tralee."

"Yes, we have all heard that story from Ariel. He had a vivid imagination; but his mind wasn't right. He rarely spoke, but when he did he seemed to have a difficult time separating his fantasies from reality. However, I do remember that when he lived in Como, Ariel kept a scrapbook filled with clippings about Lindbergh and his flight. He knew all the details. That's why his stories were so very convincing."

"My uncle believed Ariel's story. He decided to take him for a flight in the biplane he was using to practice for the performance to see if the man really knew anything about flying. That's when he crashed."

"Yes, how very unfortunate. Had your uncle not crashed we would no doubt not be having this ridiculous conversation."

The rain had increased. A bolt of lightning flashed outside the window, the lights blinked momentarily. John counted the seconds until he heard the roar of thunder.

"So why then did you keep my uncle locked away in some private hospital on an island in a large lake in Switzerland?" John spouted out.

"He wasn't locked away anywhere. He was only at the clinic so he could receive the best medical care possible."

"He wrote in one of his letters that he was kept there long after he was healed. He though he was being held there to prevent him from revealing what he had discovered about Lindbergh having a secret copilot."

"That's utter and complete nonsense!" the count interrupted. "When I heard about the crash, from Hans Hockenheim," he continued, "I was indeed distressed . . . not just about your uncle, but for the many other problems it would also present. Unfortunately, Hans had taken out no liability insurance. He was afraid, as technically your uncle's employer at the time of the accident, that he would be held accountable for the hospital bill as well as the cost of the destroyed airplane, and the other damage on the ground. The festival was also concerned about who was going to be responsible. Your uncle was in the local hospital, very seriously injured. The Swiss were worried that his American health insurance, a notoriously arbitrary system, would not pay the bills. When I received the call, as I was one of the sponsors of the festival, I did not hesitate to have your uncle transferred to my own private clinic on the Lago Maggiore. There he received the very best treatment, entirely at my expense."

"So why were you so concerned about my uncle, a man who you said earlier that you hardly knew?"

"You don't seem to understand, Mr. Vigilia . . . money is not one of my family's problems. Here was a person in need, so I helped him out."

"Just like your father helped out Ariel Angelucci?"

"Precisely."

"And so why was my uncle told that Ariel Angelucci was not in the airplane with him when he crashed?"

"Because he was not," the count said decisively. "The man in the airplane was not Ariel Angelucci. The real Ariel, the boy my father adopted, died on a boat that went down in a thunderstorm in 1942, on one of your Great Lakes; at least that is what we discovered much later. Ariel had been working with the underground, smuggling Jews by boat up the lake from Italy into Switzerland. From an informer, he learned that the Nazis were on to him. . . waiting for him in Italy when he was to return for another group of Jews. So he just stayed in Switzerland. When one of the Jews who was supposed to go to Canada was killed, Ariel took his place. He always talked of having a twin brother in Canada, but no one believed him. You see, we all knew that Ariel was inclined to make up stories."

"Or so you say." John felt he was in a boxing match now, sparring with someone who was far his superior, but he was still in the fight. "So who was the man my uncle did meet if, as you claim, the real Ariel Angelucci was already dead?"

"It is a complicated story," the count replied, turning all the way around in his chair and looking out the window, the rain was letting up a bit, but was predicted to come and go all day.

"So tell me, I have plenty of time. . . ."

"Unfortunately, I myself do not. I have a meeting with the prime minister later today; I must prepare my material. However, since we have come this far I will try to hurry to a conclusion. When Ariel left for Canada he took the Jewish man's identity papers, as this man's passage was already pre-arranged on a ship, leaving his papers behind. Why he did this nobody could understand, as he would have been safer traveling across German occupied France under his own name rather than as a Jew.

"Ariel had a good friend, remarkably similar in appearance. This friend knew Ariel was receiving money from my father for his support. He moved into Ariel's apartment in Locarno and took his identity. My father was quite unaware of what had happened, and kept sending money. The new Ariel even wrote letters thanking my father, and keeping him informed of his activities. When the war ended my father wrote Ariel to come home, but he said he would rather stay where he was. I think my father might have suspected something was not right, but he was an old man, and happy to let things be. It was no problem for him to send a small sum of money to Switzerland once a month. And the man was living in a villa that we still owned, but no longer had use for.

"The matter of the two Ariels was only made known after your uncle crashed his airplane. When the authorities were trying to identify the body, they found that the fingerprints did not match those that had been taken of

Ariel Angelucci in 1943." The count leaned back in his chair.

"So why didn't you let my uncle out of the hospital when his bones were mended? Why did he think that he would have to make an escape on his own?"

"You uncle had also injured his head. When they X-rayed him at the clinic they found he had a small, but growing tumor in his brain. As they were not equipped to do such operations, he would have to be sent to some other facility to have this procedure done. They were waiting for him to get stronger, and to hear from other hospitals that would be able to take him. The doctors at the clinic were also afraid that something else might be wrong with him. They said your uncle had become paranoid and irrational."

"Because he thought he was being held prisoner," John injected.

"Which was not the case at all, and which only made his actions more difficult to understand. He thought he needed to escape."

"And did he? . . ." John Vigilia asked. The room had been oppressively hot when John first entered, now he felt a coldness that made him shudder. The count remained silent. "And did he escape?" John asked again. Speaking the words made his throat tighten.

"So, it seems like, you haven't heard from your uncle since he was at the clinic," the count said; now it was he who was fishing for information.

"No, not since the final letter he wrote from there. In it he mentioned some woman who was going to help him to get out. Apparently it was she who mailed the letter."

"Yes . . . there was a girl. Her name was Miranda. She was my sister's secretary. Her husband had been killed testing one of our airplanes. She and your uncle had had a brief affair when he was in Como. She came to visit him at the clinic. Somehow or other he convinced her to help him get off the island."

"Were they successful? . . ."

"Yes and no. But it is a strange story, as absurd as everything else connected with your uncle. Miranda borrowed a sailboat, and came for him in the middle of the night, with horrible weather approaching. The two managed to sail to the airport at Magadino, where they stole an airplane and took off into a thunderstorm."

"Where did they go from there?"

"No one really knows."

"What do you mean by that?"

"For a long time our family could find out nothing about their whereabouts. Then we got a report that the airplane had been found. It had apparently run out of gas, and crash landed in a field in the mountains near Bled."

"Bled? Just where is Bled?"

"It is not far from Ljubljana, which is now in Slovenia."

"And so what happened to my uncle and this woman Miranda who is supposed to have helped him escape?" John asked, his tone hinting at the count's mendacity.

"The message that we got from the authorities who discovered the airplane was that there was no trace of either one of them. The report was rather vague though."

"And you accepted this *vague* report as final. You didn't think to send anyone there to look for my uncle and the woman?"

"I sent two of my best men, but they could find out nothing. You see at the time there was a war going on in Yugoslavia, the country was breaking apart. There was not much civil order. It was dangerous; the mountains were filled with rebel bands, or more accurately bandits."

"And that's all you can tell me. . . ."

"That is all I know. . . ."

"Then I will go there and look for them. So where exactly was this crash site?" John asked, a tenor of apprehension in his voice.

"All I was told, if I remember the story correctly, is that it was on a hill . . . in a clearing with a tree; about nine kilometers north of Bled, which, as I said, is now in Slovenia. The town is a well-known tourist spot. There is a famous castle there, and a church on an island in the middle of a lake. It's quite a popular place."

"So Bled is where I'll go next. . . ."

"Well then good-by, and good luck to you," the count said, abruptly standing up.

The young art history student from America had not intended his comment about going to Bled to be his final statement, but the count was shaking his hand and ushering him out the door into the hall. "Yes, go to Bled, it's not hard to get to. You can fly to Ljubljana, or take a train; there is one that stops in Bled, people there can help you find your way to the crash site." The count pressed the elevator button. "And I recommend you forget about this story of Lindbergh's secret copilot. It is a fantasy. You are only wasting your time."

The door opened and the younger John Vigilia got into the elevator with the red velvet seat. He turned around to thank the count for his help, but the man was already gone. The door slid closed.

As the car slowly made its descent, John wondered what the count had left out of his uncle's story and how much, if anything, of what he had just been told was true. He would go to Bled, wherever it was, and try to find out.

Back at his hotel room John Vigilia got out a map of Europe, laid it on his bed and planned his route. He would take a train to Bled. There he would rent a car and drive to wherever the crash site might be. More than three years had passed since his uncle's apparent disappearance. He regretted not starting his search sooner, but he had been in school. And he also had held out hope that the authorities would turn up something. John doubted that the count's lead would amount to much, if the man had been telling the truth; but he had to try. It was the only option that he had left.

Thirty-three

You do look, my son, in a mov'd sort,
As if you were dismay'd. . . .

Shakespeare *The Tempest IV. i.*

East of the Dolomites, in the rugged Julian Alps, the day to day world a person inhabited and the world one went to after death often were not very far apart. Indeed for many of these rustic people there were times when the two worlds were so near that it seemed as if their earthly existence was no more than a mere shadow of things beyond.

A dense forest blanketed the sides of a narrow valley not far from the town of Bled. Cut into the top of one of these bosky hills was a large, and level clearing, the origins and purpose of which were said to be unknown. In the middle of this bald spot a tall and lone oak tree stood like a sentinel. Although the paths through this clearing were well-worn, and quite regularly traveled during the day, there were few who would venture there after dark. Generations of old women had scared little children with bleak tales about this oak, which was reputed to have been there forever, and contained the souls of those people who had died underneath its branches.

Not far from this clearing, and the legendary oak, separated by a mass of black thickets full of nooks and niches of confused and secret darkness, were two cemeteries, the Catholic and the Orthodox. Despite their grim purpose, their location on the crest of an often windswept hill made them a popular spot for kite flying

On this day, bright and fresh with a good wind, a group of mothers and their children had gathered in the market square before making their way up the steep and curving gravel road that led to the two cemeteries from the village below. Their plan was to spend a leisurely Sunday afternoon flying kites and picnicking.

Standing under a poplar tree a bit apart from the assembling group, a very young boy named John was startled by a strange and earsplitting noise. He turned to his mother and asked her what was making the sound. It was coming from the tree, loud and shrill like a siren. The noise was so piercing that John's face made a grimace and he put his fingers in his ears. He barely heard his mother when she answered that she did not know what it was; that it must be a bug or something.

There were more and more questions John had these days that she could not answer—boy's questions. He was too young to go to school, and didn't have many friends in the village, which was not his fault. For reasons known only to her, John's mother kept him in the house most of the time, isolated from the other children. And she was often away for most of the day, when she went into Bled to work as a translator. Because his father had been an American, his mother had taught John to speak English, a language few people in the village understood. All she had told him about his father was that he had been a pilot, and had died from head injuries he suffered in an airplane crash before John was born. She told him that he had run out of gas, and was trying to land his airplane in the clearing up on the hill, and had hit the lone oak tree there.

John was not sure that he believed her story, at least not the part about the oak, as the little boy had heard too many tales spun around that particular tree. He secretly expected that his father would be coming back sometime soon. John guessed that his father had probably just gone on a trip somewhere, and would surprise him and his mother one morning when they would wake up and find him sitting in the kitchen drinking coffee.

To escape the shrill noise coming from the tree, John and his mother had started up the hill before everyone else, but now they could hear the others coming up behind them. As it was Sunday the mother and son had first gone to mass. After the service, since the weather was good, a number of the mothers, who were friends, had decided that they would take their children up the hill to the cemeteries to fly kites. Everyone in the village made kites. John had hoped his kite would be the finest, but on seeing the others in the group had conceded that it was not, not even second best. It might have been the best, he told himself, had he been allowed to make it himself.

His mother tried to help him, but she was not very good at art. He had only asked her to get him the materials. Nevertheless, she said that she had made kites when she was a little girl, and knew what to do. He remembered when his mother had once claimed that she knew how to draw, and tried to prove it by attempting a picture of their cat, which hadn't turn out very well compared to his.

Huffing and puffing, John and his mother climbed the steep road until they reached the region of the cemeteries. The first was the Orthodox. As they hurried past the closely packed stones, John tried to read the names, but could make no sense of anything. He asked his mother why some of the letters appeared to be backwards, and why all the crosses had an extra, slanted bar on them. She answered it was because they were Russian. When he asked her why Russians wrote some letters the way they did she said that it was too complicated to explain, and that he would know when he got older.

Their goal was the Catholic cemetery on the crest of the hill. From there the whole valley could be seen spread out below them. The Catholic cemetery had some open spaces, and a vacant corner where people could fly their kites. The rest of the mothers and children had also arrived, and most of the other kites were soon in the sky, bobbing and weaving on the fresh summer breeze. The brightly colored objects seemed to leap into the air right out of the holder's hands, flying high, strings taut, and tails waving. But John's no sooner flew from his mother's grasp then it would lurch up and spin wildly, before crashing to the ground.

John's little legs were growing tired from running while trying to pull his kite aloft. Given a choice, he would rather have been at home in his room working on his pictures. John loved to draw, and had decided that he wanted to be an artist when he grew up. This was Sunday, however, the day they always spent doing things with the other mothers. The fathers more often than not hung out in the village square, playing cards or bocce and drinking beer. John didn't miss having a father so much on Sundays as on this day none of the other children had their fathers around either. John had to admit that he was a little jealous of other children's fathers. He was not, however, the only child without one. There had been many wars in this part of the world and so there were more than a few children with no father, or grandfather, or uncle, and some even had no mother. Whenever John asked about his own father his mother never said much except that he had been a very good man.

When he finally got his kite up in the sky and watched it dancing on the wind, John could not deny that he had a secret desire to be up there with it, but was afraid that if he did get to fly someday that he might die when he tried to come back down like his father supposedly had.

Around noon the kite flying stopped, and the mothers and children sat down on the grass in the shade of some trees and opened their picnic baskets. John carefully laid out on a clean cloth the sandwiches and little cakes that they had brought. His mother unscrewed the lid from the glass jar she used to mix up a batch of orange fizzy water. The drink would be warm, but that was the way they always had it anyway as they were too poor to afford a refrigerator.

The group was sitting in a large, loose circle, talking and laughing, eating their food when a car slowly drove up and parked on the gravel drive, not near, but not too far away. The car's sudden arrival had been unexpected as the road was steep and rough, and no one ever drove up to the cemeteries unless there was a funeral. John and his mother could see the car clearly. It was a black Alfa Romeo, with what appeared to be an Italian number plate. There was a man inside the car wearing a dark, wide-brimmed hat and sunglasses.

Several minutes passed, but the man did not get out. He just sat in his car watching the women and children. Every now and then it seemed as if he would study particular members of the group through binoculars. John could sense that his mother was getting rather nervous. He brushed away an unknown insect that was about to crawl up his pants. The man was still looking at them.

The woman sitting next to John's mother, an elderly Jewish lady, one of the few in the village who knew some English, spoke up: "So whadaya make of that, Miranda? A man . . . a foreigner, in such a fancy car comes up to this here old cemetery . . . now what could he be looking for?"

"Johnny! Put our food back in the basket. We have got to go!" his mother said sharply, jumping to her feet.

"Why Mommy? We're not done eating yet."

"Johnny! Just do as I say."

John caught a tone of anxiety in his mother's voice. She kept looking at the man in the car as she crouched down putting things away. The other mothers, sensing that something threatening was about to happen, started to pack up their baskets also.

"Ah, Mom, we only just got here."

"Come with me Johnny, now!"

She didn't say anymore, just grabbed the basket, and her son's arm, and began to run back down the hill. The other mothers were running too. For no apparent reason, one woman started to scream. John looked back at the man, who had gotten out of his car. He seemed to be holding something in his hand, a paper, or a photograph perhaps, and kept glancing down at this material as he scanned the fleeing mothers.

"Stop looking at that man and run!" John's mother shouted, tugging at her son's arm so hard that he fell to the ground.

"Did you hurt yourself?" she shouted, helping him back up.

"No! I'm okay. . . . What's happening, Mommy?" John asked, shaking with alarm as he brushed himself off.

"Never mind, Johnny! Just run!" she shouted. Looking up from her son, Miranda saw that another car was slowly coming up the hill, a smaller car, with a Slovenian number plate.

"Let go of me and I will."

"Then run, run!" she urged releasing her grip on his arm. "Run home and wait for me. Hide in the shed in our backyard."

Some of the other mothers were racing ahead of them, some struggled to catch up. Children ran past the second car on either side, screaming and in panic, not knowing what they were afraid of, their fright set in motion by the grown-up's fears. John's eyes met those of the man in the second car. There was a brief pause, a moment of recognition, as if they had known each other from someplace before.

"Run, Johnny run! . . ." his mother shouted at him.

Stealing a glance over his shoulder, John saw that the first man was getting back into his car. Did he mean to come after them? John abandoned the gravel road and took off between the rows of tombstones. As he ran along his kite, which had been so reluctant to fly before, was now eager to take to the sky. The boy thought to abandon it, but knew he would not get another one if he should come back for the kite later and find that it was not where he had left it.

After slipping between the widely spaced stone monuments of the Catholic cemetery, and dodging the closer markers of the Orthodox cemetery, John finally made it to the bottom of the hill. A fast runner, despite his small size, he was one of the first down. Out of breath and unable to go any farther, John stopped and waited for his mother under the poplar tree where he had heard the siren-like noise earlier in the day. Thoughts of what may have happened to his mother raced through John's head, each one more horrible than the last.

The two men in cars that John had seen at the cemeteries now appeared in the village; first the black one, with the man in the hat, and then the second one that had a younger man driving it. They circled the square, slowly and in opposite directions, as if looking for something. The two drivers seemed to go even slower, and eyed each other suspiciously, when they happened to pass. The men from the village had stopped their drinking and playing games and were watching the crisscrossing parade of the strange automobiles. The group of mothers and children were nowhere to be seen, having scattered like ants did when the stone that they were living under was unexpectedly lifted. John and his mother were the only ones from their part of town, and no one was planning to meet back at the market as they had on the way up, so everyone had headed for their homes.

The two cars, having driven around the square, and up and down the few streets of the village several times, finally went away. At last John's mother came into view, walking slowly toward him. She was all alone, still showing a bit of fright, and struggling with the picnic basket.

"I though I told you to go home and hide in the shed in our backyard," she scolded, but her smile told little Johnny that she was glad to find him waiting here.

"You did, but when I couldn't see you behind me I though maybe you had fallen down . . . or maybe the man had caught you. Then I saw the black car down here, and the other one too, but now they both have gone away. "

"Don't worry, Johnny. Whoever they were they are gone now, and we are here."

"But who was he, Momma? Who was the man who got out of his car and came after us? And why did we have to run away?" John pleaded.

"I'll tell you all about it someday when you are older, son," was her only reply.

"Why can't you tell me now?" he pestered, taking hold of the picnic basket handle with his free hand while still holding his kite with the other. "Why can't you tell me? John repeated, the basket swinging awkwardly between them as his little legs tried to keep up with her rapid steps. But his mother would say no more.

A fresh breeze fluttered the branches of the poplar tree. The siren-like noise had started up again.

Some twenty years later John and his mother would retrace the steps of the day they fled down the hill. He found that the cemeteries had many more headstones now than they had back then—some of them belonging to children he had known, but who died while John was away studying in America. The once open corner by the trees was full of graves. Kite flying would not be possible here, and even if it was, John was sure it would not be allowed, along with things like dog walking, artificial flowers, votive candles except on All Soul's Day, and all the other items listed on a three foot tall sign displaying the rules that dominated the entrance. He no longer lived in this small, mountain village with its simplistic absence of perspective, where many of the children who ran down the hill with him still dwelt in the crumbling houses of their youth. The poplar trees had been cut down, so the cicadas no longer sang their siren song across the market square.

And the woman who held his kite that day, the prettiest of all the mothers who ran down the hill, now stood quietly next to him, holding onto his arm, a bit out of breath from their climb. She never told him why they had to run. It was only now, many years later, that John realized how he had thrived on the wisdom of all the questions she did not answer, and the untold tales that he still did not know.

Stephen Poleskie is an artist, writer, and photographer. His artwork is in the collections of numerous museums including the Metropolitan Museum, and the Museum of Modern Art in New York: and the Victoria and Albert Museum, and the Tate Gallery in London. His writing, fiction and art criticism, has appeared in many journals both here and abroad. Among these are *American Writing, Leonardo, Lightworks, Pangolin Papers, Satire,* and *Sulphur River Literary Review* in the USA; *D'Ars*, and *Spazio Humano* in Italy, *Himmelschrieber* in Germany, and *Imago* in Australia. He also has a story in the anthology *The Book of Love,* from W. W. Norton, and been nominated for a Push Cart Prize. A handmade book of his poetry was published by Loughborough College of Art in England. He has published three novels, *The Balloonist; The Story of T. S. C. Lowe,* 2007, *The Third Candidate,* 2008, and *Grater Life,* 2009. Poleskie has taught, or been a visiting professor at 26 colleges and art schools throughout the world, including the School of Visual Art in NYC and the University of California, Berkeley. He also holds an Air Transport Pilot license and was active in air shows and aerobatic competition flying. Poleskie is currently a professor emeritus at Cornell University. He lives in Ithaca, NY with his wife, the novelist, Jeanne Mackin. Additional information about him can be found on his website: www.StephenPoleskie.com

www.ingramcontent.com/pod-product-compliance
Lightning Source LLC
Chambersburg PA
CBHW030823310726
48980CB00006B/605/J

* 9 7 8 1 4 2 6 9 2 9 4 7 2 *